GEMINI GIRL MURDERS

TORENA J O'RORKE

ISBN: 0615834736

ISBN 13: 9780615834733

CHAPTER 1

November 23, 2005

♊

Four days break. Cassie hugged herself, feeling the giddy, spine-tingling glee that comes with the unknown. Her parents were leaving on Friday and she was going to have the biggest kick-back ever. Her boyfriend promised to bring an ounce of weed, her best friend had already stolen a gallon of whiskey from her neighbors and there would be plenty of X to keep the party rolling all night long. It was going to be awesome! She skipped up the front steps of the salmon pink stucco house and opened the door, shouting, "Hi Mom, I'm back!"

Nearly tumbling down the stairs, Cassie ran to the basement bathroom. She sighed with breathless satisfaction. Brrrr, she shivered. The three blocks from the bus stop seemed like a long walk today.

The teen stood to gaze into the mirror. She knew that she was pretty. Her hair was thick and shiny, a rich patina of color that resembled a bar of chocolate after she straightened it. Her face was small and her complexion still pimple-free. Her nose was a bit longer than she liked, but you couldn't have everything. Most people said that her eyes were her best feature. She smiled and closed them slightly, admiring her eyelids, which glimmered with bright green eye shadow. Quickly she pulled out her nose ring. Her mom would start trippin' if she saw it. Peering more closely at the spotless glass, she noticed a smudge of blush on her temple and quickly rubbed it off. She had a thing about make-up-it had to be perfect, like a painting.

Soon she would be sixteen and would have a car. Her parents were very generous and normally bought her everything that she wanted. Sometimes she liked to steal, though. She loved the thrill of the chase and the way her body felt right before she decided to snatch something. Perhaps the high from the fear of getting caught, as her probation officer had once surmised, was the real reason she had begun to steal. Jason, the youth pastor at church, had a come-to-Jesus talk with her and explained that little children in places like Vietnam had to work hundreds of hours a week to make most of the clothing that she wore. Now she thought about that every time she wanted to take something. It was very unfair to the kids over there.

Then her mom found some stolen clothes. They had a terrible fight and back to detention she went.

The sound of voices caught her attention as she swung open the bathroom door and headed to her bedroom. Her mom must have another wedding to plan. She hated when the clients came to their house. It was an invasion of her privacy. She couldn't go up to the kitchen now, or she'd have to get introduced, and smile and act all nice. That was the last thing she was in the mood to do.

She flopped down on her bed, pulling the *Little Princess* bedspread over her as she began to text a few friends, excited to make plans for the party.

Tab had texted, saying that she was going to bring some chips. She dialed Angela's number. "Hi girl, wassup?"

"Hangin' out with my man. Wassup with you?" her best friend replied.

"Just calling about the party."

Cassie heard a second beep. "Hey, I've got another call." She pushed the button on the phone, "Yeah."

"Cassie, this is Christian Vargas." The girl's heart did a little dance. Why would her probation officer be calling now? She'd just come to the house earlier in the day for one of their meetings. Did she know about the party?

"I feel pretty stupid saying this, but I think I left my cell phone on your kitchen counter when I was over today at lunch. Could you check for me?"

"Did you call the house phone?" Cassie didn't feel like running up stairs at the moment.

"Yes, but your land line isn't working."

"Can I check and call you back later…I'm kinda busy right now."

"Sure, Cassie, no problem. I can come by later this afternoon to pick it up. I'm sure I left it there somewhere." Cassie didn't mention that she'd already found the phone and had taken it back to school to show her friends.

"Ok, bye." Her P.O. was one of the better ones. All the kids who got on probation wanted to be assigned to Christian. She was young and pretty and didn't follow you around like a freakin' cop.

Cassie started to punch in the next number when the house seemed to rock with a dark, unidentifiable power. She paused, listening for a long moment. The girl sensed danger. A repressive silence, dense and cloy with potential, seemed to fill the space. She shivered, surprised to feel the hair on her arms stand to attention. Something was wrong.

She heard something fall, a crash of broken glass. Footsteps, heavy and purposeful, pounded loudly from above. Small tremors shook the freshly painted ceiling, as a man's voice, angry and echoing with menace, shout incoherently from the kitchen upstairs. Jumping up, the anxious girl opened her bedroom door and started to call out to her, but a rippling scream stopped her. Her mother's normally low voice was shrill and terrified. She could hear more arguing and then a loud slam. Another cry pierced the air, begging for help this time. Fear wound its way up Cassie's spine, clutching her insides, turning her guts to jelly. *Please God, don't let someone hurt my Mom!* She grabbed her cell phone and dialed 911 as the first gunshot reverberated through the house.

♊

Two patrol cars raced by, their sirens screaming a message of terror. Indeed, for Christian, there was no sense of safety in their high-pitched drone. Passing Daniel's truck with ferocious speed, the cops were followed by an ambulance and a fire truck. *It's too late,* she realized. *They're already dead.* She felt hollow and withered. She glanced furtively at Daniel. His face was pale with fear, or anger, she couldn't be sure. He white-knuckled the steering wheel, driving faster as they passed a stream of commuters lined up to get on the Blue Bridge. Daniel swept by a cement truck and onto Highway 395. She wanted to speak, as though sound, any sound, would release the steel band of grief that seemed to cinch tighter around her chest with every breath.

Christian knew that if she was going to be of assistance to the team, she had to muster some strength. Nevertheless, tears streamed down her face as they turned off the highway and headed toward the elegant house at the end of Canyon Drive.

The well-kept homes in Canyon Lakes belied the sense of evil permeating the neighborhood now. It was nearly six o'clock and night was soon upon them. No time for gathering clues, at least not out of doors.

As they pulled up to the curb a few houses away from the crime scene, the young woman's mind began to play tricks on her. She had been there hours earlier. What if she'd come back, as she'd intended, after accidentally leaving her cell phone on the kitchen counter? Could she have stopped the tragedy? Why had she been missed again? Daniel mumbled something and pressed the button to roll down her window. A bobbing head veered toward her.

"Ms. Vargas, may I have a moment of your time?" The news reporter was short and thick around the middle. Her aggressive manner was tamed somewhat by her polite request, but the microphone was only inches from her face. Christian reached for the door handle, attempting to climb out of the car.

"Please, excuse me," she replied and pushed the door into the squat woman, who momentarily refused to move. Her gaze darted from the reporter to the crime scene. Six cop cars and four television station vans were parked around the perimeter of the cul de sac in macabre circus formation. To their right sat the fire truck, though there was no need for that service here. The ambulance idled in the driveway of the Maltos home. The probation officer watched in horror as a pair of EMTs wheeled a gurney covered with a white sheet to its open doors. Uniformed groups of men huddled like football players, preparing to make their next move.

The mottled sky threatened snow and a pervasive chill drew frost from her breath as she made her way through a crowd of curiosity seekers.

"I understand the girl was on probation with you. What can you tell me about what happened here today?" The pushy reporter followed her relentlessly as Christian walked toward her boss and the county sheriff. The KMXN television van pulled out and rolled slowly behind them.

"I know as much as you do at this point."

"What about the girl's boyfriend? Do you think he was involved?"

"The girl? *The girl?* The girl had a name, Sandy. And until you acknowledge that, acknowledge her as a human being, I have nothing more to say." Her fury rose, slicing cleanly through her pain. Glaring at the reporter, she spun around and walked toward the large stucco house, already draped in yellow crime tape.

CHAPTER 2

September 15, 2005

♊

The probation section of the Juvenile Justice Center was quiet as Christian Vargas unlocked the daylight basement door. Built in the sixties, the place was an atrocious fashion statement of the past. Garish plastic cabinets and large flowered wall hangings competed with chrome chairs upholstered in primary colors. Miniscule offices circled the parameter while the lower level's central ceiling span two floors to an enormous skylight, which only increased the brightness of the space. Orange was the prominent color, but the administration's early attempt at color therapy had backfired. The young woman often felt she was working in a giant glass of orange soda.

Removing her motorcycle helmet, she shook out her long dark brown hair and made her way to her office door. Slipping inside, she lifted her sunglasses and squinted. Her small office was dancing with light as the sun poured in from the east. Her plethora of plants was already wilting from her absence over the long weekend. The hum of the air conditioning was the only constant sound, though far away, she could hear the haunting slam of a detention door.

Though it was mid-September, the Indian summer temperatures in the Tri-Cities seemed to be on the rise. It was already seventy degrees at seven. Yet Christian loved early mornings. There was no one to bother her and for a brief time every day, the destructive memories vanished.

She turned on the computer and waited briefly. An e-mail alert popped up first, blinking like a yellow warning light; an obnoxious reminder of her duties for the day. Opening the message, she read:

PERSON OF INTEREST

On DOC probation with Matt Ruelas (Pasco DOC)

Francisco (aka Blanks) Gomez-Cuelar DOB 4/13/1987 WHM 510 198 TATS Documented 18th Street Gang member. Known to carry firearms

Wanted for a double homicide murder in Umatilla, Oregon.

Was traveling with 2 juveniles-Tim Carson (DOB 1/12/1989) and Lilly Host (DOB12/2/1990). Lilly is a reported runaway, was last seen at Richland Wendys on 6/14/2005.

Christian quickly understood that the words, *double homicide*, had additional significance this morning. As always, she had to remain calm in order to allow the information to flow freely through her mind. If she tried to connect the messages too quickly, with too much intention, an ominous pressure would start to build in her chest, and a relentless sense of doom would become her master. Over time, she had learned this game well and knew to remain at ease.

"Hey partner, how was your weekend?" Daniel O'Callahan announced his arrival by setting his coffee cup down at the desk across from hers and flashing a winner's smile.

"Good. Yours?"

"Alright, but you look like you've been burning the candle."

She shook her head somewhat apologetically. "A few of the girls got together over at Eva's last night. I stayed a little later than I'd intended, not to mention there were several bottles of wine and lots of *dirty* stories."

"Oh, do tell," He spun his chair around, ran a hand through his thick thatch of his chocolate-colored hair and switched to a hard stare, his wide amber eyes glowing with anticipation.

"Not a chance!" Yet she couldn't help but smile. "Wine night out" with the female probation team was always full of wild confessions, derisive commentary and private bargains. "Did you see the bulletin?" she asked, hoping to change the subject. Daniel always seemed to get her talking and she knew better than to share last night's revelations. Their partnership was just shy of a year and she wasn't ready to divulge many of her secrets just yet.

"Yeah. I know that guy, Blanks. He's Juan Castillo's Dad."

"Lilly Host's is mine. She's been on the run for six months."

Daniel glanced over from his computer, "She's a handful. I had her on my caseload three years ago. She was barely thirteen and was already prostituting herself for meth." Grimacing, he grabbed a file and threw it at her. "Did you look at the photos yet?'

"Yeah... they're pretty bad." In truth, Christian had been on verge of tears after she'd looked at the series of photos of the girl. Lilly had been a beautiful child at eleven, when she'd come in for her first charge of theft. A year later, her face had begun to harden and she had swastika tats on her forearms. By the time she was fifteen, Lilly had scratched her skin to bits from the meth use. Fortunately the girl still had an alluring face and a good set of teeth.

Christian picked up the phone as their boss, Michael Faust, sauntered in. "Morning, you two." He was dressed in a too-tight golf shirt, his bulbous stomach hanging over his pants like a dangerous balloon, ready to rupture. His attire signaled an afternoon at the golf course, meaning that Daniel would be expected to supervise the rest of the staff. She had hoped for a quiet day, but by the looks of things, it wouldn't be.

Her phone rang, giving a reprieve. "Christian Vargas, may I help you?"

"Hey, it's Officer Joiner, Pasco PD. I've found your kid, Lilly Host. She was wandering down Lewis Street earlier this morning, completely wasted. She's at Lourdes Hospital now, getting her stomach pumped. Can I bring her in?"

"Hold on." Christian covered the phone. "Michael, I've got a jurisdiction transfer as of Friday out of Yakima County. She's on warrant status up there and they've found her in Pasco. I assume we have room in the girls pod. Should I tell him to bring her in?"

Michael paused for a long moment, gazing up at the water-stained ceiling tiles for an answer. His exaggerated processing time was something that the female probation officer found infuriating. "Ah...yes, there's room, but you should probably do a probable cause and get your paperwork from Yakima in order before you do."

Christian winced. "Yes, boss. I'm on it." She hoped her voice didn't sound as sarcastic as she felt. "Joiner, you can bring her in after she's done there."

Michael gave a nod. "Good work." With an appreciative smile, he waddled out. Christian released a long sigh. "Don't need any more contact with him today. Not in the mood for hand holding."

"Yeah, too much of a good thing." Daniel dug furiously through a file drawer and yanking out a green folder, issued a cry of accomplishment. "Got it."

"What?"

"I keep files on the old cases, the ones who were particularly dangerous, or were on SAP before they disappeared." SAP was an acronym for Selective Aggressive Probation, a program which targeted particularly prolific felons in the juvenile system. "I still have some stuff on that guy, Blanks."

♊

Lilly Host was screaming like a cat on fire when Daniel and Christian went to see her in detention intake an hour later. As usual, master control was humming with action. Six kids were waiting in various rooms to be processed.. Lilly had been placed in one of the open cells, otherwise known as 'the cage'. Barefoot and wearing only a black mini skirt and purple sequined crop top, she was rolled up in the fetal position. Her skin was the color of ice; her neon red Mohawk was plastered greasily to the left side of her face.

"Hey, Lilly, we're your probation officers. We'd like to talk to you." Christian leaned down to get a better look at her. The girl reared up and spit. A large bloody wet wad landed on the front of Christian's turquoise silk tee-shirt.

"I don't know why we can't wear uniforms." She glared at Lilly as Daniel passed her a tissue from the counter nearby.

"OK, Lilly, have it your way," Daniel was never happy when someone messed with his partner. "Keep her in the cage until everyone else has been processed," he said to Scott Wyer, the lead detention officer who was known for his no-tolerance attitude.

"My pleasure. It'll be a few hours, young lady." Lilly responded with another wad of spit.

Christian turned away, glancing at Daniel for a reprieve. He seemed to know her expression because he put his hand on her shoulder gently. "Try again later, on your own. She'll open up to you."

The rest of the morning was spent in and out of the courtroom where six of Christian's kids were being arraigned on new charges. Several meetings and a couple of appointments ate up her afternoon. As the sun sent horizontal rays of light across her desk, she remembered that she needed to return to detention to see Lilly.

The chalky lump in her throat was back. More sadness than anxiety, she felt it every time another youth succumbed to the ugly world of the streets. With a relinquishing sigh, she swallowed hard, stepped through the double metal doors and headed toward the pods.

"So, Lilly, how are you feeling now?"

The girl initially refused to answer. She was now sitting in a wobbly plastic chair, head down, across from Christian in the detention library, a small room housed with books from a local Rotarian club. Her complexion was pale and marked with large, red oozing sores, a symptom of methamphetamine use. Dressed in gray cotton pants and sweatshirt, her filthy Mohawk pulled back in a rubber band, she'd been transformed into an inmate. Her large brown eyes bore the look of menace.

"What happened last night?" Christian asked softly, moving her pen to an interview form.

"Got messed up."

"Yeah, I know that. But you've been on the move, Yakima, Oregon, now here. Where are you staying?"

"What's it to you?"

"Hey, you know the score. You have to give me an address and a contact, or I can't release you."

Looking away, Lilly started to dig at her face. The girl's hands were shaking.

"What are you coming down from?"

"Crystal, weed, some triple C….oh, I think I took a hit of acid, too."

Christian caught the girl's eye. She held on, hoping to find something there.

"So you were assigned a foster home, but you're staying with Blanks." Christian offered up the name for reaction's sake.

The girl blinked hard, trying to understand. Her enlarged pupils looked like deep tunnels into a private hell. "How'd ya know?"

"I know some things about you, Lilly. And I'll be straight with you until you prove to me otherwise. I know you're a smart girl. I saw your grades from middle school. Straight As until your 8th grade year."

"Yeah, so what. What did school ever do for me?"

"You didn't stay long enough to find out."

"Yeah, whatever. The teachers always have it out for me."

"Let's talk in the morning, Lilly. When you come down. Then maybe you can tell me a little bit more about Blanks."

The girl just shrugged.

Walking away, Christian left with a feeling that said, 'Loss' hanging like a heavy shingle from her heart.

Now, after reading through the police reports on the murders in Oregon, she realized that Lilly was most probably a witness, if not an accessory to the crime. The red Camaro identified by the Seven 11 security camera showed three people in the car. One was, without a doubt, a flaming red-headed female.

Glancing at her watch, the time was quarter to five. Her appointment was at five. She quickly turned off her computer and remembering that Daniel was still up in the courtroom, left on the lights of the office.

♊

"So, how are you doing today?" Sophia asked. Christian's new therapist was an engaging woman in her late thirties. Small and compact, she had long wavy black hair and an earnest face which spoke of struggle and hard-won wisdom. This was the probation officer's second visit, on the insistence of her boss who'd noticed some changes in her after one of her clients had been sent to prison.

"I had a rather busy day."

"From what you've told me, that's pretty typical." Sophia gave her client an admiring smile. "Tough work, you do. But let's talk about the assignment I gave you last week, if that's ok."

Christian nodded and opened her journal.

"Rather than read it aloud, why don't you paraphrase for me."

The old wounds begin to throb. She hadn't talk about her childhood to anyone, really, except Tony, her late husband.

"I was just a little girl, about three, when I almost died from a snake bite. We were camping, my parents and sister and me, up in the Blue Mountains. The snake bite felt like hot fire. In the next second, I was lifted out of my body. This *Being* would not let Death take me. It took us nearly an hour to reach Dayton. I should have died. It was a Sunday. I remember looking up and seeing stoplights. Then I don't remember any more. I have been told that I passed out and the EMTs were forced to give me a shot of adrenaline to keep my heart beating. I should have died that day."

Christian paused again, this time to wipe her eyes. Some of this felt like humiliation, but when she glanced at Sophia, she read only acceptance in her gaze.

"Then when I was almost four, my family drowned. All three of them. My sister was only six. We were on our sailing boat. I was the only one to survive. I don't know why." The old tears choked her and she held her head in her hands for a long moment. Finally she whispered, "That's it. That's all."

Sophia reached over and took her hand. "I want you to listen to me carefully. You have suffered many traumas. So, the fact that your husband died, too, not the only reason you're here. Your issues are deeply metaphysical in nature. You told me last week that you feel death around you as though death was an actual entity. This tells me you need to search in a different way. You think about it and I'll see you again next week."

Christian nodded and rose to leave. When she arrived home, her affectionate St. Bernard mix was chomping at the bit for her attention. As she changed out of her work clothes and grabbed her running shoes, she realized that before finding the loyal mongrel, her personal life had been pretty bleak.

"Yes, Bear, I'll give you a good run tonight," she murmured, rubbing the dog's head. He groaned and wagged his tail with excitement, his fluffy brown fur rippling with pleasure. "Just let me get my shoes on, big guy."

♊

Six hours later, Christian woke up in a cold sweat. Bear was snoring peacefully beside her as she sat up and took a ragged breath. She'd had the dream again, another sign that death was lurking. It was always the same. She was floating away on a life ring from a large ship, into the darkness of a stormy sea.

But despite two decades that had passed since her life on the coast, her memory of that day was as vivid as if it had happened yesterday. It was the first time Death entered her young life. Her parents, avid and accomplished sailors, had drowned off the Oregon coast. She had been the sole survivor of a party of six aboard a fifty-two foot catamaran in the summer of 1980. In the years of her childhood and beyond, when the nightmares started, someone in her present life had died, or nearly so. She had learned to accept the omen rather than fight it. She had also learned that sometimes, with that intuitive knowledge, she could stop Death from succeeding in his dark quest.

CHAPTER 3

♊

Tuesday morning's field visit took Daniel and Christian to an upper middle class home in the south part of town. Cassie Maltos had come through on a domestic violence assault charge a month before and they'd been assigned to her case until adjudication. The docket was more backlogged than usual, as school had started earlier in the month, so they had taken on the family in hopes of preventing further assaults.

They drove up to the enormous home in Canyon Estates. "I really like this family. They seem so together on the outside, but Mom is so vulnerable. And she seems to be terrified of Cassie," she said as they got out of the car.

"Yeah. I don't think Mrs. Maltos knows the first thing about being a parent to a teen.. That kid really messed her up."

Christian nodded. Cassie Maltos, a petite sophomore at Kennewick High School, had given her mother a broken rib and a vicious-looking black eye.

"Mom's afraid of losing her little girl and sadly, she already has."

They knocked at the door, sharing a quick glance of concern. Screaming could be heard from the front porch. Their last meeting with the family had been tense and laced with arguments. Cassie, a pretty, dark-haired girl with a singing voice like a pop star, was dating a "bad boy", Tommy Calander. He was a seventeen-year-old who'd been in a juvenile prison for two years for the stabbing of another youth. His life since his release the previous spring had consisted of sponging off Cassie's family and dealing drugs on the side. It was understandable why the Maltos family resented him in their only daughter's life.

Minutes later they were seated in the spacious living room decorated in over-stuffed floral couches and Norman Rockwell knock-offs. Cassie sat glumly on the floor, her eyebrows knotted with angst.

"She just doesn't see what he's doing to her," Mrs. Maltos recited in her singsong southern twang. "I know she could do better."

"Whatever. You don't know what you're talking about," Cassie wrapped her arms around her legs defensively.

"Hey, Cass, take it easy. Let's have your mom explain what she means by 'better'." Though Christian had sat next to Daniel on the love seat, she slipped to the beige Berber carpet across from the teenager. She worked better at eye level.

"I just want her to date a boy without a criminal record, someone who's going somewhere in life." Sue's normally sunny face puckered with doubt as she looked to the probation officers for support. "Do you know what I mean?"

"How do you know that Tommy isn't going somewhere, Mom? He got his diploma at Echo Glen and he's going to go to community college next quarter." Cassie jumped to her feet. Livid with anger, her long ponytail swung wildly as she paced the floor.

"Whoa! Take a seat, young lady," Daniel commanded. The girl meekly sat back down.

Christian took the cue. "Ok, so you're asking your mom and dad to give him a chance to prove himself. That's his job, not yours. In the meantime, you need to start thinking about your goals. I understand you're singing solo in the all-city church choir competition on Saturday. That's awesome, Cassie." The girl smiled slightly and seemed to relax. Christian felt a little burst of satisfaction. She'd found a connection.

The girl was quiet for a moment. "Yeah, I was asked to join the Christian band, called *The Offering*. They want me to be the lead singer."

"I've heard of them." The probation officer offered an admiring smile. "They played at the Battle of the Bands last summer. They're really good, but I can see where they might need a female to make them even better." Christian winked at Cassie's mom.

"Ok, I'll come home by curfew, but I want to see Tommy tonight." Cassie's voice had a slightly pleading quality to it. The adults were ahead by one point.

Daniel leaned forward. "Cassie, I'm going to ask you to reconsider. I think you need a break from one another. Just the weekend. If you do it, I'll let the judge know how well you are cooperating with us. A good word could mean no detention time." He let the probation world's ubiquitous carrot dangle as the girl perceivably thought it over.

"I guess... since I'm not allowed to drive now and he doesn't have a car. But can I talk to him on the phone?" Cassie had sat down on the couch and was petting her cat.

Christian gave Mrs. Maltos a look of deference.

"The phone is fine. I just think some time to herself." Mrs. Maltos's voice rose with forced cheerfulness. "That would be

good." Once again, she looked doubtful. That was half the problems with the parents; they all seemed to be afraid to take a stand.

Daniel stood up. "So, it's all good. Cassie. Phone calls to Tommy
only until we see you next week. If he's the man you say he is, he
can handle it. We need to get going. Remember, Cassie, you're
still on house arrest." The girl shot him a dirty look, but nodded
in agreement.

By the time they reached the Justice Center, it was nearly five
o'clock. As Daniel turned off his computer, he asked, "What time
are you walking Bear tonight?"

The question caused Christian to glance at her dog's photo
which was perched prominently on her desk like a firstborn child.

"I don't know. Why?"

Daniel looked away. A response that said things weren't good
at home.

"I could use some company."

"Sure. Let's we meet at Badger Mountain Park? There's a great
new hike up there. Besides, you don't want my hairy dog getting
that nice car of yours dirty."

He gave her a funny look. Her home was on the way to the
park.

"See you soon." She quickly walked out of the office, feeling
that familiar edge of trepidation.

♊

Once home, Christian quickly changed her clothes and put
a couple of pieces of chicken marinated in homemade Thai
sauce in the oven. That, with a bag salad, would have to do for
dinner.

As she put on her work-out clothes, she glanced at her body's image in the full length mirror that was attached to her closet door. For the past two weeks, she'd experienced some very strange warnings. Flashes of faces and the smells and sensations would not leave her day or night. She had often forgotten to eat and her pants now hung on her narrow hips like a gangster's. Kneeling down to snuggle Bear, she murmured love noises into his ear. He was a wonderful pet, but his troubled past had left its mark. She'd found Bear four years before at the edge of her property. His left hind leg had been shot and he'd nearly eaten it off in an attempt to free himself from the pain. It took the best part of a day to get him to the vet's where his leg was immediately amputated for fear of gangrene.

When Bear had finally come home, a week later, they'd fallen in love. The dog was an amazing animal that she soon learned could pick up a scent for miles. As a result, she'd spent the time and money to train him for search and rescue. Though her job description didn't actually include detective work, she'd helped the local police departments to find several missing children with Bear's unusual skills. Together, they'd become one of the more successful contributors to crime-solving in the community. "Hello! Anyone home?"

Her heart fell as she recognized her partner's voice. She hurried to the front door, but he was already inside. "Wow," he said, turning slowly in a circle while peering up. "What the hell?"

By that time, Bear had bounded into the room and nearly knocked Daniel over with a happy leap. "Hey, big boy." He grinned, pausing to rub the dog's massive head.

"This is like Walt Disney's version of an observatory." The muscular Hispanic looked expectantly at Christian as she approached.

With a heavy sigh, she sat down and nodded. "That's one way to describe it. I make them. It's a long story."

Hanging from the seventeen foot cathedral ceiling was a series of three dimensional stars that twinkled even in the daylight. Christian had made each one, using cardboard, paper mache, metallic paints and plenty of multicolored rhinestones to create her special version of heaven. The refracting light cast an ethereal glow to the entire space and gave a magical energy to her home.

Daniel sat down next to her on the L-shaped suede coach and leaned back, gazing up in awe. "They're beautiful and kind of weird."

"So now you know why I don't have a lot of people over."

"Look, you don't have to explain. You're an artist and no one at work knows that but me. I like it that way." His casual response put her at ease. She didn't want to explain that the stars dangling above represented the loved ones whom she'd lost in her lifetime. What she didn't want to explain was her strange attachment to death and the haunting way in which it accompanied her through life like an apparition, invisible and yet very much intact.

Daniel stood up and reached out his hand. "You ready?" he asked as she allowed him to pull her up. For a moment their faces were within inches of one another. The unexpressed tension between them came like a wave of hot air.

Quickly Christian moved away and went to find the dog's leash. "You weren't going to pick me up."

"I was early. The appointment with the attorney was brief this time."

"Does that mean progress, or otherwise?" Christian bit her tongue as soon as the words emerged from her mouth. She silently chastised herself. It was none of her business.

Daniel opened the door of her Volkswagen Beetle and urged Bear into the back. Once in the car, he answered, "I don't know. She's willing to split some of the assets, but others are apparently non-negotiable. Like the cabin. She wants it and I think I know why."

"I thought she refused to go to the cabin; that it's too rugged for her," she replied as they started down the street in her Bug. She'd always thought that Daniel and his wife, an interior designer whose only hobby was collecting designer shoes, were a mismatch.

"Yeah, she hates it. But I love it and she loves to punish me. We should go up there some time before the divorce is final, just in case I lose it."

Christian blushed at his comment. A weekend alone with him could only end in catastrophe. Her feelings for him were hard enough to deal with at work. An opportunity for complete privacy might take her over the edge.

By the time they'd finished their hike, the two probation officers had talked about everything from local politics to the new Sting CD. She waved good bye and turned to go into the house with Bear. Remembering that her partner had learned more about her than she'd wanted to share, she swore to herself to keep the rest of her secret sequestered away, the impervious black hole in her little universe.

CHAPTER 4

October 6, 2005

♊

"You have the right to the presumption of innocence.
You have the right to a speedy and public trial.
You have the right to legal counsel.
To the charge of residential burglary, how do you plead?"

Judge Stanzik's voice was like elevator music to the heavy metal analysis that pounded in Christian's brain. She was struggling with the fact that her new client, Lilly Host, had been released to DCFS the day before and was already on the run again, after less than twenty-three hours. She hated the way the 'department' functioned with regards to the teen population. The caseworkers would pick the kids up from detention and drop them off at a new foster home, an unknown environment that was often more restrictive than the juvenile cell. No phone calls allowed, no computers or television and general chaos reigned in many foster homes. The last three English-speaking kids on her caseload had been plunked down into Spanish-speaking homes, only to find that the inability to communicate worked in their favor. Lilly, on the other hand, had been taken to the Gaines's home, notorious for the lecherous father who, despite complaints from clients and their attorneys alike, continued to be licensed.

Christian squirmed on the bench, anxious to have her turn at testimony. She wanted to get back out on the streets and attempt to find Lilly. From new rumors floating around the office, she was fairly certain the girl would be at the Gypsy Jesters clubhouse, a Hells Angels hang-out where young girls were given enough drugs to endure non-censual orgies and other inconceivable acts. Though she had been warned by management to avoid the club-house, Christian had a friend from many years ago who had con-tacts there. The agreement was that she could get her girls out, as long as no cops came along for the ride.

One of her youth was next on the docket for a probation hear-ing. Tommy Calander was back at it with the *Sureno* gang, flashing signs at school and wearing gang-affiliated clothing in direct viola-tion of his gang conditions. He had not only breached that court order, but he had been at Cassie Maltos's home when her parents were at work, though Christian had specifically requested a no-contact order. As a result, he was now Cassie's ex-boyfriend, but according to her parents, Tommy had made several threatening phone calls to the family since they'd broken up.

Tommy offered a cocky grin as he stood up and sauntered over to the defense table. Tall and lanky, the boy sported a new tattoo on his left cheek in the sign of a tear, indicating that one of his hommies had recently gone to prison. He stared at Christian with malice in his eyes. He was refusing to stipulate to the violation. Christian had requested eighteen days in detention and he was not happy about it.

The prosecutor turned to Christian and nodded. Standing to face the bench, she said, "Good morning, your Honor. I have requested eighteen days because of several violations. I have here a letter from Tommy's principal stating he wore *Sureno* gang attire to school on September 11,12,15 and 17. He was given a month's expulsion on the last date. Since that time, Tommy has been seen with Juan Campos and Stephan Norman, *Sureno* gang members, on several occasions by Kennewick Police. In addition to that, he was at Cassie Maltos's home, according to her mother, who kicked him out when she found him there and then called the police, resulting in his immediate arrest as a result of breaching the no-contact order."

"When was this no-contact order put into place? Why I don't see it on his original disposition?"

"The order is on Cassie Maltos as a direct result of violating her house arrest conditions, your Honor."

The old judge paused for a moment. In the state of Washington, no-contact orders went both ways. The so-called 'victim' was required to keep away from the offender, in this case, Cassie.

Judge Stanzik had a big, square fist of a face which would clench fiercely at the slightest provocation. His was a zero-tolerance attitude, resulting in a steady stream of contempt of court charges. He looked down his bulbous nose at the defense attorney, who had the strange habit of rocking from foot to foot when his clients were in the hot seat. Dressed like a dapper southern gentleman down to the suspenders and a bowtie, Mark Mason was comical to watch. He strutted dramatically towards the bench and began to raise his hand, when Stanzik, losing patience, pressed on. "Mr. Mason, your client's answer please?"

"In all due respect to the court, we feel that eighteen days is too long, Your Honor. Tommy will miss too much school and based on my experience…" he began. Mason was notorious for pompous soliloquies that normally ended in his own self-aggrandizement. This judge knew when to cut him off.

"That will be enough, Mr. Mason." Christian was certain she saw the judge give her a wink. "What is the state's recommendation?" The judge peered back at the deputy prosecutor, Callum O'Connor. Callum was a sharp-witted attorney blessed with Colin Farrell good looks and predatory attitude, particularly when it came to gang activity. His best friend, a respected high school teacher, had been murdered the year before by a *Norteno* member. "Your Honor, the State would support Ms. Vargas in her recommendation."

The judge took a slow sip of water while watching Tommy. The boy continued to smirk, as though he was on stage and the courtroom was his audience. Stanzik gave him a steely glare. "Eighteen days it is."

Christian hurried from the courtroom and found Stella, another probation officer with a long history with the juvenile justice center, standing in the lobby, talking to an irate parent. She could see that Stella could use a rescue.

"Excuse me. I'm ready whenever you are." Stella gave her friend a subtle look of relief.

"Mrs. Webber, there is nothing I can do to get your son out of detention. He has to wait until First Appearance, which is on the docket for tomorrow," Stella told the heavy-set, disheveled woman who looked like she'd been up all night. "Now I have to go."

With a nod, Stella turned to her friend. "I'll meet you outside in five minutes."

Christian went back to her office to gather her files, phone and keys to the county car. On her way out the door, Kevin Stoppard, a retired detective who ran a gang abatement program, stopped her in the hall.

"Hey, I have some information on Lilly Host. She was hanging out last night with your kid in there after he left the Maltos home." Kevin's shiny bald head swiveled toward the courtroom doors. He was tall and broad with a thick, ropy neck, reminding Christian of the actor on the Mr. Clean commercials she used to see as a kid.

"Tommy Calander? They know each other?"

"I guess so. When Mrs. Maltos called the police, apparently he took off with Lilly."

"I didn't know where they'd picked him up."

"I talked to Shelly Marcin from Kennewick police. Apparently your detention officer messed up big time and inadvertently let her go. No warrant?" Christian nodded affirmatively. "Anyway, Shelly said that they wanted to interview her when she was in here regarding Blanks and that homicide in Oregon, but she was released before they could."

"I know. She was scheduled to meet with Shelly, but DCFS had placement, so detention released her. I had a chance to talk to her briefly though. Lilly said she met Blanks about a month ago. According to her, she'd been living in Yakima with her Aunt Debbie. Blanks was a boyfriend of Debbie's at one time. Lilly ended up taking off with him. She apparently wanted to see some friends and then got picked up. She didn't exactly admit they went to Oregon, but didn't deny it either. Apparently he has some business here which was why she went with him in the first place. She actually said she was scared of him."

"Lilly Host, scared?"

"I know, pretty crazy. Have they found Blanks yet?"

"No. Pasco PD thought they spotted him in East Pasco at the projects, but that's like finding a needle in a haystack. Do you think she's hooked back up with Blanks?"

"I don't know. I was just going over to the Jester clubhouse with Stella to see if she was hanging out there."

Kevin shook his head. "You know you shouldn't go over there. Let the police handle it." His wide-set eyes suddenly narrowed like a camera shutter, their black pupils boring into her. There was no mistaking his concern.

"Excuse me? You know that they won't touch that place. We'd have to call in the swat team before they'd go in there."

"If Blanks is there, you're looking for trouble. He's a Jester from way back. I'd let it go if I were you. Just get the warrant signed. They'll find her eventually. I'm telling you, you shouldn't go over there." His persistent nature irritated Christian. In her opinion, he'd spent too many years on the force. Caution had become his daily companion. Yet if she were honest with herself, she knew he was right. A deep chill run up her back as his voice continued its drone of persuasion. She wasn't about to let Lilly go that easily. Her gut told her that Lilly was as vulnerable a girl as any.

A few minutes later, the women were on their way down the highway towards Kennewick. "Hey girlfriend, what's the latest?" Christian turned onto the freeway going east.

"I hear Sara, our new officer in detention, is bonking a deputy prosecutor from Franklin county."

"Which one?" Christian's mind only partially on her fellow traveler's comment.

"Gary Taravich. And I'm jealous. He's such a hunk."

"Yeah, but isn't he married?"

Stella's laughter rattled throughout the car. "When does that stop any of them?"

"Someday I'm going to meet a man who knows what the word 'faithful' means," Christian turned down Fruitland Street towards the Jester's notorious haunt.

"Honey, if you marry one like that, you'll have to settle for boredom as a side effect."

"Come on, Stell. Your husband's a sweetheart and I don't believe for one minute he was the cheating kind."

Stella shrugged. Christian knew when to leave well enough alone.

"So you are looking for someone again?" Her friend knew that the topic of husbands could be touchy for her younger friend.

"Sometimes I'm really lonely and a good man seems to be the only cure."

"What about your partner? Isn't his divorce nearly final?"

"Hey, wait one minute!" Christian's face grew hot. They'd reached the Jester's clubhouse. She pulled discreetly to the side of the road a couple houses away from the building. "What do you think?"

"It's looks awfully quiet."

The Jester's clubhouse was an old mechanics garage that had been converted into a party house. A tall fence wrapped around two-thirds of the building. A large wood sign hung on the gate which read, 'Jesters: Rulers the Road, Mighty Motorcycles=Mighty Men.' A skull and crossbones were painted in red below the large, old gothic-styled lettering. After the doors closed for the night, evil reigned.

"I say we look around a little."

"Last time I was here, a pair of Rottweilers nearly ate me," Christian shuddered at the memory. "I brought pepper spray."

"You aren't supposed to carry that stuff on the job." Stella grinned, giving her a thumbs-up.

"Yeah, so." Christian began a slow pace toward the back of the property. On the south corner, a few slats of the wooden fence had been torn down. She peered through the open space. "The front door is open. Let move."

Climbing through the narrow opening, she held up her hand. "If those Rotts are around, we are not going in."

Creeping slowly up to the door, the women stayed close to the western wall which didn't have any windows. Christian climbed up onto the porch and pushed the door open.   "Probation. We're looking for Lilly Host." At first, there was no sound coming from the front room. Then a low moan could be heard.

"Stella, let's go." She shoved the door open. The cavernous room was filthy with beer bottles, cigarette butts and old fast food wrappers. Various motorcycle parts littered the floor. A slight smell of chemicals permeated the air, indicative of methamphetamine manufacturing. As they moved deeper into the dark and dirty space, they could make out a shape. Lying in the corner on a couch was a girl. Her bulbous stomach protruded from a too-small tee-shirt. Christian hurried over to her. "Look who we found here? Stella, isn't this Hannah Staples?"

Stepping carefully around the piles of debris, Stella came forward. "Hannah? On my god, honey, look at you!"

"Let's get her out of here, quickly. There could be some guys in the back." Together the two women picked up the girl by her arms and moved her through the room and out the door. As they did so, the sound of motorcycles could be heard approaching from the east. "Hurry," Stella pushed the girl forward as they reached the broken fence and pulled themselves through. They had just reached the car when they heard loud voices behind them.

"Let's go." As Stella helped the girl into the back seat, Christian released the emergency brake and allowed the car to coast forward down the hill before she started the engine. She continued to watch in her rearview mirror until they were out of sight.

"That was close!" Stella turned to the back seat to talk to Hannah. "What's your due date?" Hannah's face was swollen, a couple of teeth were missing and a deep purple bruise shadowed her right eye. Her arms were spotted with fingerprint bruising.

"I was due last week, but Rounder wouldn't let me go to the doctor lookin' like this."

Stella shook her head. "Hannah, when are you going to give it up? He's such a monster."

The girl released a ragged cry. "I know. I want to have my baby and get out of here. I want to go live with my Aunt Sarah in North Carolina, but I couldn't get away from him."

"Why didn't you call me?"

"No phone. Besides, don't I have a warrant?"

Stella reached out and took her hand. "You do. But Hannah, you aren't going to spend a lot of time in detention. However, you are also not going to be released until your aunt shows up to take you home with her. Do you understand?"

The girl whimpered a soft, "Yes, thank you. Thank you for finding me."

Christian slowed to a stop sign and turned back to the juvenile. "Where's Lilly Host?"

The girl looked away. Her eyes grew shiny. "Don't know." Reaching into her back pocket, she handed Stella a crumpled piece of paper. "Take a look at this. Maybe it will help you find her."

Her friend studied it for a moment and gave her friend a hard look. "We'll talk about this later," she replied in a grim tone.

II

"Screw off, or your balls will feel it," the older man snapped as he walked through the screen door. Slamming it hard, he threw his jacket on the back of the couch and sat down, cutting gas loudly in the process. Yanking a baggie from his shirt pocket, the ugly man spread a small line of white powder on the cluttered table in front of him. Placing his nose to the table, he sniffed the line loudly. With a filthy index finger, he rubbed the remaining white powder into his nostril and upper gums. Closing his eyes, he threw himself back and sighed. His long stringy hair flew up for a moment from the motion and then fell against his large, sweating head. "Man, this is good stuff. I'll give you half today and the rest next week."

"Sorry, Boss, but I need it all today." The other man who had followed him into the clubhouse was dressed in full regalia. His Gypsy Jester coat was worn and dirty, but well-decorated, none-theless. His leather chaps matched the jacket and the dark blue bandana wrapped around his head was his favorite, purchased by a fellow member from a famous Hell's Angel who was now in prison for life. With two Xs stitched to the bottom of the jacket, he'd openly announced to his tribe just what he'd accomplished. The murders were a mark of pride, and he had wasted no time in giving himself visible credit.

"You need it when I tell ya you need it."

"It's just that those spics won't leave me alone. I gotta get them the cash, or I'm screwed."

The Boss, as he was called, had never liked the other one. There was a reckless quality about Blanks that had never sat well with him. He associated with spics and niggers and generally messed with too many outsiders for his liking. Not following the Jester's creed was often punishable by death and this guy had nearly crossed the line several times.

"I'll think about it. Let me get some action with my girl first, and then I'll let you know." There was a long pause. "Hannah, where are ya, babe?"

"Hannah?" He looked over at Blanks, his eyes narrowing. "Where is Hannah?"

CHAPTER 5

October 27, 2005

♊

Christian slipped into the side door of the auditorium unnoticed. The Kennewick High School homecoming assembly was just about to begin and the lights had already been dimmed. Dressed in her American Eagle jeans, black boots and a form-fitting pale blue leather coat, she looked like any other PTA mother striving to dress like their teenage daughter. Yet at twenty-nine, she fit in with her younger counterparts. Friday was her day off and she'd decided to see Cassie's rumored singing ability firsthand.

The crowd was loud and frenzied as paper airplanes flew through the air. Several kids were talking on cell phones while others took silly pictures of one another with their expensive toys' extra feature. Skimpily-dressed girls giggled loudly, performing sideshow antics to get the attention of the football team who had just entered to the right. In full uniform, the boys looked more like men, she observed.

There was a drum roll as a tall, pimply boy came on stage and awkwardly took the microphone. He grinned with embarrassment as he welcomed the crowd and offered opening remarks.

The crowd roared and eventually settled down as a pair of novice comedians from the senior class came out to verbally bash on the underclassmen. After a few laughs and several boos, the boys left the stage and were followed up by the school dance team who performed a racy number to a famous Michael Jackson song. Following that was a group of drama kids who did a skit about the upcoming football game. A couple of cheerleaders bounced out in their orange and black uniforms to announce the details of the homecoming dance. Then the orchestra hummed, its violin section singing a warning as spotlights began to swing through the audience. One by one, various kids were announced as the homecoming royalty. Six boys and six girls strutted, slinked and squirmed up to the stage where they sat on decorated chairs and received their crowns.

"And now, before we introduce our King and Queen for Kennewick High's Homecoming 2005, please welcome Cassie Maltos singing "Beautiful".

The crowd went silent. It was obvious that they'd heard their talented peer sing before now. Cassie walked on stage in a floor-length simple black gown. Her hair was drawn up in a fancy knot on her head. Stunningly poised, she had been transformed into a performer, her shoulders back and her head held high as the music began to play. Her voice was angelic and yet strong. The crowd seemed mesmerized as the young singer moved around the stage, coaxing them into her world of heartache and hope. The girls sighed as the boys clutched their seats, struck by such talent. When Cassie sang the last word, Christian longed for more. The room was silent for a drawn moment before the applause rang through the room like galloping horses. There was a standing ovation. It appeared as though the announcing of the royalty had become unimportant. Many of the girls had tears in their eyes. She quickly wiped a random tear from her own cheek. After the announcements of Prom King and Queen, the assembly was over. Christian wandered out after the mass of students had found their way through the double doors. She was almost out of the building when she heard her name.

"Christian. Wait!"

The probation officer turned to see Mr. and Mrs. Maltos hurrying to catch up with her, their eyes still dewy with pride.

"Hi, how are you?"

"Wonderful!" Mrs. Maltos was beside herself with pride. "We're so proud of her."

Mr. Maltos reached out and lightly touched Christian's arm. "Really, you are the only one who seems to get through to her. We believe there are some positive changes on her horizon because of you and your partner. Maybe probation isn't such a bad thing after all." He offered a genuine smile.

Christian smiled, embarrassed by the complement. "Cassie is absolutely amazing. She has such a gift." She yearned to flee. It was her day off after all.

An awkward moment passed and then Mr. Maltos seemed to take the hint.

"We'll see you on Wednesday afternoon, then? We'll look forward to it."

As they walked away, hand in hand like newlyweds, Christian wondered if she had really made a difference.

After donning her motorcycle helmet and dark glasses, Christian was as inconspicuous as any undercover worth their merit. Using the bike as transportation was an advantage in a small town where people were easily recognized. She headed out of the parking lot cautiously, watching the various groups of kids as they made their way to their classes. As she reached the end of the parking lot, she glanced across the street and saw the light brown Ford King Cab pick-up that was parked illegally. Tommy Calander stepped out. Christian watched in astonishment as Lilly Host jumped out after him and climbed into the back where she quickly disappeared. Tommy then pulled his cell phone from his pocket and dialed. He began talking to someone, gesturing wildly. She pulled out her cell phone at the same time to call dispatch. It was time that Lilly was taken into detention. As she did so, she saw motion out of the corner of her eye. From her right next to the school exit, Cassie appeared. She had changed her clothes and was now wearing jeans and a sweatshirt. She glanced around and saw her mark. Running across the street toward Tommy, the girl tried to put her arms around him, but Tommy pushed her back and held out his hand. Hesitantly she pulled some money from her back pocket of her jeans. She handed him the cash and then he kissed her, however briefly, and spinning her around, pushed her back toward the school. Head hanging, Cassie darted back across the street and ran into the building.

Christian was furious. Obviously Tommy still had complete control over Cassie. This was not the girl who'd been on stage, full of confidence and so unbelievably talented for her age. What did Tommy have on her? What was the power that teenage boys, many of them emotionally crippled and mentally weak, seemed to exert over beautiful girls? The theory of the good girl going for the bad boy didn't make sense anymore. Girls had so much opportunity to spread their wings and fly in this world. Why, so often, did they settle for less?

Dispatch finally answered, jolting the tempestuous memory aside. Christian gave them the location and license plate of Tommy's car. She would see Lilly in detention, again, on Monday.

As she headed for home, the probation officer decided it was time for some reflection. At the last minute, she changed lanes and turned onto Highway 240, heading toward Pasco, to the All-City Cemetery. There were a few people whom she needed to visit.

♊

"Those girls were like a bunch of Whirling Dervishes." Christian's smile was enigmatic.

Christian's phone rang, so Daniel reached over and grabbed it before she could.

"Ms. Vargas's indisposed. She'll call you back. Matt. Yes, she's got your number."

"Daniel!"

"Look, you know I'm dumb about such things, but I don't think Matt is good for you."

"Really? I'm glad that we went to the Cougar game. It was worth the drive and I enjoyed getting to know Matt better." She shuffled through her pile of court papers as she opened the filing cabinet.

"We need to see Cassie today. I want to talk to her about Tommy. I caught a little exchange between them on Friday, after the assembly, when I had Lilly picked up. Looked like she's keeping him flush with cash."

"Isn't that what girlfriends are for? That and a couple of other very important things!" Christian threw a squishy ball his way. She kept it on her desk for just such purposes.

"Enough with the chauvinism!" she warned, shaking her head good-naturedly.

"Okay, okay, I'll be good. By the way, did you see Lilly this morning? She's back in, singing the blues in there, coming down hard."

"Those meth hangovers hurt. I'll talk to her first, find out what she's willing to tell me. Make her a little deal."

"Meet me here after court. I'll give the Maltos family a call and we'll stop by there this afternoon. We need to go over the case focus plan and set some ground rules with regards to her friend, Tommy."

♊

Christian arrived in detention a few minutes later. Cold drafts of air swept through the corridor, so she could only imagine the temperature in the cells. Grubby, disenchanted kids were lined up against the wall, shackled at the ankles and dressed in the grey sweat suits, which served as jail attire. The First Appearance group was larger than usual this morning. On the way, Matt Hiles, a handsome African American detention officer who'd accompanied them to the football game, stopped her.

"Hey, do you have a minute. I have some phone calls that I think you might want to hear between Tommy Calander, and his girl, Cassie Maltos. I heard that you asked for a no-contact order, but apparently detention didn't get a copy of the order. Wait 'til you hear this. You'll wish you hadn't."

Christian followed Matt into the detention supervisor's office where he punched a few buttons on a large console in front of him. The juvenile detention center taped all of the phone calls from the inmates to the outside. The calls often led to important information when solving crimes. There was a loud ringing tone and then a monotone voice said, "This is the Benton Franklin County Juvenile Justice Detention Center. This phone call is being recorded. Please push one to accept this call."

"*Hello?*" Christian immediately identified Cassie's soft voice.

"*Cass? It's me, Tommy. Wassup?*"

"*Tommy! How long are you in for?*" Her voice sounded childlike and hopeful.

"*F-ing-ay, six more days. That hoe Vargas has it out for me, I swear. She can go to hell for all I care. Why haven't you written me?*"

"*I didn't know how long you were going to be in there. I will today, I promise.*"

"*Yeah, whatever. I hate my life. You're probably out bangin' another dude any way. Why should I even want to be around?*"

"*Tommy, stop it. You know I won't do that,*" Cassie's voice quivered.

"*I'm going to do it this time. I'm going to call it quits.*"

"*What do you mean? Stop saying that, please!*" Cassie pleaded. "*I love you!*"

"*Whatever. What do I have to live for if I can't count on you? You don't show me any support.*" Tommy's voice had turned cruel in its accusations.

Cassie began to cry, her sobs deep and convulsive. "*I love you! Please don't make me feel bad because you're in there. I can't do anything about it.*"

"*YOU CAN WRITE ME!*" Tommy shouted. "*Cassie, you're useless. Don't you know anything about being my woman by now?*" A recording announced they had a minute remaining.

"*Tommy, I will write three letters today to make up for it.*" Cassie paused and then said gruffly, "*Get out of here.*" A muffled voice could be heard that sounded like Cassie's mom.

"*My mom says 'hi',*" Cassie mumbled.

"*Yeah. Why don't you tell that bitch to bail me out? Hi. Whatever. I gotta go.*"

"*Tommy... Tommy, wait. I love you.*"

"*Bye.*"

A deep sob could be heard. "*Bye,*" Cassie cried.

When the tape clicked off, Christian uncurled her hands. They had been balled into fists while her shoulders were knotted into ropes of tension. "That makes me sick. Tommy is such a manipulator," she grumbled to Matt.

"He's got her wrapped up tight. She is one sad little puppy around him."

"I hate to see this. Cassie is such a talented, adorable girl when she wants to be. What's with this good girl/bad boy thing?"

Matt gave her a slow smile. "I don't know, but if you have an aversion, I promise to be a good boy."

Christian blushed self-consciously. "Good boys are not always good..." she countered. "But really, I sometimes wonder what it's going to take to get these girls thinking straight."

"Didn't you tell me that Cassie was raised in a strictly religious home? Those kids are so controlled by their parents, the church. Sometimes this is the outcome. Good girls going for the bad boys to rebel against their sheltered world."

"So you're giving me a little Psych 101 now?" Christian replied with a grin.

"I'm all about it, but I've already passed 301. I'll be done with my masters in June. Speaking of which, I was hoping you could help me out. I'm in a stats research class that's kicking my butt. Would you be willing to coach me on some stuff?"

His large brown eyes locked on hers, hopeful in their steady gaze.

A foreign stirring in her abdomen suddenly happened. How long had it been since that feeling had been there? "Sure, I'd love to get my hands dirty again. I actually liked my research classes."

"I hear that you aced them."

"How do you know that?"

"My buddy, Daniel. He talks about you all the time."

She felt herself blush again. "I'll talk to Lilly now." He smiled warmly and led her down the hall to the girls pod.

"So here we are again," Christian sighed, putting down her file on the small detention library table a few minutes later. Lilly squirmed in her chair, her eyes shifting from one side of the room to the other. "Your UA was dirty for just about everything, Lilly."

"I know. I was trying to stay clean, but I got nowhere to go, so I keep ending up with Blanks. He's the one who's giving me the stuff."

"I don't want to hear any more excuses. You're not getting out until I can get you into inpatient treatment. The alternative is drug court. I'm not going to stand by and watch you slowly kill yourself."

The girl refused to meet her eyes. "So whassup with my new boyfriend, Tommy?"

"He's bad news, Lilly. He's probably going to do some more time on that drive-by shooting. And he still hangs with Cassie. Why would you want to be with a cheater?"

"It ain't him. It's that little hoebag. She better keep her hands off my man. Besides, he's only using her for cash."

"What does that tell you about him? You really want to date a guy who chooses to use girls like that?"

Lilly just shrugged.

"Let's talk about how this can look. If you let me know where to find your buddy, Blanks, then I will talk to the prosecutor about your new charges. Maybe we can get them dropped to a misdemeanor."

"Yeah, okay. Blanks is staying with his sister-in-law, Candy, out on Chemical Drive. It's a blue house with an RV parked out front, down by the lagoon."

Christian couldn't believe her ears. Could it be that easy? And she knew just the house. It was painted a dark turquoise and had a purple door with yellow trim.

They talked a few more minutes and then, just as Christian was getting up to take Lilly back to her cell, Matt burst through the door.

"You got to get downstairs right away. Daniel's looking for you. Apparently a minor emergency."

When she got downstairs, Daniel was waiting for her in the office. "What's the emergency?" she asked worriedly.

"I just got off the phone with my grandmother. I was telling her about you. She wants to meet you….tonight."

"What? Why?"

"She's a Mexican healer. Most of what she does is mumbo-jumbo, but some people believe in her kind of medicine." He gave her an earnest gaze. "We call them, *la curandera*. She who cures. And I don't mean with real medicines. She makes up the most horrible tasting concoctions and suddenly, you get well. She made me drink all kinds of stuff when I was a kid." His face looked like he just sucked on a lemon as he conjured a visceral memory.

Christian laughed. "I should have the Mexican grandmother, with my last name. On the other hand, O'Callahan conjures

Leprechauns and Guinness. That's sounds cool. When can I meet her?"

"I'm going by today after work. Tonight's her fresh tamale night. We all go over."

Christian laughed again. "How many of you do I have to contend with?"

He started counting on his fingers. A stray lock of his hair fell forward and Christian noticed for the first time how truly handsome he was. "Sixteen of us....*at least.*"

♊

Later that evening, they headed out to Connell. The evening was cool, though the sky was clear and the sunset blazed like fire in the western sky. She was relaxed for the first time that day.

"So I don't mean to intrude, but we are partners after all. And by the way, happy birthday." He handed her a card.

Christian glanced over at him. "Thanks." After she read and laughed, she said, "Go on..."

"I have a feeling there is a whole bunch of stuff you've never told me about you, about your past. Your husband's death, your parents whom you've said are not your birth parents, your sister whom you've mentioned in the past tense. It seems to me that you've had a helluva lot more loss than most women your age."

Christian nodded, feeling completely tongue-tied in the face of an explanation.

Leaning toward her, he tousled her hair. "Hey kiddo, only if you ever want to talk about it."

"I'm not too good at that. It's too hard to explain. Your grandmother, I hope she can help me, though."

They arrived at Maria's home an hour later. The small ranch-styled house was painted a bright sky blue. Its tiny fenced yard was crammed with rosebushes and miniature statues of strange-looking creatures that appeared to be something between leprechauns and dwarfs. As they got out of the car, Daniel explained the decorations with a touch of embarrassment in his voice. "My grandmother is very superstitious. Her yard art is more for protection than for decoration. She thinks these idiotic-looking things will keep the bad spirits away."

As they entered the house, the sound of mariachi music was blaring from a small television set. Daniel led her into the back where his large Hispanic family engulfed the elderly woman's steamy kitchen. He introduced her to his four brothers, three wives and several grandchildren who seem to appear and disappear in increasing numbers as he issued a sort of roll call. The group was imbued with a rowdy sense of camaraderie, joking with one another and engaging in horseplay. The spicy scent of garlic and cilantro was in equal measure to the heavy smell of corn oil and sizzling sausage. Marie made her own tortillas, but the gang of brothers lined up to help her, mixing, rolling and flipping the corn meal mixture with the expertise of someone taught young.

The remainder of the evening was full of laughter, new friendships and delicious homemade tamales. After a lifetime in the fields, Maria seemed as ancient and mysterious as a Mesopotamian riverbed. As they prepared to leave, *La Curandera* made a point of walking them to the door. In broken English, she said, "Senorita sad," as she patted her heart. "Don't be afraid. He is here to help you find answers. See me again." She handed Christian as small blue agate. "This will keep you safe until then."

"Thank you," the younger woman said graciously.

Daniel gave his grandmother a kiss and promised to bring
Christian another time soon. As they drove away, he asked, "Did
you have a nice time?'

"Of course." She grinned. "I completely forgot it was my
birthday."

"Is that good?"

"It is when you're me." She leaned back and closed her eyes,
listening to the hum of the heater and the soft jazz on the radio.
She was content and without fear, for the first time in days. But she
knew, despite what the *la curandera* had told her, that the dark man
was sometimes late with his information.

CHAPTER 6

♊

The snow was falling hard when Christian opened the door to put the dog out the next morning. From the evening before, the clear skies had thickened to a mottled white and her front yard had become an instant fairyland. She laughed at Bear as he tiptoed cautiously through several inches of the powder. His memory didn't last long, she thought, remembering last year's heavy fall. Yet his searching abilities were outstanding. Once he'd found a rape victim, naked, spray-painted with gang insignias and wrapped in duck tape who was wandering the ditch banks in North Franklin County on a snowy night. She had fallen into a ditch and in the darkness, would have been otherwise impossible to find. The track animal had won a commendation and she'd been given a shot at a new job. Since joining probation after years of working in the NGO world, she'd definitely found her niche.

Bear finally began scampering about, realizing suddenly that the snow wasn't all bad. After doing his business, he bounded in to give his master a sloppy kiss. She rubbed his big, furry head and turned to get ready for work when the phone rang. She glanced at the clock. It was not yet seven, she moaned, wondering who could be calling so early.

"Hello?"

"Is this Christian Vargas?"

"Yes, why?"

"You better watch your back, bitch. You'll be the one dead if you don't keep your nose out of my business." With that, the phone disconnected.

Glancing around, she quickly shut the front window's blind. She double-checked the front door lock and ran to the kitchen to check the door there. Then she called Daniel.

"Hey, it's me. I just got a threatening phone call. It came up on caller I.D. as unknown."

"I'm on my way. Don't erase the message."

Daniel had set up a system on her phone to tape all of her conversations after she'd received threatening calls a year before. It turned out that her phone number was still listed in some of the older phone books and a couple of disgruntled kids had made the calls. They were eventually identified and given a strong dose of detention time. Since then, any time Christian found an old phone book, she would check for her name and then, surreptitiously if necessary, throw the thing away.

Glancing at the clock, Christian figured she had enough time to take a quick shower before Daniel arrived. She stopped in her bedroom to grab her pepper spray and entered the bathroom, pausing to look behind her for a second time.

♊

By the time they'd arrived at work, Daniel was in a desperate state. He'd already called his friend at the phone company in attempts to trace the owner of the phone. Unfortunately cell phones made that a modern impossibility. He brought the tape to work to check against voices on the tapes in detention. That, too, was a long shot. The taping system was fairly antiquated and voices were fuzzy at best. Still, Daniel had a hunch that the call came from Blanks.

"Why do you think it's him?" Christian asked, trying to complete a probation violation on a kid who refused to go to school.

"I have a hunch, that's all. Hey, maybe I have a little of my grandmother in me, ya know?' He pushed his hair back and continued his scrutiny of recent phone records.

"I can't wait to see your grandmother again. There's definitely something mysterious about her. I do feel it. But there were so many of you, I couldn't get a word, especially an English word, in edgewise."

"Here," he shouted. "The phone number is here on this sheet. Dated September 16, 2005. Lilly Host calling out to a cell phone. Same number as the one the phone company said came through on your phone. So there you go!"

Christian gave him a nod of admiration. "I love your tenacity. Now let's call the phone from our office cell. They can't trace it back to Juvy that way."

Daniel grinned. "Here we go." He dialed the number and moved closer to her where he bent to her ear as they listened together. A loud rap song came on, a full minute of derisive lyrics, and then a raspy woman's voice said, "Hi. This is Candy. All's good in the Hood, yo, leave a message if you would."

Christian rolled her eyes. "*Please.* That woman's probably older than me."

"At least we know it came from Blanks, or one of his hommies. Now we've got proof that he's hanging with Candy, which might just give the Kennewick Police Department what they need to get a warrant."

"You know that piece of paper that Hannah found at the Jester's clubhouse, the one with the numbers on it? You'll never guess what those numbers were. The phone number and the street address of that couple who were murdered in Oregon, along with the date of the robbery."

Daniel's face was grim. "As long as he's out there, you are not going to be alone. Bring Bear and come to my house until they pick up that piece of dirt. We can go up to my cabin. It's the holiday weekend anyway."

She hesitated, unsure and nervous at the thought of being alone with Daniel. Finally she agreed. "I still have to visit the Maltos family. You can pick me up at six."   A few minutes later she left work, arriving at the Maltos home fifteen minutes later. When she got there, Mrs. Maltos was in a frenzy.

"Please, come in. I must apologize. I've been doing the books all day for my wedding business. The house is such a terrible mess!" Sue Maltos explained, flitting around like a frightened bird, wiping the kitchen counters in a frantic way.

Christian took her time in responding. Gently she took one of the woman's hands in hers and looked her directly in the eyes. "Sue, your home is beautiful and has never been anything but perfect whenever I've come by. Please relax, ok? Is Cassie here?"

"She should be here for lunch any minute. Please, sit down. Would you like a cup of coffee?" At that moment, the phone rang. As Sue turned to answer it, Cassie burst through the door, singing at the top of her lungs.

"Hey, how are ya?" the girl called out as she jogged down the stairs to the basement. "Be up in a minute."

A few more minutes passed before Cassie bounded into the room. She was wearing a plaid mini skirt, black tights and an orange and black sweater, which were her school colors. Her large, almond-shaped eyes were ablaze with a new life. She'd discarded the sullen, slit-eyed look along with her normal EMO dress style.

"Hi, Cassie. Cute outfit."

"Yeah, today was school colors day," she replied, biting into a large peanut butter and jelly sandwich that Sue had generously placed in front of her. "I guess I'm what you'd call prosocial-looking." She giggled.

"You're an interesting girl, Cassie. You're somewhat of a chameleon."

"Whaddaya mean?"

Sue hovered nearby, as though gleaning the younger woman's every word.

"You can be anyone you want, better than most girls. One minute a singer, the next a school leader, then a bad boy's girlfriend." Christian gave Cassie a hard stare. "What's it going to be for your future?"

Cassie looked down and began to pick at her sandwich. "I broke up with him yesterday. He's been cheating on me. I'm done with him." When she looked up, her expression was a vivid mixture of pain and remorse.

Christian nodded. "I know it's hard. My first boyfriend did a number on me, too. But I was so much stronger for leaving him. I'm proud of you, Cassie. I know it's not easy, that it hurts a lot. But I'll bet you there are a hundred boys that would like to take you out."

Cassie blushed. "Yes. The good thing is that I'm starting over, with everyone. Check it out. Three guys called me last night, *including* Jeremy Smith! He's the bomb and he asked me to go snowboarding this Sunday."

"I know Jeremy Smith. He's the center for Kennewick's varsity basketball team, right?" Christian received an affirmative nod.

Sue walked in and clapped her hands, signaling her cue to join back into the conversation. "That's my girl. She is so beautiful and smart and talented. She deserves a nice boy like Jeremy. You know, he's a member of our church as well."

"*Mom*! Use to be. He used to go there. Both of us aren't going anymore." Cassie issued a warning, but unlike other times, her tone hinted of a new tolerance. Christian was cautiously surprised by the girl's softening attitude.

Sue smiled. "Well, you might change your minds. And in celebration, I think a shopping trip is in order. Your ski coat is looking pretty ragged."

Cassie squealed. "Really? Oh Mom, you're the best."

"Speaking of best, I want you to know I see a big change in your attitude toward your mom, Cassie. I hear respect coming out of you now."

Sue piped up. "I feel so much better about things, too. That homework assignment that you gave us, to write down our answers before we speak them. I enjoyed that. Sometimes I react to Cassie rather than act, if you know what I mean."

Christian nodded. "Of course. We're all conditioned in our families to behave and react in a certain way. It requires a lot of perseverance and courage to change what we know. What about you, young lady? What's different for you now?"

Cassie gazed up, her large brown eyes solemn and forgiving. "When I started answering your questions, the ones you gave me for my journal, that I always tell myself my mom is wrong, before

I think about whether or not she might really be right...does that make sense?"

"Yes. We call that our defenses. We put our defenses and make other people wrong because we are afraid, or we don't want to change the way we do things. What is your mom right about?"

Cassie looked over at her mom, stuck out her tongue and crossed her eyes. Her playful attitude was the charming part of her personality. "Ok, so Mom's right about other guys liking me. And she's right that I can be smart in school and still be cool with myself. I have been raising my hand a lot more in class lately. My friends are telling me they didn't know I was smart and they like it. Now they call me to help with homework and stuff." Sue nodded and uncharacteristically, didn't respond with an "I told you so." There were some nice changes going on, perhaps enough so that the violence in this family may finally come to an end.

"You all have a wonderful Thanksgiving. I'll call you next week, but I'll probably hook up with Cassie at school, okay?"

Cassie grinned. "Oh, great, my P.O. comes to school." She shrugged good-naturedly. "That's cool with me."

Back at the office, Christian finished a few e-mails and got ready to head home. A nagging feeling had started in the back of her mind. She sensed danger again, and this time it was regarding the Maltos family.

As she drove up to her house, Christian realized she'd forgotten to stop at Cassie's house to get her work cell phone. Her partner's truck was idling in the driveway. Her porch light was on and he was standing in front of it, studying something on the door.

"Hi," she called as she locked her car doors and walked toward him.

"Damn!"

"Really? That's the greeting I get?"

"No, I mean it. Look at this!"

He moved to let her see the cause of his reaction. On her door, painted with blue paint were the numbers #187.

"You know what that means?" His eyes blazed with anger.

"No, what?"

"187 are the police call numbers for homicide. I think we'd better get your stuff and get out of here. I've already called RPD." Daniel slowly pulled a Glock from his jacket pocket. "Let's go."

Christian's gut twisted as she stared at his gun. "When did you start carrying a gun?"

"I have one in my truck, all the time. You should have one, too."

"Guns won't stop someone who's intent on killing us." At that moment, his cell phone rang.

Flipping it open, he began to listen, his eyes narrowing and his hand reaching out to grip Christian's arm in a tight vise. "We'll be there."

"What is it? What's going on?"

"Get in the truck! Now." He'd never spoken to her in that tone. She responded almost robotically, climbing up in to the cab and waiting as he finished his call.

Moments later, he climbed into the vehicle and slowly turned to face her. "I'm not sure how to tell you this. It's the Maltos family. There's been a double homicide."

Christian's body sunk into the seat, melting away as she took in his words.

She shook her head. "No. That can't be. I was just there. I was going to get my phone. I left it there."

"I know. Cassie used your phone to call for help. That's how they tracked it back to probation. That's why they called me."

A tortured sound peeled from the depths of her, leaping from her mouth, an alien sound both animal and inhuman. She jumped from the truck and made it as far as the front porch where she plunged into convulsive motion as her body tried to purge itself from the truth. Daniel came up behind her, his hand on her back, rubbing softly. She wanted to push him away, scream at him to leave with his bad lies, but she knew he was not lying and that he would do whatever he could to console her.

"We can leave right now, for the cabin. We can get Bear and go. They don't need us there. It was simply my first reaction, to say we would come."

Christian wiped her face with her coat sleeve and shook her head as she wobbled to her feet. "No. We go. Now. Let's get my dog first though. Let's hope he can help somehow."

She ran in the front door, hastily threw some things in a suitcase, grabbed a bag of dog food and brought Bear out seconds later. The dog was wiggling with delight at the sight of Christian. Opening the door, she reached out and half pulled him into the truck, ordering him into the back of the King cab. The creature moaned with joy and continued to squirm, his thick tail slapping the sides of the doors. She reached back and stroked him, a brief sense of happiness flooded her, despite what they were about to face.

Daniel sped onto Highway 240. Within the next mile, he was forced to pull off to the side as several patrol cars passed them. Christian shivered as he repeated his phone conversation. He thought they should turn back, that she was too vulnerable to face the horrific scene, but he was the one who'd turned green when he'd described Randy's message. Sue Maltos had been shot first as her daughter screamed into the probation officer's phone for help, according to the 911 operator. Then a scuffle and another gun shot as the phone went dead.

"Hey, can you hear me?" her partner started again. She had opened the window and hung her head out, gasping for air. They had reached the next exit.

She must have realized his plan because she yelled, "No. Take me there. I want to see. I want to help."

"Randy just passed us. It appears the sheriff's department is not sure of jurisdiction. They've called in KPD. If you're sure you're okay to go, we'll follow them in."

She turned, giving him an anguished look. "How can we do anything else? We know this family. They're one of ours. We've been there for them." At that, she collapsed into sobs.

"Listen, if you don't pull it together, you're going to feel foolish once we get there."

Christian nodded. Straightening up, she rubbed her cheeks as though she were trying to remove paint. "I'll be okay. You're right. It's just that sometimes I know when something bad is going to happen."

"You knew about the murders before they happened?' His face scrunched in disbelief. "Because of the 187 on your door?"

"No. It's not like that. No, not exactly. I feel this feeling sometimes. Before things have happened in my life. I can't explain it." She shuddered and closed her eyes. "I promise I'll explain when this is all over. I'll try anyway."

As they turned off the highway and took the roundabout that led to the Maltos home, Christian offered a silent prayer. *Please give Mr. Maltos strength, dear God. Please help him to survive this nightmare.*

As they reach the cul de sac, the activity level suddenly increased a hundred fold. The quiet side street off Canyon Drive had become of circus of sorts. Spotlights had been set around the perimeter of the house and the crime lab was now working against the clock with only a sliver of sunlight left on the horizon. Bear immediately started growling and began to paw at the window of the truck, eager to get out and go to work.

"He needs to stay in the car for now. I'll ask Sheriff Gomez if he's interested in hiring my one and only."

"Great! I'm getting my partner back." He had gone to the Gulf War and had seen death. It was part of their job, in the line of duty and all that. He didn't have the bleeding heart temperament of his female counterpart, but she knew that he was ragged with disillusionment. There were just so many ways they could help these families. Sometimes, it didn't matter what they did. As she contemplated the circumstances, she decided that it was Tommy Calander who'd had a hand in this. He'd been in on several assaults, and there were 2 assaults against Cassie that had never been reported, according to Jim Maltos. The boy was angry and impulsive. Indirectly, the restraining order could have been the impetus to this crime.

They cautiously approached the front of the house where Detective Jensen and his assistant, James Doughtery, stood, immersed in deep conversation. Michael, their boss, who had turned around to talk to the press, didn't acknowledge their arrival. Christian groaned. "That stupid reporter. If she comes at me again, I'm going to knock her down."

"Now there's a side to you I rarely see." Daniel chuckled softly. They stopped on the grass in front of the taped barricade near the porch and instantly began to scan the area for anything unusual.

The front door of the house was open and the sharp metallic odor of spilled blood blew in the icy breeze. She felt her stomach reel and she thought she might be sick. Turning away, she gulped some fresh air, trying to remember the layout of the Maltos home. The front door opened into the living room, with the stairs to the basement on the immediate right. A walkway led in front of the stairs to the kitchen. The master bedroom was to the left of the front door.

Just then the coroner's team brought out a second body, one that appeared to be headless from the shape beneath the body bag. She heard the coroner's assistant say that they'd found Sue Maltos in the master bedroom with her head blown to pieces. Christian felt dizzy as they passed with the gurney and grabbed onto the porch railing to steady herself.

Fighting to stay in control, Christian forced her mind back to the present. She recalled that Cassie's bedroom was in the basement, out of sight from the top of the stairs. She'd learned to make note of her surroundings as an in-home therapist. There had been many occasions when she'd walked into a home to do her magic and noticed drug paraphernalia, weapons and pornography, camouflaged in corners like an 'I spy' page out of a kids book. Yet since becoming a probation officer and working with Bear, her observation skills had developed into a fine-tuned machine.

"Daniel, look, behind us." They turned slightly as a figure in the shadows moved from the side of the front porch. "Mr. Maltos is up there on the porch. He's trying to get our attention." Christian felt her insides clutch into knots as Jim stepped out, motioning them to come closer. It was as though a courageous separate self moved forward and climb the steps, taking the man's hands into her own. For a moment they stared at one another, both hesitant and then she pulled Jim toward her, whispering, "I'm so sorry, so sorry. Oh Jim, what can I do for you?" The broad-shouldered man then seemed to curl like a child against her, his muscular back lifting and dropping in a shuddering rhythm of heavy sobs.

"This can't be true. I don't, can't live…without…my…girls." While attempting to keep the large man from falling, she vaguely remembered that Cassie had an older half-brother who was in the Air Force. Certainly he had not yet been notified. There were things that she could still do to help.

After a long moment, Jim Maltos pulled away from her. He appeared somewhat embarrassed by his momentary collapse. He wiped his eyes as she continued to hold his hands. "Jim, have you notified your son? Can I do that for you?" Behind them, her partner tried to stave off the press. Obviously Mr. Maltos had been hiding from the media. They reminded her of ravenous dogs, eager to take a bite out of the devastated man before them.

"They want to interview me at the station. I don't want to do it alone. Will you two come with me?"

"Of course we will. We'll stay with you and then take you wherever you feel safe."

"My best friend lives over in Richland. I work with him out in the Area. But how can we avoid those TV folks?"

"I don't think we can go through the house. It's a designated crime scene. Let's…" Christian paused and glanced around. Her boss was enjoying his moment in the spotlight, literally, along with Sheriff Gomez and the Kennewick Chief of Police. The coroner's van had pulled away and the crime lab techs were packing up their gear for the night. Though Jim Maltos had previously identified the bodies, he would be a prime suspect in the murders and wouldn't be finished for the night until he'd made a statement. Glancing around, she noticed a door from the porch to the garage.

"Jim, is there another door that leads out of the garage on the other side?"

He nodded. "It goes to the back gate that leads to the field behind the house." Quickly she pulled her phone from her pocket and turned her back to the crowd where her partner was standing less than twenty feet away. Within seconds of her dialing, she could hear the distinctive Creed song indicating his ring tone.

"This is the Big D."

"Don't look back at me. Just listen a minute. I'm going to take Mr. Maltos through the side door of the garage, off the porch. You can't see it from where you are. We're going through the other side of the garage and out the back gate. Have Officer Rusk meet us on the west side of the field behind the house."

"Sure thing."

By the time they'd hiked through the sagebrush-dappled field to meet the awaiting police car, large white flakes of snow had begun to fall from the sky like stars.

Ⅱ

It was nearly dawn. Scarlet and tangerine streaks painted the sky to the east as he finished cleaning up. Smiling with satisfaction, he wiped his hands on his jeans and then looked down to see the damage done. The crimson red of the blood spray still stained the sweater, but his precious car looked perfect again. He considered throwing the sweater out with the rest of the stuff, but had an attachment to it due to the fact that he'd stolen it from his local nemesis. If he returned it to its rightful owner and some of the evidence remained, the crime could be pinned on the other guy.

Sauntering down the narrow dirt path between the corn rows, he thrust the first bottle as far as he could throw, which was quite a distance. Even if the car tracks were found, the cleaning product remnants would be far enough away. Flexing his muscles, he admired his own strength and physical prowess. He'd been the state champion in the shot-put and javelin during his senior year of high school as well as the state wrestling champion in his weight class. The Windex bottle was the next to disappear into the ocean of golden stalks along with the small can of leather cleaner. The latter was an expensive product, but he didn't want to leave any traces of a recent cleaning should his car be the subject of anyone's investigation. Though normally a risk-taker, he also had a cautious side to his nature. In fact, he was a systems guy. Everything required a procedure in life and he prided himself on creating systems that worked for him.

Shivering from the cold, he hurried back to the car and climbed in. The fully-loaded sports car was parked dead center in the middle of Penny Stockton's Dad's farm where he'd taken her a few times, hoping to get some ass. She was a tight little bitch, he thought wryly, placing a mental bet with himself that he'd fuck her before the year's end. Just thinking about it got him aroused. He unzipped his pants and went to work. It would be hours before the workers arrived to finish cleaning up the popular Corn Stalk Maze where he now pleasured himself.

As his member grew in size and tautness, he sped up his rhythm, his muscular arm feeling no stress. Due to his athletic history, he had an exceptionally strong right arm, but occasionally he would switch hands to give his left side a workout as well. As he deftly stroked, he thought about the killings and noticed that he became even more aroused than would be expected. Still, violence had titillated him in the past. Raping that cute little redhead a couple of summers ago was the most memorable thrill to which his mind often dwelled, but this was completely different. His mind methodically recounted the details of the last twelve hours. He had stopped at the Maltos home to tell Cassie that it was over between them, not expecting to find her mother at home. Sue Maltos had let him in and had then asked him to step into her bedroom to have a private talk. Though the woman was old enough to be his mother, she was quite attractive and so he'd found himself mildly excited by the idea. However, once they'd gone in, she'd immediately launched into a verbal attack. She'd become hysterical as she confessed that she'd found out about Cassie's pregnancy and forced abortion. Initially she'd just raged with words, but finally lunged at him in anger. At that point he had responded by pushing her up against the closet door and telling her that he'd kill her if she didn't shut up. He aimed a warning shot at the ceiling and fired. Then suddenly Cassie appeared. Her face had shifted from fear-induced anger to utter shock when she'd recognized him. She'd stumbled as she stepped towards him while her mother screamed. Without pause, he'd leapt on her, pinning her to the bed as the gun went off, hitting Sue Maltos directly in the face as she'd moved forward to help her daughter. Normally feisty, Cassie had instantly turned into a rag doll, screaming in horror as she watched her mother's face rip into a thousand fragments of tissue from the bullet's impact. Fortunately she'd warned him that she'd called 911 before the first shot, so he killed her, too. The act of killing gave him an orgasm of a lifetime. He groaned loudly, shaking with the effort and bursting power of it all.

Minutes later he opened his eyes and noticed that some blood was on the steering wheel. Cursing loudly, he pulled off the sweater, upon which Sue and Cassie's blood had dried. He wiped the leather-encased wheel and got out of the car.

By the time he started the car and drove through the field onto the main highway back to town, the sun had risen. "Like the rebirth of a new day, I, too, am reborn," he sang the popular Christian tune as he drove south towards the glittering lights of the city.

CHAPTER 7

Thanksgiving Day

♊

"It was horrible," Christian moaned, dropping her face in her hands. "They wouldn't let me go in, but I managed to convince him to keep his statement short. I only know that from television shows. He's retained an attorney, Dwight Sellum, but from what I know of the guy, he's pretty lousy in the courtroom."

Daniel nodded in agreement. "How can they even think Jim Maltos is guilty? The guy loved his wife and daughter more than life itself. I'm willing to testify to that."

"Me, too. But apparently he left work early that afternoon and no one knows where he went. So if he doesn't have a witness to attest to his whereabouts, our sometimes lame law enforcement will definitely take the easy route."

"Yep. I've seen that before, plenty of times." He briskly stirred up a batch of scrambled eggs. Their Thanksgiving feast was made up of bacon, eggs and hash browns, the only supplies they'd had time to grab from a local store before heading up to the cabin later that night. The evening before the murders, Christian had attempted to make her famous Dutch Almond rolls, with the initial thought of going to her brother's home in Bellevue for the holidays, but the weather had made the trip impossible. Though their extended rising time had produced the largest lumps of dough this side of Amish communal kitchen, Daniel had insisted the marzipan-filled gems come along for the ride. They'd had to place them on the dashboard in order to preserve their self-inflated status.

Christian stretched out on the plaid couch, which faced the Pullman kitchen. Bear lay on the hook rug beside her, snoozing contentedly. The cabin had turned out to be a delightful surprise. Tucked into the Blue Mountains on the west side of Lake Wallowa, it was named The Sherwood Cottage and had the magical qualities of a true mountain retreat. The central room was lined with pine paneling and a sharply pitched ceiling. An enormous river rock fireplace hugged the north wall while large eastern windows offered views of the lake. A wood-burning stove was the centerpiece of the blue and white tiled kitchen. The walls of the two tiny bedrooms were decorated with hand painted scenes of forest picnics and Bambi-like wildlife. Brightly colored Star quilts covered the beds and the bathroom had an original claw foot bathtub.

"I can see why Tammy wants this cabin, despite the fact we had to dig our way through the snow to reach the front door. This place is adorable in every way. Besides, if it's not worth a fortune now, it will be in a few more years."

"Yes. I think I've finally convinced her that the upkeep would be her downfall. We've renegotiated. I'm giving her the ski boat instead, along with all the furniture at the condo. Surprisingly, she seems satisfied with that."

"I know you don't want to spend all weekend talking about this, but you and I both know that Jim is innocent. By the time we get back, if he's still in the hot seat, we're going to start our own, albeit secret, investigation."

"Good plan, but until then, just for the sake of stress interference, can we take walks, sled, play cards and watch the moon rise?"

Christian laughed. "Are you talking about that remote and rare commodity some call relaxation? Yeah, I think we could both use a little of that right now. Grubs up!"

Standing up, she walked to the kitchen door to retrieve the fruit platter that she'd prepared earlier. Her love of fruit was evident in the neatly sliced piles of fresh pineapple, papaya, blackberries and kiwi. The sweet aroma of almonds and smoky scent of bacon filled the cabin as they sat down in front of the fire to eat.

"If this isn't a perfect Thanksgiving dinner, I don't know what is," he said, diving into his meal.

"You're a good sport. I'm just a little curious about the next few days. I don't know if I can live on canned soup alone." In fact, it was a nearly perfect setting, though her pain for Jim Maltos stirred from time to time.

"We'll go into town, to Joseph. It's one of the most unique little places. They've actually got a famous bronze artist who lives here and has his own foundry. I think you were asleep when we drove through town last night, but you'll see. There are large bronze sculptures all over town. It's the wild west with a touch of class around here."

Christian giggled. "I don't think of you as the type to really like art."

"What's that supposed to mean? I liked your art stars, didn't I?"

"That's not art. It's an obsession."

"So what. I want you to make some stars for in here. The A-frame ceiling would be a perfect place to put a few. Would you do some?"

Hesitation mounted silence. A long moment passed. "It's not like that. I make the stars as a means of emotional survival. Each star has a deep and profound meaning to me. They represent people, deceased people whom I've loved and lost." She tugged on her long brunette ponytail, feeling self-conscious.

Daniel stared into the fire as though searching for words. "The Maltos women, they were somebody to both of us. Would you turn their memories into your beautiful stars? If they hung in here, we could both come and honor them."

In that instant, Christian felt a sense of belonging unlike anything she'd felt before. They were mutual survivors to a tragedy. Together, they had become witnesses to terror and for that they shared a very special bond.

"We're like soldiers in the same trench, watching our buddies fall," he replied softly. "Remember, I was supposed to go back out there with you. If Mike Sanchez's mom hadn't come in and held us up, well, who knows if we'd be here right now."

"I know I said I didn't want to talk about this, but I guess I need some details. I know you have them. I heard you talking to Rusk this morning, even if I did appear to be sleeping. He was the first on the scene, right?"

He nodded as he tore into his second almond roll. "These are awesome. I'd marry you if I could get these every morning," he joked. She appreciated his repartee, but her tenacity meter was on now and she wouldn't be satisfied until a few things had been answered.

"Please, tell me what else you know."

Daniel put his plate on the coffee table and leaned back into an old oak rocker. Closing his eyes, he began to share. "The 911 call came in at four-forty-two. Apparently you had left their place around twelve-thirty or so, right?"

"Yes. We'd agreed to meet that afternoon at lunch. I was there for about an hour or so."

"Okay. So apparently Cassie had already found your phone when she heard her mom scream. There were no signs of forced entry, so whoever came into the house walked right in."

"Yeah, I know they didn't lock their doors, like so many people in this town. Ours is such a naïve community in so many ways. When I lived in Portland, everyone locked their doors and most women I knew at school carried mace."

"That's the Tri-Cities. We've grown faster than we can emotionally and socially handle. We're a government town inside a farming community. It's a dichotomy, kinda like forcing the Moslems and Christians to be best friends. Most people are more intimidated by the Department of Energy than they are by crime."

"So Cassie called 911 from the basement?"

"Apparently. Randy said that the 911 operator told her to get out of the house or try to find a place to hide. Instead Cassie replied that she was going upstairs to protect her mom."

Christian pushed down tears. It had been a long road with this family and the relationship between Sue and Cassie was a tortured one. Sue had never truly believed her daughter really loved her. Now sadly it was obvious that her daughter loved her so much as to place herself in harm's way. Cassie's love was exceptional and courageous and single-minded and the sad waste of their lives was breaking her heart.

The fire in the large hearth crackled cheerfully, subtly changing the mood as the flames danced hypnotically.

"Hey, what size shoe do you wear?"

"What, you're going to buy me a pair of shoes now?"

Grinning, he threw a pillow at her. "You could use some ass-kickin' boots, but no, I was thinking about going cross-country skiing. Tammy's about your height, size eight shoe. What do you think?'

"Really? I'm a downhill skier. I'd love to try cross-country."

"Great. I'll grab the gear. It's out in the shed. You grab that loaf of French bread and a hunk or two of those cheeses you threw in the cooler. Meet you out front in ten."

The next two hours were the closest thing to heaven that Christian could remember in a long time. The sky was a bright periwinkle blue without a cloud in sight. The powdery snow glistened like a bridal veil as they made their way through the woods. The cedars trees moved slightly in the light breeze as though swaying to an imperceptible song. Bear leaped through the snow, full of excitement, his enormous head bobbing as they skimmed along behind him. Cross-country skiing was easier than she expected and soon she found a rhythm that felt like synchronized skating. Daniel led the way, glancing back every so often to give her an admirable grin.

"You take to this like a fish to water. Sure you've never done this before?"

She returned his generous smile. "No, but I skated a lot as a kid, at Lloyd Center. Ever heard of it?"

"No. Where's it at?"

"Portland, where I mostly grew up after my parents died." She paused in shock. She'd never said that so easily. In the past, it had always come out of her mouth, bitter and burning, a sour residue of pain. There was a rush in her ears, a sudden awareness that she was safe and could speak freely, without the fear of internal emotional chaos.

"Tell me about your childhood. I know a little, but only through Kathy, and, of course, your magical stars."

She took a deep breath and began. "My parents and older sister drowned when I was about four. I was taken in by my mother's sister and her husband. They had four kids already and I was smack in the middle in terms of age. I had two older male cousins, one seven years ahead of me and the other ten years older. The oldest one, Scott, is more like a Dad than a brother or a cousin. He still worries about me. My 'little sisters' as I call them, were one and two at the time I joined the family. I was loved, but also left to my own devices a lot of the time. I took up skating when I was ten. My best friend's mother got me into it. I had to work at the rink after class to pay for my lessons. Later, when I started to compete, I taught the younger kids to pay for my trips."

"Is that the reason you traveled so much?"

"How did you know I traveled?"

Daniel gave a goofy grin and tapped his temple. "It's not like I'm the scarecrow from Wizard of Oz. I've got a brain, girlfriend. Our office is full of stuff. Let's see-you have a rug from Turkey, pottery from Greece, photographs with your signature from Italy and Spain."

Christian felt playful. Plunging herself at him, she toppled them both into the snow. She landed on top of Daniel, her face inches from his own. They paused for a long moment, looking into one another's eyes. Something tingled and move inside her, like a slippery silver bullet deep within her belly. Embarrassed by her unexpected desire, she rolled off, her skis tangling as she did so. In a clumsy attempt to stand up, she fell backwards again and collapsed into a fit of giggles.

"Ok, be the wizard now and help me stand up." Daniel, now standing over her, poised and relaxed, laughed.

"Tell me the rest of your story, then." He reached down and hauled her up. He waited as she brushed the snow from her face and coat. She watched him expectantly, awkward with the moment. Looking away, he pulled out a flask and offered her a drink of Irish coffee. She took a long sip and handed it back.

"There's not much more. By the time I was a teenager, my aunt and uncle were fairly well-off. My uncle worked his way up in Nike and eventually became a vice president. We spent a couple of our summers in Europe while my uncle did business over there. The younger girls looked up to me and I was basically in charge of them, particularly when we traveled overseas."

"So I take it you weren't left with a lot of time to hit the European discos?"

"If you're asking me, did I hook up with some of those gorgeous Italian men, the answer is no. I had a few boyfriends in high school, but nothing serious. Not until I met Tony. What about you?"

"What about me? I grew up here, in farm country. My parents were migrant workers before I was born and eventually settled down and worked for Lamb Weston. The most exciting thing I did as a teenager was cruise Court Street."

"Yeah, but the military was your ticket out, right?"

"Yes, and that *was* exciting. I spent a lot of time in the Mediterranean, primarily in Cyprus until I was sent to the Gulf. That was a short duty, thank god. I didn't get exposed to the gases, didn't end up with the syndrome, like so many guys."

"So that's a real thing. I've read a bit about it. A lot of psychiatrists think it's more psychological than physical in nature."

Daniel shook his head. "It's a poisonous part of the world, all the way around. They think differently, live to die, you know. We live to live over here. We strive to live better and do better. Those poor folks don't have much to look forward to, unless of course they're in with the oil people and the old monarchies."

"I feel that way about our people, too. Look at the kids we work with. They are so distressed in so many ways, relative to our world. No computer means you do poorly in school, no discretionary income means no sports or extracurricular activities. No Dad means no role model, which effects the girls as badly as it does the boys. You can see why our kids join gangs. To fit in, to have a family to belong to and to get the material things they can't otherwise acquire."

"Yeah, it sucks. Not to mention their mental illnesses. Sometimes kids walk in and I think, *this one's a mental health fruit salad…got every diagnosis from ADD to schizophrenia.* Take those genetics combined with an abusive home life…no wonder we have serial killers. Still, I do this job because I feel we're doing the work to make their lives better, little by very little." He turned and threw a well-packed snowball hard against the trunk of nearby tree. His anger was evident in his thrust, spring-loaded with frustration. Christian knew enough about her partner to know the Maltos murders were eating at him.

The Maltos family. She tried to harness the pain, scoop it up or shove it down, but it was too late. A smooth stream of tears rolled down her cheeks. Would this ever stop? Daniel sensed her change in mood. Without turning around, he slowed his pace as they approached the edge of the frozen lake. Pointing to a bench, he murmured. "Let me clean it off. We'll stop for lunch here. You okay?"

Christian watched as he laid out their lunch, her mind now ready for analysis. Grief was just an energy-consuming distraction. "It's crazy! The whole thing doesn't make sense. Let's say someone knew that Mrs. Maltos kept money at home. If they wanted to rob her, why in broad daylight, when her car was in the driveway? And why kill them? Why not just scare them, take the money?"

"You're assuming robbery was the motive."

"Her cash box was empty. I overheard Jensen talking. There was a bank withdrawal slip from the day before in the box for five hundred dollars."

"What if the robbery was just a cover-up for another motive? What if Jim was the perp, or someone who had some secrets to keep? Secrets that the Maltos family knew about and might divulge."

Christian rolled her eyes. "Now you're sounding like a spy novel. And you don't believe any more than I do that Jim killed his beloved wife and daughter. Besides, what kind of ghosts could that family have in their closets? They are good, church-going folks. They hold down jobs, do the right thing in their community."

"Everyone has secrets. You, me, everyone. We all have something we don't want people to know about. If you really want to start looking for answers, start with Cassie's friends. I have a gut feeling you'll find something that links her to this murder. See if you can get a hold of her stuff, like journals, emails, you know."

As they sat down and began to eat, Daniel's phone rang. He pulled it out and looked at the caller's name. "It's Randy. I'll take it, okay?"

She nodded and watched silently as he answered. "Hey buddy, what's going on?"

He listened without saying anything for a long time. Then he gave a low whistle. "Wow. Who was he with? Really? How much?" Another long pause. Then, "Do they think he had something to do with it? How about Saturday? Good. See you then."

He flipped the phone closed and with a nonchalance that nearly took Christian over the edge, he cradled a hunk of brie atop a chunk of French bread.

"Well?" she cried, "Tell me! What's going on?"

Daniel took a large bite and slowly chewed his food, further tempting her curiosity. After taking a swig from the flask, he finally replied, "Blanks was picked up last night around nine at Candy's place in Finley. He was caught in the middle of processing some meth, already had six ounces of it, apparently freshly made as well as a serious amount of China White. He also had $470 on him. He's being considered as a suspect for the Maltos murders."

"Why?"

"Tommy Calander was with him. That kid had access to their house. He also knew that Mrs. Maltos kept money at home. It makes sense."

She nodded and closed her eyes, quieting her racing mind. Slowly a sensation crept forward, pushing out logic and replacing it with an ancient knowing. If her intuition was right, Blanks had absolutely nothing to do with the murders. As sure as the sun rises, Death confirmed her hunch like a shadowy figure stepping dead center on her heart.

CHAPTER 8

December 4, 2005

♊

Black, nebulous clouds framed a sullen sun one week from the day that Sue and Cassie Maltos were murdered. The dawn had come and gone. It was nearly eight o'clock in the morning and yet the thought of going to work was only a vague consideration. Christian hadn't slept much since Saturday and felt the heavy lethargy that accompanied insomnia. Her limbs moved as though underwater and her heart ached with a low-grade fever, one brought on by frustration, grief and helplessness. The only rest that she'd been able to sequester had brought nightmares and vicious memories. Ambien hadn't touched her tempestuous state, nor had self-hypnosis, which was an antidote that, in the past, had been successful in curing sleeplessness.

On Saturday afternoon, she'd returned home from the cabin and had subsequently met up with Randy, Daniel's old friend and key player in the investigation. Over several beers, the story of Blanks arrest and the torrid details of the Maltos murders were revealed. Cassie had been in the basement, out of sight, when the perpetrator had first arrived. She'd called 911, pleading for help and was told to hide, or if possible, leave the home without drawing attention to her presence. Cassie had chosen otherwise. According to the 911 operator, the girl had climbed the stairs to confront the monster who had then left her slain, flat on her back, her hands covering her breasts like a priestess from an ancient tribe, succumbing to the sacrifice of the gods. She was shot in the heart, once, and still cradled Christian's cell phone in her right hand, though her words of despair had been smothered by death.

Christian had spent Sunday in bed, watching Marilyn Monroe movies. It was her feeble attempt at comedic distraction. She'd been a fan of Marilyn's for years, ever since she'd read a book about the fabled actress and learned of her sad and tumultuous life. She identified with the icon's sense of abandonment and admired her acute acting skills. During a time when movies and television still feigned innocence, Monroe was an example of a sensuous idealism that had long been lost to a world of reality TV and live war footage.

One Monday night, in desperation, she'd left a message for her therapist, but in her heart, didn't believe for a moment that Sophia had the ability to sooth the type of pain that she was experiencing. Both in her personal and professional experience, therapy was better for every day problem-solving and cognitive distortions of the past, rather than a curative for the destruction of the soul.

Through Randy and a friend in the sheriff's department, Daniel had managed to get her phone returned, after they'd scanned, dusted and recorded evidence. She found the Motorola wireless on her desk on Tuesday morning, wrapped in a plastic bag, and without enough juice to boot it up. After a three hour charge, she turned it on and began a thorough search of all recorded messages as well as text messages. The county had inadvertently received a free text message service with their cell phone contract, though the department was generally discouraged using the extra feature. However, she could see that it had been accessed late in the day of the murder and was unequivocally certain she hadn't been the one to use it. In seconds, Christian was able to trace a message at 2:06 p.m., a message that could only have been sent by Cassie. Obviously the detectives hadn't considered this feature when gathering evidence, or if they had, they'd left it there for her eyes only.

As with all teen talk, it was difficult to decipher at first. The message had been sent to a 'Sista T' and read: *Got my P.O.'s cell, n.s. Dickbreath's going down. Meet me here at five. He'll be on his way to the pig house. We're awesome!*

She poked around at her memory, trying to catch the message's meaning. 'Sista T' had to be one of Cassie's friends. She recalled that the teen had once mentioned a friend named Tabby with whom she'd grown up in their church. She'd called her, 'her big sister'.

The rest of Tuesday had been filled with the normal daily dramas in the world of juvenile delinquents. As a result, she'd not had time to pursue anything else. A day later, still wet from the shower and trying to get it together for work, Christian flopped down on her bed and called information. Asking for the intended phone number, she pressed 1 for immediate dial. After a few rings, a high-pitched voice answered, "Hi, I mean, good morning, Desert Evangelist Church."

"May I speak to the youth minister? Christian tried to sound casual against the rush of adrenaline in her brain.

The rather distracted receptionist replied, "I don't know… just a minute. Oh, well, the board says that Jason Roads is out for the day." The probation officer thought quickly. Aware that Cassie had recently been to a church retreat and had brought along her Kennewick High choir friend, Sara, who was not a member of the church, she created a ruse.

Keeping her voice a notch higher than usual, she explained, "Hi, I'm Sara Harter and I was at the last youth retreat with Cassie Maltos." The woman's voice caught. The receptionist was all ears.

"I accidentally took home a sweatshirt belonging to Tabby and wondered if I could get her phone number. I can't get it from..." Christian didn't have to perform. Her voice instantly became thick with emotion as she continued, "From Cassie anymore." She heard another gasp as the receptionist fell neatly into her trap.

"Of course, Tabby Smithson. Here's her home. Wait, it appears Jason has her cell number on this list. Ready?"

Inspired by that simple success, she jotted down the number and thanked the woman. Now she was on her way to finding out some answers. Determined to learn the meaning of the message, she continued her mental wanderings as she pulled on a pair of black slacks, a pale green cashmere sweater and her Doc Martins. Brushing her hair, she reflected back on the girl's reaction when, while she was first in detention, Daniel and Christian had interviewed her for the case risk assessment.

The CMAP Risk Assessment tool was used by all juvenile departments in Washington State to determine a youth's propensity to re-offend and then to develop a case management plan to assist the youth in avoiding any re-offense. Covering twelve domains of a teen's life, the tool recreated a picture of aspects such as their friends, drug and alcohol use, school experience, home life, and attitudes and behaviors to name a few. One of the questions was whether a youth had been abused in any way. When they'd asked the adolescent about sexual abuse, a haunted look had crossed

Cassie's features as she simultaneously shook her head 'no'. That was all the proof necessary. In the meantime, Christian had been building trust, waiting for the right moment. Something told her she'd been close to Cassie's secret before Death had snatched the beautiful young one away.

By the time she arrived at work at eight-thirty, there were twenty-seven voice messages on her recorder. Before she dug in, she stopped at her supervisor's office to explain her tardiness. Thomas was, as always, kind and offered his now-daily condolences for her 'situation', adding that her request for a half a day off was approved in order that she attend the funeral.

Her caseload detention headcount was one. Tommy was in again. He'd been picked up with Blanks, charged with possession of meth and due for his arraignment that afternoon. She had not yet visited him in detention. The wound of Cassie's death was still too fresh. Rumor on the street was that he'd given Blanks the address to Cassie's home, encouraging him to rob the place. The investigation was still underway and both Blanks and Mr. Maltos remained suspects.

Daniel was at a Pasco Gang task force meeting all morning so she had the office to herself. A blessing, she decided, though she normally loved his companionship. She'd almost completed the arraignment report when she heard a soft knock. The door was partially open, so she called for the visitor to come in.

Matt walked in slowly and said, "Hey girl, I heard the horrible news. I'm so sorry. That girl was a sweetheart, just a little mixed up, that's all." The compassion in his gentle baritone voice touched her deeply. She gestured for him to shut the door.

"I'm glad you stopped by." She bit her lip and silently ordered her tears to withdraw.

Matt moved toward her. "You look like you need a hug." She nodded in spite of herself and stood up, allowing him to wrap his muscular frame around her. She could smell his aftershave, a familiar scent she recognized as the one that Tony had worn. His chest was hard and yet yielding. She pressed her face to him, just reaching below his collarbone, and tried to steady her legs. If nothing else, the man was sturdy and held her completely.

He gave a single caress to her head, murmuring sounds of reassurance.

"I should have been there, Matt. I could have stopped it. Why did God spare me?"

"Ah, Christian, how do I know? You weren't supposed to be part of this one."

She pulled away and looked up into his eyes. They were a deep brown, but with flecks of gold, like a polished piece of amber. "Thanks." There was nothing else to say, though her mind was filling with new thoughts. This was not her typical reaction, allowing someone she hardly knew to comfort her. Yet he was such a tender man; it had been easy to relinquish.

"I'm glad for your company. Did you just get off your shift?" Christian felt flushed suddenly.

"I should have been out of here at six, but we had a couple of no-shows. One of the things I hate about working in detention."

"Yeah, but you're almost done with school and I understand the budget was approved. I'm guessing they'll be hiring soon."

"Fingers crossed I'll make it to graduation. Statistics is the worst class yet."

"I'll help you like I said. I'm pretty good at numbers."

"Really? I wanted to ask again, but thought twice after what you've been through." Matt appeared caught off guard, his handsome face registering surprise. Why did men always react to her that way? She wrote her numbers on a sticky note.

"I've got my personal cell and home number on here. Call me. I'm home this weekend. Anyway, statistics should help to get my mind off things."

"Awesome. I'm working swing starting Sunday. Does Saturday work for you?"

Christian smiled. "Where and when?"

"Are you okay with my place? I live in those condos down by the river, near McDougalls. Number three."

"Works for me. Say about one? I have a few things to do in the morning."

"That's good." Matt turned to leave and then paused. "Hey, if you want to bring Bear, it's no problem for me. He probably gets lonely when you're gone all week."

Christian felt another tug. The man was well-known for his generous nature and apparently he didn't mind dogs, especially those that were joined at their owner's hip. After all, she was a package deal. "That would be great. We'll take him to the park afterwards, if that's ok."

After Matt left, a sense of peace arrived for the first time in days. She tried to shake off the soothing sensation that moved through her veins like warm water from a faucet. Some happiness was acceptable, despite the circumstances. Her life would go on, regardless of her guilt and temporary disillusionment.

The answers were now hers to find.

She closed her eyes and said a little prayer, "God, help me now. Mr. Maltos is the innocent. Help me prove it to be true." She crossed herself, out of habit. Raised a Catholic, she'd erased a lot of its rigid creeds from her belief system, but ultimately she

still had a superstitious nature. Never throw the baby out with the
bathwater, as her aunt had always told her.

The outer door of the hallway slammed. She looked up to see
Lilly standing in front of her. The girl appeared anxious and har-
ried, but otherwise fairly healthy.

"Look at you! I hardly recognize you!" The adolescent actually
looked better than she'd ever seen her. Her multi-colored crop of
hair was tucked under a Mariner's baseball cap, her complexion
was clear and her eyes registered reality.

"I'm in trouble. I need your help." Lilly's face crumpled simultaneously to her collapsing knees. She melted into a chair as
Christian moved to shut the office door.

"What's up, honey?"

"It's not what you think. No drugs. I've been clean for a month.
It's just that last weekend I left my grandma's house to see my
Mom, for Thanksgiving. Gram reported me to your manager and
I'm sure there's a warrant now."

"Maybe. He's been gone since last week, so maybe not. But
that's not all, is it?" The girl rubbed her nose hard and sniffed
back tears. "The cops came to my gramma's house and talked to
me this morning. She told them I was with her. Blanks dropped
me off about two. I would never do that. I swear to you, I might be
an addict, but I'm not no murderer. I told them that this morning.
I wasn't there that day and I got proof of it."

Christian considered the child carefully. The world of drug
abuse brought the strays and mongrels into the pack. The alpha
dog would require certain favors. Who knew what the girl had
done and seen? The girl had evidently been through an intense
interrogation. Her demeanor indicated a stressful event. Her va-
soconstriction was evident by the paleness in her cheeks and the

vivid flush of color on her throat. Fear emanated from her like a bad accident. Her strong reaction indicated that she'd been traumatized by the interview and was still feeling the pain.

Was the girl telling the truth? Earlier in the day, the probation officer had been disheartened to learn that Jim Maltos was the primary mark on the detective hit list. He had an apparent motive. The month prior, Maltos had taken out a life insurance policy on his daughter and wife, with himself as primary beneficiary. The policy was worth two million dollars.

The week prior to the murders, Maltos had been sent to collections for failure to pay his mortgage, which was three months in arrears. A neighbor had reported several domestic violence incidents over the summer, indicating to police that Mrs. Maltos was the aggressor in some of those conflicts.

Rusk had told Daniel in confidence that Jim Maltos's boss reported that his normally efficient employee had been less than so over the past few months and that on the day of the murders, the man had left work at noon and had not returned for the remainder of the day. None of that proved he was a killer, but provided enough grounds for serious suspicion.

In a community as tight-knit and frightened as hers, people speculated and wanted answers so that they could go back to their simple, small town lives. They didn't want to believe that random acts of violence existed as near as next door.

Christian glanced at her watch. It was only nine-thirty. "Were you planning to go to Cassie's funeral?" Lilly nodded earnestly.

"Let's go."

"Where?"

Christian leaned toward her and cupped the girl's small chin in her hand. "You are far too pretty for that hair. You also need some appropriate clothing. If nothing else, you will appear inno-cent today. Come on. We're going to my salon and then to T.J. Max to find something for you to wear."

Three hours later, they were on their way to Riverview Memorial Gardens. Lilly had succumbed to a color and cut and now sported a short, shaggy blonde style that was popular with younger girls. After the salon visit, they'd stopped and bought her a pair of black corduroy trousers and a dark green DNKY sweater. While she was changing, Christian had dug through a bargain box and found an interesting Celtic cross necklace and a pair of earrings, which finished the outfit.

As they turned into the church's massive parking lot, they drove toward a volunteer parking team, busily pointing the cars in different directions. The place was teaming with activity.

She turned off the engine and gathered her wits. Lilly had turned a pale shade of gray. "Christian, I have something to show you. It belonged to Cassie. I found it a couple of weeks ago in the backseat of Tommy's car. It's a diary. I think you might want to take a look at it. I think you'll find it..." the girl seemed to be search-ing for the right word, "*enlightening*." With that, she slipped a small book onto the dashboard of the car.

Lilly stuck close to Christian's side as they got out of the car and wandered around, looking for Daniel. Eventually they moved toward the church's massive series of double doors. This mega-church had become one of the more popular places of worship in the Tri-Cities in recent years. According to the general teen population, the youth groups there were some of the best around. Christian was intrigued by the way today's churches used modern language to hook their members. Cassie had told Christian that she belonged to a 'cell'. In fact, the nearly two hundred kids now attending the church had all been divided into cell groups, with cell leaders and specific activities often kept secret from other cells. It was oddly reminiscent of the HBO television program about terrorist cells in America. Frankly, the concept set off warning signs in her head. Secrecy was never a good thing. It hadn't worked for the Catholic faith, proven obvious through the countless revelations regarding pedophile priests.

As they were ushered to their seats, Daniel appeared and slipped into the chair next to Lilly. His face registered astonishment. "Could this be Lilly Host?" Directing his question at Christian, he winked. "When did she turn into such a beauty?"

Lilly blushed and gave him a smile-laced glare. The tough girl image was a hard one for her to relinquish. In the meantime, Christian's eyes were everywhere. She was determined to find Tabby and was relieved to see she was on the program as one of the speakers. Once she cornered the girl, Daniel would have to keep an eye on Lilly. Privacy and timing were going to be the clincher in getting the girl to talk about the text message.

A synchronized hush spread throughout the enormous space. How over a thousand people knew when to be simultaneously quiet had always amazed Christian. The auditorium was built like a theater in the round. In lieu of expensive stained glass, large swatches of multi-colored fabrics hung from a soaring ceiling at the front of the church. Amidst the rainbow of color, there hung a massive bronze image of Christ on the cross. Like a Renaissance sculpture, the larger-than life representation was stunning in its realism and detail. The altar was raised and appeared to be about the size of a tennis court. Several pots and tall sprays of flowers, flowering trees and towering candelabras filled the floor space, making the podium nearly invisible. It was a festive sight except for the mute reminder of tragedy: two closed caskets sitting end to end.

Two young men in white and gold robes appeared from the side aisles and slowly lit the candelabras. Each held approximately thirty candles and brought fire play onto the billowing yards of transparent fabrics that moved to and from, guided by the large fans mounted high on the ceiling above. The sight was ethereal and evoked deep emotion in Christian.

Soft piano music filled the sanctuary from Bose speakers mounted on tall platforms. The sound was acoustically perfect. Then the minister stepped out and walked toward the podium. He was a large man with a penetrating gaze. Even from where they sat, one could feel the essence of his power over this congregation. Turning to face the audience, dressed in a deep purple robe with gold braiding, he raised his hands and said in a booming voice,

"Welcome, my children of God. Today we celebrate the lives of two beautiful souls, Susan and Cassie Maltos. They are with our Great Maker today and we bless them and hold them in esteem, for their journey home was fraught with pain and suffering. And yet we know, our magnificent God and his beloved Son are with them. We are assured they have returned safely home. Now let us pray.

Dear Lord, we have come together today as witnesses to the lives of these two women, who have become angels of your calling. Susan Jennifer Maltos and Cassandra Rhea Maltos are with you, our Great God and will forever walk the paths of heaven, in peace, their sins forgiven and their spirits free. For as it was spoken by Christ, 'I am the resurrection and the life. He that believeth in me, thought he were dead, yet shall he live. And whosoever liveth and believeth in me shall never die.' And so, we know that our coura-geous sisters live on, though they've sacrificed their time on earth to teach us and guide us to be strong, be faithful and to remain true to our Father in heaven as they both did so well. We ask that they be wrapped in the great light of our Christ. In Jesus's name we pray, amen."

He lifted his bison-like head, smiling beatifically around the room. "My dear ones, we are more fortunate than we know to have been acquainted with Sue and Cassie Maltos. They were women who led by example, faced their greatest fears and willingly asked for God's guidance. May we all lead our lives as they once did. May we become better humans for their suffering, remember at all times to help our neighbor and heed the call to act with heroic intent. For what is a hero, but someone stripped of their dignity and strength who chooses to fight instead of fail, and who chooses to stand for what is right rather than turn to face the wall of conformity. There are lessons in our pain, my people, lessons, which we will reflect upon in the days to come. And so, in honor of these two cherished women, I would like to invite Tabby Smithson to the podium to share."

Christian craned her neck. She could just see a young blond woman stand up and to walk up the stairs to the podium. She was tall and willowy and walked with a graceful stride. She took the microphone from the minister's hand and faced the crowd.

Tabby was lovely, if not fragile. She was a Nordic ice princess and probably wouldn't hold up to the pressure of the task. Then she began to speak. The voice that came from the girl was one of wisdom and self-assurance. It was the voice of someone with a great respect for the mysteries of life. Her tenor was clear and elevated the room's vibration with its conviction.

"Last week I lost my best friend and sister of the heart, Cassie Maltos. The meaning of best friend has been trivialized in my lifetime, so that often when I hear the phrase in passing, I wonder as to its accuracy. I can honestly say that Cassie was my best friend in the old-fashioned sense of the word. She loved me regardless of how many times I let her down. She knew my faults and self-imposed fears and fed me strength and hope to combat those undesirables. She laughed and cried with me and never left me alone when I was facing loneliness. She held sacred my secrets and made promises that were always kept. She was a true friend in every way possible. To lose her was to lose a part of my soul. And yet I know she and Sue are with us and yet together, as they should be, safe now, happy now and beloved in the eyes of our Lord. I am proud and blessed to have known both of them." With that, Tabby seemed to look out past the audience and to somewhere no one else was entitled to see. Then a soft murmur as she finished, though her voice was still strong. "Thank you, Cassie. I love you."

Christian felt a tug at her sleeve and looked over at Lilly who was incongruously handing her a pretty white lace hankie. "Here, you look like you need this," she whispered. "Don't worry. It's clean. My gramma gave it to me for today."

The rest of the funeral became a private expedition into Christian's past. She had been to so many funerals and wept so many tears in her lifetime, and yet the death of an innocent continued to torment her, rather than become a thing of familiarity. Something in the way Death had come this time, with a strange sort of warning, caused her deeper anguish than in her prior experiences. She was at the edge of an abyss and could look down and nearly make out the miniature markings in the pit below. This time she would find the answers to these senseless murders. She knew this with absolute and unwavering certainty.

A few vocalists from Cassie's school chorale sang the song, 'Beautiful', the same song that Cassie had sung at the homecoming assembly. Their rendition was a simplistic version of the anguished soul song that Cassie had once performed. Sue Malto's sister then stood up and cried her way down memory lane. Sue was talented, loving, giving and basically perfect, according to Cindy Thomas. Christian made a mental note to contact her after a few weeks had passed.

The audience was becoming restless when the last speaker, the church's youth minister, stood up to speak. Jason was young himself, probably close to twenty. Tall and well-built with wavy brown hair and a toothpaste ad smile, Jason radiated goodness. Even from where they sat, nearly twenty rows back, his spiritual charisma touched her. He was one of those young men that every girl dreams of marrying and every mother hopes to find for her daughter. When he began to speak, his voice wavered slightly, as though he was using all of his inner strength to control himself. His steely grip on the podium and the intimate way he leaned toward his listeners gave her the feeling that he was talking to her and only her. You could hear a pin drop in this room when he paused momentarily. He spoke of Cassie with tenderness and conviction. "She was a girl of God," he said, "A child of the universe."

The rest of his speech was lost to Christian. Her head began to pound suddenly and her vision blurred. She grabbed Daniel's arm. "Get me out of here, fast." Immediately he stood up, against murmurs of protest from the others around them and firmly took her arm. Lilly also stood up, confused. The two of them quickly guided her out of the sanctuary. By the time they reached the vestibule, blackness had enveloped her as she felt herself falling.

When she opened her eyes, she was lying in the backseat of her partner's truck, her legs dangling from the seat where Lilly stood in the open door frame, holding vigilance. Daniel was talking from the front seat, mumbling about a water bottle and where in the hell was it?

"It happened again. What is wrong with me?"

"You did that pass-out thing you do," Daniel replied. "Christian, you need to get your blood pressure check. From what I can tell, your pulse is non-existent."

"This is getting ridiculous. Give me the water, please," Christian took a long gulp and felt the soothing cool begin to ease the heat in her throat and chest. "Something's wrong. I can't explain it. It was like the world flipped on its back."

Lilly hovered near her, a worried look on her pixie face. "Lots is wrong. There are two dead bodies in there and you look like you're next on the list. Man, you look like you seen a ghost."

"She's right. You don't look so good. Did you eat today?"

Christian sat up. "Give me that mirror out of my purse, please." She pointed to the leather bag that Lilly held tightly in her hand.

She fished around inside the large purse and eventually pulled out a small pocket mirror. Gazing into it, she shuddered. Her cobalt blue eyes were laced with dark red lines. Her face seemed gaunter than usual and her normally Irish rose complexion was a sickly green. She was shaking so hard that her jaw was rattling.

"You look like you seen death, that's for sure. That's the way Tim looked after Blanks killed them two people in Oregon. When they came back to the car, I thought…"

"That's enough, Lilly." Daniel barked. His normally gentle voice was harsh. "Don't upset her any more than she is. Besides, we don't want to hear the evidence of that case."

"What can I do for you?" Daniel leaned over the front seat and placed his hand on her forehead. "Man, you're on fire. Let me turn on the air conditioner."

He twisted the buttons on the car's interior above their heads. Icy cold air shot out as Christian leaned back and closed her eyes. Slowly she began to speak.

"This has happened to me before, a couple of times. It's not because of the funeral, that I'm upset. Someone in that church killed those women. The killer was in there."

"Yeah, Mr. Maltos. That's what some of the kids were saying outside juvy this morning," Lilly replied quietly.

Christian kept her eyes shut, waiting for an image to come to her, but after a long moment, there was still nothing but blackness behind her eyes. "I just don't believe that. It's not Mr. Maltos. Cassie once said something to me. I can't grasp it right now, but I know what she said, the first day I met her, I know that is the answer to who killed her, who killed them."

CHAPTER 9

♊

His heavy hand gripped Christian's throat as she thrashed to get free. Her skin was on fire and her breath was shallow and constricted. Her pounding heart felt like a pressure cooker ready to pop. She swung her legs up, trying to hook them around his neck. It was a feeble attempt; her body felt like it was stuck in quicksand. In the darkness, there was nothing but his smell: rancid and yet sickeningly sweet like baby's feces, or piles of manure baking on a hot summer's day. Her mind whirled with fear and the desire to fight. She slid a hand from his grip. Ah ha! He could not hold both her hands and her neck at the same time. He leaned forward, dumping deadweight on her chest, and gave a guttural groan of repressed fury. With her last remaining bit of strength, she took advantage of the moment and stabbed her fingers directly into his eyes. There was a wild howl as he pulled back. Then as if in reflex, his grip tightened on her neck, hitting a pressure point so that she couldn't move at all. She tried to scream, but it was no use. Her voice was gone.

Just when she thought she'd lost the battle, the phone rang. Ah, life again! Christian opened her eyes from the nightmare and saw the room as it was. Pale light was coming in through the cracks of the blinds. Bear was snoring peacefully beside her. It had only been another bad dream, but one of tactile realism. The skin on her neck still tingled from the monster's grip as she breathed deeply. Finally her heart rate began to slow, but she had no energy to pick up the phone. She let the message run and felt her body cool and become chill to the bone.

"Hey, it's Daniel. Just got a call from Randy. Jim Maltos was arrested early this morning for the murders. I'll tell you more when you get here." Then there was the click of disconnection.

She climbed from bed and shuffled to the bathroom. Bear was now awake and already trotting out of the room in the direction of the back door. Christian sat down on the toilet and closed her eyes, reflecting on the dream. She didn't feel fear, but instead curiosity. Whatever the dream signified, it taught her that an attack would probably leave her paralyzed. She finished in the bathroom and headed for the kitchen. Pushing the coffee machine to 'on', she slowly opened the door and caught sight of a raccoon running away from Bear. He immediately bolted when he caught sight of the creature running toward the river. He was a quick hunter, but would only chase the creature for the sport of it. He'd had his encounters in the past. The dog knew when to relinquish power.

Christian thought about that concept as she sipped her coffee. Unless driven by severe hunger or extreme fear, animals seemed to know when to back down and leave their fellow creatures be. She couldn't count the times that she'd relived the Maltos murders in her mind. What would she have done had she been in the home? If Jim Maltos was the killer, she would have taken one approach: that of territorial familiarity and her wits advantage. But she had never believed that Jim was the perpetrator. That left someone like Blanks. A crazy man, hooked on methamphetamine with little or no sense of conscience. She would have been out of her element with someone like him. Psychological magic had little if any power when dealing with the fried brain of a drug addict.

Slowly she showered and dressed for work. It was a court day, so she chose a pale pink silk blouse, a fitted cinnamon brown jacket and an A-line plaid skirt of brown, pink and cream. She added her favorite brown suede boots and brown tights, grabbed a pair of gold hoop earrings and called it good. Then came a jolting reminder: Jim Maltos would probably have his first appearance today. The media would make a Jerry Springer series out of his arrest. He would be deemed guilty before innocent in this town. The local stations had already interviewed everyone even slightly connected with the Maltos family

Christian pulled her Daytimer from her purse. She'd have to cancel some appointments in order to attend adult court. Her supervisor had graciously indicated that he would accept her request for time off during any trial that might ensue. Her manager agreed, but indicated she would be required to make up the time or take vacation while simultaneously handing her a card for a free E.A.P. grief counselor visit, a proverbial consolation prize. The recollection of Michael's lackadaisical attitude sent her anger to savage on the Richter Scale. The probation staff were always expected to take their clients' murders, rapes and assaults in their stride. Only in her former profession, she'd been trained to show empathy, get in touch with emotions and work from a place of forgiveness. She wondered if she'd ever get to the place called 'jaded' before her time was up. She certainly hoped not.

Christian gave Bear a rawhide bone as she prepared to leave. She returned to check that the doors were locked. Since the graffiti message on her door, the Richland Police had been keeping a close watch on her house. Her home was at the end of a long, winding road, difficult to see and far enough from bus routes to deter easy access. Her neighbors were always on the look-out, too. She didn't believe for a moment that a gang member did the markings.

In fact, Christian believed that the graffiti threat was a link to the Maltos murders. It seemed she was alone in this concept. Daniel and the rest of her co-workers were certain it was one of the youth on her caseload who'd done the crime. Though the blue paint was the notorious color of the Surenos, often used by the gang when marking their territory, anyone could be the culprit.

As she turned to close her bedroom door, Christian realized that she was truly terrified for Mr. Maltos. He was the last person in the world who deserved this kind of humiliation and pain. She needed to do something quickly, find a way to help him. She glanced around, looking for a sign or a direction from whence to embark. She had fallen asleep the night before with her most recent book in her hand. It now lay open on the opposite side of the bed, her paperback partner, a reminder of her single status.

Despite her loneliness, she managed to get by. Christian knew that she had an inexplicable gift, one that she had yet to truly tap. Psychic was a term used too often, with a new-age fad connotation. Yet in her gut, she knew that she was right. The Maltos murders had a different ending than the story that was now being written. Without another moment's hesitation, she picked up the phone and dialed, embracing the moment. A man's voice answered.

"Scott here."

"Scotty, it's me, Christian."

"Hey sis! It's been ages. How are you?"

"I'm good and I'm sorry to be calling under the circumstances. I know I owe you and Jasmine a visit."

"Honey, what is it?' Her cousin-come-brother's voice was tender and searching.

"A friend, no actually a client, needs your help. He's just been arrested for the murder of his wife and only daughter. He's innocent, I just know it." Her words were rapid-firing. She paused, took a deep breath and waited.

It seemed that she could hear Scott thinking during the silence that ensued. A big brother in the best of ways, he had taken her under his wing after her parents had died. His role modeling had continued into their adult lives. As a principal in one of Seattle's most prestigious law firms, he'd been involved in several notorious Seattle trials and had won countless federal cases. Best of all, Scott never hesitated to help her in any way he could.

"Why is this case so important to you?" he asked.

"I worked closely with this family, Scott. And I'm lucky to be here. I was on my way back to the house when and where the murders took place. I haven't told anyone this, but I should have been there. I didn't go…because…"

"Because what?" His warm voice melted her armor. She had to tell someone.

"Because at the last minute I knew. I knew something bad was going to happen over there that day. There were signs, the snake, the message on my door and the dreams."

"Whoa, little sis. Stop right there!" There was a long pause as Scott sighed heavily into the phone. "Good lord, girl. You and death have some kind of a pact going on." *Don't I know it*, Christian thought, waiting eagerly to hear his answer.

"Have they already arrested your man?"

"Yes, apparently early this morning." Holding her breath, she crossed her fingers and toes, like she used to do as a little girl when he made her grand promises.

"Things are a little slow at work. I can take a day or two. I think Horizon Airlines has a flight out around eleven. Can you pick me up at the airport?"

"Absolutely," she cried, feeling about fourteen years old. "Thank you so much, Scotty. I'll pay you back. Promise."

She heard a low chuckle in response. "You still owe me for that bet we made when you were sixteen, little sis. But we'll call it even if this guy is worth representing."

Christian smiled at the reminder. She had made Scott a bet when she was sixteen years old that she would never get married. Ten years later, he'd given her away at the altar.

Hanging up the phone, she did a little jig around the room and sang an off-tune version of 'Celebrate'. Then she hugged Bear, who watched her in adoration, not quite sure why his mistress acted so strangely sometimes. Then she snapped her fingers and said to him, "The diary. Bear, I completely forgot about the diary."

Christian had left the girl's diary in her car console. No wonder she'd forgotten about it. After the funeral, they'd sat in Daniel's car, watching people leave for a good hour with the idea being that she might catch sight of the perp and have another reaction. No such thing happened. Eventually they'd found Tabby Smithson. The girl was cool toward the probation officers and obviously anxious to get away. Christian only had time to give her a business card before the girl disappeared back into the crowd. By the time they all got back to the office, there was another crisis to deal with, a call from Jim Maltos, received before the funeral, in which he said that there was something at the house he wanted her to see. Unfortunately her return phone call hadn't made a connection.

She hadn't left the office until nearly ten that night and had fallen immediately into bed, only to wake up to the phone call regarding the Maltos arrest. Locking the house, she went to the garage. Climbing into her car, she opened the console and took out the small pink leather book. The cover was embossed in gold print and read: *The Diary of Cassandra R. Maltos.* Someone had chosen this gift carefully; someone who had dearly loved this girl. In flowery script the words: THIS IS PRIVATE!!! IF YOU FIND THIS, PLEASE RETURN IMMEDIATELY. Cassie's address and phone number followed.

"Cassie, I'm sorry if I'm invading your privacy, but I'm trying to save your father's life." She glanced quickly at the car clock as she started the engine. The restored 1967 Volkswagen Bug had belonged to Tony and didn't have a working radio or CD player, but it did have a decent clock. It was only 7:05. She could take a little peek before heading out. Turning off the engine, she began to read.

April 15, 2005. Dear Diary, Mom and Daddy gave me this beautiful little diary for Easter. I've always wanted one of these and Mom PROMISED she would never read it. I am still going to hide it, just in case. The sweetest, most adorable boy in the world asked me out today. Tommy Calander. He's kinda skater and kinda gangster, but he's got the most awesome blue eyes I swear I've ever seen! Still my parents will probably HATE him. He's not in the church. Yuck to all the dudes at church. They're all gay, except for Jason. (Tabby has a crush on him, too.)

Back to Tommy. He said he heard me sing at the assembly yesterday and fell hopelessly in love with me. That's exactly what he said, exactly! Hopelessly in love. It didn't sound as stupid as it looks on paper. It was not gushy. Just like, "hey, you made me fall hopelessly in love just now. Do you want to go out?" Ok, so he's one of the hottest boys at Kennewick. I mean, probably THE HOTTEST. Anyway, I don't want my parents to know, so Tabby said she would lie for me and tell them I'm with her tomorrow night. She's such a cool friend.

April 28, 2005. Sorry I'm skipping days, Diary. So much has been going on. I can't believe my suddenly incredible life. Last night...oh my GOD!!! My new man is the bomb. He took me out to dinner at this cool little biker restaurant in the Y. I didn't even know it was there. He knows the owner, so we got served drinks. I had my first martini. I didn't even really know what a martini was, but I pretended I was down. Then he took me out to Bateman's Island. We drove down this bumpy road to the beach. He actually drove his car down there. It was totally cool because he drives one of those awesome old collector Mustangs. The moon was like sick huge and we were just staring up at it and talking for the longest time. We talked about pretty much everything. Then we smoked some weed. He said it was ok, there was nothing sinful-that God put weed here for a reason. I'm not going to let church garbage get in the way. I felt SO GOOD. Then we started making out. He was touching in a way...well I can't describe it, even in here, except to say my body was on fire and I know what it means now to want a man inside you.

We didn't do it though.. We wanted to, but he didn't have a condom, so I gave him head instead. He said I did it pretty good. I would have taken my clothes off right there, but I didn't want him to think I couldn't control myself. I can't wait until we do it, though. CAN'T WAIT!

May 20. Tommy took me to an awesome rave tonight. I told my parents I was going to prom, even dressed the part and we took pictures at our house. It was the first time my parents met him and they were not acting too happy. I don't care. He is so much fun, but more like a best friend. He's funny anyway. The whole time, he was whispering little things to me, like how proms were for geeks. He wore his brother's wedding tuxedo and my parents totally fell for it. By the time we left, my mother actually gave Tommy a little hug. She is so gullible (new vocab we learned in class last week).

After pictures we went to his house. His mom works night shift so we took off all our prom stuff and then he asked me to take a shower with him. I can't even describe what happened in there. It's kinda like he's practice for the big stuff later on. We eventually got out and got dressed to go to the rave. We took some ecstasy before we got there. It was like being in a fairy land. Everyone was dancing and hugging each other. The DJ was sick, like totally sick. We stayed until about 1:00. Then we hurried back to his house, I put my dress back on and I was home by about 2:00. This time I was on top!). My mom was waiting up, of course. But I didn't drink anything, no booze so no stumbling around. She acted all happy I was home on time. She's so dumb, but I like her that way. And she OBVIOUSLY can't tell when I'm rolling on X!

May 30. We just got back from Seattle. My parents took me to see the new EMP. I was totally amazed they'd take me there. I guess my Dad used to be a Jimmy Hendrix fan. He was all over it. Mom was acting her stuck-up self, but Dad and I had loads of fun. We even made our own music video and I sounded damn fine. I'm thinking American Idol next year...DEFINITELY! We also went shopping at Nordstroms, which was pretty cool. Mom bought a couple of outfits for me and some jeans for her. The jeans are called, "These aren't your daughter's jeans." How stupid is that!

June 2. Eight more days and school is OUT. That's so tight! My job at Taco Bell is going good and they said I can work extra hours in the summer. I really like my boss, Erik. He's cute and REAL. I think he kind of likes me, too. After work last night, he took me out for a Starbucks. I never dreamed I'd have so many men in my life. Tabby will be jealous now.

June 12. It's been exactly 1 month and he hasn't called. Apparently he's been really busy with his new business. That's what Tabby said anyway. She is acting really weird toward me lately. Like she's jealous that I've got it going. She's always had a million boyfriends. It's my turn now. I left him 3 voice messages at his work, but then I thought that might not be such a good idea. I feel like I'm two people. Cassandra and Cassie. One side never hangs with the other. It's really cool, though, leading a double life. I just have to keep my parents out of it. Mom is prying all the time. Where did I go after work, why was I late coming home from youth group, etc. Dad is clueless. He thinks I walk on water. I think he's going to buy me a car for my birthday this year!!!!

June 25. I got the extra hours at Taco Bell. I'm making bank now. Finally my parents will be off my back and I can use work as my excuse whenever I want to meet up with… or… or… I love this. It's going to be a total sick summer.

July 5. I HATE MY MOTHER. She is such an f-ing b. She found my diary and told me, under no circumstances, can I ever see Tommy again. She'd promised me she'd never read it. And I will see Tommy. She can't control me!

July 16. Finally HE called. He said that he had some stuff to get done for some kind of family emergency. Anyway, he's picking me up after I get off work. I told my parents I have to work overtime tonight. We are going to our favorite place. I'm wearing my best Victoria's Secret bra and matching panties. They are a pink lace and so cute! I went tanning yesterday, too. And best of all, I'm on the pill now, so we're safe!!!!

July 20. Oh my freaking God!!! Tommy read you, Diary. He was over yesterday and we were downstairs in my bedroom, hanging out. Anyway, I went to the bathroom and while I was gone, he found you. I guess I wasn't careful hiding it again. Anyway, he freaked out when he found out there's someone else, but it was like it was a fantasy when we first started going

*out. After a while Tommy believed me and then said he would have taken
me down there by now, but that I was so stupid, because there are no roads
onto the island. I thought, yeah, you're the stupid one, but thank god for
that. Then I said I thought that he was done with me before he called from
Juvy. I'm finding out he's pretty dumb. He believed me after I gave him
what he wanted. But I've got to be careful. If he figures out I'm lying about
youth group night and Sundays after church, he'll kill me. I'll be good until
he goes back in to detention next week. I guess I should feel guilty that I'm
playing him, but he'd probably do the same to me if he had the chance.*

*July 30. Tabby is freaking out. I think she'd like to beat me up, if a
perfect little Christian girl like her was allowed to do such a thing. I don't
give a rip. She should have known better than to break up with him in the
first place. I can see why she set me and Tommy up now. Ever since I told
her about our affair, she's been a freak. And now with JJ in the picture,
I'm losing it, trying to keep track of three of them. Two is bad enough. I'm
finishing things with Tommy. I told him I just want to be friends now. I
ran out of the pills today. I've got to remember to get some more. Still JJ was
a bit weird about me being on the pill. Apparently he's all about making
babies, but NOT ME!*

That was the last entry for the month of July and there were
no additionally entries until nearly a month later. Glancing at the
clock, Christian saw that it was time to head out. She put the diary
back in the console and started the car. This was a typical teenager's diary: sex, drugs and negative commentary on parents. But
there was something about the way that Cassie talked about her
love life didn't sound right. When Tommy read the diary, he'd
found out about another man. Who was her mysterious lover and
what might he know about her murder? And who was J.J.?

Christian noticed that her car was in dire need of gas, so she
pulled over at the Shell station around the corner from the house.

She was climbing out of her car when she noticed Tabby Smithson standing at the fuel pump across from her. She watched her for a second and then, after hastily shoving the gas hose into the fuel tank, she headed in the girl's direction. Standing next to her sporty green Mazda, Tabby was wrapped in a white wool coat with a fake fur collar. With her pale hair and complexion and statuesque height, she was an ethereal sight in the dull of winter.

"Tabby, do you remember me? Christian Vargas?" She casually approached the girl who was now trying to clean her window without getting her expensive coat dirty.

Glancing up from her task, Tabby gave her a long, incipient gaze. Finally recognition passed over her perfect features. "Yes. You're Cassie's P.O."

She stopped her cleaning, but remained stoically silent. Her self-composure was somewhat unnerving. "I have wanted to talk to you about Cassie. I know you weren't in the right space the day of the funeral, but I was hoping we could meet up and talk some time."

"What do you want to know about Cassie that you don't already know? I mean, really, you were her probation officer."

"And you were her best friend." The girl seemed to blanch slightly at the comment.

"What do you want to know?"

"Who was she dating besides Tommy Calander?'

"Why does it matter now? She's dead." Tabby looked down, but not soon enough. Tears gathered in the corners of her eyes. Maybe she'd come on too strong, Christian thought. The girl was grieving after all.

"Look, I'm so sorry for all you've been through. I really cared about Cassie and her mother, but I don't believe for a minute that Mr. Maltos killed them. Do you?"

Tabby shrugged, unwilling to meet the probation officer's gaze. "No. He really wouldn't do that. I don't believe he would. He's a really nice man."

"So Tabby, what's your thought? Is there anyone you can think of who would want to hurt Cassie and her mother?"

When she looked up, Tabby's face was sullen with pain. Shaking her head, she said, "I don't know."

"Tabby, I have her diary. I'm reading it. She talked about another boyfriend, one who has a car, dabbles in drugs, has some kind of a hold on her. It's like she was afraid that Tommy would find out, but that didn't stop her from seeing this other guy. It sounds like you knew who the guy was, from what she wrote in July. Do you remember a fight that the two of you had over a guy last summer?"

Tabby seemed to have pulled herself together. She stared directly at Christian now, her eyes dry and her features composed. "I know she was seeing a few guys. You see, Mrs. Vargas, Cassie was a bit of a slut. We were not happy with a lot of the things she did."

"*We* meaning who besides yourself?" Christian pushed on. She was finally getting somewhere.

"Jason Roads, our youth minister at church and a few of us girls in the youth group. She was starting to embarrass us. I was actually happy when she stopped coming to church. I didn't have to feel responsible anymore."

"Responsible for what?"

"For what happened. Now I've got to go. School starts in ten minutes. I don't want to be late."

She climbed quickly in her car and drove away. It was just like Cassie had said. Tabby was all about being perfect, even if it meant discontinuing a conversation that could save a man's life.

By the time Christian arrived at work, her brother had already left her an e-mail stating that he'd contacted Mr. Maltos and had convinced him to accept his counsel. Furthermore, true to his nature, Scott had googled the local papers and read the story. Apparently it had touched him deeply. He was willing to do the case pro bono.

Christian glanced at the copy of the Washington Bar Review that she kept in a basket in her office. Her brother's photograph was featured on the cover nearly four years ago, as the public defender of a woman on murder row, who had killed her husband after years of physical abuse and torture. She'd originally gone to Seattle to hear the trial's opening arguments and then had stayed on, riveted by the grotesque and inhumane treatment of the defendant by her husband. Over a dozen police reports, six hospital visits, nine broken bones, several burns, fourteen CPS reports, a no-contact order and a criminal restraining order hadn't stopped that monster. Her observation of that trial had been excoriating for her and yet she stayed. The woman still had three small children at home and a prison sentence for her had meant a prison sentence in the foster system for them. In the end, after three weeks, Scott had gotten her off with a suspended sentence and a requirement that she seek counseling, specifically dealing with domestic violence victimization. That case had been Christian's impetus to take the job in probation as a domestic violence counselor. Little did she know that she'd be facing some of the same trials in her own life.

Scott was the only one in her extended family of whom she resembled. Her mother and aunt's Irish features were prominent in both their faces- the clear blue eyes and freckled skin. Over time, her hair had turned to a rich mahogany color while his had remained the glowing red of their youth. Both of their expressions exuded determination, or so she'd been told of her own. Scott was the ultimate Jungian hero archetype. He'd saved as many stray dogs and lost children as she had and over time they'd made a sort of running joke out of it. Often he'd called her and say, "who'd you save today, little sis?" and she'd inform him that her numbers were now higher than his own.

Her phone rang just then, jolting her out of her reverie.

"Good morning, Christian Vargas."

"Hey, it's me. I'm on my way to Spokane to drop Jose Valdovinos off at inpatient treatment. I just heard the fabulous news!"

Christian took a deep breath. *Dear God, news travels fast in this town*, she

marveled, awaiting Daniel's next line.

"So, Mr. Maltos apparently collapsed into tears after a phone call this morning, per Stephanie Conley who works the morning shift at the jail. When she asked him if he was alright, he told he was *very* good, considering the circumstances. Then he told her that Scott Halverson is representing him. Wow, girl! You work fast."

"You and I both know that the public defender is," she lowered her voice as Michael walked in her office. "is Carl Howes. Anyway, Michael's here for a visit. I'll see you when you get back from Daybreak."

She set down the phone and smiled up at her boss. "Morning, Michael, what's up?"

"How was the funeral?" he asked casually, as though talking about a lunch date.

"Very moving and very, very sad." Christian started moving papers around her desk in an effort to look busy.

"I'm sure it was. I just want to encourage you to move on. It isn't easy, this work we do, but we need to put this behind us. I can't help but think you'll have a hard time doing that, though." His gaze was expectant. He wanted reassurance.

"Look, Michael, if you're worried that this case is going to come between me and work, it won't. I may take a day or two of vacation come trial time." she paused, wondering if she should mention her brother's involvement. The time was probably better now than later.

"But that's only because my brother is defending Mr. Maltos."

Michael's ruddy complexion turned a shade redder than usual. "What? How'd that happen?"

Christian steadied her temper. Why did this guy have such an easy time triggering her?

"He does read the newspapers *and* we talked about it. He was really interested because of the work he does in his practice. He was a public defender for King County for nearly 12 years. He had some time and he wanted to help. He's good, Michael. He'll get Mr. Maltos off."

"I thought they had Blanks in custody for the murders."

Christian wanted to roll her eyes, but she stopped herself. "Blanks was released yesterday. He had a solid alibi. He was filmed on video tape at that motorcycle bar, Dirty Momma's, in downtown Kennewick. He was there all day, getting sloshed with his buddies."

Michael nodded his head. "Yeah, right, I think I remember hearing that now."

Christian kept her voice as polite as she could, "Got anything else for me?"

"Ah, no. Just keep up the good work." Michael turned and walked out, flustered as he often was when she, or anyone else for that matter, knew something before he did. He was notorious for ignoring the news, though he was the first one to want to be seen on camera.

She was still reading her e-mails when the phone rang. "Hey, it's Matt. How are you?"

"Hi. I'm good. What's up?" She tried to sound nonchalant, but to her private embarrassment, her heart was now racing like a fifteen-year-old waiting to be asked on a date with the coolest guy in school.

"I've been thinking a lot about you. I heard the funeral was pretty brutal."

"Oh. Actually it was...very upsetting. Those women were loved by so many people. It was hard to be in a room of a thousand people grieving. Like something out of a war movie. I didn't make it through. I had to leave."

"Yeah, I heard. The Big D said you were a bit traumatized. It's like that, you know, when you care about someone as much as you cared about the Maltos girls. You're going to have to toughen up, honey."

She shivered. Did he just call her 'honey'? "I don't want to toughen up too much, Matt. So how are things with you?"

"Good. I was thinking that maybe we could hook up this week-end. If you still want to, that is."

As her nervous habit would have it, she interrupted eagerly, "Of course we're still on."

"Good! I know this sounds really dumb, but my brother be-longs to a Mustang car club and they are having a big Christmas party out at Hog Heaven, spelled like I said it. It's this wacky place, a friend of his, Doobie, owns. He fixes old collector cars and vans. Anyway, these parties are a kick, just the kind of thing to get your mind off the sad stuff. Do you want to come with me?"

Christian yanked in her emotional reins. "This is starting to sound like a date."

There was a soft chuckle. "If this is our first date, then I owe you big time on the second, a promise I intend to keep."

"The answer is yes to Saturday night and yes as in I'll hold you to the promise."

After they hung up, a warm humming started to emanate from her lower belly. It was a very powerful sensation. There was definitely a connection going on with Matt. It was the kind of magnetism that hadn't come along, but once or twice in a lifetime. Even her relationship with Tony had once had a solid beat to it, nothing as delicate as the strange song that sang within her now.

By ten-thirty, Christian had finished the detention report for afternoon court. She'd requested that Tommy Calander be held on his new charges pending a $5,000 bail. There was talk about Tommy's possible involvement in the murders, so she prayed that there was no one who would bail the boy for that amount of money. She was disappointed that Blanks had been exonerated, but at least he had been arrested and would soon be on his way to Oregon to face homicide charges there. An earlier email from Detective Jensen, who had been officially assigned to the Maltos murders, indicated that he was very interested in talking to Tommy. The youth's alibi, according to the detention log notes, was a weak one. Upon intake, Tommy had told Pam Hudson, the detention supervisor on night shift that he'd been out partying with some friends from Connell. These witnesses were boys who were both known felons and couldn't be trusted to tell the truth. In the meantime, Christian was anxious to talk to Tommy, though she knew it was imperative that she didn't interfere with the prosecutor's investigation.

Glancing at the clock, she grabbed her purse and headed out the door to pick up Scott at the airport. She would take an early lunch and get him where he needed to be. Then she'd tackle the rest of her day, with a visit to Tommy next on her list.

Jumping into her car a few minutes later, she pulled out Cassie's diary and set it on the passenger seat so as to remember to show it to Scott. As she did so, the book fell open to the page upon which Cassie had written about her late night visit to Bateman's Island. Looking down, she saw something that caught her eye. On the page, a series of words seemed to jump out at her. *Old collector Mustang.* Didn't Matt say that the Christmas party was for some kind of car club his brother belonged to? A Mustang car club?

CHAPTER 10

December 10, 2005

♊

The Tri-Cities Regional airport had a small town, good ole' boy ambience. Rental car company representatives, consisting of young, pimple-faced men and overweight girls with tummy tires, their low-slung pants accenting their obesity, stood in small booths lining the east wall of the wing of the T-shaped building. They milled around one another, chatted on their cell phones and, on occasion, offered eager, rent-from-me smiles. The only two carriers that serviced the bi-county area filled the other wing. In the waiting area, wine country posters hung on large billboards, displaying oversized photos of local girls standing in vineyards wearing brightly colored scarves and lederhosen-like attire, as though they'd just stepped off the set of *The Sound of Music*. Meanwhile local advertiser displays demanded that you buy a used car from Russ Dean, visit the Franklin County Historical Museum or stop at the Broadmoor outlet mall for thousands of dollars in savings. Grimy plastic chairs surround the interior perimeter and a demo Jacuzzi tub sat in the middle of the entry.

Christian walked in to meet her brother. She loved Scott's sarcastic commentaries on her community. A hot pink hot tub would really put him over the top. There were still a few minutes before the flight arrived, so she wandered into the Chukar Cherries store. This was the one and only purveyor in the airport with the exception of an Italian restaurant that served around the clock. The little gift shop was choked, literally, with every kind of cherry, nut and dried fruit under the sun. She sampled a dark chocolate-dipped blueberry and a couple of white chocolate-coated macadamia nuts. Buying a gift box was her next decision. Scott loved chocolate. It was the least she could do.

Soon she heard the sounds of a plane's arrival and watched through the plate glass window as her brother disembarked the 18 seat Horizon jet. He was trim and healthy-looking, a good sign in her mind. It had been nearly six months since she'd visited Scott and his beautiful Asian wife, Jasmine. They had been together for nearly ten years, had a couple of adorable children and seemed to enjoy their life in the big city. He waved at her once he was inside and as he came through the security doors, she found herself diving into his arms. Tears came to her eyes as she nestled her head against his broad chest. "Thank you for coming. You don't know what this means to me, Scott."

"Oh, I think I do. You've never once asked me for help like this. What could I do, but be your hero?' He grinned, his wide mouth splitting his sunny Irish face in two. Wearing a gorgeous brown Armani suit and Italian shoes, he was a rare sight in the Tri-Cities based on the appreciative stares of the women around them.

"Now, before we go any further with this, I want you to know one thing. This will be a pro bono job on my part, but I'm going to be paying you."

Her mouth fell open. "What are you talking about?'

As they headed out the doors toward her car, Scott explained. "You're going to be working a lot harder than me. I need you to be my investigator. I can't be here all the time, of course, and I will need someone who can figure out who might have done this murder. Between your contacts and your tenacity, I expect you'll be able to solve this crime. And what's with that neon pink hot tub back there?"

Minutes later, they were on the highway to Kennewick. After a bit of catch-up conversation, Scott began to ask questions about the case while skimming the pages of Cassie's diary.

"So why are they holding Mr. Maltos? What do you think they have on him?"

"In this town, everyone wants life to go back to normal as quickly as possible. Naming a suspect keeps the peace, if you get my drift. Apparently Mr. Maltos can not account for his whereabouts during the time around the murders. He had also just taken a life insurance out on his wife and daughter. He says he had left work early to run some errands, but it appears there is no one who has come forward to confirm that. He didn't attend our meeting earlier that day."

"So how long were you at the house?"

"I arrived a little early and stayed until around 1:00. I left my phone on their kitchen counter, but I didn't realize it until around three. By then, I was teaching a class, one of our remedial classes. Anyway, I'd planned to go back after the class." She shuddered as an involuntary stab of emotion flooded her. "Scott, I was so lucky. We don't carry guns, you know."

Her brother reached over and put his arm across her shoulders. "You have a dangerous job. Jaz and I worry about you...a lot.

But let's stay with this. While you were at the Maltos home, did anything unusual happen during your meeting?"

"Jim Maltos called to say he wouldn't be able to make it. Then... hmmm." Christian thought back. What was Sue's reaction to that phone call? Something nagged at the back of her mind.

An errant memory stirred. Sue Maltos had received another phone call shortly after Jim's call. She had been very friendly with the person on the phone and she'd said something about meeting later. What else?

Christian pulled into the Justice Center parking lot and parked the car. Scott was quiet as she closed her eyes and attempted to remember. "Mrs. Maltos took a second phone call while I was there. She was familiar with the caller. She said something about meeting up at the house later that afternoon and that she'd baked the caller's favorite cookies. It was someone she knew well, Scott. Someone who made her smile."

"So we can assume they were killed by this person."

"Not necessarily. Perhaps that person never went to the house," she paused. "There was only about two hours from the time I left their house and when the murders occurred." Christian strained to capture that tragic day. What had she observed? Her eyes darted under their lids as she scanned the Maltos living room in her mind's eye, remembering the afternoon's events as closely as she could.

She cast her eyes on Scott. "Cassie was relaxed that day, but also excited about something. She looked pleased when her mother came back in the room, as though she knew who was on the phone. From the living room, we could overhear Sue's one-sided conversation. When she replied that 'around two-thirty sounded fine', Cassie had hugged a pillow, giggled and said something under her breath like 'got him now'. What do you think it all means?"

"I think Cassie knew darn well who was coming to the house. And we know that there didn't appear to be a break-in, right? It sounds like she had something planned, a surprise for her mom? The phone call was a confirmation for her."

Christian raised her hand to interrupt. "Scott, I remember now. Cassie had begged me to stay longer that afternoon. She said she wanted me there to help her with a surprise. I told her I had to teach the ART class and couldn't stay. She acted very disappointed, but then she said something like, 'you'll hear about it soon enough. It's going to change everything'. I can't believe I'd forgotten all of this until now. It's all coming back. I feel so stupid." She put her face in her hands, frustrated and relieved at the same time.

"No. Yours is a typical reaction. Memories get locked whenever there's a trauma. You're the one who taught me that. Now I'm going to go in and meet my client. Is there anything you'd like me to tell him for you?"

"Just that I'm thinking about him, that I'm concerned. When should I pick you up?"

Scott glanced at his watch. "Court starts at one-thirty. He should be in and out of there quickly. First appearances normally don't take long. I will be named his attorney and then we start the real work. Any chance you could take Bear up to the house and have him snoop around the yard a bit?"

"I get off about five. It gets dark by then. How about if I go tomorrow, at lunch?"

"That might be better. I'll see if Jim will tell me where we can find a house key. I'd like to go in there before I leave tomorrow night. I'd like to get a feel for the crime scene."

Christian smiled. "Thanks so much for coming, Scotty. I'll see you in a few hours."

On the way back to her office, her cell phone rang. Every time she'd used it since the murders, she felt strange, as though Cassie's energy was still with her through the touch of the phone. "Hello."

"Hey, partner, it's me. I just heard from my *abuela*. She wants to talk to you as soon as possible. I think she laid some cards for you."

"Who's *abuela*?" Christian asked as she pulled into the parking lot and climbed out of the car.

"My grandmother, Maria. She's called me a couple of times and has wanted to talk to you. I've been so busy, I've forgotten to tell you."

"Yeah, been so busy with Sophia. I heard you guys went out for coffee and lunch!" Christian stifled a giggle. She'd given her partner the therapist's phone number. He'd wanted to interview her for individual therapy, and from what she'd heard around the office that morning, they'd ended up on a lunch date. "So what's with seducing my therapist anyway?"

Daniel was silent for a long moment. "Okay, so you found out. So what! She's a babe and very nice. We decided it wouldn't be such a good idea to do counseling after the murders, with you seeing her and all, but that friendship was an option. Frankly, a new friend is just what I need right now, considering my separated state of affairs."

"Uh-huh, but remember, *successore novo vincitur omnis amor*," Christian quoted.

Daniel replied slowly, "Every love dies when a new one comes along."

"You got it!"

"Spanish isn't that far from Latin, Professor. And I know what you might be thinking. No, we're not planning on sleeping together. Remember, I'm still a married man."

"And oh, so Catholic. So what do you think Maria wants to tell me?"

"She wants to see you. Something about the Gemini Girls."

After she hung up, Christian flipped through her address book and found Maria's number. She was surprised to learn that Maria read animal cards, but under the circumstances, she was willing to listen to anyone with some advice, esoteric or otherwise.

A quick phone call to the elderly Mexican woman ended in arrangements to meet after work the following day. In the meantime, she had enough to keep her busy. As she walked into the building, the courtroom buzzer sounded. The afternoon docket was about to begin.

Judge Stanzik held Tommy Calander pending bail. As she headed back to her office after first appearances, Christian decided to stop at Stella's office to say hello.

"Hey girlfriend, how are you?" she asked, standing in the doorway as Stella glanced up from her computer.

"Good, but how about you? I've been worried about you." Stella lifted her reading glasses from her face and offered a hopeful smile.

"I'm okay. This whole thing is becoming an obsession around here. Did you hear the news?"

"There's so much to hear! If you mean about Mr. Maltos's arrest, yes and I'm sick about it. If you're referring to your handsome brother taking the case, another yes, and I'm happy about that. How did you manage to get him on board?"

Christian put her finger to her lips. "Shhh. I told Michael that Scott had read about the murders in the papers and came on his own volition. My brother is the best!"

"Yeah, too bad we're both married, or I'd be all over him."
Stella took a sip of her Starbucks coffee. "I'd love to catch you guys
for a glass of wine while he's here. Any chance?"

"Probably not this time, but he'll be back. Sorry, but I've got to
get going."

"Wait. I heard something about your girl, Cassie, from one of
my girls who was doing community service hours with her at SARC.
Crystal Rodman-Casey, you know her?"

Stella continued, "Crystal said that one day she and Cassie were
talking to one of the counselors there, a young gal right out of college. The counselor was all worked up about a date rape case that
had come through. Apparently the girls didn't really understand
what a date rape is. Anyway, Crystal said that Cassie was really upset
about the case and left early, before she was supposed to. Cassie
also hinted to Crystal a few days earlier that she thought she was
pregnant." Christian stared at Stella while processing the information back to the diary entry in which Cassie had said she was
taking birth control pills. She needed to talk to Tommy as soon as
possible.

"Thanks, Stell, that's good information."

With a shrug, she added, "I don't know why, except if she was pregnant, who knows, maybe the killer was the illegitimate father, huh?"

"That's what I'm thinking. Stay in touch." With that, Christian
raced out of the room and headed toward the detention center to
find Tommy.

♊

"So, what's with your alibi? It sounds pretty flaky to me."
Christian was seated across from Tommy at one of the metal tables

that kids used for eating. The pod was quiet. The remaining inmates were in detention school down the hall.

Tommy flexed his arms and gave her a malice-laced grin. "You
shouldn't asked me anything about it. I don't have to tell you nothin' and you could screw up the investigation if I tell them you're
asking questions." His hair had grown long and hung over his face
in lumpy strands. She could see a new tattoo on his forearm, the
number 13.

"Look, Tommy, I know you're upset. This whole thing sucks.
I feel sorry for you whether you like that or not. You loved Cassie
and I know she loved you. You have every right to be mad, at the
killer, at me, at the world."

The boy hung his head. She wondered if he was really crying
or if it was just an act on his part. He was a sly one. Christian stayed
quiet, but stood up and handed Tommy a Kleenex box that sat on
a counter nearby.

"It wasn't my idea to keep you in here. I would've released you
to go to the funeral, but that wasn't my call." Christian was stretching it. She couldn't have released him in time for the funeral and
she knew it, but it was an attempt at getting the upper hand.

Finally the boy lifted his head. His eyes were bloodshot and he
looked forlorn. Despite his ragged appearance, she noticed he was
a fairly handsome kid. She could see Cassie's puppy love attraction. "She was seeing some other dude. Some older guy. I don't
think she told you about him, did she?" His gaze was clear now, as
though he needed confirmation from her answer.

Christian shook her head, "No. I was just her probation officer.
She didn't tell me much. How much older was this guy?"

"Not a lot, some college geek, I think. I know he drove a
Mustang and had a little money. I only got bits of it when I read

her diary. I stole it from her room when I got out of Juvy the last time. She was acting weird back then. She quit doing it with me, you know, cuz she was doin' him. But the little ho kept sayin' that I was the one cheatin' on her with my friend, Lilly, which was complete b.s.. Lilly and I are hommies, that's all. We were in the same foster home for a while when we were little kids."

"Yeah, I figured you were loyal to her." Again Christian gambled. "That's a good thing, Tommy. You're smart. Did you ever follow Cassie around to find out who this guy was?"

"I tried. Then I got really mad and told her I'd tell her parents if she didn't stop seeing him. She acted like she was going to, showed up to get high with me and bring me a little money sometimes. But I caught her one night leaving the church in his car. She always went to church on Wednesday nights, to youth group, you know. Anyways I was hidin' up there at the church behind some cars and watched her sneak out of the church after everyone else left. He was waiting for her in the parking lot, in the fuckin' fancy car of his."

"You really did care about her." She paused to let her words sink in. "So you wouldn't hurt her, but someone, this guy, do you think he killed her and her mom?"

Tommy shrugged. "Who knows. But if I find out, I'll kill whoever done it. I miss her so much." The boy started crying now in earnest. Christian felt for the kid. His whole life was about loss, something she could relate to.

"I had someone that I loved very much die, too. I understand how badly it hurts."

The boy's eyes were still wet as he said, "Really? Who?"

"My husband. About two years ago. He had a heart attack, when he was training for a marathon. He was only thirty."

Tommy stared at her a long time. "You ain't so bad for a P.O., ya know that? Thanks for coming to talk to me. Will you come tomorrow?"

Christian offered him a smile. "Of course I will. I do want to help you, if you'll only let me."

She stood up to leave and on impulse, caressed the top of the boy's head. He looked up and returned her smile as she walked out the door.

Scott was waiting at the curb when Christian picked him up a few minutes after five. She'd invited Daniel to meet them at her house for dinner and had left work a few minutes early to buy the ingredients for a Caesar salad and Chicken Alfredo. Italian food was Scott's favorite, especially her homemade versions which were generally laced with fresh mozzarella cheese, garlic and lots of cream. His great love of food was not wasted on his younger cousin.

"So how is Mr. Maltos?" Christian asked as Scott climbed into the car.

"He's good, all things considered. Bail was set at a half a million, so he'll be in there awhile. He's a really nice man, and I don't believe for a minute that he killed his wife and child. He said he left work early that afternoon, but instead of coming home, he was shopping for a birthday gift for Cassie. He says that he was going to buy her a car, but he has no witnesses as to his whereabouts as far as we can tell... When he told this to the detective, the guy just laughed at him. We need to find some kind of proof as to his whereabouts."

Christian turned on to the freeway. The sky over Rattlesnake Mountain was turning a vivid mandarin with streaks of bright pink. The sunset was the first she'd seen in a while. The gorgeous sight distracted her momentarily.

"Will you look at that! Do you guys get the sunsets here," Scott commented as though reading her mind.

"See, there are some positive attributes to our little country town," she replied cheerfully, recalling an entire winter in Seattle where she never once saw anything but grey skies and rain. "I read in Cassie's diary that her Dad had talked about getting her a new car on her birthday. I didn't get very far, though. I think I stopped reading in the July entries."

Scott pulled the small book from his briefcase and flipped through the pages. "It looks like she wrote quite a bit in September. The last entry was in October."

"Yeah, that's right. Her boyfriend, Tommy Calander, said he stole it from her after he was released from detention around that time."

Scott flipped on the dome light. "Let's see, here's one on September 5: *I'm madly, crazy in love. My man is awesome. I'm not supposed to write his real name, I promised. That means....that man makes me so hot. I'm on fire down there just thinking about him...*" Scott flipped the pages in the book. "Hmm, teen love has gotten pretty sophisticated. It appears I'm going to have to keep my daughter locked in the basement in the future." He continued to read, emitting occasional sounds of surprise and disgust.

Her impatience had begun to fester when he finally said, "Okay, now she's writing about her part in a homecoming assembly, something about a church retreat, her grades....here, September 24, she's writing about that guy again. Here goes: *Tommy really takes me over the edge. I don't want to hang out with him anymore. He's totally on my case about other guys. Still my guy and I are getting serious. I can tell my mom hates him. She says that he's a phony and that he can't really do what he says he can do. She has no clue about us, though. God, he is so beautiful. He mentioned getting married some day, but then he got freaked out after I told him about my periods stopping. Still, he brought me a back-to-school present, a pink sweater from the Gemini Girls catalog. My big sis has one just like it. She acts so weird about us. She keeps saying that J.J.'s the one for me and that he's going to drop me one of these days if I don't cool it with...."* Scott paused and looked up again. "Dang that's a beautiful sunset."

"Obviously J.J. and Tommy are two different people, but there's another guy in the mix. Keep reading," she ordered as she turned off the highway and headed down the riverside road to her home.

"Okay, Miss Bossyboots. Still true to your name, I see." Scott grinned teasingly and turned another page. After a few minutes of silent reading, he released a slow whistle. "Jesus, this is bad."

"READ!" Christian cried as she turned into the driveway. She could see Bear's head poking through the blinds of the front window as she waited to hear the rest.

I forgot to get my pills from Planned Parenthood again. I told him and he said that if I'm pregnant, he has a way to fix it. We'd smoked a bowl at our secret place and he wanted to have sex, but I told him not until I got back on the pill. He refuses to use condoms. Anyway, he forced me to have sex with him. It hurt this time. I begged him to stop, but he wouldn't. He acted like someone I didn't know. He held me down and said some really mean things to me. I got scared! What a jerk. I pray to God I'm not pregnant.

Scott closed the book and released a loud sigh. "That's it. No more entries after that. But that girl was raped and I'm willing to bet if her partner raped her, he could also be the one who killed her. Most sociopaths who enjoy that kind of violence are capable of murder."

Christian's mind was beginning to drop information into neat little internal boxes now. Things were beginning to make sense.

"Grab those bags of groceries in the back. Let's get in the house and start sorting things out."

Daniel arrived a few minutes later with a bottle of 2001 Leonetti Cabernet. It had come highly recommended from their English friend, Erick, a true connoisseur who waxed poetry about wine like some lit major who'd just fallen in love with Shakespeare. Daniel grinned as he handed Christian the bottle.

"Erick told me to tell you this." He winked and pulled a note out of his pocket. "I had to write it down," he admitted, rolling his eyes. Putting on the best English accent that he could muster, Daniel recited, "This elegant vintage is reminiscent of the early Mondavis. Rich raspberries flirt with a subtle, but potent hint of rosemary, though the heavy oak influence bleeds through, give it an erotic finish that leaves you begging for more."

Christian laughed. "Very well *said.* Some day that guy needs to write this stuff down for real...for the <u>Wine Spectator</u>."

Daniel shrugged. "I think he prefers being a nerdy Hanford scientist. That side of him insists that we decanter it and let it sit at least twenty minutes before tucking in."

Nodding, she found him a decanter and then began dinner, boiling some noodles and tossing a salad while the men took the chicken out to the gas grill on the patio. By the time the two returned, they were laughing like old friends.

Christian ceremoniously lit the candelabra on the dining table and went to the stereo player, inserting the latest *Pink Martini* CD. A hip Latin beat played softly in the background. After they'd offered a toast all around, Scott got down to business.

"Okay lady and gentleman, we have a job to do. It's not going to be as easy as you think. They have very little in the way of motive with regards to Mr. Maltos. He appears to be, after all, a stand- up guy. However, you never know. From my experience, about ninety percent of all murder cases have a domestic violence element to them. And that was why you were working with the family in the first place, right? Anyway, I don't think we'll find any dirt on him, but just in case, that will be your job. Dig around, check your sources, talked to his boss, his friends, the neighbors. Be cool. Don't let people know who you really are. The good news is the weapon has not been found and there doesn't appear to be any guns registered to Maltos."

"How do you know that?' Daniel took a slow sip of the delicious wine.

"I made some calls after court. However, just because he isn't a registered owner, doesn't mean he didn't have a gun. This community is a little gun happy by the sounds of things. Anyway, we take the angle of his innocence, but in the meantime, your job is to find out who committed these murders. So far we're guessing that it's someone the family knew well."

Daniel nodded as he tore off a piece of garlic bread, "These folks are the PTA, clean-living, church-going types. I think it was one of Cassie's gangbanger friends. She was dating Tommy and he's involved with some bad people."

Christian added, "I saw Tommy today. He just got a new thirteenth street tat."

Scott's face drew a question mark. "Remind me, please."

"Thirteen is Sureno's number. Tommy hangs with the gang down in East Kennewick. There are a lot of them and some are associated with the local motorcycle gang, the Gypsy Jokers. They run drugs, mostly meth and some heroin. They are responsible for a lot of crimes and all of them pack heat. Nobody is too anxious to mess with them, except maybe your cousin here."

Scott gave Christian a hard stare. "What's your partner trying to tell me, little sis?"

Christian glared at Daniel, but the damage had already been done. "Ok, my friend Stella and I went into the clubhouse a month or so ago. I was looking for a girl on the run. No one was there, except another girl who needed our help. No big deal."

"Yeah, *big* deal. Anyway, Tommy is a felon, been to juvenile prison and has a group of friends who would do whatever he told them to do. If he was upset with Cassie's mom, say, for trying to keep them apart, he might have gone in to hurt her."

"On the other hand, if Cassie was pregnant by another guy, maybe Tommy found out and was looking for a little revenge."

"What makes you think that she was pregnant?"

"Stella said that one of her girls was doing community service hours with Cassie at SARC. Cassie had spoken to her about it."

"And in her diary, she mentions that she might be, too." Scott reminded her.

"Nope, she wasn't. I've already checked with the coroner's office. I have a friend who works there as a lab tech. He says she was not, under any circumstances, pregnant. She did have some kind of a venereal infection, though. One we can assume came from Tommy," Daniel opened a second bottle of wine from Kestrel Cellars.

"And now my *Lady in Red*," he announced loudly as he filled their glasses.

"I assume you're talking about the wine, not my sister," Scott grinned, looking from one to the other expectantly.

"I'm confused...sister or cousin?"

Scott gave Christian an appreciative look. "She's technically my cousin, but in reality, by far my favorite sister."

Christian pushed her plate away and smiled. "There's only brotherly love on Daniel's part, too. Don't worry, he's a married man." She shot Daniel a sly wink.

Daniel turned a deep shade of red. "It was just a lunch date. Now back to our crime analysis. What else do we have to go on?"

"My wipe-out at church. Every time I get faint, it's around negative memories or energies. I know that sounds weird, but I react physically to perceived or real danger."

"That's something you might want to ask Maria about. She'll give you some weird potion for that, I'm sure. You might not want to faint when chasing down bad guys. But let's go back, so what, or should I say *who* was in the church who could get to you like that?"

"I don't know. There were so many people there. But I did talk to your grandmother today. I get a gut feeling Maria's magic might give us an answer."

Scott pushed his chair back and rubbed his belly. "Now that was a fine meal. As far as potion-making, magical grandmothers go, do I really want to know?"

After dinner, the three of them took Bear for a stroll down by the river. Typical for the Tri-Cities, the early snow had melted long ago with a Chinook wind and the temperature now hovered around 40 degrees. In the distance, the dissonant howls of coyotes could be heard. A beaver slipped into the water as they walked along the bank, loudly splashing his tail in warning. Neighbor dogs barked sporadically, but the evening was calm and quiet for the most part. A giant full moon hung low and golden in the cool solstice sky. The magnificent astral rock's face smiled in mockery. Like an illustration from a child's storybook, it gave a benign portrayal to an otherwise terrified town.

♊

Maria had laid five cards out on the card table in a T shaped pattern. She'd also crossed herself several times before the reading, praying in Spanish to her Holy Father and a few other deities that Christian couldn't identify. Her partner had assured her that his grandmother was a stoic and proud Catholic, but that she mixed a little Mexican folklore into their lives as was standard practice for Mexican healers. Christian was silent, more in awe of all of the paper mache and clay death statues that surrounded her than of the odd incantations that she was hearing.

"Maria, what are all these figures for?" she asked when the woman had finally finished. She pointed to the wall-to-wall shelves packed with gruesome, skeleton figurines whose gaunt faces all seemed to be staring directly at her.

"Mexican traditional art. We are not afraid of death, my Chiquita. We are lovers of all states of being. Death is a step closer to the Great Mystery. Mother Earth has an energized connection with every creature on the planet. We are all connected. The animals of the Medicine Wheel speak to us if we will listen. On the great Red Road, the animals show us the way through the patterns in their lives. Pick seven cards now. Hold them close and listen as you do." Christian took the well-used cards and held them to her heart. Slowly, one by one, she pulled from the deck, handing each card to Maria as she did so. The healer was quiet as she looked over the cards and began to place them in a two-three-two spread.

"This is Pathway." She furrowed her eyebrows. "The first card is the old times, the past. The Otter. In your past the otter was present. Always on the move and very curious." She pointed to the card depicting a dog. "You are loyal and have this friend." A gnarled finger poked at the card's face. "This creature looks out for you. But here you are. As you see, it is the Snake. The snake is very good. She is the animal of transformation. You shed your skin and become new. You can listen? Learn to listen and trust the snake energy. You doubt sometimes, yes?"

The probation officer nodded. "Yes. I think that's what happens when I faint. I stop listening because of…" she stopped. There was too much explaining to do.

"Because of all the death you have seen. No worry. You will learn. I will help you." The old woman adjusted the multi-colored scarf she'd placed over her shoulders. It was chilly in the small niche off the main house. Maria's reading room had originally been a screened-in porch. The house was wedged in the hills several miles north of Pasco. The old bungalow-styled building was probably over a hundred years old. Several space heaters burned fitfully around their feet. Their electric glow gave the hundreds of statues a life-like presence. Christian felt as though she was in the middle of a New Orleans Halloween Horror house.

She gazed at Maria as the woman shook her head, concerned at something only she could see. The grandmother was plump and as wrinkled as a raisin, but her luxurious black hair hung in a single sheet down her back. There was more Indian to her features than Spanish and she wasn't more than five feet tall.

"Now we look at this card over is here." She pointed to the far right card. "This card is the Horse. Man could not fly until the horse became their way. The horse gave us freedom. You have freedom to fly, but you must not go too fast. You are a rider now, on a journey of discovering." The woman stopped for a moment, shook her head. "I see this butterfly. She is like an angel, but she will make your journey difficult. It will be confusing and dangerous.

There is danger of betrayal. This card, the coyote. It is the sly creature, the trickster, who hunts at night. Beware. The coyote is from another den. He is the alpha, very fierce and territorial." Maria nodded, as though pleased with herself.

Christian pointed to the last two cards. "What are these two cards for?"

Maria scowled. "Life not so simple. You know that, Miss. You're a scarred woman; you have had bad times. Never simple, is it?"

"This card. Look at the card. See the Hawk. He is a messenger. Life is the initiation. You are learning and the magic of life is being brought to you. These are directions, the map." Maria paused and cocked her head in confusion.

"The messenger could be my brother."

"Perhaps. Yet I see my grandson, Daniel." She smiled widely, showing gaps in her yellowed teeth. "Man and woman should be together. He is a very brave man."

Christian smiled as embarrassment crept up her neck and into her face like fire. "I don't understand. He isn't really involved."

"No?" The old woman made a 'tsk, tsk' sound. "This does not mean you can not solve this crime. This is for you. The snake is a growing card. You will mature through this difficult time, become a stronger woman. There is always crime, you understand? Always pain in the world. We try to fix one and then another one comes along. We can only grow closely to our voice. Remember this card!" Maria pointed to the snake. "You must learn to listen to your inner voice. You will become better woman, better crime-solver."

Christian was suddenly exhausted by all that she had heard. "I'm so glad that you asked me to come, Maria. I will think about all of this, let it sink in. This is my first time with a healer. I hope you will let me come back."

Maria smiled, her deep brown eyes twinkling. "Of course. Now I have a special tea for you to drink. My grandson asked me to give you something for your fainting spells. It will make your blood hot, but it will keep you upright. Drink a little every morning, especially now." Her face suddenly turned grim. "Be careful, Miss. This is dangerous job. You will have to keep your eyes open all the time. Look with your inner eye, too. God will protect."

With that, the woman handed her a plastic baggy filled with dark burgundy leaves. As the woman stood and turned away, Christian surreptitiously slipped a hundred dollar bill under the cards. Daniel had warned her not to directly pay Maria. It had something to do with superstition and money. The healer turned back from her shelves of figurines. When she faced the young woman again, she was holding one of her paper mache dolls.

"Here. You must take my Contessa. She will protect you. She is very charming and very wise." Maria then handed her a delicate statue of a skeleton, nearly a foot in height. She was dressed in a lovely blue gown, her black hair swept elegantly off her ghoulish scull. Her sunken eyes, however, were not fiendish, but rather seemed to emanate wit. "She came from Vera Cruz. A beautiful place in my country. She will be your guide. You pray to God, no? Also pray to Contessa. She is good for you."

Christian thanked her and gave her a hug. As she left the side door, she turned back to ask about the Gemini Girls reference. The door to the strange sanctuary was wide open and she could see the room in its entirety, but Maria had completely disappeared.

On the drive home, she replayed the woman's words in her mind. Who was the betrayer? Was the phrase Gemini Girls significant? Then she remembered Cassie's diary entry. *He calls me his Gemini Girl.* How did Maria know that?

CHAPTER 11

♊

Christian got up early Saturday morning with the intent on taking Bear over to the Maltos home before meeting up with Matt. Jim had told Scott where to find the house key and was very encouraging with regards to their desire to uncover any possible remaining evidence. The Kennewick detectives and crime scene folks had exhausted their search and the home was basically locked up until further notice.

The sky looked like raw skin after a brawl. Bruised clouds filled the horizon and a freezing chill permeated the air. As quickly as the balmy weather had come, it was gone. The forecast called for snow flurries. Hopefully, there would be snow for Christmas this year. She'd invited Scott, Jasmine and the kids down over the holidays, promising to take them to a local church Christmas pageant, a winery tour or two and sledding on Carmichael hill if the weather cooperated. It would be the first time that she'd she spent Christmas at home since Tony died, but with Scott's family for company, she expected it to be a happy occasion.

As she tidied up the kitchen, Christian was surprised to find the *Dia de los Muertos* doll sitting on the windowsill in front of the sink. She stared at it, trying to figure out when she'd moved it from the living room mantel. The *calaca* or skeletal figurine looked at her wisely. Contessa's face was both grim and strangely beautiful. After Maria had given her the doll, she'd spent some time researching the meaning of the Mexican art. The Day of the Dead was as ancient to the culture as the Mayan pyramids. The early Mexicans believed that the soul was in a perpetual dream while in the body during a lifetime and that only in death, when the soul was finally set free, did real life begin. She remembered a quote that she'd found which had impressed her in the simplicity of its message. 'Don't fear dying; fear not having lived'. She smiled at the funny little paper mache woman and she seemed to smile back.

The drive to the Maltos home was a little unnerving. She hadn't been there since the night of the murders and felt as though she was reliving those terrible moments as she drove down the deserted highway and up towards the lifestyles of the local rich and famous. Most homes were overdone with Doric columns or great stucco cupolas. Most garages housed three cars while driveways held the extra family vehicles: jeeps, boats and the occasional Winnebago. Upon her arrival, she noticed that the newspapers had piled up against the garage door and a couple of empty flower pots had tipped over in the wind. She picked up the scattered papers and threw them in her trunk as Bear leaped around, smelling every bush and tree he could find. The house reeked of sadness and neglect. She hesitated as she whistled to Bear and moved toward the front door. There was a darkness that seemed to envelope her as Death hovered near. He was watching, waiting to see if she was able to move forward. He played with her impending defeat, a well-fed cat toying with a languishing mouse.

Her hand found the key beneath a small welcome urn. She relinquished to the dread that raced through her limbs, though it threatened to cripple her. She knew this feeling…nausea, fatigue and an energy-stifling consumption. Then, because of Maria, or her own desire to overcome the anticipated humiliation, she waited patiently to resurrect her strength. Garnering her resources, Christian imagined a mystical surge of power and stood tall. Unlocking the door, she uttered, "As it should be."

At her feet, Bear was full of excitement, pumping his tail hard against the outside wall of the house until she opened the front door. Suddenly the dog froze and gave a low growl She'd seen this behavior before from the canine. He reacted to blood and this house, no doubt, was full of it.

Christian whispered soothing sounds to Bear as she pushed the door open and stepped in. A bank of light switches were lined up on the wall to her left. Quickly, she flipped them on and took a deep breath.

"Okay boy, where do we start?" She'd brought Cassie's diary, but had left it in the car. She didn't see much point in Bear tracking here. Even the scent off Tommy's shirt, which she managed to swipe out of detention's personals locker, was pointless. The boy had been in this house dozens of times. If the killer had left his DNA, the police department hadn't found anything to point to who that might be.

She grabbed Bear's leash and turned to go down the hall to the master bedroom. On the way, she winced several times, swallowing hard. Thank goodness she'd had some of Maria's tea that morning. Though it was disgusting to taste, it seemed to be making a difference. She felt strong and clear-headed. Blood streaks could be seen on the walls as she moved closer to the room. Outside the door, where Cassie was shot, the carpet was black with dried blood. Christian grabbed Bear tighter and steadied her legs. The

bedroom was a paint fest of blood. The walls, bedding and curtains were streaked as though someone had come through with a
spray gun. The smell was tangible and hit her deep in the gut, but
the nausea didn't come. She forced herself to breath and walked
slowly in, feeling a sense of both honor and horror.

"This is where they were killed," she said more to herself than
to Bear. "This is a sacred place. These women, God bless these
women." She sank to her knees in a spot where the carpet still
gleamed white. She bent her head and folded her hands, offering a prayer for their souls and for the strength. She begged God
to help her find the killer, to give her the courage to see this
through. Bear growled and sniffed, moving methodically from
one side of the room to another. At the closet door, he began to
whimper. Then he scratched at the door and pushed at it with
his nose.

Christian stood up. "What is it, boy?" Though the room was
bathed in light, she pulled a flashlight from her pocket and got on
her knees to see what he was sensing. On the edge of the folding
closet door in the gap between the two panels was a snagged piece
of fabric, basically just a dark blue bit of fabric. The closet door
had splintered slightly and caught the piece in its fine grip. Bear
wouldn't have reacted, she thought, unless he sensed that it was
something that didn't belong in this room. She started to pull a
baggy from her pocket to remove the evidence when she decided
she needed a witness. She grabbed her cell from her other pocket
and dialed Daniel's number. At that moment, Bear uttered a different kind of growl, one of dire warning.

The hairs rose on the back of her neck. Slowly she turned and
looked toward the door. Standing there, illuminated by the hall
light like an angel, was Tabby Smithson.

"Easy, Bear," she murmured, placing her hand on the dog's head. "Hi, Tabby. What are you doing here?"

"I guess I should ask you the same question," the girl replied with a sarcastic bite. "I came to write on the memory wall outside. I saw your car and the front door was wide open."

"Mr. Maltos asked me to come by and check on the house and water the plants." Christian hated to lie, but suddenly felt trapped by this perfect specimen of a woman-child.

"That's weird. Why wouldn't he have one of us do it, or someone from the church?" Tabby continued, her face marked with suspicion.

"That should be obvious. I carry a badge," Christian countered, unwilling to give up her ground.

Tabby looked around the room, suddenly noticing the blood-drenched space. Her face became a frozen mask of horror, but almost too late. From Tabby's belated reaction, it didn't appear as though the gory scene had really come as a surprise.

"So, do you care if I go down to Cassie's room? She still has a few of my clothes that she borrowed."

Christian now offered the girl a warm smile. "Of course. I haven't been down there yet. I need your help on something, Tabby. My dog, he's a search dog. He has sensed something in this room that doesn't seem to belong here. Look, over at the closet door. See the slight splinter in the wood. There's a tiny piece of fabric there." Christian held the flashlight on the door as Tabby walked over and leaned in to take a closer look. She was dressed in jeans, high-heeled black boots and a short white fur jacket. Her fluffy blond hair created the halo effect again. Not a typical Saturday morning outfit, Christian thought as she took a baggy out of her pocket.

"I'm going to collect this fabric piece for the lab. I just need you to be a witness should they ask where I found it. You never know with people. Sometimes juries question stuff like this. So are you okay with that?"

The girl nodded strangely and stepped gingerly away from the closet and backed out of the room, avoiding any bloodstains on the carpet. "Are they going to clean this place up before Mr. Maltos comes home?" There was a note of hysteria in her voice.

"Usually there's a cleaning company who will come in. But that is if Mr. Maltos is coming home. He's still being held for the murders." Once the evidence was bagged, Christian stuffed it in her pocket. She pulled out her cell phone, which was still lit up; she'd completely forgotten that she'd dialed Daniel's number. She pushed the off button and proceeded to follow Tabby downstairs.

"It's really creepy in here. I kind of feel like I'm going to be sick," Tabby said as she flipped on the basement lights. "Thank goodness there's no blood down here."

'It's tough, honey. I often get sick in these kinds of situations. I'm actually quite amazed at your courage."

Tabby flashed a set of very white teeth. "Thanks. I guess I didn't know what to expect." She walked into Cassie's room with Bear close behind. The room was painted a bright turquoise color, like a Caribbean sea. The white wicker furniture was glazed in a pale yellow with turquoise and yellow flowered pillows. Matching curtains and a bedspread finished the tropical look. It was once a happy room still filled with choir trophies, school pictures and other typical teenage memorabilia. Tabby had already moved to the closet and was flipping through the hangers of clothes, almost hungrily, Christian observed.

"What are you looking for? Maybe I can help," Christian offered gently. The girl seemed agitated. It was no wonder, considering she was in the room of her deceased best friend.

"She has…had a couple of my sweaters. A pale pink one and a dark burgundy. She always wore them whenever she and…" All of a sudden, the girl stopped talking.

A pained look crossed Tabby's face as Christian attempted to keep her tone neutral. "Go on."

Tabby looked away and wiped her eyes with her sleeve. "Never mind. I can't find the pink one, but here's the burgundy. It's his, I mean, it's my favorite." Tabby held the sweater close to her and said, "It's too hard to be in here. I've got to go." She spun on her heels and raced up the stairs before Christian could say another word.

"Bye," she called up the stairs, just as she heard the front door slam.

"That was interesting. Now let's find that pink sweater." She began to open Cassie's dresser drawers. In the back of her underwear drawer, she found a number of condoms and some lubricant. She also was surprised to find a couple of catalogs which sold erotic lingerie and sex toys, but no sweater. Next she moved to the computer desk. Cassie's computer was missing, undoubtedly taken in for evidence. The desk had a neat pile of books next to where the computer would have been. She flipped through a pile of school books and papers, and eventually came across a letter to the infamous J.J. dated October 29, 2005.

Hey!

You're my man!. You give me so much lovin'. I want your mouth on me, making me squirm. But I'm scared, too. You seem to be distracted lately and I found her number on your cell phone. Why would you call her? I checked the messages. You left three on her phone just yesterday. Are you really just trying to plan the Halloween party or do you guys have more going on?

I sometimes think you call us your Gemini Girls for a different reason than what you say you do. I know you have a dirty mind. I bet you want to do all of us, eventually. I don't want to share you. Don't think I can't hurt you. I know you could get in big trouble for what we're doing. This is for real. I'm your one and only Gemini Girl and if you mess around on me, well, I guess you'll pay.

I'm sorry to say it this way. I've done what you asked, and broke it off with Tommy. He wasn't important to me anyway. Only at the beginning, when you and me first started hanging out. Once I slept with you, Tommy was a joke. You know that. I get hot just thinking about having you inside me. I want you every second.

I'm coming to your house this weekend. My parents are going to be out of town and we can be together the whole three days. I can't wait.

I love you, babe, Cassie. XXXXOOOOXXXX

Christian slowly folded the letter and put it in her pocket. It was never sent, but why? Her frustration level was beginning to climb. Who was her man?

She wandered around the room, looking for anything else that looked like it could be of investigative value. Opening the closet, she glanced at Cassie's wardrobe. There were more clothes in there than most women's closets. Her shoes alone could have filled a small shoe store. Tucked in the corner was a laundry basket. Christian pulled it out and noticed something on the floor behind it. She reached in and grabbed a lose article of clothing. She gasped as she realized what it was. A pink angora sweater with the tag ripped out. It had several stains across the front. Though the stains themselves were nearly invisible, they had matted down the angora wool. She looked at the sweater for a long time, and then it came to her: a voice, the inner voice that Maria had told her to listen for. *These are semen stains left here by the killer.*

Great. My first message from my inner voice is a discussion about sperm! Christian thought. *What an auspicious beginning to enlightenment.*

She made one more sweep through the house with Bear. The place was beginning to get to her, though she was happy that her fainting spells hadn't appeared. Once they were on the highway to town, she flipped on her phone to check messages. There was one from Daniel.

"Hey, where are you? You left a message on my phone a few minutes ago. I couldn't really tell what was going on...someone as your witness? I'm confused. Call me." His voice sounded tense.

Nevertheless, she grinned. His phone had caught her conversation with Tabby. That could be a good thing down the road. In the meantime, today was for another man. A small fluttering in her belly began as she turned off the highway and headed toward his condo.

She pulled into a parking space next to Matt's ground level unit. The condos were built to give a view of the Columbia River from a series of balconies and patios that ran along the north side of the development. Matt was standing on his patio as she drove up and waved before he stepped into the house to meet her at the front door.

She hesitated to let Bear out, but as she opened her door, she heard him call, "Bring Bear in. I want to meet this wooly mammoth of yours."

She turned and said to the dog, "A wooly mammoth...that's just about right, boy."

She walked toward Matt with her dog at her side. Bear seemed relaxed even when Matt pulled her into his arms to give her a hug. "I hope you don't mind my way of saying hello. The Hiles family are an affectionate lot," he said as they separated.

"No, not a bit. I need more hugs than I generally get. It gets pretty pathetic when the only one you hug is your dog!" Matt smiled as he continued to hold her arms. He looked into her eyes and replied,

"I'd never pass up the opportunity, honey." There it was again. Honey.

She wandered around the lower level of his place as he went into the kitchen to pour some coffee. It was definitely a bachelor's pad-decorated in a dark brown leather couch and matching chair set with a slate coffee table. On the east wall was a ceiling to floor bookshelf. On the other was a big screen television. The windows that faced the river were covered with heavy wooden blinds, now open to see the view.

"Here, take a seat and have some of my southern style coffee. It's a little like mud. I hope you don't mind." Christian sat down on the couch. Bear immediately curled up at her feet and released a heavy sigh.

She took a sip of coffee and smiled. "Yummy. This tastes like the coffee that's served in New Orleans."

"Yep. I love it this way. So, Bear looks beat. What have you two been up to already this morning?"

Christian looked down at her hands. She had wanted to keep her visit to the Maltos home a secret. She looked back at Matt. He had sat down next to her and was leaning toward her, alert and interested.

"I went over to the Maltos home. You see, the deal is, now that my brother, Scott, is Jim's attorney, he's asked me to do a little behind-the-scenes work."

"Good for you. Obviously we can never be sure, but I don't think Maltos did it. When he came to pick his little girl up from detention a few months ago, he was in tears. She ran into his arms and he just held and held her. It was actually quite touching. I think a few people in master control had tears in their eyes. A father like that doesn't murder his only daughter. Anyway, that's my opinion, if it counts for anything. I've worked in detention a long time, and I've seen a lot of things in there. A lot of horrible parents."

"I trust your opinion. I just wish our prosecutor did. We got a job on our hands, especially now that Blanks is off the hook."

Matt nodded thoughtfully. "Well, I'll help you if you'd like, whatever you need. I don't want to see Maltos go to prison."

"Really? Okay, first I'll help you get through this school stuff. Then I want to take a trip down to Bateman's Island."

The next three hours were an intensive cram session. Matt's quick mind was impressive. He struggled a little with his math skills, but she'd always had the knack, so between the two of them, his math paper was printed and ready to be turned in by the Monday deadline.

"So, how about I take you out to lunch next door and then we'll hike down to Bateman and see what we can find." Matt suggested, stretching his arms and flexing as he pulled away from the kitchen island where they'd been working. Christian admired his muscular frame as he stood up and offered his hand. As he pulled her up, she stepped forward and lost her balance when Bear decided he was going to get up at the same time. As she tried to untangle herself, she fell into Matt. This time, as he steadied her, she paused, her face only inches from his and took the plunge. To his surprise, she kissed him deeply on the lips. There was no use denying the chemistry anymore.

Matt kissed her back. His lips were soft and his tongue seemed to know exactly where to go. When she pulled away, her heart was racing. "It's been a long time since I did that."

Matt smoothed a piece of her hair away from her cheek. "You can do that any time."

She wanted to kiss him again, but felt awkward, like she'd come on too strong. "Now I'm embarrassed," she mumbled, moving to the couch to get her coat. "That's not me, to do that, but there's something about you, Matt."

"There's *definitely* something about you. I've wanted to spend time with you since I met you, when you first started in probation." He looked away, as though the embarrassment was contagious.

"What, tell me!" she encouraged, turning back to face him.

He studied her in silence, his eyes flashing with unspoken longing. "At first I wanted to respect the fact that you'd just lost your husband. Then I thought maybe because I'm just a detention guy, that you wouldn't be interested. Besides you're such a beautiful woman." He glanced at her, showing a bashful side. "Then I heard that Big D's marriage was on the rocks and you guys might have something going."

"What!" Christian's voice came out louder than she would have liked. "Sorry, but I *hate* the office rumor mill. We're just partners. That's it. There's no contest. He is a nice guy, but I've just been a little gun-shy since Tony's death. I don't want to have anyone that I care about to get hurt because of me."

Matt reached out and pulled her to him again. He kissed hard and pressed his body into hers. "You can't hurt me," he murmured when they'd paused for the second time. She felt his heat and considered pulling him directly into the bedroom, but it was too soon. *Let the fire build,* she said to herself. *Give this time.*

Matt hesitated, watching her, allowing her to take the lead. "I think we'd better get some lunch," she said, trying to ignore the pleas of her body.

"Let's go. Shall we leave Bear here while we're gone?"

By the time they'd finished lunch, it had started to pour. Sheets of rain drenched them as they ran to his car. "No Bateman's Island today," she remarked as they drove to his house to get the dog.

"Are you still interested in going to Hog Heaven? That shop of Doobie's is not too well insulated. In this weather, it's going to be cold in there. I could just as easily stay in with you and rent a movie."

Christian smiled as the blush of desire spread through her again. "Are you sure your brother won't be disappointed?"

Matt shook his head. "No. He'll be fine with it. Those Christmas parties are pretty crazy-lots of drinking and car talk. To tell the truth, I was looking for a way to get some more time with you. Pretty lame invitation, huh?"

Christian grabbed his hand and gave it a squeeze. "The thought was a sweet one. I'd love to just hang out. I'm not much of a car connoisseur, but at some point, I need to ask your brother about the Mustang Club."

"Why's that?"

"Cassie Maltos was having a secret affair with a Mustang owner. It may be a lead in the case."

Matt's face was bright with admiration. "I'm impressed. You can be tenacious when you want to be. I'll call my brother tomorrow and get a list of the members. I'll also talk to Doobie. He knows everyone in town who owns a Mustang, club member or not."

"Thanks. You know, I feel like I could have stopped this somehow, but just didn't have the prescient knowledge. This is going to sound really weird, but I had a strange phone call, and then someone painted 187 on my door the day of the murders. I feel like those were warning signs, but I didn't know what to do with the information. And when I was at the Maltos house one time, I saw a snake."

Matt raised his eyebrows. "A what?"

Christian took a deep breath. What a relief it would be to tell someone everything about her, her secrets and superstitious leanings, her fears and developing talents. She had often wondered if she were to share herself completely, if the burden wouldn't be so great and in turn, she could be more effective.

"Okay, get comfortable," she instructed. With a hardy nod, Matt threw a couple of logs and a fire starter in the fireplace that was the centerpiece to his picture frame windows. She watched intently as he lit a match and threw it in. Then he pulled a sheepskin rug out of the hall closet and laid it next to the fire. "One more thing." He grinned and trotted off to the kitchen. A couple of minutes later, he walked out with two glasses of white wine.

As they settled onto the sheepskin, she smiled, "How'd you know I'm a Chardonnay girl?"

"I ask questions. Wine night out?" He looked so pleased with himself, that she had to laugh.

"Okay, I'm all ears." Matt said as he lay down on the sheepskin. Acting out of character, she scooted over and leaned against his hips, nestling against him.

"Here goes. I was bitten by a rattler as a toddler. I should have died. Everyone from the EMTs to the emergency room doc said so. But here I am and since then, whenever anyone else is going to die, I see a snake. It doesn't matter the time of year or where I am. I think the snake is Death in disguise. Like it's a vision telling me to watch out."

She could smell Matt's cologne and a slight wave of body odor, but not an unappealing one. She watched him intently. Did he think she was crazy?

"Extraordinary. I've heard of this stuff before. My grandmother down south, she's a bit of a voodoo queen. She says death visits her all the time, but only when she is calling on him. I'm not a complete believer, mind you. She's a batty old lady, but this stuff isn't new to me. Go on."

"I have this unsettling feeling when Death is around me. Like I know that he's... it's... whatever, around. He is like a shadow that I can't shake. I used to get really scared. Now I just get annoyed. I feel helpless, too, because I don't have the ability to stop the inevitable. When my husband died, I knew something was going to happen for weeks. Of course, I didn't know that Tony was going to be the victim, which was the worst part of all. I have such regrets."

Matt lifted his hand and stroked her cheek. "What could you have done? You can't lock someone in a room and hold them captive until the feeling passes."

"That's just it. We had no idea that Tony had a heart problem. He'd just had a physical only a few weeks before and supposedly he was in perfect health. I feel horrible about that. Now here's another case. I saw a snake at the Maltos home, *in late October!* So if there's anything I can do now to help Mr. Maltos, I'll do it. It's not a choice anymore."

He stroked her back and murmured, "You're a brave woman. You seem so troubled by all of this. You can't control the universe.

Bad things happen to good people. We don't know why and we are not responsible."

She nodded, feeling soothed by his calming words. "Please don't tell anyone what I've told you. Some people wouldn't believe me, or understand."

"Like who?"

"Like Daniel, for example. He's so black and white. He only sees the facts. I work with him, but sometimes I have to keep my mouth shut even when I need to share. It's not worth the effort of trying to convince him of my instincts."

"In my experience, detective work, police work, whatever you want to call it, is about eighty percent instincts. How do I know when to watch my back with a kid and when to relax? My experience and well-honed instincts. Kids don't come with signs on their backs that say, 'I'm dangerous, watch out.'"

Christian started to giggle and then suddenly collapsed into a fit of laughter. When she finally got her wits about her, she looked back at Matt, who wore a surprised look. "Sorry. I know that's not so hilarious. I just feel such a sense of relief."

"So why did you feel you could tell me? I mean, we really don't know each other that well."

Christian looked into his attentive eyes and replied, "I used my instincts?"

With that, Matt took his wine glass and then hers, setting them aside "Good girl. Now I'm going to use mine," he whispered as he pulled her into his arms.

♊

On Sunday morning, Christian got up early and decided to go for a run. Passionate flashbacks of her time with Matt were inescapable as she dressed and drank her coffee. Trying to read the front page of the Tri-City Herald was like trying to read a philosophy essay with a hangover. His voice, his touch and his smell invaded her thoughts.

Christian knew that the best bet for gathering her senses was a good workout. The weather was balmy and warm for December and Bear was thrilled to get out after the prior day's rainstorm. She drove to Columbia Point, a hip new development where a running and bike path wound alongside the river. Several high-end restaurants, hotels and a marina had sprung up in recent years, as well as expensive condominiums that offered stunning views of the Columbia. As she put a leash on Bear, she noticed a red car coming into the parking lot. The sun was bright and her vision was somewhat compromised, but the vehicle looked like a Mustang. As the car drew closer, she saw that it had tinted windows. The driver slowed as though to park and then hesitated and turned sharply back toward the parking lot exit. As the car pulled back onto the road, a Richland police car passed it and drove in.

Christian smiled as the cop approached. Randy Rusk hung his head out the window and said, "Hey good-looking, what's up?"

"We're just headed out for a run. How are you?" She smiled, pushing off the hood of her sweatshirt.

"I'm good. I hear that Jim Maltos won the jackpot. I'm sure that was your doing, too."

Christian put her finger to her lips. "Mum's the word. My brother reads the newspapers, after all."

Randy gave a sly wink. "Uh, huh. At least the poor guy stands a chance. I talked to Harry Frances at the crime lab. They confiscated a diary that belonged to Sue Maltos. Apparently she wrote something about her husband having an affair. Bad news for his defense. You probably want to let your brother know that before discovery, especially if Maltos isn't talking. Give him a head start, if you get my drift."

"Good idea. Randy, do you know if Donna Spencer is working day shift this week?" Donna was a jailer who was one of Randy's main squeezes.

"As a matter of fact, she is." He grinned and turned slightly red.

"I guess you two are still hanging out a bit." Though Randy was a well-known player in police circles, he often seemed to be embarrassed by his reputation.

He shrugged. "There's a lot of fish in the sea, baby. I can't just eat one variety."

Christian shook her head and returned his smile. "Whatever keeps you happy. Looks like Bear is about to take me for a ride here. I'd better go. See you around." Bear was pulling hard against the leash, but promptly relaxed as she turned away from Randy and began to jog.

As they passed Anthony's Restaurant, Christian pulled her cell phone from her pocket and dialed her brother's number. She got the answering message and quickly relayed the information that Randy had shared. Then she added, "I'm going over to the jail tomorrow to see Jim. I'll use my badge to get in. Call me tomorrow night and I'll let you know what I've found out."

Three hours later, Christian slipped into the back pew of The Desert Evangelist church for the eleven o'clock service. She was sure that this was the Maltos family's chosen service, based on an argument she'd once had with her parents about getting up in time for Sunday church services. The probation officer did her best to be invisible as she sat down next to an elderly couple. The service began with the youth band playing a peppy Christian rock tune. Halfway through the song, the bombastic minister appeared, wearing a navy blue serge suit and shiny black patent leather shoes. His thick hair was combed back pompadour style and his face looked ruddy from too much time spent in the outdoors. Christian knew he was an avid hunter and encouraged the young men of his flock to take up arms and learn to use them properly.

All of the boys in the C.E.L.L. youth groups had been encouraged to participate in Boys Scouts. According to information she'd gleaned from the church bulletin, the organization's firearms badge was the most coveted. C.E.L.L. was an acronym for *Christian Excellence in Leadership and Love.* The girls group had a different acronym, The GIGIs, which stood for *God Incarnated Girls Inspire.* The girls were encouraged to assist in the nursery, perform one-act plays where they danced and sang various Biblical stories and otherwise work in the kitchen in order that the men be fed. The deliberate separation of the sexes and the traditional roles expected therein bothered her. Though she didn't necessarily agree with many tenets of her own faith, in her observation, this church embodied conservative fundamentalist values far more effectively than the Catholics.

The music soon quieted and the minister recited a prayer. Then he began a lecture on the evils of modern media and the sinful opportunities available on HBO and the Internet. He thrust his arms about and turned various shades of red as he hollered that television and computers were the devil's playthings and that the youth in America were doomed for moral failure as a result.

Several murmurs of agreement could be heard in the audience as he went on to rant about other indiscretions of youth. He ended the sermon with a Biblical quotation: *Rejoice, O young man, in thy youth: and let thy heart cheer thee in the days of thy youth, and walk in the ways of thine heart, and in the sight of thine eyes: but know thou, that for all these things God will bring thee into judgment. Therefore remove sorrow from thy heart and put way evil from thy flesh: for childhood and youth are vanity.*

Suddenly an overweight teenage girl shot out of her seat. The parishioners grew restless as she moved to the front of the room while speaking rapidly in a gibberish that could only be identified as the odd phenomenon called speaking in tongues. Several men came forward and grabbed the girl's arms, holding her steady as her eyes rolled back and she started to jerk and roil as though having a convulsion. Her display prompted others to stand up as more high-pitched screeches and cries of an unintelligible manner filled the church. In moments, the room became an insane asylum.

As though to calm the storm, a young man stepped out from behind one of the fluttering curtains and held his hands up. Introduced as Jason, the minister left the stage, now a self-ordained sycophant, and allowed the newcomer to take over. The room became completely quiet as he softly began to speak in a language that sounded somewhat like French Creole. Christian watched, mesmerized, as the people left the front of the stage and slowly staggered back to their seats. For the next few minutes, Jason seemed to grow larger as he stood trembling as strange, melodic words poured from his mouth. His 'gift' in this group was the most powerful. The others 'speaking' were rudimentary and perhaps even feigned whereas this young man had a countenance of spiritual energy that inspired belief in even a skeptical, half-ass Catholic like Christian.

She watched as the congregation began to sway in time to the beat of Jason's words. He could have led an army over a cliff with the way the group held their breath on his every move and utterance. Despite the fear she was experiencing, Christian felt very strong and serene, unlike she had before in her life. Perhaps Maria's strange herbal concoction she'd taken to drinking was the sedative. Soon the older minister stepped back up to the podium and motioned for the elders to lead Jason out of the room to the 'recovery chamber'.

Breathing deeply, Christian remembered Maria's instructions. She closed her eyes and counted to ten. In the next instant, she saw a vision, as clear as an image from a television screen. A wall splattered with blood appeared in her mind's eye. Over the spray of blood, written in large blue letters was the phrase: 'The Gemini Girls shall die'.

CHAPTER 12

♊

Monday morning started off with a literal bang. A kid was being arrested as Christian drove up to the parking lot. He had arrived at detention to free his girlfriend and had unloaded a 9 MM magazine on the outer detention intake door. Fortunately he had used all of his ammunition by the time the police arrived whereby he was immediately taken into the cage for processing. Though Christian had arrived with plans to go immediately to the jail to visit with Jim, she had other impending duties to attend to. Three new kids had come in over the weekend and before she could go to the jail, she had to meet with them. Allison Maclair, a promiscuous thirteen-year-old, had been picked up while trying to sell herself on Lewis Street in Pasco. She was mentally ill, had three psychotropic prescriptions, which she refused to take, and generally used sex as a form of self-medication.

Then there was Willy Stedman. He was a black kid from West Richland who had a penchant for fire-starting. According to the probable cause statement that she'd found in her office mailbox, he'd burned down part of a playground over the weekend. Lastly, there was Jonathan Cap, a squirrely sex offender who was caught with his younger cousin, a victim from a recent molestation with whom he had a no-contact order. Christian poured a second cup of coffee, downed a couple of vitamins and got to work.

By eleven, she was finally on her way to the county jail. Fortunately or otherwise, she had an incarcerated client, Steve Banks, who was sitting out a probation violation for thirty days. He had continued to use meth despite her attempts to get him into treatment. She'd finally given up after he was found with his newborn infant sitting in a car while lighting up a meth pipe. His child had been removed from his care; the baby's mother long gone for darker worlds. Another child in the foster system was disheartening to Christian, as much as she knew the baby would be better off than with either of her parents. On the pretense of visiting Steve, she would also have the chance to meet with Jim Maltos. Her brother had encouraged her with a list of questions, but she had plenty of her own to ask.

Daniel sauntered in just as she was about to leave. "Good morning, partner. Where are you going so soon?" he asked as he dropped a pile of files on his desk.

"More like, where have you been?" She reached in to get her coat from the small closet they shared.

"I was at the Richland Focus meeting. Then I saw a few kids at the high school and met with Cassidy Smith at Richland P.D. She's working on the Maltos case. I guess they've interviewed quite a few people and someone in their neighborhood said they saw a red Mustang leaving the cul de sac around two-thirty that day."

Christian shivered as a voice in her head replied, '*same one you saw yesterday.*' "I saw a red Mustang yesterday, when I was down at Columbia Point. I swear the car was about to approach me when Rusk turned up. It was pure coincidence, but probably a blessing.

Matt has a contact in the Mustang club. He's going to get me a list of everyone who owns one around here."

Daniel raised his eyebrows. "Are you seeing him?"

Christian blushed and looked down. "Is that your business?"

Daniel's voice turned brusque. "Apparently not, *partner.*"

Christian glanced back up and gave a small smile, a sort of half apology.

"Look, I just don't want to become part of the gossip mill around here, so please keep it quiet. Yes, we're seeing each other."

His face became stony. "Well, good for you. You finding yourself a little rusty after, what's it been, nearly four years out of the sack?"

Christian felt her heart shrink. "Why would you say such a mean thing?"

"I don't know, just being truthful. Or maybe you haven't been so pure and like this time, you just haven't mentioned it."

Yanking on her coat, she grabbed her files. "See you later, or not!" she fumed and stomped out of the room. Why was Daniel acting like such an ass?

By the time she arrived at the jail a few minutes later, she was feeling somewhat calmer. Christian had never seen him act like that and it was a part of his personality that she wished she hadn't experienced. Jealous men were an irritation at best. In her college days, she'd dated a jealous guy and once she'd figured it out, she'd ended their relationship quickly and without a second thought.

She stopped inside the jail door, showed her badge and placed her purse and files on the security conveyor belt. Passing through the metal detector, she gazed around the lobby. She felt an immediate shift in the energy - the energy of desperation, poverty and greed. Screaming babies, tattooed women with haggard faces, shifty gangsters and poor-looking elderly people milled around the oblong room, waiting for their turn on the video monitors. All of them had someone inside that they loved or otherwise had reason to talk to. Gangsters were notorious for talking to their friends on the inside, but generally used a coded ghetto talk that even the jailers didn't understand. Deals were made, retaliation murders were planned and drugs were delivered through various channels. Plenty of jailers could be persuaded to deliver heroin for a few bucks. Though the only folks who were allowed into the jail itself were legal professionals, nurses and chaplains, there was still an abundance of contraband that found its way into the inmate's pockets.

Christian went the window and gave them her I.D. The woman at the counter gave her an entry badge and she walked through a locked door to a set of elevators that led her to the male living pods.

From her brother, she knew that Jim was in Pod B. Fortunately so was Steve.

Randy's girlfriend was working. Through the window, she could see her and pointed to the door. The sucking sound of air could be heard as the heavy metal door opened to the Pod. The room was as large as a basketball court. The upper perimeter was banked with bunk beds. A metal railing offered the only privacy. On the bottom floor, the room had numerous tables and chairs, all which were bolted to the floor. The entire place was color-less except for the orange jumpsuits worn by the inmates. A half a dozen showers lined one wall and several men were shower-ing as she entered. Cat calls and whistles filled the space as she walked over to Donna and asked to see Steve. He came down the stairs, his face puffy from sleep, and gave her a dark-toothed grimace. Despite his young age, he'd already lost several teeth from his meth use. While she talked to him at one of the tables, she could feel eyes on her, especially from the showers. She was certain that the men were pleasuring themselves behind the curtains. She could hear a number of them grunting as they stared in her direction. Any sight of a woman would give them reason to get excited. Christian never offered eye contact to anyone in the pods, and intuitively hardened herself with a sort of psychic armor while she was visiting at the jail. Nevertheless, she always felt dirty when she left and often went home at lunchtime to take her own shower as a result.

After she'd spent a few minutes talking to Steve, who was so blown out on meth that he was only able to utter gibberish, she asked to see Jim. Donna was more than helpful, allowing her to take Jim into a secured room away from the view of other inmates and staff.

Jim was brought in immediately. His expression was vigilant and marked by despair, but when he saw Christian, he offered a smile that reminded her of the happy guy who had a deep love for Jesus and his family.

"Hi, Christian," he greeted her softly as he sat down. "Thank you so much for calling your brother for me. You don't know how much that means." Tears gathered in his eyes as he began to sob silently. His broad shoulders heaved as she reached over to touch his arm.

"Jim, I believe in you. I know you didn't do this and I think my brother can prove your innocence, but you have to help us. I know you didn't talk to Scott about where you were that afternoon, but everyone is speculating, and it only makes you look guilty. Please, if you can, tell me what you were doing and who you were with. We can't make a good case without knowing."

The prisoner's breathing slowed and he lifted his head, wiping his face on his sleeve as he did so. "Okay, but I don't think it will help you. Probably, if anything, it will only make things worse."

Christian gazed into his eyes. "Go on."

"Sue and me, we were having problems. You might have picked up on that. Part of the issue was the way she was with our daughter. She was so wishy-washy, and always kept things from me. Tommy used to come over to the house all the time after school. Sue would leave the house so the kids could have time to themselves. Then I'd find out somehow and we'd get into a terrible argument. And she was also pressuring me to get a better job. Then I ran into Cindy Wright and things went from bad to worse."

"Who's Cindy Wright?" Christian pulled out a steno pad and began to take notes.

"She's a gal who I went to high school with. We had our thirtieth class reunion in August. Cindy and I used to date back in school. It was so great to see her again after such a long time. She had been living in Washington D.C. with her husband of twenty-five years. Then they got transferred back here. Anyway, long story short, we became friends again. *Friends*, mind you. Nothing else. I kind of leaned on her with the stuff that was going on with Cassie. She has two girls of her own, both grown now. I thought she was pretty good with advice. Of course, any time I would repeat what Cindy told me to my wife, Sue would come unglued. After a while, she was certain that Cindy and I were having an affair. I promised her I would cut off our friendship, but I was going to do it in person. Furthermore, Cindy is an important person in town. She's the president of Compliance Northwest. I don't want her reputation put at risk."

"So you were seeing Cindy that day, to say goodbye."

Jim nodded. "It was no big deal. But I know that Sue's diary was confiscated after the murders. She once told me that she wrote about Cindy and me in there, that if I ever left her, she would show it to Cindy's husband. After all the lives that have been ruined, I'm not going to ruin another one."

Christian reached out and patted his hand. "What an honorable man you are. But if the detectives already know about your relationship with Cindy, there's no reason to worry about keeping this part a secret."

"Yes, but if Cindy's last name wasn't logged in the diary, I'm guessing that Sue wasn't even sure what her last name is, won't she just be some woman they can't identify?"

"No, Jim. Ever heard of testifying under oath? You will be required to tell the court her name either way. If you come forward now, openly and honestly, it looks better all around. If she will testify to your whereabouts, you have an alibi. You need to call her. Here, use my cell."

She held her breath, waiting for his refusal. Instead, he slowly took the phone and began to dial. As soon as he said hello, he began to sob again. Christian stood and turned her back to him, watching the pod in action instead of invading his privacy.

The space outside the double-paned windows was greased with despair and bad deeds. She considered how so many innocent people could end up in a place like this, people like Jim Maltos, and eventually, when they were finally able to leave, they would be forever changed inside. An invisible plague of remorseless revenge, lascivious desire and incorrigible greed created these monsters who lived for the next crime, many of them using the penal system as a way to gain prestige in their otherwise pathetic existence. Christian watched with feigned nonchalance as a motley crew of convicts paraded past the window, staring hungrily at her. One particularly ugly guy, with dark circles under his eyes and a mop of filthy, shoulder-length gray hair, played with himself as he walked by. She shuddered to see the look of pure sexual evil that permeated his gaze. Jim was surrounded by rapists and murderers.

"Cind, it's me. Yeah, it's pretty bad in here. Hey listen, I'm going to have to tell them I was with you that day. I don't…you will? Are you sure you want to be associated with…ah, Cindy, thanks so much, thanks so much."

When the phone clicked closed, she turned. "It sounds like you have a true friend there."

Jim shook his head and sat up a little straighter, as though trying to recover some of his dignity. "You know, I'm having a hard time trusting right now. This is such a mess."

She sat back down. "Jim, my brother and I are going to get you off. I have a few leads, but I need you to think for me. I got a hold of Cassie's diary. It's a long story. Just let me say that there are references in there about another guy she was dating, someone who drove a red Mustang on occasion. He's an older kid, probably in college. I think Tabby Smithson knows who he is, but she's not talking yet. In fact, she's not cooperating at all. I'm sure the detectives will get to her sooner or later, but I'd like the information first. Who called Cassie? Who did she talk about?"

Jim stalled, as though trying to recollect a lost history. "She seemed to be fixated on someone. Of course at first we thought it was Tommy, but she seemed nonchalant whenever he called, especially toward the end there, but if she got a call from a cell number that was labeled 'out of the area', she got all excited. What college do you think this kid attends?"

"I have no idea, but her diary talks about an older boy, someone who she spent a lot of time, especially during the times that Tommy was incarcerated, which was quite a lot in the past six months. She looked up to this kid, like he's someone really special. I'm doing some investigating as to who owns Mustangs in town, but if you can think about anyone."

They'd been talking long enough. As she did, Jim snapped his fingers. "There was a guy she called J.J. She was very secretive about him. I overheard her talking about him once to a friend, though she didn't know that I was listening. They were making a film of some kind. She was upset, though, when she was talking about it."

"When was this?"

"About a month ago. I'd come home from work early, with a headache. I was in the kitchen when she came upstairs. She didn't see me and went into the living room. She didn't know I was right next door. Cassie was crying and kept saying, 'how could he do that to me?' Something about the film was only supposed to be for her, or she was the only one who was supposed to be the star and now he was using all the Gemini Girls. A few minutes later I heard something that nearly made me lose my lunch. She screamed, 'Who else is he screwing besides me?' She hung up then and I could hear her sobbing. I wanted to go to her, but I was so shook up at what I heard, I didn't want her to know…dear God, I should have asked her about it. Maybe I could have stopped… maybe it was that kid, the one she was having sex with, maybe he came after her and Sue got in the way." Jim began shaking, his face turning white. He gasped for air and gripped the table. Christian became concerned and opened the door to call for help.

Donna immediately led Jim out of the room toward the nurse's station. She motioned for Christian to leave through the set of opening doors and began to speak into a walkie-talkie. She thought to wait and then decided that she'd better get going. He was probably having an anxiety attack. She shouted goodbye and grabbed her notebook. She had some work to do.

♊

Despite the craziness of her day, Christian left work in a festive mood. Though her real desire was to dive into the investigation, she was on hold while waiting for a call back from Scott and Matt's list of Mustang owners. She sensed that Tabby Smithson was the link to much of the mystery, but she didn't feel ready to approach her yet. Once she learned of the Mustang owner's identity, her plan was to pay Tabby another visit. That girl knew more than she was willing to say, but Christian realized without something solid, she wasn't going to get the girl to talk.

Christmas was less than two weeks away and she'd already planned to do all of her shopping at one of her best friend's local stores. Rosalie Lahear owned a quirky little shop in downtown Kennewick called *The Party Girl*. Flush with party supplies, books, a smattering of antiques, wine and Rosalie's unique and personalized masks, the place was lushly decadent in a fairyland sort of way.

Her gift list was fairly short. She still sent a basket of goodies from the Harry and David catalog to both her Aunt and Uncle and Tony's parents. The siblings in her family normally picked names and this year, she'd fortunately drawn Scott and his clan. The little girls would be easy to buy for. Rosalie had a section in her store for children's games and books. Her sister-in-law was a jewelry nut and several local artisans displayed their wares at *The Party Girl.* Finally Scott, an obsessive oenophile, would appreciate one of the famous Columbia Valley wines that Rosalie stored in high wine racks that lined the walls of the store. Those folks and a few girlfriends completed her Christmas obligations.

Strolling into the store, Christian immediately found Rosalie and gave her a hug, but there were plenty of customers milling about, so she left her friend to cope and began wandering around, looking for gifts. On a table in the back of the store, there was a pile of inspirational books. The title of one read, <u>Miracles, Saints and Satan.</u> She flipped over the book to read the back. The first paragraph talked about the quest for sainthood. She hadn't realized that in order for a person to be canonized a saint, they had to perform one miracle before death (made sense) and then two miracles after death. (weird...how to attribute thereafter?). Then the book's description posed the question: if someone can inspire us to believe in God, can another be responsible for one's loss of faith in God?

Lost in thought, Christian stared at the book. Her faith had been challenged by events, not people. And death had only seemed to strengthen her belief in someone or something greater than herself and mere humanity. Death's presence in her life was not Satan, though some might argue that. Her sense of his presence was now in the process of transformation. Once she had viewed death as an evil apparition, but her views had changed. Her meeting with Maria was the catalyst. Reflecting back on a Jungian psychology class, she recalled that according to Carl Jung, all humans had aspects of themselves, which were represented by archetypes.

These 'parts' appeared symbolically as king and queen energies or magician, warrior and lover energies. It was Jung's position that these energies functioned within one's personality in both positive and negative ways. When the shadow warrior was in charge of the personality, assaulting and destructive behavioral patterns resulted. On the other hand, when the warrior of light took action, a person was in a position to fight for others' rights. A diplomat working to reach a ceasefire was the warrior of light. The mercenary hired to kill was the shadow.

Christian began to realize that the inexplicable relationship that she had with Death was a powerful tool. If she was receptive and allowed her intuition to work, she could use her strange friend to solve problems. Her mind began to race then, as though the mere thought of trusting his power was enough. She closed her eyes as a movie began to play in the back of her mind. Flashing images of Cassie, Sue and Jim appeared. Then she saw Tabby and their encounter at the Maltos home and then again at the gas station. She slowed her breath, the sounds of the store fading away as another face appeared, one that soon left her trembling and confused. Jason, the youth pastor, with his arms raised to the heavens, was the final image.

"Christian, are you alright?" As she opened her eyes, Rosalie was standing before her, her face a mask of fear. "What's wrong? I've been calling you for the last few minutes. Sit down."

Rosalie guided her friend to a nearby chair. The store had emptied of other customers and the only sound was Enya's floating voice coming from the background music system.

"Dear, you look like you've seen a ghost. Are you feeling alright?" Rosalie was a motherly person by nature and Christian would not get out of the store without an explanation.

"I'm not sure what just happened, but I think I know who killed Sue and Cassie Maltos."

Rosalie sat down hard on the chair next to hers, a look of dark disbelief crossing her normally sunny features. "What in God's name are you talking about?"

♊

The church appeared empty when she drove up. The parking lot was void of cars, but there was a smaller one behind the church where employees parked. Christian walked up to the double glass doors and found them unlocked. Stepping in, she called out, "Hello, is there anyone here?"

There was no answer, but the building was vast and the offices appeared to be down a long hall to the right. She followed the hallway around a corner and came to a large office marked with the pastor's name. She knocked and heard someone reply, "Come on in."

Opening the door, there was a young woman sitting at a desk. She guessed it was the receptionist who'd answered the phone when she'd called about Tabby's phone number.

"Hi." She offered her best smile. "I'm an investigator for Scott Halverson, Jim Maltos's defense attorney. I was wondering if I could ask you a few questions."

The young woman stood up. She was dressed in a plain blue shift and wore her hair in a severe bun at the back of her neck. Her conservative dress made her look older than her twenty-something years.

"I've already talked to the police. I don't know what else you need to know." The girl's tone was curt, but as she looked more closely at the girl, it became apparent that her demeanor was a defense mechanism. Unfortunately, the receptionist was an over-weight plain-Jane type with enormous breasts and the chin of a turtle.

"I'm so sorry to bother you. It's just that they don't always share information with the defense and poor Mr. Maltos! He told me you were the one who I should talk to, but never mind. I can see you're busy."

Christian turned as if to go and as she did, the girl countered, "Wait. I can spare a few minutes for Mr. Maltos. He's such a wonderful person. I can't stand to see him locked up."

Relief flooded her body. "You're so right. It's horrible what has happened to him. I hope we can help him."

Pulling a chair closer to the receptionist's desk, she sat down. "This will only take a few minutes. I know that Cassie had a lot of friends here at the church and was involved in the choir."

"Yes, the Gi Gis. That was their secret name. I only know that because Jason told me in confidence. He wanted me to join, but I don't really sing and those girls...well, they're all the beautiful type."

"You're being modest. I bet he thought you would have fit right in." Christian watched as the girl turned a bright crimson. She probably could look okay, if she'd try to look like a young woman instead of an old lady, she thought. A little make-up, some foiling on her hair would help.

The girl piped up with a Biblical quote about chastity and then frowned. "You know, I don't really like those girls. If you want my opinion, and I'm trying not to judge them, of course, but they act rather, umm, indiscreet. Especially with Jason. Shelly and Tabby, actually all of them have a huge crush on him and when they get around him, they act ridiculous. Except Cassie. Jason really likes, I'm mean liked her because even though she was a lot younger than him, she acted plenty mature." *Really?* Christian thought. *You should have seen her with her parents and Tommy Calander.*

The girl smoothed back her hair and continued with a wistful and yet sad look on her chubby face. "Cassie was always so nice to me. I think the other girls thought they were better than her, too."

"Why better?"

The girl's eyes became slits.

"Cuz Cassie didn't interpret for Jason. You see, in the Bible, speaking in tongues is a gift and so is the interpretation for the speaker. All the other girls have claimed to have that gift. Pastor thought it was amazing, but Cassie, she didn't pretend to be able to do it. I think the others did. All except Jill. She had the gift, but she's dead now."

"Dead?"

"Yeah." Just then the phone rang and the receptionist briskly answered it. She chatted amiably to the caller, discussing particulars on the next church potluck. Christian did her best not to pace, but her anxiety had risen into her throat. Another dead girl?

Finally the young woman hung up. Christian offered a neutral smile. "Do you mind me asking how Jill died?"

The homely girl shrugged. "Killed herself. I think she was…" she put her finger to her head and twirled it. "…crazy. Anyway, Cassie was real and talented, too. She used to make really pretty hemp bracelets. See, I have one on." The girl thrust a thick wrist in Christian's direction. On her wrist was beaded bracelet that read, 'I luv JC'.

"That's beautiful. It sounds to me like you and Cassie were pretty good friends. Anything else I might want to know about her friends?" She pressed on.

The receptionist lowered her voice conspiratorially. "I think Tabby Smithson had it for Cassie." She made a face as though sucking on lemons.

"I'm sorry. I don't know what you mean." Christian had an inkling, but she wanted the words to come out of the girl's mouth.

"I think Tabby is a homosexual, you know. A lesbo. I haven't told anyone this, but one time, after choir practice, I heard Tabby and Cassie fighting in the choir room. I went in to see if I could help and watched as Tabby grabbed Cassie and tried to kiss her. Cassie was grossed out and I about fainted. It was disgusting."

"What happened next?"

"Cassie was really angry. She pushed Tabby away and ran out the back door. I was afraid that weirdo would come after me next, so I ran back to my office and locked the door. It was horrible. I felt so sorry for Cassie. She and Tabby had been friends for a long time. Just think, all the times they spent the night together, even changed clothes in the same room and the whole time, Tabby was looking at her like *that*."

"Miss......"

"Snodgrass. Kelly Snodgrass." The girl's name nearly made Christian laugh aloud.

"Kelly, you've been awesome. No wonder Jim suggested that I talk to you. Thanks so much for your time." Christian hesitated for a moment after she shook the girl's hand. "One last thing. Did you tell the detectives about Tabby and Cassie?"

Kelly shook her head emphatically. They only asked me about Mrs. Maltos. They didn't ask much about Cassie, so I didn't think to tell them about it."

"You know, I didn't even ask about Mrs. Maltos. Do you think that she was the original target for the murders?"

"The police said she had a business at home. They said it might have been a robbery, but I don't know anyone that would want to hurt Mrs. Maltos. I think she was one of the nicest ladies, really. She was always helping out at the church. But there was one time that she and Mr. Maltos almost left us. It was a weird thing. Sue, I mean Mrs. Maltos, didn't like Jason Roads, our youth director. One time I read a letter from her to our Pastor. I saw it on his desk. It was a complaint letter about Jason. Mrs. Maltos wrote that she thought that Jason was not genuine-his speaking in tongues. She said that she'd grown up in Louisiana and that Jason was just talking some language from down there. She said he was saying nasty things about girls, but nobody else in the church knew what he was saying except her. I don't know what ever happened after that. It was a long time ago, last year sometime. After that, I'm pretty sure that Jason and Cassie started seeing each other, but I don't think Mrs. Maltos knew about that. If she did, I don't think she would have approved."

Christian took the opportunity at hand. "You know, Kelly, we wouldn't want anyone else to know you read that letter. I'm sure you didn't mean to, but I'd hate to have you lose your job. You might want to keep that to yourself and maybe, with regards to Tabby and Cassie. We wouldn't want people to think bad things about Cassie."

At the mention of Kelly reading her boss's correspondence, the girl turned pale, her deep-set eyes growing large in her wide face.

"I agree. I won't tell another soul," the girl replied, biting her lower lip. "I won't tell if you won't."

As she left the office and walked down the long hall, there was a set of stairs and a sign that read: Youth Pastor's office and choir rooms upstairs. She glanced back to see if anyone was around. Kelly was behind the closed door and the rest of the church was dead quiet. She tiptoed up the stairs and headed down the hall. The second door had a sign with Jason Roads's name on the door. She knocked softly. There was no answer, so she slowly opened the door. The office was very dark with a number of football trophies and framed awards on the wall: **Best Christian leader, 1998. Camp Cross International Delegate 1999, Young Christian Counselor of the Year 2001**. The youth director had plenty of credentials as well as a diploma from a Christian College in Louisiana. Christian was convinced that she'd heard a French Cajun dialect during the church service now.

Draped over a chair was a blue sweater. On a hunch, Christian went over to it and examined the garment. Checking the desk, she found a pair of scissors and carefully cut a piece of the sweater pocket lining.

She was about to look in the other desk drawers when she got a bad feeling. Quickly she moved away from the desk and got out of the office. She had only gone a couple of steps when she heard someone bounding up the stairs. She tried to act lost, looking at the doors across the hall. She glanced up to see Jason Roads coming toward her.

"Hi there! Can I help you?" he called out in a friendly voice.

"Oh, yes, thank you. I was just looking for the Ladies Room. I thought it might be up here."

As the man came closer, she could smell his aftershave. She recognized the male's version of Jean Gaultier, a rather expensive brand for a youth pastor. He was smartly dressed and moved with confidence. With casual aplomb, he took her elbow and gently moved her in the other direction. His voice was velvet as he said, "Down this way, lovely lady. Have I seen you at our church before?"

Christian could feel his magnetism on her arm like a soft electrical pulse. "Actually last week was my first time. I enjoyed the sermon and I believe you were one of the 'speakers'."

Jason released a husky laugh. "A speaking in tongues speaker, yes. It is an amazing gift, don't you think?"

"Yes, absolutely." Christian looked directly in his eyes as they paused in front of a closed door that had a shape of a woman painted on it.

"My name is Jason. I hope to see you next Sunday. Please, don't hesitate to find me after the service. I'd love to show you around." He slipped her a boyish grin.

Christian thanked him and walked into the restroom. After the door shut, she waited, wondering if he was still outside. She pretended to use the toilet and washed her hands. When she walked out, he was gone and as she passed his office, she noticed the door was closed. A faint sound of music could be heard. He was talking on the phone to someone. She pressed her ear to the door to hear his words. Her knees became jelly as she heard him say, "You're my new babe. I'll pick you up tonight. Yes, I have condoms. I'm hard just thinking about you."

That was all that she needed to hear. Afraid he'd come out, she hurried down the stairs and out the door. As she drove away, she circled the church into the back parking lot, wondering if she'd see a red Mustang there. There was only a white Chevy van, a blue Honda Civic and a bicycle chained to a rack.

♊

"Matt, hi, it's Christian."

"Hey, how's it going?" Matt's voice warmed her all over.

"I'm good. How about you?"

"Good, too. I passed the math test, thanks to you. Am I bragging when I say I got an A?"

"Of course not! See, I knew you could do it. Math is just one of those languages we forget if we don't use it." She could almost hear his smile over the phone.

"So I wondered if you have time for dinner tonight. I've got a surprise for you, but only if you're also free on Saturday."

"Yes to both, but only if this is the real thing."

"You mean, a real date?"

"Are we there yet?"

"Yes, definitely. After all, I'm getting A's out of the deal." He chuckled good-naturedly. I'm getting a lot more than that, she thought as he continued, "So how about Anthony's at six? Their oyster plate is fabulous, but we've got to get there early."

"Sounds good!" As Christian hung up, she wondered what he was up to. The one thing that whetted her romantic appetite was surprises. This was more than a good start.

She filled her afternoon with paperwork, got hung up in the courtroom on a couple of probation violation cases and didn't get out of the office until nearly five-thirty. She hardly had time to walk Bear around the block before her dinner date. Quickly she brushed her teeth, changed into a silk blouse and added a pair of diamond drop earrings that Tony had given her as an engagement present. They were expensive and she rarely wore them, but Matt was worth it.

Anthony's Restaurant was only minutes away from her home, but it was dark by the time she headed out to dinner. As she left the driveway, she noticed an unfamiliar car parked down the street. It's probably an unmarked cop car, she decided as she continued on her way.

The dinner date was beyond Christian's expectations. Though he was working the night shift and had to leave by nine to get to work, Matt was in unusually high spirits. He attributed it to her company. By the end of the evening, she realized that her sense of an unique synergy between them was mutual.

As they were walking back out to their cars, Christian said, "Thanks so much. I'll see you soon, I hope." She wondered if Saturday night was no longer in his plans.

"Geez, I almost forgot!" Matt paused. With an act of flourish, he added. "And now, the surprise you've been waiting for. Since I never would have passed my stats class without your help and I mean that so…" His dark eyes twinkled in the ambient light as he swept an envelope from his coat pocket like he was doing a magic trick. "For you, oh very smart friend of mine, I have tickets to the Chris Bodie concert on Saturday night. Interested?"

"Are you kidding me? I'd love to go!" Christian reflected on their animated conversation a few weeks before when she'd stopped to see him in detention. Out of the blue, they had found themselves on the subject of music history, particularly New Orleans-styled jazz. He'd obviously remembered that she'd said she loved Bodie and knew he was coming to town soon.

"Awesome. He's playing at Timber's Jazz club. I have a front row table."

"How about if I make dinner at my house first?"

"Sounds good. What can I bring?"

"Just your yummy self. Oh and Matt, I need you to do me a big favor. Will you come to church with me on Sunday?"

"Yeah, but I'm not much for the whole Catholic kneeling thing."

Christian laughed. "No kneeling at this church. This one is a speaking-in-tongues kind of place."

"Oh, whoa. I don't know about that. I grew up around that as a kid, down south. I'm not fond of all that screaming and seizing up." His face had the look of a scared kid.

Christian laughed again. "This isn't my church, Matt. I'm doing some investigating for the Maltos case. I remember you told me you knew a little Cajun and there's a guy at this church. I want you to check him out for me."

Matt put on a thick French accent. "Of course, Mademoiselle. I would be happy to be your interpreter. It makes me so happy to help you in your time of need. However, if you decide to sway that way, I won't be dancing your step."

"You do that well. So, what time on Saturday?"

"The concert's at eight, so how about six?" Christian paused for a moment. She knew that the minute he walked into her house, she'd want to lead him to the bedroom. Would that evening constitute their third date? After all, she wanted to keep to some set of rules.

"How about five-thirty…just in case we run late?"

Matt gave a husky chuckle. "I can't imagine how that might happen," he replied as though reading her mind.

This time it was her turn. She reached up and put her arms around his neck. In the sexiest voice that she could muster, she said, "Now, kiss your date goodbye." The kiss was long and sweet. As they pulled apart, she whispered huskily,

"Good-bye, Matt."

"Bye, honey."

Christian was in a butterflies-in-the-tummy daze by the time she got home. She walked into the house and went straight into the bedroom, falling back on the bed with a happy sigh. Matt was simply wonderful. How had he remembered that she loved Chris Bodie's music? Her fear-of-failure radar was still up and running, ready for the vaguest hint of a let-down, but so far, so good. She hummed to herself as she pulled off her slacks and blouse and went into the master bathroom to run a bath. A sea salt bath sounded like a great way to end her day. She waltzed around the bathroom, still walking on air from her evening with Matt. Suddenly she froze. Contessa was sitting on the edge of the bathtub as though waiting for a night of girly conversation. Christian shook her head, trying to figure out how the death doll had made her way into the bathroom. If Christian's memory served, the figurine had been on the mantel before she'd left that morning for work. A cold chill of premonition passed through her as Bear traipsed in, growling low in his throat.

"What is it, boy?" The dog had her corduroy slacks in his mouth. She bent down and pried them loose. 'What are you doing with my pants, you silly dog?" She put them up on the bathroom counter, but before she'd turned around, the dog had pulled them down again. As she watched in curiosity, Bear began to paw at the left pocket.

She reached down and slipped her hand in there. Perhaps she'd left a piece of candy or a mint? Instead she pulled out the envelope with the fabric piece. She mentally chided herself for forgetting to drop it at the Kennewick Police Station. Quickly, she picked up her cell phone.

"Randy. It's Christian. I found something that I think you might be interested in."

The cop's voice sounded tired. "Please tell me it's a break in the damn Maltos case. Otherwise, that father is in trouble."

"Actually, I am hoping so. Stop by on your way home tonight and I show you my new treasure."

Flipping the phone closed, she patted Bear on the head. "You're so smart, big boy. I might have forgotten that if you hadn't reminded me." Then she poured some salts in the tub and climbed in. Norah Jones was playing on the stereo. As she closed her eyes to relax, her phone rang. Climbing out to grab it off the counter, she quickly returned to her soak.

"Hello?"

"It's Scott. I have some good news. My source in the prosecutor's office is looking at some felons who were picked up over the weekend as possible suspects. They were found with some stolen property and a 9 MM. The same type used in the Maltos murders. They are checking the casings as we speak. As you know, Mrs. Maltos had quite a lot of money stashed in the house from a home business. The guys that they arrested had over three hundred dollars in cash and some stolen property. The property came from a house in Richland. Apparently the owners were not home, but when they talked to the police, they told them that they didn't have cash in the house."

"Thank God, they weren't home or maybe we'd have more dead people. It doesn't sound right. Remember, the intruder was not really an intruder. Their house wasn't broken into."

"Unless they didn't lock their doors."

"But it wasn't like that. Not according to the 911 call. I really believe that whoever killed those women knew those women."

"What did you do with that evidence you collected from the house?"

"I still have it and I've collected a very interesting piece of evidence as well. When you said investigator, I took it to heart. I was at the church today and snuck into the youth pastor's office. There was a blue Abercrombie sweater in there. I cut out a piece of it to see if it matches the fabric I found in the closet door. It seems to match the stuff from the crime scene perfectly."

"Take it to the crime lab rather than the police department. I've made a couple of contacts over there, a guy named Pete and younger kid, Harry. Pete is very knowledge and very keen to help us. He needs to take prints off her diary and the letter you found as well. Did you get anything else?"

"Yeah, the pink sweater, remember?"

"Take in a.s.a.p. If there's semen on it, we can get a subpoena for some semen donors as soon as we make a concise list, if you get my drift. Every person who has ever entered that house can be subpoenaed if necessary. The door in the Maltos bedroom closet, did it look broken or smashed at all, like there had been a struggle?"

"I'm not sure. I can go back and look, though, if you want. I'll take a camera this time."

"Do it. If that fabric piece can't be matched to any clothing in the Maltos home, and there's evidence of a struggle, then whoever owns that blue sweater is definitely a suspect."

"I already believe he is." Christian replied. "I know you know I'm a little crazy, but this whole thing is coming at me like a chapter book. I see it now, Scott. It's a very blurry picture, but I see it. I think the youth pastor is our man. He was the one who was the secret lover, I'm almost certain. And judging by Sue Maltos's dislike of the guy, he might have gone in to 'handle her' and Cassie was just in the way. Either that, or he wanted them both dead."

"But you said Mrs. Maltos seemed happy about the call. Why would she react that way if she disliked the caller? And if he thought that Cassie was pregnant, maybe his little Jesus trip was going to come to an abrupt end. I can see a motive at the end of the tunnel. Anyway, it's time for me to do bedtime. The kids send their aunty big hugs and kisses. Call me after you've met with Harry from the lab. He promised he'd put a rush on things, but we still only have a few more weeks before we're back in court. Oh, one more thing. What's that youth pastor's last name?"

"Roads. He graduated from the Gallant Soldiers Christian Junior College just outside of New Orleans in 2000."

"I need you to run a check on his name. From what you told me about the weapon junkies at that church, we'll see if he has a registered gun or maybe a handgun license."

$$\text{II}$$

"So what's up with you?" Christian asked after they'd sat in the office together for more than an hour without a word between them.

"Probably my cholesterol. Definitely not my friendship meter." Daniel's voice was flat, but Christian heard a subtle scorn between his lines.

"Why are you acting this way? I have every right to date. As a friend, you should be happy for me."

"Whatever you say," he said sharply. "I guess I have a different concept of partner than you do. I wanted to help you with the Maltos case and suddenly Matt's become your number one guy. I'm sure he knows a lot more about what's going on at this point than I do. Not to mention that I've been trying to help in every way and haven't heard one word of thanks out of you."

"Is that's what's really bugging you?" Christian still felt it went deeper than that. According to her therapist's secretary, Sophia and Daniel were not seeing one another.

"Hey look, I'm sorry things didn't work out for you and Sophia."

"*Great!* You know about that, too. I must be the last on everyone's list this week," he snarled. She wanted to soothe him, but at this point, she knew that it was no use.

Instead she suggested, "I really do need your help on something, if you don't mind me asking." She waited for him to take the bait. There was a long pause, but she knew that he would respond. If there was a job for him to do, he wouldn't be able to tolerate himself if he didn't step up to the plate.

After a heavy sigh, he replied, "Okay, what is it? And what are the paybacks?"

Christian tried not to grin. "Three dozen homemade chocolate chip cookies and part of my cut from Scott. I need you to check on some gun license stuff. For a Jason Robert Roads. I found him in I-Leads. His birth date is 2/2/1980."

"Anything else?"

"This is a bit harder. This guy's the youth pastor from the Desert Evangelist Church. He went to college down south near New Orleans. I wrote down the name and the year that he graduated." She handed him a piece of paper. "I'm curious to know if he has any priors down there. He only has a couple of traffic infractions up here, but you never know. College is a wonderful time to get into trouble. Especially for kids who've grown up in over-protective religious backgrounds. I figure with all of your contacts, you can find out for us."

"So are you going to fill me in? I know you've been sneaking around." Daniel turned to face her directly. "And sorry I was an ass. I just can't see you dating…"

"What?" Christian coaxed.

"If you want to know the truth, a detention officer. It just doesn't seem right somehow. And he's Black and from the south. In other words, a completely different culture."

Christian felt hot with anger. "Hey, I married a Hispanic and you didn't think that was wrong, did you?"

He shook his head. "No, of course not! I'm Hispanic. It's just that, I don't know, he's probably got a bunch of illegitimate kids off somewhere that you don't even know about."

"I can't believe I'm hearing this. You hate it when people stereotype Hispanic people, but you're doing the same thing. Please, think about what you're saying for a minute." Christian was fuming.

Her friend hung his head sheepishly, knowing that he had disappointed her. He retorted with humor, as always, "Well, at least if you have babies with him, their skin will be my peeps' color." He stroked his own cheek and gave a comical smile.

Christian shook her head. "Whatever. Okay, so listen up and I'll let you know what I've been doing so far." Her partner was all ears as she began to recount her escapades over the past week. She left out any mention of Matt, however.

CHAPTER 13

December 16, 2005

♊

On Friday, Pete Johnson called from the crime lab to give her the scoop on the sweater fabric. "It's un...un...undoubtedly from the same sweater," he said. His high-pitched voice seemed to exacerbate his stutter. Christian wondered if that's why the young man had chosen a life in a laboratory. "It's a wool synthetic blend commonly used in high-end garments and that in....in.... in....deed, both swatches were from the same fabric blend," he squeaked.

"So how could I find out where it came from?" Christian asked impatiently.

"You know, I think we could i...i....isolate the company who sells this sweater," he'd added. "We can usually trace through a dye batch. It would be easier if we knew the label."

"I think it's an Abercrombie, but anyone and everyone owns their stuff."

"Do you think you can isolate the buyer from credit card re... re...records. I know a guy who can trace that kind of thing."

"Awesome. His name is Jason Roads, lives in Kennewick on Thompson Street with his parents. I can get his social if you need it."

"Yeah, that would be great. Also, this is go…go…going to surprise you, but the residue on the girl's sweater….it's not just semen."

"What else is there?"

"Ple…ple…plenty of female genital fluid. A girl was apparently using that sweater to clean up, if you get my meaning."

"Could you match that sample to Cassie's DNA?" Christian was beginning to feel uncomfortable with the subject matter. Despite the disgusting topics in her office circles, she couldn't imagine what else lab techies discussed.

Pete gave a snort of humor. "I'll check. If you have a DNA sample for a guy to send to me, I can see if there's a match. As far as diary fingerprints, there are too many to count. I guess everyone's had a read, huh?"

Christian frowned. "I got it from a couple of kids and then forgot to wrap it. I need a little more practice, as you can tell. With regards to the male DNA, I've got a couple of thoughts. Check it against Jim's DNA. Not that I think he's involved. Just to cover our bases. Also, Tommy Calander. He's in the system. I have one more suspect, but I don't have anything on him yet. I'm working on it. Thanks for all of your hard work. We owe you."

"Yeah, well I'm look…looking to move to Seattle. I'm hoping when this is all over, your brother can get me hooked up with a job over there. The crime lab in Seattle is CSI compared to what we do here."

"I bet. Thanks again." As Christian hung up, she realized that Jason Roads lived only a few miles from the Maltos home.

♊

"Got the list," Matt said as he walked through the front door. He was also carrying an armful of flowers, Stargazer Lilies to be precise.

Christian felt awkward as he gazed around the living room and then up to the ceiling, his face marked with surprise. When he looked at her, he smiled. "First, a kiss for my beautiful girl." He pulled her to him and his mouth met hers. She relinquished as a hungry heat spread through her body. As he disengaged, he added, "Got to keep my priorities straight!" He handed her the flowers. "I hope these are okay."

"They are my absolute favorites. How did you know?"

"A little bird named Kathy told me." He grinned and spread his arms.

"This place is terrific. Love the stars, too. I wonder if you'll make one for me."

Christian laughed. "Not if I don't have to-ever. This is going to sound morbid, but the stars represent departed loved ones. I pray you don't go up there anytime soon."

Matt tilted his head and pursed his lips. "No, baby. I'm not planning any departures any time soon."

"Come in," she laughed girlishly. "Sit down at the island while I cook. We can look at the Mustang club list in a minute." As Christian turned, she could feel his eyes on her. She was wearing her new 7 jeans, a chocolate velveteen pair accented by a very sexy brown lace top and high heels. He gave a low whistle as he followed her into the kitchen.

"I hate guys who whistle, but man, I can't help myself. You're lookin' good, girlfriend." Christian blushed and poured him a glass of Hedges merlot. "This wine won some awards last year. I hope you like it." Matt nodded and pulled the Mustang car club list from his pocket. "I've checked this out with my brother. Most of the guys on this list are old farts. Two of them live in Connell, seven are from West Richland, ten are from Richland, six from Pasco and four from Kennewick. Where does your suspect live?"

"Kennewick. Out on Thompson Road." Matt scanned the list as she turned to start the grill. She was preparing a California Sea Bass with fresh mango sauce.

"There's only a couple in that part of town. A Kevin Tanner and a Jerald Smithson."

"What did you say?" Christian turned to face him, a dripping spoon still in her hand.

Matt repeated the names. As he did, Christian leaned on the island and gasped, "That's got to be Tabby Smithson's dad."

Christian's meal turned out perfectly and it was all that they could do not to retire to the bedroom after supper. The heat between them was more a forest fire than a slow sizzle, but they both agreed the concert was too good to pass up. All evening, as they relaxed to the jazzy melodies of Bodie's trumpet and sipped Grey Goose martinis, Christian had two continuous and contradictory thoughts in her head: making passionate love to Matt and nailing that little brat, Tabby Smithson.

♊

When they made love, it was as though her body was experiencing ecstasy for the first time. She didn't recall ever feeling the way she had with Tony as she did with Matt. Her new lover was all sensuous eyes and soft words. He moved slowly, almost methodically, yet the rhythm of his body meeting hers reminded her of lapping waves on a beach-a part of nature that wanted no interruption. She woke up in his arms. Bear was now on the floor, a place he hadn't occupied at night since Tony's death. The dog didn't seem to mind. He groaned a morning dog groan and stood up to go out. She slipped out from the sheets. She was completely naked, but despite a tendency toward modesty, her robe was in the wash. Matt was sound asleep, so she tiptoed out and let Bear outside. Then she went to the kitchen and ran some cold water over her face and took a gulp of orange juice out of the bottle. She had just finished putting on the coffee, when she felt Matt's lips touch her shoulder.

"Please, delicious woman, come back to bed." Christian turned to him, no longer aware of her nudity. She felt her body respond as he pressed himself against her and began to kiss her neck and face. Slowly he lifted her up and she wrapped her legs around him as he slipped inside of her. She allowed him to hold her completely as she rocked against him again and again. Throwing her head back as he nuzzled her breasts, she heard her own voice as she released a deep moan of pleasure. Without missing a beat, he turned and carried her back into the bedroom. They climaxed in seconds, after which she held him close and tried to stop the tears. She was no longer a prisoner of her dead husband's memory. It had been long enough. Tony would have to be happy for her and his ghost would have to find someone else to haunt.

It was still early, so they lounged in bed and sipped on coffee. Christian had pulled one of her almond coffee cakes from the freezer the night before, in hopes of an overnight guest, and it was now warming in the oven. The house was filled with the aroma of almonds and Chris Bodie's CD played softly on her Bose. They talked for a while and then made love again, this time drawing it out for long moments. Matt was the kind of man who could wait for his pleasure and did so very willingly. Later, they munched on fresh fruit and the coffee cake in sweats and slippers. Christian had kept a few of Tony's things and though he'd been somewhat shorter than Matt, he had been nearly as muscular, so his Adidas running suit fit Matt just fine.

"Does it feel weird to wear Tony's clothes?" she asked while putting another slice of cake on his plate.

Matt smiled gently. "As long as you don't mind, I'm fine with it. Remember, I grew up in a poor household. Everyone borrowed everybody else's clothes from time to time."

"Do you miss your family?"

Rubbing his hand over his smooth cap of hair, Matt looked beyond her and out the window, as though thinking of an old image. "You know, having my brother here helps a lot. I miss my momma and my three sisters. They're all amazing women. My sister, Casey, is a lawyer in New Orleans. She's still working down there to get things right for folks after Katrina. Josephine, my middle sister, is studying to be an archaeologist. She's actually in Tunisia right now, working on a dig. My youngest sister, Candice, well, she's the baby and kind of a mess, but a beauty, yes ma'am. She just turned sixteen. A couple of days after her birthday, my mom called in hysterics a couple days ago. Candy's pregnant. My dad's a good man, but he's away lot, works on an oil rig out in the Gulf. I think it's been hardest on Candy, without the rest of us at home to keep her straight. I've got to fly down there this Easter, to see everyone. It's been over a year since I was home."

Christian decided to venture into unknown territory. "So you're not going home for Christmas?"

"No. I've already asked for time off for finals this year, so I'm kind of stuck. I'm working the day shift though, so at least I can spend it with the kids in detention. I've got a few ideas to make their Christmas a little better. My brother's coming over and we're going to have a basketball tournament on Christmas morning, boys against the girls. We've got some silly prizes, slippers and comic books for the boys and some hair stuff and fashion mags for the girls, approved of course. A bunch of us have collected some money for Christmas treats. I'm in charge of the pies. Then the chaplain is coming by to do a little church service. After that, we've rented *The Grinch who Stole Christmas* and that new Christmas movie with Chevy Chase. We'll have desserts during the movies in the gym."

"That's so cool. You really care about the kids. So many people who work at BFJJC seem to have lost that."

"So what's the point in working there? Helping kids, isn't that what it's all about?" Matt pushed back his chair and sighed. "That was a perfect beginning to a Sunday. Utterly perfect." He gave her a sly smile. "Want to try again?"

Christian stood up. "One more time, but this time, we need to make it quick." She fluttered her lashes and gave him a seductive look. "After all, I'm a church-going girl and we've got a sermon to attend." As she took his hand to lead him back into the bedroom, she added, "Hey Matt, do you want to come over here for Christmas dinner? You can bring your brother along."

"Really? I'd love it. He's probably working night shift, but I'll catch up with him later. Who else will be here?"

"My brother and his family."

Matt slipped off his clothes, revealing an erotic sight. He didn't show any hesitation as she stared at his body, drinking it in. "So I get to meet the family."

"Yeah, big boy," Christian murmured, pulling him down to her. "You're not just some hot fling, you know."

" I definitely hope I'm that, too."

Ⅱ

They arrived at the church a few minutes after eleven. There were a few people still milling around the lobby as they hurried in. The band played an upbeat Christian tune and the congregation swayed and clapped to the music for the first ten minutes. Then the pastor swept onto the chancel and stepped up to the pulpit. He was dressed in a navy black double-breasted suit and his hair was gleaming. He smiled and nodded at the band, welcomed the audience and recited a prayer.

Pastor Maxwell congratulated his people on their great success at the Christmas bazaar and reminded everyone of the work party that afternoon for the completion of their outdoor nativity scene. He mentioned a few other holiday activities and then, as his energy rose, the verbose man began his sermon like a political speech, all goodness and gratitude, before launching into a diatribe on Christian passivity and its dangers. Flinging his arms upward, he shouted the word 'repent' as he cited several Bible verses. He warned the people of the evil in their hearts and the heat of their passion when it was used for immoral purposes. His voice echoed off the walls and filled the room with a roar. Christian closed her eyes momentarily to ward off his angst.

Matt looked over at her several times and raised his eyebrows. Leaning in, he whispered, "This seems like the kind of church that has ranting faith healers and holy rollers falling down in the aisles." Surreptitiously he slipped his arm around her waist and pulled her closer as if to protect her from the message and its fury.

Eventually Pastor Maxwell calmed down and Christian began to listen. As she allowed the message to penetrate her mind, it seemed as though his words were directed at the Maltos murders in some inexplicable way.

"It's a vicious cycle, my people. Because of your passivity, the evil spirits are encouraged to come in. Upon entering, they manifest themselves through everyday activities and our blessed believers misinterpret these activities, not knowing that they originate with the devil. The cycle goes on and on and eventually the believer, in his passivity, is certain that his thoughts are directed by God, rather than by Satan. Beware when you seem happy in your inertia and be vigilant in your actions. Lust, greed, envy…these are the activities of the devil! Especially you, young people!" He paused to point to the young men and women sitting in the front row. "My soldiers of God and my maidens of the Lord, beware. You are entering a time in your life where your desires can overcome your devotion."

Christian watched the sides of the room for Jason to enter, but instead a couple of other young men stood up and began to sway and cry out in their strange language. As they did so, a couple of girls walked out of the room to their right. She started when she realized that one of them was Tabby Smithson. She nudged Matt and whispered, "I'm going to follow them. Meet me after Jason comes on."

Christian slipped out of the nave and watched as the girls headed toward the stairs. When they reached the top of the stairs and disappeared from sight, she quickly followed and caught the view of Tabby's back just as she entered Jason's office.

She heard the door shut and the lock click, so she quietly moved down the hall and to the door. Positioning herself at the left side of Jason's door, next to an office which fortunately had its door slightly ajar, she leaned her ear to Jason's door to hear what was going on.

Initially there were only rustling sounds. After a few minutes passed, Jason began to speak. His voice was soft and seductive, and at first, Christian refused to believe what she was hearing.

"Angie, do it faster. You know I can't do the talk unless....yes, that's right. Now Tabby, you touch Angela, there, that's right. Breathe, feel it!"

"Yes, I do. I feel it," a girl replied.

"Oh, you are good girls, my girls." She could hear Jason emit a guttural moan while one of the girls uttered a sharp cry. The next thing that Christian heard was a girl whining, "After church it's my turn." Her voice was petulant and angry. Jason said, "Yeah, baby, after church. You know what to say, right? Did you memorize it?" Christian thought the girl must have nodded in response as Jason continued, "Okay, good. Now let's get the hell out of here before someone comes looking for us."

Christian slipped into the office next door just as she heard the sound of the lock click open. She listened as Jason bounded down the stairs and the girls came out and continued passed her to the ladies room. As they did, she heard the other girl say, "That was awesome. Can we do it again, after the next cell meeting?"

Tabby snapped, "Maybe later. And by the way, this is just between the three of us. The cell doesn't know about this, you stupid ho."

Christian waited until the girls had returned to the service and then decided rather than return to the sanctuary and risk being seen by the girls or Jason, she would wait out by the car. By the time Matt found her, he was furious and muttering with disbelief. As they exited the church parking lot, he hissed, "I can't believe what a piece of work that guy is and the girl that was interpreting had to be faking it. There is no way this guy's the real thing. Doesn't anyone up here understand Cajun dialect?"

"Apparently Sue Maltos did. What did Jason say?"

"Oh, he's good. It's like he's speaking double talk, a code really. He knows our language, the deep, dark swamp talk. He's talking about screwing 3 or 4 virgins and how he can make them scream with pleasure. It's not a gift from God, that's for sure."

"Who was interpreting for him?"

"A girl with shoulder-length brown hair. I think the pastor called her Angela."

"Did she recite scripture?" Christian tried to focus, but her glance kept returning to the church doors. Several people were clustered at the entry while others gathered to chat on the sidewalk or otherwise return to their cars.

"She got some of it right…at least the snake part." He shook his head, obviously sickened by what he'd heard. "She quoted Mark 16:18 which goes something like this: 'And they shall take up with the serpents and if they drink anything poisonous, it won't harm them. If they touch the sick, they shall recover, and so on. It's basically the part of the Bible that talks about the gifted or blessed have powers to defy death by the grace of God. However, Jason was actually talking about his trouser snake and laying his hands on young girls, the bastard. Still I bet that he coached that girl ahead of time as to what to say."

Nodding, she watched out of the corner of her eye as Jason stepped out of the cluster and began walking directly toward them.

"Oops, here he comes," Christian murmured. "I'll give it my best shot."

Jason was nearly upon them when she met his gaze. Ice-cold arrogance draped his eyes like a veil when she refused to look away, but he continued walking. Angela suddenly appeared closely behind the youth director. She scampered past them like a faithful puppy as Christian whispered, "She's next on my list."

She paused, lost in thought and then glanced back at Matt. He was visibly shaken by his experience. "Hey, I'm sorry. I didn't mean to ruin our date."

Matt shook his head. "No, this is the stuff you can use against him. I wrote down as much as I could without being obvious. Here," Matt pulled an offering envelope from his pocket. "What we need to do is go back with a tape recorder. Who knows, maybe next week, he'll 'tongue' a confession."

"You know, when we first arrived, I saw him in the lobby. He started to come toward me and then he must have seen you standing behind me, because he literally did an about face. I wonder if he's afraid of you."

"Lots of white guys who go down to southern colleges form strong opinions about my people. They do their so-called charity work in the Bayous, but there's some heavy duty black magic that goes on out there like voodoo and witchcraft. He's probably been told that enough times to dislike my race. Not to mention that there wasn't one other African-Americans in the whole church. Cassie must have hated it there."

"Because she was part Asian?"

"Yeah."

"But she was so pretty and talented, I'm sure people gave her plenty of kudos."

"You know that doesn't really matter. When you can sense a person's prejudice, it doesn't matter how much they suck up to you."

"I'm sure you're right."

"See, that's what I worry about, with you and me dating. You are such an innocent that way. You don't see color. But other people do. There were people in that church today who were sickened by the fact that we appeared to be together. That's why I didn't hold your hand. I don't want that for you."

"How awful for *you!*" she cried as they pulled into her driveway. She shut off the car and turned to him. "I will always be proud to be with you, Matt. Don't forget that. You're a wonderful man, a good, caring, intelligent man. The next time you drop my hand in public, I'm going to grab yours and not let go. Do you understand me?"

Matt started to laugh until tears were streaming down his face. Christian was silent, but still incensed by his description of human nature. "You are one stubborn woman, Christian Vargas," he muttered through his laughter. "Don't get me wrong. I love it. I'm crazy about it." He shook his head again, his laughter finally subsiding. "I'm in for some fun, I can tell."

Christian finally smiled back. "Tony hated that about me. He said I was a control freak."

"No, that's not what it is at all. You're a woman of your word. And that's a good thing…a very good thing."

By the time they'd sat down to eat a lunch of leftover pizza and a Caesar salad, Christian began to give Matt a watered down version of the scene in Jason's office. She was too disgusted to talk at length about it, though it seemed there were definite implications to the Maltos murders now. Later, when he kissed her good-bye after an afternoon of movies and cuddling, she whispered, "Thanks so much for all of your help. This is such dirty business!"

"I think, no, *I know* that you're going to get to the bottom of this. Don't ever hesitate to ask me for help. I'm here for you and I'll do whatever it takes to keep you safe. Remember that."

After Matt left, Christian called Scott and filled him in on the morning's events. He encouraged her to corner Tabby and Angela as soon as possible. The conversation turned to their holiday plans. By the time she'd hung up, the distasteful experience at the church was at the back of her mind and she'd decided to put her latest obsession aside. With the talk of Christmas, it was time to get out her decorations and put up her tree. Over the years, she had collected many ornaments from her travels. Hand-blown glass balls from Venice hung next to straw-wrapped Stars of David from Israel. There were little velvet camels from Morocco and rosy-cheeked Danish St. Nicholas dolls, miniature German beer steins and delicate lace angels from Portugal. Christian hauled the boxes from her garage and rolled the Norwegian pine tree in off the patio where she kept it in a large, wheeled pot. That evening, to add to her festivities, she called Stella and invited her over for a glass of wine. Standing in her living room, watching her funny, homemade stars twinkle above her, Christian hugged Bear and laughed aloud. "Things aren't so bad, old boy," she whispered to the dog, as she looked forward to happy dreams, with Matt in the forefront of her mind.

♊

Despite Sunday's horrible revelation, Christian floated in a dream world most of Monday. Though Matt was working day shift for the rest of the week, she decided that it was best if she didn't go back to the pods to see him. She was certain her dreamy girl look would announce to the world that they were having a love affair. Christian considered what Matt had said about her disregard for color. At first it had seemed like a complement, as though there was some sort of purity in her ignorance. But now, as she thought about it further, she realized that she was missing a whole range of issues that affected her friends and co-workers alike. Daniel was in awe of Matt on the basketball court. He made comments about it all the time. Yet he thought Christian was too good for his team mate. She wondered how a guy who had worked in the fields for slave wages as a kid could see himself differently than a man from the south who had essentially experienced the same.

In the meantime, she'd heard back on Jason Roads's criminal history. Christian's contact at the Department of Corrections had sent a rap sheet on a Jason Robert Roads who shared the same birth date and social security number as the evangelistic youth pastor. The records came from an obscure county just south of New Orleans. There were only two entries on Jason's adult record, both minor offenses-a speeding ticket and a trespassing charge. However there was a confirmation of a DNA sample. The DOC contact tried to find out what had prompted the DNA requirement and soon found a reference to an expunged juvenile record out of Georgia. Eventually through backtracking and back scratching, he discovered that Jason Roads had an indecent liberties charge. In 1996, at the age of seventeen, Roads pled guilty to it. The victim was a thirteen-year old girl.

Upon learning of this, she called Scott immediately. He was cool about the information, adding that such a relationship in the south was common and didn't mean someone was a killer.

"You never know. Lots of juvenile perps go on to lead fairly normal lives. A sixteen-year old boy lives in a hormone haze. Throw a sexually-budding teenage girl at him and stupid things happen, more often than you think."

"But whatever happened in that office on Sunday proves that he is still engaging in perverted sexual behaviors."

"What? Screwing a couple of nubiles? That seems pretty normal for a young man to want to do."

"Scott, they're teenagers. He's nearly twenty-eight."

"Yikes."

"Okay, but I'm allowed to keep him on the suspect list. Who else could be involved?" she asked stubbornly. Christian could almost hear her brother grin at her tenacity.

"Yes. Keep him at the top of your list. Motive is the key here, however. What motive did Jason have in order to want to kill his girlfriend and mother? On one hand, if Mrs. Maltos was on to him, threatening to expose him, he might have killed her to protect his relationship with Cassie. But that's a stretch. However, he might have overreacted to a threat, or …I don't know. It just doesn't make sense yet. Remember something like eighty percent of the people murdered in this country are killed by someone they know, most as a result of domestic violence. That is why everyone is looking at Jim. By the way, there's good news on that front. His friend, Cindy, is going in to make a statement today. She's attesting to the fact she was with Jim that day and has a credit card receipt to prove it. We should have him out before Christmas. Tomorrow if I get my way."

Christian thought about Mr. Maltos and what a horrible Christmas he had to face. The murderer was still free, so the department would probably give him some security protection, but that wouldn't, couldn't alleviate the deep pain and suffering he would experience. Christian remembered her first Christmas without Tony. It was more a blur than a memory. There were constant tears despite family surrounding her and grief so deep that she felt she'd fallen to the bottom of a well. It had taken weeks after his death just to want to take a shower, and Christmas had forced her back a step. Three steps forward, two steps back. That was her Aunt's adage after her parents had been killed. "Honey, some days it's a good day and then, you'll have many bad ones. Then a few more good. But someday, in the near future, you will feel good most all the time again. I promise." She missed her aunt after whom she'd been named. Her aunt and uncle's retirement had taken them down to Mexico years ago and despite her good intentions, she rarely visited the little village outside Mazatlan. As she prepared for another meeting for Lilly at the DCFS office, she breathed a sigh of relief. It would be good to tell her aunt that she was in love again.

Daniel arrived back in the office shortly after lunch. He was in a surly mood, after learning that his soon-to-be ex-wife was planning to file bankruptcy after their divorce was final.

"She's such a piece of work," he fumed, shoving paper around his desk, refusing to look at Christian. She knew that his wife had charged up plenty of credit card debt during their marriage. If she filed bankruptcy, he'd be responsible for all of the payments.

"But you got the cabin, right?" she asked, searching for something positive in the messiness of it all.

"Yes, I got the cabin, which I'll probably have to sell in order to pay off debt in the form of a hundred pair of designer shoes."

Christian wondered how he'd ever let it go this far. She thought for a long moment and then replied, "You know, I have some money. I could help you. I just sold our property in the Gorge. How about I buy the cabin from you? On paper only. It will belong to you, but in the future, I can use it when I need a get-away and we can split the upkeep costs."

Her partner's face had an incredulous look on it. "Really? You'd do that?'

"What am I going to do with the money? I could invest it in the stock market, but it's so volatile right now. Like you said, the real estate market down there is only going to go up. Have you checked out the prices of property in Hood River? Same thing. That rental that Tony and I owned just outside White Salmon had tripled in value since we bought it. That's one of the reasons I sold it. And it's a hassle to find good renters. As I see it, it's a great deal for me. Someday, if we ever sell it, you can pay me from the profits."

"I'd rather not complicate our relationship any more than it is."

"But it would be fun to share it with you." Christian heard the subtle sound of want in her voice. What was she doing, sharing a cabin with her partner while making love to one of his friends?"

"You can always share it with me." He was looking at her now, with appreciation and something more. Admiration, or a deeper, more complex emotion, but she didn't allow herself to ponder. Instead she changed the subject.

"So I'm going to start by spying on Jason. I'm pretty sure that he was driving Mr. Smithson's red Mustang when he would take out Cassie. I can't tell you why the old guy would allow him to borrow a car like that, but I'm going to find out. Jason probably kept a low profile which was why he would take her down to Bateman Island. It's really secluded down there."

"But for all you know, he wasn't the driver of the car. He might not be her lover. We don't have anything to prove that he is. We need to check Tabby, see what she's up to. Why don't I do a little spying in her direction and you stay on Jason."

"Hey, remember the diary's reference to J.J.? You can't tell me that J.J. and Jason Robert Roads are not the same person."

"And the DNA sample for Jason is being sent up from Louisiana as we speak. If we can match the semen samples, that proves their love affair.

At that moment, the phone rang. "Hold on," she said. "Hello?"

"Christian, it's me, Matt. Hey, I've done some research on this whole glossolalia thing."

"Excuse me?"

"The speaking in tongues phenomenon. It goes way back to biblical times, but ironically, the most famous 20th century charismatic was from Seattle. A Father Bennett from St. Luke's Episcopal church. He really started the movement in America."

"I've been to that church, once anyway. Go on."

"Speaking in tongues is one of the gifts of the Holy Spirit. When a person feels the spirit, they speak gibberish, or sometimes speak a language unknown to all but one or two around them. It's like imparting a secret message. If Mrs. Maltos understood, partially anyway, what Jason was saying, then perhaps he was warning her of something."

"Do you think that what I heard going on in his office during the service yesterday was not what I thought it was?"

"I'm guessing from the little you told me that you thought they were having sex. Think about what they said again. Could it be they were doing something else?"

Christian shook her head as she felt tension fill her body. Whatever those kids had been doing hadn't sounded holy to her. "Ok, let's just say they weren't having sex, that instead they were contacting the Holy Spirit somehow. If he was speaking that French swamp talk as you call it, and no one else in the church can understand it, what's the point now?"

"But I could understand it."

There was a long silence. Christian felt like a complete fool. "Of course, Matt, I'm sorry."

"No, it's alright. But I'd be curious if he's been speaking Cajun the entire time, since the murder, or if something happened yesterday, something we mere mortals can't understand."

"What else did you learn from your research?"

"For one, Tabby Smithson has an older brother named Jerry, but I've got to go. They need me in master control."

"Matt, thanks so much. Call me later."

After Christian hung up, she was buzzing with the sweet energy that she felt whenever Matt had touched her in some way. He must have spent last night doing the research, she realized. This case seemed to be as important to him as it was to her.

"So are you going to talk to me, or just sit there in a daze? Jeez, you look a little pathetic really," Daniel quipped.

"Stop it. You're just jealous." Christian felt her joyful state recede.

"Of what? Or what are you trying to tell me something, like perhaps Matt is more than just a weekend one nighter. Could it be you are falling in love?" Daniel smirked as though in fun, but his eyes spoke of betrayal.

"You're just going through a really hard time. I know that. You'll find someone else. It just takes awhile. Look at me. Two years alone. But you know, it's better that way. You need some time to heal."

"Whatever. It's just hard to watch, I guess. I want you to be happy. I really do."

"Thanks. Enough said." She turned to her computer. The conversation was over.

After an hour of paperwork and phone calls, Christian dialed Angela Harper's number again. The girl's name had been in the church newsletter as a new member to their youth group, so it had been easy to trace her phone through the city of Kennewick's dispatch. On the ninth ring, a woman answered the phone.

"Hello?"

"Hello. My name is Christian Vargas." Christian paused, searching quickly for an excuse for the call. Then she remembered one of the church announcements from the service. "I'm calling from the Desert Evangelistic Church youth group to remind Angela of the Tuesday night gathering for girls. It's at seven o'clock."

There was a long pause before the woman replied in a very terse tone, "Angela's not allowed to go to your stinking church anymore. My husband and I don't believe in your form of Christianity. If you want to know my honest opinion, I think ya'all are working with the devil. Now don't ever call here again, do you hear me? If you and that Jason, if anyone from your ridiculous church calls here again, I will have the police pay ya'all a visit." With that, she hung up.

Christian sat very still, trying to process what she just heard. There was a sting in the air, like an electric shock, as though the woman's fear and anger had actually penetrated her psyche. She took a deep breath and stared at the door, willing herself to stand up and walk out. She knew where she had to go. Grabbing her backpack, she headed out to her car. It was time to pay Jason Roads a little visit.

CHAPTER 14

December 22, 2005

♊

Snow was falling lightly as she pulled into the back parking lot of the Desert Evangelistic Church. With Christmas now only a few days away, it was a welcomed sight. As she slipped from the car, Christian noticed an immaculate blue Honda Civic parked near the back door. There was a sticker on its back bumper that read "Jason's detail service, call 628-7177."

Glancing around, she didn't see anyone in sight. The Honda Civic was the only automobile in the parking lot. Wandering slowly toward the car, she grabbed a piece of paper from her purse and wrote down the license plate and detail phone number. Once she was close enough, Christian peered in the driver's window. The car was spotless, though in the passenger's seat was a blue sweater. She looked up and scanned the parking lot and church again. There were no windows facing toward the parking lot. She tried the car door and it was unlocked. Her heart began to race as she made the decision. Quickly she pulled out her phone. She began to snap pictures of the car. First the license plates, then the decal. With a hard jerk, she yanked open the door and grabbed the jacket. She laid it out on the driver's seat, exposed the cut-out pocket and label.

Her hands were trembling as she stepped back and took a panoramic photograph of the car in the church parking lot. Jason's name was a blur from where she stood, but she knew that Harry could enlarge any photo to a microscopic degree.

Slick with nervous energy, she grabbed her driver's door to leave. She felt that dreaded feeling and was finally learning to heed her own internal advice. The old Bug was temperamental and the lock was notorious for sticking. She pushed the key back and forth. As she did so, the back door of the church swung open and Jason sauntered out. Just as the lock turned, he caught sight of her and waved. She smiled weakly and opened the door, surreptitiously shoving her notes into her purse as he approached her. This must be what a thief feels like, she realized.

"Good morning!" Jason tilted his head questioningly and put out his hand. "I'm sorry! I've forgotten your name already."

"Christian. I'm the counselor who worked with Cassie Maltos." Her hands were shaking, more from nerves than from temperature. She hoped that he thought it was the latter. She also wanted to curse herself for revealing her profession. It would have been safer to adhere to his first impressions that she was a new church member.

"Oh? Yes, I remember now. She said that they were going to family counseling. It's such a terrible thing that happened to those two women." He bowed his head and gave her a miserable look.

"It's horrible." She didn't know what else to say. All she could think of was how to get away from the scumbag. His phony forlorn act had given him away." She waited, tapping her foot anxiously on the floorboards, wishing that he would go away.

But didn't I see you here the other day?"

Christian shivered violently. "Brrr, it's cold out here. And to answer your question, yes, I was here. I'm interested in joining the church. I was very touched by the Maltos funeral service and met some nice folks that day. I thought I'd stop by to find out about the adult singles group."

Christian, Stop rattling on and don't tell him another thing about yourself.

"You're single? So am I. It gets lonely sometimes, doesn't it?" Jason was leaning slightly toward her. His closeness gave a sense of intimacy to their conversation. Snowflakes laced his heavy lashes and thick, wavy hair. With a shake of his head, he gestured toward the church. "I'm getting wet. Why don't we go inside and warm up. I'll make us a latte. We've got an espresso machine in the lobby."

Christian inwardly cringed as she noticed that there were still no other cars in the parking lot. It was lunch time, after all. "Okay." Her voice squeaked as she followed him in. As she did, she slipped her hand in her purse and pressed the redial button on her phone. If she was right, Matt's number was the last one that she'd dialed.

"So, lovely lady, what's your flavor?" Jason led her into through the dark sanctuary. She felt the hairs go up on the back of her neck as the door slammed behind her.

"Anything's fine."

"One shot or two," he added as they walked through the double doors into the brightly lit lobby. The church seemed exceptionally empty now.

"One's good."

"You know, that snow is really coming down. We might get a white Christmas after all. I'd love that. How about you?"

"Yes. It would be really nice. So did you grow up in this church?" It was high time that she began to run this show.

"Actually I grew up in Seattle. My father was a pastor at St. Lukes. I grew up Episcopal, but after learning about the gifts, well, I decided to follow God's lead. I ended up going to college in the south, down in Louisiana, where the gifts are still quite prevalent. However, snow is not!" He winked at her as he poured some coffee beans from a large container, quickly grinded it and began to fiddle with the machine. He seemed to be an expert at working the presses.

"I'm sorry, but I'm confused. Gifts?"

Jason handed her the latte. She took a small sip. It was perfect. He looked at her and offered a genuine smile. "Good?"

Nodding, she replied, "Wonderful."

"I insist on ordering the coffee from New Orleans. None of that Starbucks around here. Anyway, the gifts. Have you ever read the Corinthians, or the Book of Acts? Both talk about the gifts of the Holy Spirit. As true believers, we have the right to those gifts. Prophecy, the laying of hands, and of course, speaking in tongues, are gifts from God. Many Christians don't believe, but here, at Desert Evangelist, we rejoice in these manifestations."

"So how do you get the Spirit to come to you?"

Jason grinned boyishly. She was finding it hard to look away; her attention was being drawn in by his passion alone. It made her sick to her stomach.

"We come together. It's hard to explain." He paused and closed his eyes, as though listening for something. As he clenched his fists and drew them to his chest, she noticed the muscles in his forearms ripple and wondered if he used steroids. The rolled-up sleeves of his crisp cotton shirt only exacerbated his well-toned physique. Then his eyes popped open and he said, "I don't normally do this so early on, but are you willing to let me show you something?" Before she could reply, Jason moved toward her and took the coffee cup from her hand. "Do you mind? It won't take long."

Christian suddenly felt a little woozy as he took her hand and led her back into the dark sanctuary.

"Follow me," he said and took her to a long table on the stage behind the podium.

"Now, lie down here," he said, his voice delicately stroking every word. "I should have grabbed my coat out of the car. Are you warm enough?" She nodded. Though she was wearing a thick turtleneck, a lined tweed blazer and wool trousers, the room was chilly. But if he went to get the jacket, she was in trouble.

"I won't hurt you. I promise." A voice in her head started to protest, but she ignored its warning. This was a moment that she shouldn't pass up. He wouldn't hurt her here, would he? She set her purse down and climbed onto the table.

"Now what do I do?" she asked as Jason gazed at her. His eyes radiated something bordering on possession as he placed his hand on her forehead and slowly pushed her to a lying position.

Softly stroking her hair, he said, "Just relax. I'm going to call upon the Holy Spirit. You are tired, exhausted in fact. I will help you to feel God's energy through my hands." With that, he placed his other hand lightly on her belly. She flinched, but forced herself to go along with it.

"It's ok. I know you're a little scared. Just let me touch you... feel it? Ahh, yes, you can, can't you?" His voice had taken the tone of a hypnotist.

Christian closed her eyes and concentrated. She could feel an electricity- a slow, steady pulse as he slowly moved his hand back and forth across her torso. Though he wasn't actually touching her, his fingertips were only a hair's breadth away from her breasts. If she breathed in deeply, his hand would make contact with her.

Still she waited. Why, she didn't know. To experience his power, to see what the younger girls couldn't seem to resist.

"That's a girl. I feel you now. I feel the demon of death around you. You are lucky to be alive. You are… ouwww"

In the next moment, Jason yanked back and stared at her wildly, shaking his hands as though they were on fire.

"What is it?" she cried, sitting up.

He backed away, shaking his head. "There's something wrong. This has never happened before. He stopped as the door of the sanctuary flung open.

"Looks like we have company." His face was burning with an emotion, rage of fear, either she couldn't be sure. Christian sat up and saw Matt standing in the doorway, his silhouette haloed by the light from the lobby. He was her hero.

Christian sat up, her mouth falling open. "He's a friend of mine. He's interested in joining too. I asked him to meet me here." Her words sounded hollow as Matt stepped through the door.

"Hi, ya'all. Hey, sorry I'm late." Matt played his part with ease. There was a total sense of trust as he strolled in.

She climbed off the table and grabbed her purse. It all seemed so surreal. Why was Matt so calm in the face of such a strange encounter?

"So you guys are doing a little laying of the hands, I see," Matt said casually. "It's been a long time, but I used to do some of that myself."

Jason looked from one to the other in utter surprise.

"It really works. I could feel his, I mean the Holy Spirit through his hands. I feel better, in fact. Not so tired."

For a moment, Jason's face betrayed him. Then he turned and jogged down the aisle and back into the lobby. As though nothing had happened, he called back, "May I get your friend a latte?'

$$\text{II}$$

Jason was deeply perturbed as he walked out to his car. That damn counselor had seemed sincere at first, but there was something later, when he did the healing, that frightened him to the core. He'd only seen it once before, when he was working on a nigger in Louisiana. He shivered when recalling their encounter. As he attempted to lay hands, she'd gripped his arm with unbelievable strength and had said, "I know all about you, little boy. You are bad...very bad." He'd immediately feigned illness, stumbling out of the healing room before any of his parishioners could see his terror. Within minutes, his entire body had grown feverish, as though she was contagious with some lethal disease. He didn't return to church for nearly a month. Wracked with nightmares and unpredictable anxiety, he was afraid that he would see her again. She never came back to the church and later, when he'd asked around, no one remembered seeing her there at all.

During the attempted healing, Christian hadn't said a word to him, but his power had dissolved almost instantly, like steel turning to mush. She seemed unaware of her effect on him and it was by the grace of God that the big nigger had walked in when he did, though that was a problem unto itself. Jason couldn't lie. He hated those people with a passion. Living in

the south had taught him to distrust their kind and had solidified his convictions that their race was inferior. However, he'd
made exceptions when it came to the yummy little black girls
with perfectly round booties, perky breasts and tight pussies.
He loved their hairless skin and wide eyes that gave them the
look of idiots, but enhanced his ability to manipulate them to
his gain. He'd had sex with more of them than he could count,
especially after the issue with the pastor's daughter. Fortunately
the indecent liberties charge was long buried. He'd been convicted just a month before his eighteenth birthday and had
therefore avoided any adult criminal history.

Jason shivered again. He definitely wasn't feeling well. He
reached into the back seat to grab the jacket that he'd left there.
Looking around, he didn't see it on the backseat. Instead it was
laid out smoothly on the driver's seat. "F-ing ayy!" he cursed aloud.
His friend's jacket had a hole in the pocket. Jason's power suddenly returned the form of rage. Peeling out of the parking lot, he
headed toward Kennewick High. He needed to talk to his woman
as soon as possible.

♊

"Have you ever heard of the Stockholm Syndrome?" Matt asked
after Christian had spent a few minutes gushing over his appreciated arrival at the church. They were standing in the parking lot of
the Juvenile Justice Center. Matt had just finished explaining that
after he'd heard her phone call, he'd become concerned when
she didn't speak, had then asked to leave on his lunch break, and
had eventually learned from Stacy, the front desk receptionist, that
Christian had left for the Desert Evangelist Church.

"So you see! Checking out with the front desk does have some value. I got to be a hero." He grinned proudly. "Now, back to my question."

"Yes. The Stockholm Syndrome is a psychological reaction of victims in captivity. After awhile, they begin to identify with their captors," Christian replied, following Matt toward the detention doors.

"Ok, so what happened today? Why did you trust Jason to lay his hands on you? How did you know he wasn't going to hurt you?"

"I don't really know. I felt somehow I could trust him. Besides, it's not the same at all."

"My point exactly. You hardly know him and he's your number one murder suspect?"

"I know. I'm completely crazy."

Matt stood at the detention entrance doors. Christian just wanted to put her arms around him as he looked down at her with a quizzical sort of tenderness on his face.

"You're a very intelligent woman, but you succumbed to his charm or whatever it is that he has on people. Those girls are no different."

"Yes, Matt, they are. They are younger and more naïve. I'm simply stupid to let him go ahead with his weird magic, but I had to know what all the fuss is about. And now I'm rethinking that incident I overheard on Sunday. Maybe it wasn't what I thought it was."

"Let's talk later. I have to get back to work. I'll call you tonight." He leaned forward and squeezed her arm. "Glad I could be the good guy. Only next time, I hope I'm the one with my hands on you!" He winked and pushed open the detention door, quickly disappearing from sight.

When she returned to the office, she quickly called Scott to let him know she'd taken the photos of the car and jacket.

"Good work. Turn those in immediately. Call our detective friend and confirm the dates on the phone as well. The bullet casing was no match to that stolen gun. If we don't have a weapon, we've got nothing."

Christian felt entirely dejected. 'I know, but there has to be a way. I am certain this guy's the one."

Scott interrupted. "This information is enough for a search warrant. I'll start that process as soon as I can. We'll make that kid's house and office look like a tornado came through if we have to."

By the time Christian got home that night, she was truly exhausted. After swinging by the KPD to drop off the new evidence, she'd stopped by Costco to buy a turkey and other items for the Christmas holidays. Matt had volunteered to bring dessert in the form of his famous maple pecan pies. He swore that his version was better than Emeril's, a famous chef for whom he had worked while in high school. As she hoisted the boxes of food into the house, she realized that she was dating a man who was probably a much better cook than her. The thought of it was more inspiring than intimidating. Tony had been an awful cook and she had been consigned to the kitchen during their marriage. In fact, Tony hadn't been much of a domestic at all. His contributions to the marriage were primarily financial in nature, but his bent for investing in real estate had paid off, she admitted, as she gazed around her beautiful home. From the patio doors, she could see the Yakima River glistening in the evening light. The snow had stopped for the time being, but the inch or two on the ground cast a glowing sheen of white across her triangular-shaped property. As she gazed out, a figure appeared at the edge of her lawn. After nearly knocking her over upon her entrance, Bear was still shaking and moaning, an indication that she was probably correct.

"Hey boy, what do you see?" Walking over to the east wall, she reached for the switch for the yard lights. Her home was at the end of the road and the last city street light was a block away. When they'd first moved there in 2000, Tony had put in a security system as well as several standing lights on the perimeter of the property. When she flipped the switch to the outer lights, she saw two people start to run toward the marsh on the other side of her property. She considered letting Bear out, but thought twice. Whoever it was, he would probably tear them to pieces.

Instead, she grabbed her old Nikon camera off the kitchen counter and quickly set the aperture accordingly. With the zoom lens, she shot a series of photos until the mysterious duo disappeared from sight.

♊

Christian awoke to the telephone the next morning. A five am wake-up was earlier than she liked as she glanced at the clock on her bedside table. "Hello?"

"Hi, it's me."

"Why are you calling so early?" Her tone was a bear's growl.

"Sorry, sleepy head. I'm on the way to the cabin, remember? I want to get on the road while the pass is still open. I was just in to check my messages before I leave. Guess what? You won't believe it, but the lab called. Harry got the DNA sample on Jason. It matches the semen on the pink sweater, some of the semen. The thing is, there's another boy in town. This one doesn't have his DNA on record. Cassie was getting some action, lucky girl."

"We're talking about a dead girl here. Try to stay professional."

"Sorry, I just haven't had any lately. It's rough. But you wouldn't know about that."

"Listen, I've spent many a night with just me, myself and I. I understand what you're feeling. Even if you're a horny male, I don't enjoy chastity any more than the next guy… or girl for that matter."

"Okay!" His voice was mocking. "So what's the next step?"

"I'll call Scott. I'm sure this needs to be given to the prosecution. Maybe the lab has already alerted them. However, again, it only proves he's a lover, not a killer."

"But it's the little steps, girlfriend! Now get your butt out of bed and walk that poor dog of yours."

"Yeah, yeah, I'm on it." She felt weary by this investigation. "Later."

Christian stood up and stretched languorously. Walking to the window, she gazed out at the winter morning. A few inches of new snow had fallen and her lawn was a glistening sheet of white. An energetic thought crossed her mind. She headed for the walk-in closet, but paused in front of her dresser. There, standing regally in the soft morning light, was Contessa. Christian froze and then, with a flippant toss of her head, said aloud, "I don't know how in the hell you keep moving yourself around, but I'm beginning to find it rather charming." The statue's blank gaze seemed to follow her, like a ceramic Mona Lisa. The room seemed to grow a little brighter as she turned and stepped into the closet. Grabbing her sweats, an all-weather coat and some boots, Christian hollered, "Come on, Bear. We're going tracking."

Bear frolicked across the yard, nipping wildly at the snow as they headed across the lawn toward the edge of the river. For the first few yards beyond the patio, no imprints appeared in the snow. However, as she ventured to the eastern perimeter of the property, on the other side of the garage, she could see two sets of tracks. She called Bear over and pointed at them. "There, boy."

Tracking in snow or other extreme terrains was the most difficult for dogs, though the slightest of scents undetectable to humans were apparent to good tracking animals. Sometimes it was only a strand of hair, or a littered gum wrapper that gave them the first clue. Generally the animal had been shown an item with which to associate, especially in the case of a lost person. But sometimes there was nothing more than the beginning of a trail.

Christian had first decided to teach Bear the Koehler tracking method as a result of a strange coincidence. In hindsight she realized that once again, Death had been hovering. It was the spring of 2001. Tony had been out of town for over a week on a work assignment, so Christian had believed her dark hour fears and troubling nightmares were simply a symptom of being alone. Bear had come into their lives only a month before and was still in the process of healing. The vet had indicated the dog was not yet two years old, based on the size of his three remaining paws. He'd mentioned that dogs like Bear, who appeared to be a cross between a Labrador Retriever and a St. Bernard, were well-known for their tracking abilities.

Christian had envisioned the great canines of the Alps who were famous for saving skiers trapped by avalanches, but she'd never expected what happened next.

About midnight of that fateful night nearly five years ago, Debra, her neighbor, had come to her door. The pounding had a hysterical sound to it. She remembered clearly the terror in Deb's face when she'd opened the door.

"Deb, what is it," she'd asked, rubbing the sleep from her eyes. Bear was standing next her at the door, moaning softly. Debra was crying.

"It's my granddaughter, Andrea. She's gone. One minute she was tucked into bed, the next she is absolutely nowhere to be found."

"Did you check your studio?" Christian was referring to her neighbor's outbuilding that acted as a stained glass studio.

Debra shook her head, unable to speak. In her hand, she'd held a small, tattered blanket. Bear had begun to sniff the blanket and then took it into his teeth.

"Stop it, Bear," Christian had scolded.

"It's Andy's blanket. I don't know why I have it. What should we do?"

Then Christian got an idea so instantaneous and simple, she didn't reply. Running to her room, she threw on a pair of shoes and grabbed a sweatshirt. Her boxer shorts were skimpy, but at this point, modesty didn't matter.

"Deb, you call the police. Bear and I are going out. Can I have the blanket please?"

With that, they were out the door. Within ten minutes they'd found the five year old and none too soon. She had wandered out to the edge of the river in search of her doll, which apparently she'd left in a row boat the family often used. She'd slipped and was caught up by a Russian olive branch only inches from a small, but slippery slope that led directly into the river. When Bear had found her, her night dress was slowly

tearing. Another rip and the girl would have been dumped in the river and presumably drowned.

After that episode, Christian had realized two important things about her life. She was destine to forever live with the transitory presence of Death and sometimes, she could actually do something to stop his insidious plans. The other important discovery that night was, of course, Bear's uncanny abilities as a natural search dog.

By the time the police had arrived, Bear was becoming a neighborhood legend. Two weeks later, the book on Koehler Dog training arrived in the mail. Another six months passed and Bear had completed the first three training levels.

Tonight, as they moved methodically along the edge of the property, Christian recognized how truly fortunate she was to have the dog. He was company, protector and assistant. With no children, no husband and fairly little extended family contact; Christian relied on the Bear as a partner and friend. She wondered if Bear was Death's way of saying that she was worthy.

Suddenly Bear darted into the bush. Thick willows and Russian Olive trees lined the east side of the property where the river curved from east to west. Her property was shaped like a unilateral triangular with one apex of the land meeting a bend in the Yakima River. The river was extremely dangerous at the curve with whirlpools and an undertow that was more powerful than the current. The Yakima was known as a fairly innocuous river, popular for its seasonal tubing and rafting populations. During the hot summer months when temperatures in the Tri-Cities reached the low one hundreds, large groups of kids could be seen in makeshift boats made from barrels, plywood and old tire tubes floating near her property. Many traveled with various accoutrements including illegal substances which impaired their judgment.

A couple of months after Andrea had been found, Bear had hauled two pre-teen girls from the river near the spot where they now stood. He was a strong swimmer, despite his handicapped condition and once again, he had been written up in the newspaper as a super dog.

Prior to the dog's heroics, Christian had allowed him in and out of the house through a doggy door in the garage. After he'd rescued the girls, their property had been on the front page of the newspaper and as a result, Tony had reluctantly forbidden the dog's free access. Now, on good days, he was locked tight in a large kennel. Her late husband was a little paranoid at times, but he'd also known that if Bear was ever stolen, Christian would have been the one who was lost.

Bear appeared out of the brush with a paper bag in his mouth. He trotted up to her, dropping it at her feet. Then he sat very still, looking up at her with his enormous brown eyes, as he'd been taught to do when he'd finished his tracking process. Christian bent down to pick up the bag and then hesitated. Pulling a pair of latex gloves from her pocket, she put them on and lifted the bag to peer inside. Carefully she reached in and pulled out a can of blue spray paint along with a wad of gum wrapped up in a piece of paper. She paused, thinking back. The spray paint on her door, of course! She'd spent a better part of an afternoon sanding off the paint and staining her door, but not before the Richland Police took a sample. She put the paint and gum back into the bag and pulled a baggie out of her other pocket. Opening it, she pulled out a hunk of stew beef and fed the dog his treat.

♊

"So Scott, do you think there's a chance that the same person who painted my door, and left the paint can behind has anything to do with the murders?" she asked her brother later that day. Her anxiety was humming like a bad air conditioner. Christian had called her brother's office several times and wasn't able to reach him until after lunch. In the meantime, she'd dropped the evidence off at the crime lab, just in case. His lecture on exculpatory evidence and the process of discovery had convinced her that she should never hold on to anything any longer than necessary.

"It's a stretch. What have you done about Tabby? Also, now that Mr. Maltos is out of jail, you need to get over to see him again. He's still a suspect until we prove otherwise. I'm guessing that his house is still ripe with answers. I hate to sound critical, but there is no such thing as a Tri-Cities CSI unit. Most of the evidence that they receive is tainted in some way. They do the best they can, but your locals are truly yokels when it comes to crime investigation. However, the photo of the sweater's tag was a good call. My Microsoft hacker buddy did a little investigating for me. He got into Jason and Tabby Smithson's bank accounts. As it turns out, Jason doesn't own a credit card, so we can't track any of his purchases except the ones paid for by check. In the past year, he did not buy an Abercrombie unless it was with cash. However, Miss Smithson did buy one, in September. The strange thing is, she didn't buy it for herself. She bought a men's size large. I matched the purchase date with Jason's birthday. It doesn't fit. However, it does fit with another man in her life. Her brother, Jerry, who is a student at WSU, was born on October first. What do you want a bet the jacket was a birthday gift?"

"Then why would Jason have it in his car?"

"Who knows? The boys are probably friends. Acquaintances at least. Maybe Jerry left it in his car, or in his office. Anyway, it's another good lead. Harry told me that he found a several threads of fabric were found on the edge of Mrs. Maltos's closet door. We need to get it and see if there are any tears in it. It's a long shot and it's not going to convict anyone of murder yet, but it definitely works as evidence. However, we need to prove that whoever was wearing that jacket was wearing it the day of the murder and was the one that fired the gun. Now, little sister, go! Figure out a way to corner that cagey little lass, Tabby. Get her to talk. She knows what happened. I'm sure of it. She's acted too odd not to. Maybe her brother had a crush on Cassie and found out she was dating Jason. Again, motive is jealousy, with mom in the way. Maybe Jason found out about Jerry and he became jealous. We've definitely got a complicated case on our hands. By the way, have you seen your psychic recently?"

"She's not really a psychic. More like a healer and no, I haven't. Why?"

"You need a little encouragement. Your intuition is usually spot on, but you still don't trust it. Go see someone who can help you with that."

"Do I believe what I'm hearing? Are you suggesting that you actually might believe, I repeat, *believe* in my hocus pocus theory? If so, I might faint with shock this very minute." Christian released a satisfied chuckle.

"Yes, okay, I'm the chump. Last year we solved a very strange case of a brother abducting his sister. Do you remember?"

"Yes, as a matter of fact. I believe you found the two of them in Mexico. Wasn't he trying to sell her?"

"He was using his five year old sister to pay off a drug debt. Sick. The parents hired me to find them. Frankly, I didn't have much to go on until my partner suggested that I get in touch with a famous psychic, Shirley Teabo. She lives around here. Anyway, she told me where they'd gone. We had Interpol on them within twenty-four hours. Thank god, because he was set to do the deal the following day, the little jerk."

"So you used a psychic and were successful. I love it and with your advice in mind, I'll call Maria, but not until after Christmas. Next question. When are you guys going to be here?"

"I'm hoping to get out of here early tomorrow, before rush hour. The kids are so excited. Do you still have snow?"

"A bit. Hopefully we'll get a little more before the big day. Can't wait to see you." Christian paused and swallowed hard. "Hey, Scott, you're going to meet my boyfriend."

"Daniel?"

"God, no! His name is Matt."

"That's cool with me. Between you and me, we seemed to go for the cultural experience when it comes to serious relationships."

"He's been amazing through this whole thing. He works alongside me all the way. I hope you guys will like him."

"Of course we'll like him. Don't worry so much. I'll see you soon." With that, Scott hung up. Christian cradled the phone in her hand, imagining her family meeting Matt for the first time. He was so handsome and engaging, but she hoped he was nothing like Tony with regards to power. Unfortunately Tony had been competitive with her big brother from the very beginning. He looked up to Scott when he wasn't around, but once they were in the same vicinity, Tony had played the game of one-upmanship with everything from politics to tennis. Scott was a tolerant man and so he was a good sport about it, but Christian had found Tony's behavior to be infuriating.

She glanced out her window as a cloud passed overhead, creating a slight shadow in the small room. Scott was in luck, she thought with a smile. It looks like it was going to snow.

The rest of the day was a complete wash. The lunchroom and secretaries' corner were overflowing with butter-laden holiday foods and many of her co-workers had already taken off for the long weekend. Daniel had left that morning for the cabin before she had given him his gift. He'd taken a couple of his still-childless brothers and their wives along as well as a secret date whose name he'd refused to reveal. Her partner's divorce had been final the week prior and he was still on an emotional rollercoaster. However, his Catholic guilt had otherwise been assuaged. Her hunch was his latest squeeze was one of the assistant prosecutors, Helen Ramsdell. She was a well-known barfly, but had the body and brains to attract most any man. Word was she'd had more cosmetic surgeries than Michael Jackson. Nonetheless, she was a dead ringer for Courtney Cox, another one of his favorite femme fatales. Fortunately his departure had left her without the complications of a holiday visit from both men in her life.

She cleaned up her desk, changed her phone message to indicate she was out until the following Wednesday and snuck out the back door around four. The raucous holiday reveling taking place down the hall was simply not her cup of tea.

CHAPTER 15

♊

Five days of pure joy. Five days of friendship and family and laughter and love. Christian couldn't remember a happier time in her life, she thought as she got ready to go back to work on Wednesday morning. Her brother and his family had been wonderful guests. Her Christmas dinner of orange-glazed turkey, fresh walnut dressing, a sweet onion tart, various vegetables and a perfect sweet potato soufflé had been the best meal that she'd ever created. Matt was supremely impressed and impressive as well. Her brother and Matt had spent the evening playing cards and talking about baseball while her sister-in-law and Christian had watched Rudolph the Red-Nosed Reindeer with the kids. Her niece and nephew were both at deliciously adorable ages and had been excited by every activity- everything from the Christmas Street of Dreams holiday lights tour on Christmas Eve to the Monday afternoon sledding on Carmichael Hill. On Sunday morning, after Santa's arrival, they'd all gone to the late church service at the Cathedral of Joy, a popular mega-church known for its family-orientated and musically-driven services. The experience lent a truly spiritual quality to the holiday festivities.

Matt had not spent the night during her brother's visit for the obvious reasons, but he was coming tonight, bringing dinner and hopefully staying over. In anticipation, Christian had told her boss she'd be in late on Thursday. She was chomping at the bit for some of Matt's loving and she wasn't going to cut the pleasure short by an early morning call. He was off for a few days and then going back on to night shift, which severely limited their time together. The greatest part of all was his desire for her. She had felt his eyes on her all weekend and his touch and few stolen kisses had drenched her with passion.

By the time she left for work, the road was a sheet of ice. An early morning rain shower had frozen solid and the temperatures remained too low to induce a thaw. Cars were veering all over the road as she slowly crept toward the Juvenile Justice Center. Several small accidents had already occurred and police sirens could be heard in the distance. It was a rare day in hell when Benton County would close their local government offices, an issue that irked probation officer and client alike. As she came off the highway onto Edison Street, she lost control of the car and began to careen into the opposite lane of traffic. To her astonishment and terror, she was headed directly into a red Mustang. Pumping her brakes, Christian tried to maneuver her car away from the unfortunate target, but it was too late. As her car crossed a set of the railroad tracks, she slid into the Mustang's driver's side. Despite minor speed, her car was tossed back by the impact and began to spin in the opposite direction. As it did, she was shocked to see the bars of the railroad crossing begin to come down.

Her car came to a stop with a crossing bar over the front hood, holding the Volkswagen captive. Panicked, she glanced to her left to see the train's location. Still a half a mile away, she breathed a sigh of relief and reached to open her car door. As she did, two faces appeared at the driver's window. A girl wearing sunglasses and a ski hat began knocking on the window and pointing wildly at the train. A young man then moved to the other side of her car and tried to raise the crossing bar as the girl grabbed the handle of her door to pull on it. The door did not release. Instantly Christian realized that it was one of those times when the door was stuck from the outside. She turned off the car and rolled down her window frantically, watching as the train blew its whistle and drew closer, showing no apparent signs of stopping. "Sorry, the door's stuck. It does this all the time. Here, take my keys and open it from the outside. *Hurry!*" Fear gripped her innards, turning them to jelly.

The girl stared at Christian as recognition crossed her face. Then she paused and looked away from her. She gave a hand signal to the man and looked around as though to see if there was anyone else who could help. Then a horrifying thing happened. The girl dropped the car keys on the ground and backed away. At the same time, the young man left the tracks and disappeared. As Christian looked into her rearview mirror, they were in their car, driving away.

The train appeared to be slowing somewhat, while continuously blowing its whistle. Christian was taking no chances. *Thank god I've lost so much weight,* she thought, as she rolled down the window and quickly pulled herself through. She was only fifteen feet away when the train broadsided her car. The sound startled her with its whine of metal and roar of resistant engines. The conductor was doing all that he could to slow the enormous vehicle, but the industrial animal fought against friction, groaning like a wounded dinosaur. The crunching of metal competed with the screeching of brakes and high pitch of breaking glass. Her car was now the size of a large cardboard box squished by a trashmasher.

Her knees buckled as she slumped to the ground near a telephone pole. Slowly she turned her head as a car crawled up from a side street and yelled, "Are you alright?"

A couple quickly pulled their blue Ford to the side of the road and the man jumped out. He was lanky and spry, around the age of twenty-five. Christian gratefully allowed him to escort her to his car. She climbed in the back, shaking badly as his companion turned to her and said, "That was a close call. I'm dialing 911."

"I was scared more than anything else. Did you see the car that I hit first?"

An older woman looked at the man and shook her head. "No, but we just came around the corner up there." She pointed behind her. "I wasn't really paying attention to the train."

"Yeah, she's thinkin' about the kid. Ain't got nothin' else on her mind." The young man gave a grin, displaying a jumble of disintegrating teeth.

The woman reached out and gave the man a sharp slap on the arm. "He's talking about my son, Tommy. He's locked up in the kids' jail up the street for a while." Christian shuddered. What were the chances?

Smiling, Christian put out her hand to the woman. "Thank you so much for stopping. That was really scary. I think I probably need to go talk to the police now. They'll be here any minute."

Christian slowly walked toward the hunk of crushed junk that had been her only car. She didn't want to meet Mrs. Calander, or whatever her name was at a time like this. From her records, Tommy had been living with his Dad. Mom lived in Spokane. Obviously she'd made the trip to see her boy in his incarcerated state. There were no visiting hours at eight in the morning, but she probably didn't know any better, assuming that she was from out of town. Even bad boys have mothers who care, she thought, as the first police car pulled up.

Upon hitting her vehicle, the train had pushed her car another ten feet before finally coming to a stop. Her Beetle was finished, but she really didn't care about the car. It was old and less than reliable. She'd wanted to get a SUV Hybrid for a long time. She was more astounded by the first couple's failure to help her. The brief flash of the girl's face had registered in her mind, but so fleetingly it had not materialized into identifying memory. Was the familiar girl's reaction out of fear or was it a purposeful act of abandonment? Adrenaline was a powerful chemical, she thought, as she gingerly stepped toward the police car, skirting the rubble and chunks of broken glass.

After she'd given the two officers her version of the accident and they'd called a tow truck, Christian accepted a ride to work from Officer Fallen. He was an old friend of Stella's and was therefore eager to find the other accident victims, especially after she'd explained their urgent departure.

"It's like they knew you," Fallen scratched his sparse beard that looked like it belonged on an ailing goat. Rick Fallen was a bulky weightlifter type with a shaved head and a penance for blondes. Stella had set up a fair number of the office staff on dates with him, only to discover that he spent most of the time bragging about his weightlifting records and offering a constant stream of sexual innuendos. Now his reputation preceded him and no woman with a brain would get close. Christian was grateful that she was a brunette as she climbed out of the car, thanking him for his help.

"Hey, you got any single girlfriends? I prefer blondes, well-built blondes, if you get my drift." Rick gave her a wolf-like grin. He was an animal all around, she decided.

"No, Rick, no one that I can think of. Have a good holiday."

"I plan on it. What are you doing for New Years? A bunch of us are going to The Pub. Free tequila shots for the first fifty people to arrive all night!"

"Tequila's not really my drink, but thanks anyway. I've got plans of my own."

Rick's face turned sour. "I hear you're dating Matt Hiles. What's a juicy chick like you doing dating that detention dude. Ain't he a bit beneath you?" He narrowed his eyes, awaiting a proverbial slap in the face.

"Take it easy." Sarcasm oozed as she turned and stomped off, but she was determined not to respond in any way that would feed his ego. What a jerk, she thought, as she stepped into her office and threw off her coat in a gesture of rage. I should have Matt kick his ass. She laughed aloud at her mind's commentary. Really!

She looked up to see her friend, Stephen, standing in her doorway. "I'd like to find out why you're laughing. I saw your car a couple of minutes ago. It looks toasted."

"Yep. Looks like I'm finally going to have to buy that hybrid that I've been drooling over."

"Now that's a good reason to laugh. Are you all in one piece? What happened out there?"

She motioned for Stephen to come in. "Sit down. It's pretty weird, let me tell you."

By the time that she'd finished explaining what had happened, Stephen was pacing the office, though his bulky frame didn't have far to go before he'd end up wedged between the desks. "Damn, I need a smoke after that. That sucks, mamma. I mean, what kind of person just leaves you there to get hit by a train. After that story, I definitely need a smoke!"

Christian grinned roguishly. "Do you want to do me a favor?"

"Sure, whatever," he replied, fishing in his pocket for a cigarette. "I'm going to have to go outside for this, but go on."

"I've got a list of all of the Mustang owners in the area and I've already narrowed it down to the four red ones in town. I think you and I need to go on a little witch hunt, as soon as this ice melts."

Stephen raised his hand and waited as she raised her open palm to his. Slapping her hand, he added, "I'm with you, mamma. I got a couple of kids that I need to see on the way."

By noon the ice had melted and the bulk of her messages and emails had been answered. She'd learned that Lilly had just found out she was pregnant, and that Tommy Calander was all about marrying Lilly and cleaning up his life. The message was both disappointing and dismally sad. The boy had been sentenced to two years in a juvenile prison facility for his role in a drive-by shooting. He was to be transported to the institution the following week. There was no way that he was going to be of any help to Lilly and a baby. Tommy couldn't care for himself much less a family. And so the cycle goes on, Christian thought as she wrote up a probation violation on a Richland High track star who insisted on smoking marijuana during the off season.

She picked up the phone and dialed Stephen's extension. "You ready, Steve?"

"Yes. By the way, how in hell, after a car accident, did you recognize a Mustang? I can understand a red car, but man, for a mamma, you are *good!*" Christian loved Stephen's banter and replied with her form of street talk.

"Dude, this mamma don't mess around! So let's take your car, for two reasons: I want to bring my dog and I don't want Tabby Smithson to see that we're county if she looks out the window."

Stephen answered, "You're a piece a work. Now I know why Daniel is always a bit confounded."

"Hey. I keep life interesting."

A couple of minutes later they were on the road. The ice had melted gone and the sun was blinding in a robin's egg sky. They drove directly to her house where they picked up a very happy and eager Bear. Christian had kept a piece of the Abercrombie sweater for her own investigation and retrieved the baggie and some supplies from her entry hall bureau as well as Bear's leash.

"Hey, boy," she said. "We've got some work to do."

Though Christian hadn't actually been to the Smithson home, she knew the street and basic location. They headed down the highway as Christian gave Stephen the directions. Bear had taken an immediate liking to the big man and had his head resting on Stephen's shoulder most of the way.

"Man, this dog's got bad breath. Give him a mint, will ya?" Stephen complained good-naturedly. Christian laughed. He was a fun guy to hang out with. She needed to team up with him more often.

Christian dropped the bomb as they made their way into the Canyon Estates development. "Hey, after we stop at Smithson's, let's stop by the Maltos house. I need to see Jim."

Stephen took his right hand off the steering wheel and pointed his finger at her "You ain't getting' me into the house, girl. I'm in no mood to check out a crime scene, and a bloody one at that. Jeez, it's still Christmas time, remember?"

"Don't be such a scaredy-cat. If you want to wait in the car, be my guest." She playfully replied, watching Stephen from the corner of her eye. With a huff, he whipped the wheel and pulled up to the Maltos driveway.

"Okay. Let's do this first and get it out of the way," he grumbled.

Mr. Maltos's car was parked out front. It looked like it hadn't been moved in a while. Withered maple leaves dotted the front hood and roof. Piles of leaves had gathered around the front porch and garbage containers were stacked along the front walk. Several flower pots had tipped over, spilling out dead stalks of marigolds and geraniums, sad reminders that a woman no longer lived here.

They got out and walked up to the door. Christian had put a leash on Bear and had him in a tight grip. She took a deep breath and knocked. The deep bark of a big dog caused her to jump. Stephen looked significantly paler than usual, his tawny Hawaiian complexion now a sickly green. "Great. A greeting attack dog," he complained.

Slowly Mr. Maltos opened the door, holding the collar of a large German Shepherd. The dog issued a low growl, but when Jim saw Christian, he responded with his own warning. "Stop, boy, it's alright. She's a friend," he said, a broad smile crossing his face.

"Hello, Mr. Maltos," she cried as Bear gave a happy whine. He was a sucker for other dogs. "I was hoping to talk to you for a few minutes and perhaps use my dog to do a little work for us."

"Of course, but I'd better put Chance away first. He's about ready to pull my arm off. My new guard dog was a Christmas present from my son. It'll just be a minute."

He shut the door. Christian turned to Stephen and said, "The best thing that can happen now is if you will use your charming personality to keep Mr. Maltos busy. I need to get this dog into their bedroom for awhile and then downstairs to Cassie's room."

Stephen nodded. "I don't have to go in the bedroom then?"

"No. You accept his offer of coffee. Sit down with him and keep him relaxed. His step-son is in the military. Ask about him."

Mr. Maltos opened the door a few minutes later and welcomed them in. The home was in complete disarray. There were no signs of Christmas and all of the blinds were closed. Old newspapers were piled in a corner of the hallway and several plastic bags of garbage were lined up inside the front door."

"Sorry about the mess," Jim mumbled sheepishly. "I haven't really had the energy to do much."

They followed him in and immediately Christian introduced Stephen and Bear. Then she offered Jim a hug. "How are you?" she asked after a long minute. He pulled away and wiped the tears from his face.

"Not good. Ever since I was released, it's like I don't know what to do with myself. My step-son, Charlie, was home for a couple of weeks. You might have seen him at the funeral in his uniform." A momentary mark of pride crossed the man's face. "He couldn't stay long, but he was still here when I got out. He got the cleaners in here, but you couldn't tell now. At least I've got the dog to keep me company. He's a former police dog and very protective."

Bear had wandered over to the door leading to the garage and was sniffing as a low growl could be heard from the other side.

"That's a good thing, to have a dog. He'll be good company. Jim, I have a favor to ask. I like to put my dog to work, if that's okay with you. Stephen, here, is good company. I don't need much time."

"Sure thing. Would you like a cup of coffee?" Mr. Maltos asked, looking in Steve's direction. The man was unshaven and had lost considerable weight.

"Sure. I'd love a cup," Stephen replied. He glanced at Christian and added, "Did I hear your son is in the Air Force?"

With that, Christian took Bear by the collar and said, "See you in a couple of minutes." She wandered down the hall toward the master bedroom. The door was slightly open and the smell of blood was gone, replaced by an equally strong chemical smell. She pushed open the bedroom door and pulled the baggie from her backpack. Bending down to Bear, she opened the bag and put it up to the dog's nose. Immediately Bear reacted. He pulled back and began to sniff the floor around the bed. As he did, Christian scanned the room, taking into account any changes. The bed was properly made with a dark brown comforter that clearly didn't match the pastel flowered curtains. The original comforter had gone into the evidence box. She also guessed that Mr. Maltos wasn't sleeping in here anymore, based on the tidiness of the room. It was almost shrine-like, she thought, as she sat down on the bed and closed her eyes.

Maria had told her from a recent phone conversation that if she could return to the crime scene and allow herself to go into a trance-like state (Maria had referred to it as 'the state of grace'), she might have some burst of intuition and gain some answers. Christian knew how to meditate, so clearing her mind was a fairly easy process, though she was a little out of practice.

She leaned back against the headboard and took several deep and sustained breaths. She could smell a pungent combination of cleaning fluid and laundry detergent. Her nose was sharp, more often than not to her dismay, but as she relaxed, new subtle scents became apparent. Beyond the sharp acidic clean were the faint and lingering woman's perfume and the musty smell of sweat. She thought about Mr. and Mrs. Maltos making love in this bed for how many years. Sue had once told her friend that they'd been married almost ten years before they'd adopted Cassie. How did people make love year after year and not get bored, she wondered briefly. Would she ever get bored with Matt? He had a beautiful body, but of course that could change. His bedroom voice gave her goose bumps in the right places and his approach to sex was unique in that it was all about her. How many guys were like that? No, she decided. She would not get bored.

Don't be ridiculous. Get back to work, she chided herself. As Bear continued his sniffing, she began a rhythmic breathing exercise. Forcing out her delightful sexy man fantasy, Christian imagined instead a big blue balloon that began to expand until her mind was full of emptiness. The thoughts now tried to race in through the little whole at the bottom, but she envisioned closing it up with a tight knot. Now thoughts floated around, but not inside the center of her mind balloon. She concentrated on her breathing, finding stillness in the breath. Eventually Christian disengaged completely and went into a trance.

Slowly Mrs. Maltos appeared in her mind's eye. The woman's face was creased with anger. Next Cassie's image appeared, looking very afraid. Then an explosion, blood and screaming. The vision was fast, like a sped-up movie and ended with one more face, a face tortured by terror and disbelief.

Then her eyes popped open and she gripped the edge of the comforter. Her skin had become clammy. Her breathing was constricted and her heart began to race. Death had been there, lurking in the background like the shadow that he was. She didn't want to see any more. It felt as though she was exploring unforgiving territory. Her greatest fear, one that was realistic based on her own mother's history, was that she would someday gain the ability to see tragedy before it occurred. Already she had a sense of it, but was unable to stop impending horrors from occurring. Her mother had been a seer, though few people knew of her skills. Christian had only recently learned of her mother's gift from her aunt, who'd waited until she was a young adult before she told her the truth.

It had been at Christmas in 2001, after the terrible disaster of 9/11. The family had been discussing the incident and several subtle comments by older family members were said that had confused Christian. When one of the grandchildren raced in with a deck of tarot cards, her aunt had turned a deathly pale and had yanked the cards from five year old Lucy's hands. Her reaction was so unexpected that she knew this was something more than a child snooping where she didn't belong. Later she'd cornered her aunt and forced her to explain. Christian soon learned that the cards had belonged to Denise, Christian's mother, and apparently had been hidden in a hat box under Aunt Fran's bed where they'd been held in safe keeping for years. Finally Aunt Fran, through long-suppressed tears, shared the secret of how her mother had foretold her own death, but without the details. Denise had simply told her younger sister that she would not live to see her youngest daughter's fifth birthday.

She'd fought her entire life to avoid any type of connection to her mother's psychic past, but it was not to be. Despite her resistance, Death had decided to be her companion from time to time, but if nothing else, she was determine to master what she could from him.

She closed her eyes and took another deep breath, disturbed by the revelation in her mind. Nonetheless, she had to face it: the last fleeting image was undeniably the face of someone whom she'd seen before and the same girl that morning at the railroad tracks. Tabby Smithson

She shook her head, now trying to convince herself that the vision was only a product of her imagination. She knew enough about psychology to know that when your mind is on something specific, it conjures images accordingly. Perhaps the experiment was bogus. Just because she was a bit sweaty didn't mean that her intuition was correct. Tabby was a nice girl, well-liked and by most accounts, pious in nature. As she discarded the information, something unexpected occurred. Bear began to paw frantically at the base of the maple dresser.

He caught a few of the Berber fibers in his nails. "Stop, Bear. Let me look." Christian pulled a small flashlight from her pocket and got on her hands and knees to get a better view. She could see something shiny under the dresser. Slipping her hand in her coat pocket, she found one of her tools. A long pair of tweezers came in handy at times like this. Excitement raced through her veins as she struggled to dislodge the tiny object. This could be it, she thought, though in all likelihood she could be nose-diving for an old safety pin. Still, Bear was worked up, panting softly and moaning like he'd found a rabbit. His fervor was contagious as he leaned over her, trying to get a better look. A long string of drool dropped from his open mouth and hit Christian on the side of the face.

"*Bear!*" she cried, "Get back a bit. I don't want a dog shower, okay?" He looked her with a slight disdain and sat down on his haunches with a 'humphhh'. "Good boy." she handed him another bone.

Her heart was racing now as she felt the tweezers meet their prey. Then she paused. She needed to call Harry at the crime lab, or Detective Jensen. This could be a piece of evidence that could turn the case. She reached into her pocket and pulled out her cell phone. She scanned for the number. At her brother's request, the detective had given her his private cell number.

The phone rang several times and finally Jensen picked up. "Mark here. What can I do for you?"

"This is Christian Vargas. Get over to the Maltos house a.s.a.p. I think I've found something." She heard a loud sigh.

"I wish you would stop your private investigating games. We've scoured that house from top to bottom. There's nothing left."

"Please come over." She tried to keep her voice neutral.

"Okay, okay. I'll be over in a few. Just don't get any bright ideas. I'll collect whatever you *think* you found."

Christian flipped the phone closed and rocked back on her heels. Detectives could be such arrogant asses, she thought. Bear was sitting on his haunches, staring intently at his master.

"Sorry, boy," she said, rubbing his head.

She left the room and paused at the stairway, listening briefly to Jim and Stephen's dueling repartee. Jim was actually laughing over a story about Stephen's short stint in the army. The probation officer had apparently gotten caught with his pants down, literally, while screwing his commander's daughter in a parked helicopter. That, among other ridiculous situations, had gotten him an honorable discharge. Though general consensus believed that Stephen's stories were pulverized accounts of reality, he was forgiven. The guy was a natural comic and kept his audience well entertained.

She tiptoed down the stairs with Bear in tow, avoiding any interruption. Turning to go into Cassie's bedroom, she noticed something she hadn't seen during her last visit. A group of pictures on the wall near her room displayed several of the girl's friends. She paused to look a picture showing a group of kids on a beach.

Three girls had their arms around one another while six boys stood behind them in a semi-circle. The girls were Cassie, Tabby and another girl. The boys were unfamiliar to her. All of them were wearing tee-shirts which read, "Camp Camelot".

She took the picture off the wall and tucked it under her arm. Then she stepped into Cassie's room and glanced around. Nothing was out of place except one thing. The stack of papers that she'd originally found on the desk were gone. Leaning down, she checked under the bed. The shoes that she'd surreptitiously placed under it were missing. She moved to the dresser and opened the top drawer. The small piece of paper that she'd placed on top of Cassie's underwear was gone and the drawer had obviously been rifled through. She opened the other drawers and found the same thing. Someone had been in her room and she doubted it was Jim.

After pausing to check the closet and nightstand, she began to watch Bear. He had been sniffing his way around the room. He pushed the bedroom door closed with his nose. Behind the door on a hook was a girl's bomber-style jacket that hadn't been there before. Bear jumped up and put his nose to the jacket, smelling it intently. Then he yanked the jacket off the hook with his teeth and dropped it at his master's feet.

"Good boy," she praised Bear. Slipping on gloves, she searched the pockets of the jacket. The outer pockets were empty, but the inner pocket held a silver necklace with a small, heart-shaped charm. On the back of the charm, there was an engraved message: *To my favorite G.G., Love, J.J.* She slipped the necklace into her backpack and left the room. When she reached the top of the stairs, the doorbell rang.

Quickly she stepped into the kitchen and said, "I'll get it, Jim. It's Detective Jensen. I think I've found something, so I called him to come over." Jim started to stand, but Stephen reached out and touched his arm.

"Sir, if you don't mind, I think you'd be better off letting them handle this," Stephen said softly. Jim nodded as a look of relief passed over his worn face. He'd obviously had enough.

Jensen was a tall, thin man with a terrible comb-over. His hair had been tousled by the wind and one long strand hung over his left ear, nearly reaching his shoulder. Christian did her best not to laugh.

"Whacha got, Vargas?" Cops always called one another by their last name when working a job.

"Follow me. My dog's found something." Bear was watching the detective carefully, as though not entirely convinced that the guy had a reason to be there. She led him into the bedroom and pointed at the floor. "Under there. Here, let's move the dresser out."

They each took a side and moved the piece of furniture to the side. There on the floor was a drop earring made from beads that looked like something a young woman would wear. Detective Jensen bent down to pick it up, but before he could touch it, Christian said, "Here, some latex gloves." Jensen looked irritated as he snatched the gloves from her and put them on.

He picked up the earring and together they gazed at it. It was made from wooden beads and wire and the light colored wood was stained with a dark red color.

"I do believe this is blood," he said. "You know, the mom's head was blown to bits. She might have been wearing earrings before he shot her."

"He?" Christian felt a shiver run down her spine. The detective was insinuating that a suspect had been identified.

"We're still working the case, but the suspect is believed to be male." Jensen paused, his stoop more pronounced as he bent to pat Bear. "I can't say any more. Good work, dog."

"His name is Bear. He worked on the Delgado case in 2004, remember?"

Christian looked Jensen in the eye. He was a nerd at best and she wasn't the least bit intimidated by him.

"Oh yeah. Thought he looked familiar. Okay, so we'll get this to the lab, test it for human blood and prints."

"I think we need a search warrant, Mark."

"For what?"

"For Tabby Smithson's house. I have a feeling that she's involved, seriously involved."

"And what makes you think we'll find anything?"

"We might find a matching earring for starters. And then there's the stuff in Cassie's room that's gone missing. She was here the first time I came over at Jim's request." she added when Jensen's face showed disbelief. "She might have a house key. Who knows?"

"No, I let her come in." They both turned to see Jim standing in the doorway.

"She said that Cassie had borrowed some of her clothes. I've known Tabby since she was four years old. There's no way that girl would hurt my family. You guys got it wrong."

Christian was surprised to see Mr. Maltos so angry. She tried to sooth him by saying, "Jim, we're not accusing anyone, but she might know more than she's told us. By the way, who are these kids in this picture?"

Jim was clearly disgruntled as he walked over to her and took the photograph from her. He pointed to Cassie and Tabby. "Of course you know these girls," he murmured. Infinite sadness seemed to ooze from his pores as he continued. "This girl is Shelly Nunamaker. She lives next door to Tabby. The three girls were friends throughout their childhoods. The boys, let's see. That's Toby Jones, Joey Segado, Jess Thompson, and Jerry Smithson, Tabby's older brother. Then of course, Jason, our Youth Pastor from church. Why?"

Christian gently took the picture from him and looked again. Jason was wearing a baseball cap, which hid his eyes. She hadn't noticed him before.

"Tell me about Shelly."

"She's a nice girl. She dated Tabby's brother for a while. I'd heard they were engaged at one point. If I remember right, they broke it off sometime last summer. Jerry's a bit of a troublemaker. He was arrested a few times in college. If you want my opinion, his parents spoil him rotten. They gave him a brand new car for his graduation. A sports car!"

Christian's breath stilled. "Jim, what kind of car does Jerry drive?"

"You know, I'm not sure. It was red and sexy, as Cassie used to say. I couldn't tell you what he drives now. He's been up at WSU for the past couple of years." Just then the phone rang. "If you'll excuse me." Jim turned to retrieve the phone. Christian wondered if the bedroom phone had obviously been confiscated for evidence.

As they started to follow Jim from the room, Bear trotted over to Christian and raised his paw. He gave a low whine."

"What is it, boy? No more bones, Bear."

He gave another high-pitched whine and tilted his head back and forth. Jumping up and placing his paws on her shoulders, he looked quizzically at her and whined again. Then he walked over to the sliding glass door that led onto a balcony and began to scratch it furiously. Christian looked at Jensen and said, "This is the way he acted when my husband died. He would whine and paw at me until I let him into the garage. Then he would go to my husband's canoe and climb into it. He would sit in the boat for hours. The sound he's making…it's that same sound."

"Dogs have different sounds?" The detective shook his head. "Whatever. We've already searched the balcony, but let's see what he's trying to tell us."

They opened the door and stepped out onto a small wooden balcony that faced east. The dog pushed past Jensen and headed to a corner where he dragged out an empty flower pot. He put his nose deep into the pot and lifted out a bag with his teeth. Christian walked over and took it from him. "Back, Bear," she ordered, staring down into the bag as the blood drained from her face.

The next few hours were surreal. Jensen took the bagged gun from her and after a quick glance, identified it as a 9 MM handgun. Next he called headquarters and requested back- up. He wasted no time in telling her that though his men had searched the balcony, it was possible that they didn't see the pot, which was tucked under a stack of plastic chairs and fairly well concealed. A gun found at the crime scene was a huge coupe for the police department and Christian had no doubt that Jensen would take the credit.

Telling Jim that a gun had been found was a chilling experience. The man's response was to collapse onto the living room couch and begin to cry. It didn't bode well for his innocence, especially when he blabbered that it was his gun, but that he'd forgotten all about it. Since his previous statement had been that he didn't own a gun, the latest disclosure could result in his arrest again, though Christian wasn't completely sure of the basis for that. Scott later explained that the discovery of the weapon and Jim's omission of ownership could be construed as a confession.

After returning home, she pulled an old whiteboard from her garage and took it into the living room. It had suddenly occurred to her that her favorite television program, *Law and Order*, might have taught her a few tricks of the trade.

CHAPTER 16

♊

Christian's mind was boggled. There were too many pieces and too many scenarios to make sense anymore. It seemed like everything was a half-truth or a lie and she was sick of surprises. Their team was scrambling for answers and, as a result of Jim's second arrest, her guilt for Bear's discovery was beginning to outwit her logic. Galvanized into action, Christian had decided that the only thing that would give her some measure of equilibrium was the gigantic white board that now sat on her window ledge. The board was nearly as large as the picture window and on it, she'd drawn three distinct columns. The countless crime dramas that she'd seen on television didn't hold a candle, she assured herself as she grabbed the green marker and looked down at her notes.

Matt was sitting on the couch, half watching football and half listening to his woman. A bowl of popcorn and an open Heferweisen along with a drooling dog completed his picture. New Year's Day was perfect- sunny, but cold and definitely conducive to snuggling and couch-surfing. She and Matt had already made love three times that day and both of them agreed it was time to take a break. Most new love affairs often had the high sex element, but it had never been like this with Tony. He was far too regimented and hated to waste too much time. Pleasure was definitely on her late husband's priority list of life, but not several times a day.

"Chrissie, you're struggling. I think we should get out. Let's take a hike!"

Matt stood up and pulled her into his arms.

She nodded. "You're right. I have to stop think about this for awhile. "I'll get my coat."

♊

New Year's Day brought cerulean skies to the Tri-Cities. From where they stood on the top of Badger Mountain, Christian and Matt could see the jagged tips of Blue Mountains, to the east nearly one hundred miles away, still frosted with snow. Beyond them, to the west, there were rolling crests of land, not hills, nor mountains, but long camel humps of sand-the remnants of an ancient flood. Below them, the narrow Yakima River snaked into the shimmering Columbia, which flowed open and wide. Pockets of islands, popular as picnic grounds and bird sanctuaries, dotted the deep blue waters. On the far side of the magnificent river was the city called Pasco, originally named for the Pacific Rail and Steamship Company, a line that had first brought industry to the desert community. Bike paths and elegant homes, some the size of hotels, utilized the prime real estate there while on the Kennewick side, parks, camp grounds and marinas gave the populace a reason to enjoy the great outdoors.

After their morning romps, Matt had hunkered down for nearly three hours, finishing a term paper for his Psychology and Research class. The man had a quick brain and a strong ability to conceptualize, but to her surprise, he struggled with the charts and graphs required for the last assignment's completion. She'd been delightfully surprised, too, by his decision to invite her to New Orleans the following month. In addition, he'd planned a special treat which after much cajoling and begging from Christian, he'd admitted was a Caribbean sailing cruise. After working on a private sailing vessel during the summer after high school, he'd remained close friends with the mega-yacht's owner who, in turn, had offered Matt a week of sailing as a graduation present.

"So I'm not sure I can get on a sailboat. I have some bad memories." Instantly she swapped her explanation for silence.

"I know, Christian, but you won't be sailing in the open seas, like off the Oregon coast. This is inland and very safe. We can hug the shore and stay in shallower waters. Furthermore, you can go naked it's so warm out there."

She blushed. "I don't know about that. Let me think about it. It's going to take a shot of vodka just to get me onboard, I'm sure. So how did you get into the cruise business?" They come to the top of the mountain and were breathing hard.

He smiled broadly, his perfectly-straight teeth a glacial white against his smooth coffee-colored skin. "I was a cabin boy. I served some coffee and made some cream. Eventually I made enough to pay my way up here. Yeah, see, some of the white folks down south still think it's our duty to wait on them. But it wasn't so bad. I learned the valuable skill of swallowing my pride early in life. My mother's maiden name was White and for years, whenever we'd go out to eat, she'd pause at the front door of our local diner and tell us, 'When I was a little kid, I was always so confused. There was a sign above the door, right here,' and she'd point to the old nail holes, and then say, 'It read: for Whites only. You can imagine my frustration when my momma took me through the back door instead.' She told us things like that so that we'd remember our second-class roots, I guess." Matt threw back his head and laughed at the sun.

"You don't mind your history?" she asked cautiously.

"Mind? What can I do about it now? Wear it like some of my brothers, a noose and a badge at the same time? No, girlfriend. I just a soon leave the past where it belongs-behind me." He smiled again and took her hand, as natural as opening a door and guided her to a bench nearby. They were alone and the only sound to be heard was the quiet whistle of the wind through the power lines. His hand was warm and dry and hers felt very small. She shivered slightly as the cool air moved through her hair. She had never felt this safe with a man. Life felt right with Matt, easy and without expectation. Though at times, she still had the urge to flee. He was a lot of man: smart, strong, kind and sensuous with a self-effacing nature that was very attractive. As she spent time with Matt that Tony had been somewhat the opposite. Hard-driven, compulsive and highly energetic, sometimes Tony had worn her out with his obsessions. Saturdays had been dedicated to marathon preps, Excel spreadsheets and yard work. No laziness was allowed during their marriage. By Tony's standards, even their sex life required measuring- how long, how good, how extreme. It was his lack of spontaneity that Christian had found the most disappointing. Performance sex was not her idea of eroticism. If she were honest to Tony's ghost, he had taken something from her. With all of his desire for organization and directed living, she'd forgotten how to be quiet inside. Now, with Matt, she felt a sense of peace. As they sat, in silence, it seemed that they'd entered a state of communion where talk was not required.

Slowly she turned to him, staring into his liquid brown eyes. "Thanks, Matt, for today. I've really enjoyed it."

Matt squeezed her hand. "I think you might be a glutton for punishment, but a darn good tutor nonetheless." Leaning forward, he whispered, "And did I mention you're one tempting vision?" Before she could answer, his soft, encompassing lips melted against her mouth while his tongue hungrily probed for hers. He wrapped his arms around her and she leaned into him, pressing her chest against his.

He held on to her for a long moment before pulling away. Reaching down, he gently moved a piece of her hair from her cheek. "You need to know, I think you're amazing, what you did for Mr. Maltos. Your courage and tenacity is something to be admired." Pausing, he took her other hand in his. "I hope this is the real thing for us, Christian."

She felt a wave of sudden shyness and paused to look down at their interlocked hands. "Thanks, Matt. And you can call me Chrissie. Christian has always sounded so…I don't know, religious, to me."

"I will if you want me to, but your name is an elegant name, and I think it fits you just fine."

She smiled and leaned in to kiss him again. As she did, there was the distinct sound of rattlesnake's warning. Like a shaking rain stick, the explosive sizzling buzz was unmistakable. She looked around and then said, "He's behind you about two feet. Stay here and don't move until I tell you to." Christian stood up and slowly stepped in a wide circle away from where Matt was sitting. She didn't take her eyes off the snake. Brown and mottled in color, it was about five feet long with a girth nearly as thick as an irrigation pipe. She hadn't recalled seeing such a large snake in the Tri-Cities. Besides, it was too late in the year for the things. She continued her pace until she was completely opposite to where she'd been sitting, though only a few yards from the snake. By then, the reptile had followed her movements and was slithering toward her. She said quietly, "Now move, Matt. Go quickly out toward that pile of rock, but be careful. There may be another one over there." Matt's face had turned ashen. He looked at her with bulging eyes and slid down the bench, quickly sprinting away. Christian now stood completely still as the snake rose up and began to bob its head in her direction. A black tongue darted in and out of its mouth. She was safe enough, unless the creature decided to move forward. She knew that snakes were deceptive in their speed and could lunge up to three feet in direct relation to their size. She figured this one would have no problem biting her if he so chose. She carefully reached into her coat pocket and pulled out a small dart gun that she carried just for this purpose. It was spring-loaded and ready to use, but her desire was not to kill the snake. She slowly lifted her hand and pointed the gun, but the snake suddenly appeared to grow lethargic. Its bulbous head teetered to and fro and then eventually dropped to the ground. In seconds, the snake had disappeared behind a boulder.

Christian nodded. "Good boy. Go back to your snake den." She walked backwards a few steps and then caught up to Matt. "Ok, it's all good," she chirped. "However, we should get out of here before he decides to wake up again."

As they trudged back down the path, Matt finally spoke. "What the heck did you just do?"

"This time of year, especially this late in the year, that guy should be in their dens, hibernating. Obviously that was one confused snake. He was out, probably to catch a few more rays before winter truly hits. Remember, though they're cold-blooded, they love to sun, just like the rest of us."

"Hey, I ain't cold-blooded!" Matt tried to joke, but his laugh had a tinge of hysteria to it.

"You, my darling, are as hot-blooded as they come." Christian smiled and took his hand, giving it a squeeze.

"But really, why aren't you scared?"

"It's a long and strange story. Let's just say I have this snake thing going on. I look at them long enough and they leave me alone. Like dogs. Don't you think it's odd that snakes rarely bite dogs, though our area has plenty of hunting dogs running into rattlers all the time? It's a species thing, I think."

"So they see you as their bitch?" Matt continued the levity as he began to relax. Christian grinned and squeezed his hand again. "More like a snake goddess like Shiva, the goddess of life, death and rebirth...all that good stuff."

Matt gave a shiver and smiled weakly. "I've seen a few coral snakes in my life and well, just the sight of them nearly gave me a heart attack. So, I'll vouch for that...the rebirth part anyway."

♊

Christian passed the crowds of people milling around in the courtroom's antechambers and walked through the double doors into courtroom C. Inside Scott and Dallas Chillen were arguing about something; she could see the grim line of determination on Scott's face as he pointed his index finger at Dallas. Dallas looked positively intimidated. With simian eyes bulging, his receding chin had disappeared into his collar to the point where he looked like a bullfrog. She waited at the end of the aisle, watching as their conversation turned heated. Finally she could hear Scott say, "If that happens, I'll appeal this faster than you can spit."

Scott spun on his heel and headed in her direction, his face was marked with fury. When he saw her, he gestured her to him and whispered, "That ass is questioning the DNA evidence from Jason Roads."

"Why?" Christian's stomach dropped at the news.

"There are a growing number of litigators who are starting the question the validity of DNA from sources other than the FBI national crime base," he hissed. "It's primarily a civil liberties issue. Jason's defense attorney is arguing that using his DNA violates his privacy rights because he'd originally submitted it to prove his innocence on that indecent liberties charge and he was never found guilty of that crime."

"Because the girl recanted?"

"Yes and has failed to change her story. I've called her several times and she continues to refuse to talk to me."

"Jason was a minor at the time. Therefore the submission of his DNA could be considered to have been given under duress. There is a big argument going on because though many crimes have been solved this way, there is a question as to the validity of using the DNA of suspects never actually convicted of a crime."

"What about his indecent liberties charge?"

"Again, he was a minor. Besides we can't use his priors. It's not allowed. I was banking on the DNA."

"What about fingerprints on the gun?"

"Actually, no. The gun had been wiped clean, but since it is registered to Jim Maltos, he was brought in again this morning."

Christian's knees buckled. They had solved the crime, hadn't they?

"Sorry, Christian," Scott said, grabbing her elbow to steady her. "At this point, it's going to be nearly impossible to prove Jim's innocence without something else. His friend's testimony isn't going to do it. Her timeframe isn't clean enough. The receipt from the restaurant was stamped at 1:10pm. If he had wanted to go out to eat and then kill his family, time would have allowed him to do so. Dallas will use that slant, despite my legal tactics. Right now he doesn't know about the receipt, but he will soon enough."

Christian fought to keep from screaming. They had it all stitched up. It was done, or so she thought.

"Look, there's nothing you can at this point. I've asked for a continuance. I'll talk to the judge. We'll see if we can't get this straightened out."

"There must be something we can do," she cried. Her fear for Mr. Maltos was only tender to the fire of anger that grew inside her. "I'm going to find that Tabby, the one who left me on the railroad tracks. She knows something. We need to get her in to interview her."

Scott shook his head. "Don't intimidate anyone. We are riding a fine line. At some point, someone will screw up. Somebody will say something that will implicate someone else."

"What about Tabby's brother? He drives the Mustang." Christian's voice was shrill as she gripped her brother's arm.

"Listen to me, Chrissie. Go out tonight and have some fun. Didn't you tell me your girlfriends were getting together for their monthly wine group? Put this out of your mind for a few hours. Something will come up. Just the fact that you found that fabric sample and there's a match. Who knows. Maybe Mrs. Maltos and Jason were having an affair."

♊

Christian didn't move from her chair, though the knock grew louder. She recognized her partner's insistent pounding from the numerous times that they'd gone out to homes on field visits. She released a sigh and called out, "Coming." Her voice was reed thin. Her night out with the girls had turned into a fiasco. Sitting in an alcohol-induced daze, she shuddered with embarrassment. Daniel had just happened to stop by Stella's house to talk to her husband and her girlfriends had insisted that he drive her home. She didn't remember much else, except that he had nearly had to carry her into the house and how she got into bed, she had no idea.

Though Christian hadn't showered yet and was still wearing her Dalmatian print bathrobe, she'd washed up and run a comb through her hair. Feeling somewhat presentable, she stood up and went to the door. Opening it, she saw Daniel standing there, a big grin on his face. He carried a Starbucks traveler tray in one hand and a large bunch of Stargazer Lilies in the other.

"Wow, look at you!"

Christian shot him a discouraging frown.

"No, I'm serious. You look great in the morning. Here!" He shoved the bouquet toward her. "For my *Law and Order* babe!"

"These are my favorite! How did you know?"

"I pay attention." He grabbed her for a hug. At first Christian collapsed into him and then pulled back with a start. The situation felt ripe with sexual intonation.

"Thanks. I'll put them in water. Sit down. Do you want me to reheat the coffees?" He looked at her strangely, his face marked by an edgy hope. She knew now that he had feelings for her and had for some time. She needed to be clear with him. Her heart was with Matt now.

She took the Starbucks traveler from the entry table where he'd placed it and walked into the kitchen, leaving him to sit down on his own. Popping the coffees in the microwave, she slipped into the bedroom to quickly put on a pair of jeans and a tee-shirt. When she returned with the coffees, Daniel was talking on his cell phone.

"No way! When? Chrissie's going to have a conniption. Yeah, okay. I'll call you back later." Daniel closed the phone and looked at Christian as she sat down at the table across from him.

"That was detention. Your kid, Jonathan Cap, has just been brought in on child rape charges, first degree."

Christian held up her hand. "Stop! I don't want to hear it. You may like the 24/7 connection with detention, but I don't. I'm hung over and completely humiliated. I can't think about what I'm doing today much less Monday when all hell is probably going to break loose. You seem to have an obsession with our work, or is it your way of staying connected to me? I mean, it's pretty obvious how you feel about me." There. She'd said it. If all hell were to break loose, it would happen now.

There was a knock on the door. "Come in."

Daniel shook his head. "I locked the door when I came in."

"He has a key." Daniel flinched as anger spread across his face. Christian turned around and crumpled onto the couch, putting her head in her hands. Her brain was throbbing and she felt like she might be sick. Why did I drink that ice wine last night? she chided herself as the key turned in the lock and Matt strode in.

"Hey honey! Hey Big D, how's it going?" Matt said cheerfully as he took off his coat and through it over a chair. "What's going on here? You guys look upset."

"He was just leaving." Christian offered an apologetic smile. "And I drank too much last night."

"Yeah, I had to bring her home and put her to bed. She was a mess," Daniel answered. His voice oozed with sarcasm. Matt faced him with a steady gaze.

"Thanks for taking care of my girl," he replied. Matt held a posture of vigilance, his eyes steadily focused on Daniel. The tension was thick enough to slice.

"She was just telling me that I'm obsessed with work and apparently with her."

A low groan emerged from the woman. "That's not what I said. I said I think you have feelings for me."

"Whoa, what am I missing?" Matt glanced from one to the other.

Christian sat up a little straighter. "You're not missing anything. My partner has indicated that he's not too pleased about our relationship. And I have a gut feeling that it's because he has feelings for me."

"That's bull. You're my partner." Daniel was pacing now, his face raw with rage.

"Then why did you try to kiss me last night? What did you think? That I wouldn't remember?"

The air in the room now had a frigid quality as Daniel marched toward the door. Yanking it open, he turned and shouted, "You think you're so special. Like you have it all figured out. Fuck you. I'm not interested in you and I have no idea where you're coming from. You were in such a drunken haze, you probably wished that I'd kissed you."

With that, he stormed out and slammed the door. Matt walked over to Christian and ran his hand over her head. "You okay?"

"Yeah. Just angry at myself for drinking too much. As you well know, Daniel lives conveniently around the corner from Stella's house. When it was time to leave, Stella called him to give me a ride home. It was just my luck that he was home on a Saturday night."

"Did he try to kiss you?" He sat down next to her and pulled her close, whispering another message.

"Yes," she answered into his chest as the hot tears flowed. "And he was pretty insistent. I feel so ashamed. I didn't let him, but then I sort of passed out and when I woke up this morning, I was only wearing my underwear. I don't know if I took off my clothes, or if he did. Are you angry?"

Matt squeezed her against him and murmured something into her hair. Christian pulled back. "What did you say?"

He gazed at her. "I'm not mad at you. Things happen. I don't believe you were intimate with him, but I do know that he's jealous as hell that I'm seeing you. So I'm angry that he might have taken advantage of you in some way."

"But what were you saying, a minute ago?" Christian wanted to know if what she thought she'd heard was true.

Matt looked down at his hands, the heat of embarrassment flooding his face. "I...I said I love you. I know it's too early to say that. I'm sorry."

"Matt." She leaned into him and kissed him.

"You know, I haven't said that to a woman in a long time. And I've only ever said it to one other woman. I guess what I'm trying to say is, when I say it, I mean it."

"That's the way it should be." She put her hands on his broad shoulders and smiled. "I can't say it, not yet. The feelings I have for you run deep, but I have so many ghosts still hanging around. Everyone I've ever really loved always seems to disappear. I think my love might be a curse."

Matt's eyes twinkled. "You're no curse, baby. You're one big blessing. But you take your time. If you decide to love me, I'll be the happiest man on this big old planet. In the meantime, I'm almost there just being with you. And as far as Big D is concerned, let it go. You have to work with him and there's no need making things worse than necessary. You've put yourself under a lot of pressure to solve the murders and last night is an example of what pressure can do to a person. You're lovely, by the way. A hangover suits you."

She grabbed a pillow and threw it at him. "Right. Red face, messy hair, puffy eyes. Just lovely."

He grinned wickedly. "Isn't that what I'm supposed to say?"

"No… yes..I don't know. Hey, I really need to get some more sleep. Do you mind?"

"I was hoping to take big boy here for a walk. You crash and I'll get him some exercise."

"Awesome. Wake me in a couple of hours, though. Okay?" Matt took her arm and led her back into the bedroom.

"You know what I really want to do, don't you?" he grinned.

"Can I be on afternoon shift for that?" Christian ached all over and couldn't imagine sex right now.

"Honey, whatever you want." She climbed back into bed and Matt tuck her in and rolled down the shades. "Sleep sweet, bo peep. That's one of our southern sayings," he added after she giggled.

Christian fell immediately back to sleep as Matt took Bear out, locking up the house as he did. An hour passed before Matt returned with the dog. She heard them come in and called Matt to her room. She sat up and turned to face Matt.

"Matt, I didn't realize this until now. Do you remember when I told you that the girl at the railroad crossing, the one who dropped my keys, was Tabby!" Christian's voice began to rise again as the hysterical feelings returned. "She looked different. She must have changed her hair, pulled it back or something. She grabbed the keys and then, when she saw me, she dropped them and ran."

"You probably need to pay the girl a visit as well. If nothing else, you can rule her out once you've talked to her."

"You're right. I'll go over there today."

"Good plan."

Christian stretched against his body and ran her hand down his belly. "So you think I'm a psychic?"

Matt nodded, his smooth chin grazing the top of her head. "Something like that."

She laughed knowingly. "I predict we're not leaving this bedroom until we've made love."

Matt groaned in pleasure. "Yes, I'd say you're definitely psychic."

CHAPTER 17

January 16, 2006

♊

The sky was the color of ebony. There was no moon and the ambient light from the small city had all but disappeared from a heavy curtain of storm clouds. Christian had walked to the edge of her property, her backpack filled with the supplies that she'd bought from Maria weeks before. She'd finally drummed up the courage to participate in her enigmatic friend's prescribed rituals, but she'd not done so without a trip to the local parish priest. The gnarled old Irishman with a perennial grin had married Tony and her and was someone with whom she still visited from time to time. However, if she was looking for absolution, Father Donovan wasn't the one who could give it to her. She loathed to tell him the truth of her mission, and so was somewhat comforted by the fact that he was a busy man and could only spare a few stolen moments with her.

Afterwards she had gone to the cemetery and spoken to her late husband, in her odd, one-way fashion. Then she'd stopped to visit her lost baby and had left pink roses on her grave.

She squatted down near the old fire pit at the edge of the river. Splays of light danced on the water from the occasional passing car on the highway above. She smoothed out the dirt and ash with a gloved hand and carefully pulled the bundle of mesquite chips from her pack. Dumping it into the shallow pit, she lit the pile of dried wood which quickly caught fire and gave off a sweet, earthy aroma that reminded her of summer barbecues. The seven Devil's Claws were next. The dried sticks came from a weed in Mexico and were about four inches in length. Three sharp, claw-like fingers curled up from the base stems. Each claw had a series of small spiny needles which served to torture anyone stupid enough to tread on it. The pastel green peyote powder seemed to glow in the small jar that Maria had given her. She opened the lid carefully and set it to the side. The honeycomb, said to be from a special hive in the Sonora desert, was dripping with sweet nectar as she pulled it from the plastic baggie. Finally she found the jalapeno pepper, a shiny greenish black in the light of the crackling fire. The wooden cross, adorned with Jesus made from the finest Mexican silver, was nearly a foot tall. Digging a small hole, she stuck the cross in the dirt a safe distance from the fire. It faced north toward the White Bluffs which were just about visible from her upstairs bedroom window.

Christian whispered a spontaneous prayer, asking for guidance and protection, though she didn't address Jesus or any other deity in particular. Slowly she began to sprinkle the peyote powder into the fire. As she did, the flames leapt and waved a bright blue. A pungent aroma drifted toward her and she inhaled it automatically. A strange lucidity seemed to clear her mind as she laid the pepper to roast. According *La curandera*'s instructions, the honeycomb was to be burned last. Placing the sticky, burrito-size roll gently next to the pepper, the young mystic watched as the flames reacted with ferocity, popping and throwing sparks.

Maria had explained the magical process to Christian. The mesquite tree was known in Mexico as a protector against the evil eye. The Devil's Claw, of course, was to pacify the Being of Darkness. The shaman had explained that from the clouds of smoke produced by the Devil's Claw, the evil one would get lost and unable to find his way to the woman at the fire. The crushed peyote buttons provided the vehicle for Christian so that she may cross to the other side. Maria had hinted at the idea that she should ingest the hallucinogen, but she'd flatly refused. A trip on magic mushrooms during her college years had cured her from any desire to go that way. The honeycomb was to sweeten those loved ones on the other side as they were often made cranky by the state of death. Finally, by its very nature, the chili pepper provided a special kind of power in order that the contact with Death be strong and sustaining. According to the old woman, all of these elements were essential for the attainment of magic.

Despite her insulated winter clothing and the fire, the cold crept into Christian's bones as she crouched on her haunches, watching the flames dance and spin. Bear sat dutifully by her side, made anxious by his master's strange actions. He whined and grunted before he eventually curled up next to her. His warmth helped, she thought vaguely as the space around her seemed to recede. She focused on the sounds of the night: the fire's crackling, the delicate gurgle of the river's current and the swish of the cars across the way. Then she began to hear less obvious sounds: the rustling of a bird in the cattails, the mournful cry of a coyote, the slap of a beaver's tail and then her own breath…only her breath.

When Christian awoke, Bear was standing over her. The fire had nearly gone out and her body felt heavy and warm. She opened her eyes slowly and tried to focus in the darkness that was night. She could have sworn someone was there, in the cattails, or perhaps at the river's edge. She searched herself for fear, but found none. She only felt a deep sense of peace as Bear's hot breath assaulted her nostrils.

"It's okay, boy. I don't know where I was, but I'm okay." She reached up to pat the animal.

Whatever magic was supposed to have happened was still a mystery. There had been no encounter with swooning specters or evil ghouls. There were no disgusting odors, nor had the hair stood up on the back of her neck. She didn't recall the sound of moaning and no icy hand gripped her. So much for Halloween horror movies, she thought wryly. Rather, Christian was content and completely relaxed. As she sought for something remarkable, there was only this: her soul sensed a kind of calmness unlike anything she'd ever experienced. It was as though she were floating above the gravity of life. She pinched her arm hard, trying to recall her normal reality, but the subtle relief didn't budge. Refraining from her habitual need to analyze the situation, she forced her mind to simply accept the process. Perhaps the bells and whistles of mystical encounter were not boisterous by nature.

The fire had nearly gone out as she gathered the leftovers from her shamanic adventure and put them in the backpack. As she began to shove sand over the fire's remaining embers, a flat, square object appeared. She picked it up and tried to see what it was. It felt like a square of glass. Reaching in the backpack for a small flashlight, Christian flipped it on and directed the beam to the object. A deep shudder ran through her, nearly lifting her from the ground in its violence. There, in her hand, was a framed photograph of her father.

II

The Benton county jail was quiet as the probation officer marked her way through the security obstacle course the next morning. She found herself marking time, though a tiny doubt had begun a steady mantra in her mind. As a result, she felt compelled to talk to Jim Maltos again. A security screening, a metal detector scan, a computerized badge, four locked doors with camera visuals, a guard behind glass for verification, an elevator, four hallways, another set of security badge scans and a pair of double doors were the only way to reach her destination. Jim Maltos was in isolation this time. He was considered a suicide risk, based on an incendiary comment that he'd made to a guard shortly after his arrival. After a day in the suicide prevention smock, a glorified name for a strait jacket, he was put in the isolation cell with around-the-clock surveillance monitors. He was also subject to random body cavity searches, in case he was able to fashion a weapon from a dropped paperclip or bobby pin. She felt queasy at the thought of a cavity search. "Inhumane treatment for inhumanes", a jailer once said to her. On the other hand, inmates were famous for sneaking in contraband. Females prisoners often stuffed drugs into their vaginas while the males would bring in small knifes by way of their anus. The swallowing of bagged drugs was also common and Christian knew that at least two inmates had died the year before when their bags of heroin exploded in their stomachs before they could expel them through a bowel movement.

While waiting nervously in the interview room for Jim, Christian wondered at the percentages of drug addicts and alcoholics who were housed in the county jail. It seemed that a large number of prisoners were held for a disease that could be better treated elsewhere. Yet without a lock-down facility, addicts would rarely stay put in treatment centers. The Svengali power of their drug was like that of her nemesis, Death. She didn't have the constant desire of his presence. Like many addicts, she'd passed that stage. Now she was simply his controlled subject, driven by his will while she lived in fear for her and other's lives. Matt's suggestion that her encounters were supernatural in nature had taken her aback at first. Could it be so simple as to believe that the dark one was nothing more than a ghost, a soul trapped in the earthly plane? She had dabbled in metaphysics in college and once knew a woman who was known as a 'housecleaner', though her job was to clean homes of ghosts and other unwanted apparitions. Christian had always thought that it was an insane concept...helping the trapped souls to reach the 'other side'. Yet if James Van Pragh and other mediums had the power to communication with other worlds, maybe she could, too.

The inexplicable discovery of her father's photograph would not leave her, no matter how she tried to force it from her mind. She'd never seen the photograph before. In it, her father was standing in the woods with his back against an enormous tree. Next to him sat a dog, a Black Labrador from the look of it. Though her family had owned a dog before their deaths, this creature was unfamiliar to her. Earlier that morning, she'd called her Aunt to ask her about the photo. Perhaps it had been in her adopted family's possession and had inadvertently been put into her backpack during their last visit, though that had been nearly two years prior. That was the only plausible explanation for the photo's appearance. However, after talking to her Aunt, she learned only one thing. The photo was probably taken in the Redwood forest in northern California. Apparently her father had owned a Black Lab named Taz when he'd fought fires in California in the late 1960s. He and Christian's mother had actually met in California at a commune in Berkeley shortly thereafter.

She continued to ponder the mystery of the photograph as she watched Jim being brought to the interview room. The man looked as if he was sick with the flu. His face was wan and the shadow of a beard was evident. His hair was matted on one side and his eyes bloodshot and swollen. It was obvious that he had been crying. As the guard opened the door, Christian stood to offer her client a hug and then thought better of it.

"Hi, Jim," she murmured softly. "Please sit down." The man melted into the greasy metal chair as though he had no bones. He slumped over, his eyes glazed with fear.

"I can't do this, Christian. It finally hit me about a week ago... my girls are really dead. They're not coming back and now *this*. The other men in there, they're treating me like I'm a monster. I've been punched, spit on, kicked and one guy, he basically tried to rape me. Luckily a guard came by and then I was put in isolation."

"I'm so sorry. No wonder you talked about killing yourself."

He gazed up now, his face drained of life. He was a destroyed man in every way. Christian knew that she'd never witnessed anyone in such pain. It was terrifying to see, as though he had a contagious disease. She forced herself not to pull back. Instead she reached out and took his hand.

"You're going to make it through this, Jim. You have to. You have a son to think about and in some small, or perhaps big way, you're going to have a chance to change the world for others.

Believe me, I've lost so many people in my life and I'm still here fighting. You can do it. For them, Jim. For Sue and Cassie. Now tell me, what gas station did you stop at? Chevron didn't have any camera footage showing you, but you said you stopped for gas. You had to have stopped somewhere. Think hard."

The man closed his eyes. A long time seemed to pass as Christian watched as his eyeballs moved back and forth behind their lids. Eventually his eyes popped open and he cried, "I remember now. The car was on empty. I was on my way down Wellsian toward the highway. I'd already been to the car lots down on Lee Street not far from the restaurant where I'd had lunch with Cindy. It was about four-thirty or so. I'd wandered around a couple of lots, but didn't see anything I liked. As I got close to the gas station by Fred Meyers, I decided to pull in and get some gas. I remember now, because I stopped in at Freddies, too, to pick up a birthday card for Cassie."

"So if there isn't a camera there, there is a birthday card with a receipt somewhere. Where would that be?" Christian felt the anxiety of discovery churning in her gut.

Jim shook his head. "Probably still in the car, in the glove box."

She squeezed his hand tightly. "That will be your best alibi, Jim. We will get you out of here again. I promise."

As she left the jail, Christian called Detective Jensen and told him the information that Jim had shared. Then she crossed her fingers, gave a silent prayer and headed up to Canyon Estates. There was a young lady and her brother that she was going to visit.

♊

"I'm sorry, but Tabby isn't home yet. She should be here soon. School gets out in a few minutes. My son is on his way home from

Washington State University." Mrs. Smithson was small-boned, pale and rather homely. Nothing like her angelically-beautiful daughter or her well-chiseled, athletic-looking son, Christian observed. After politely refusing the coffee that the woman offered, the P.O. sat down in the living room to wait.

The room was decorated in the style of the 80's. Everything was white-the carpet, walls and furniture, which were relieved by occasional touches of color. The pictures on the walls were southwestern pastels-large, garishly-framed paintings of sad-looking Indian children standing into front of pueblos. Along one wall were family photos, mostly of the children. Mrs. Smithson was an obvious collector. Little porcelain figurines that Christian had often seen at Hallmark stores filled a glass-faced cabinet. Though the room had a rather cold ambience, there was nothing there that spoke of the ugliness of murder. If the Smithson kids were involved, Christian would have to come up with some strong evidence against them to convince a jury.

A black lab mix suddenly bounded into the room from the kitchen. The rather overweight canine had a large rawhide bone in his mouth, which he immediately settled down on his haunches to chew. He looked at her once, but didn't offer any friendly greetings. Mrs. Smithson followed him in a moment later and said, "That's Charlie. He won't hurt you. I just gave him one of his bones. It should keep him from bothering you."

"Don't worry. I love dogs. But I think I'll wait with you in the kitchen if that's okay." Following the older woman, she paused in front of the dog. "Hi, Charlie. What do you have there?"

The dog dropped the bone and grinned, wagging his tail furiously. She noticed the bone was the same type that she'd bought for Bear on occasion. It was a special brand for large dogs which was supposed to prevent intestinal problems. She patted the dog on the head and wandered into the kitchen where Mrs. Smithson was preparing dinner. It was time to ask some questions.

"You don't mind if I chat with you for a minute before Tabby gets home, do you?"

The mousy housewife pushed a piece of hair from her face and gave a weak smile. She was chopping onions. "Not if you don't mind my chopping."

"What are you making, may I ask?" Christian asked, feigning interest. "Beef stew. My boy loves it. I promised him I'd make some for him to take back to school. They don't eat very well at college."

Christian surreptitiously took in her surroundings. The kitchen had the once-popular country look to it. A border of wallpaper featured stout ducks and geese while old milk jugs and several ribbon-wrapped baskets sat on the top of the knotty pine cupboards. The white lacy kitchen curtains were pulled back with bright blue and yellow striped bows and the countertops were covered in dazzling yellow Formica. The outdated, overly cheerful style made Christian want to gag. The house décor seemed almost schizophrenic in its decorative contrasts. She wondered if that was somehow reflective of its inhabitants.

"Does your son enjoy school up in Pullman?"

"Oh yes, and he's doing so well. He's studying engineering. But of course he loves to come home, too. He's really close to his sister and mother." She gave a sappy grin and she pointed dramatically to herself.

It was strange that woman referred to herself in the third person. She noticed a photograph of Jerry and Cassie on the refrigerator and decided to throw out the bait. "Does your son have a new girlfriend?"

The woman put down her big chopping knife and looked down, rubbing her eyes momentarily.

"Are those raw onions getting to you?" Christian asked sweetly.

"No, I'm just so worried about my boy. J.J. was really hurt by Cassie's death."

A fit of shivers shook Christian as she wrestled to stay calm. "I beg your pardon?"

"Well, I probably shouldn't have said anything, but he was definitely in love with that girl. He was always asking if Tabby could have her spend the night. The three of them spent a lot of time together. Then when we heard what Mr. Maltos did to his..." Now Mrs. Smithson grew shaky and grabbed on to the counter. "I just can't believe it. He is such a monster. Who would do that to their own family?"

Christian took a deep breath, trying to control her outrage. "I understand your despair. If your son loved Cassie so much, I'm wondering why she never mentioned him to me during our time together. As I said before, I was working with the family. I wondered if Tabby could help me think of a way to honor Cassie's death. The agency has a little money to spend, so I thought she and I could design a bench to put out in front of the building, or perhaps a plaque for the lobby."

"Hmm. That's a nice idea."

"So what makes you think that Jim would do such a monstrous thing to his family?"

The woman threw a conspiratorial look. "Mr. Maltos was so strict with Cassie. She wasn't allowed to date older boys, though apparently they allowed her to see that boy, Tommy, who was no good, according to my daughter."

Christian cringed. Didn't Cassie write in her diary that Tabby encouraged her to date Tommy? Without acknowledging the insult, she replied, "I heard about that."

"That's why whenever he was home, we invited Cassie over. Our son is such a good boy and we felt that the kids should have a chance to get to know one another in a supervised setting."

"Did your son ever take her out?"

"On occasion he'd take her for drives, but they were never gone long. I was planning to talk to Jim about it eventually, once Cassie turned seventeen, but I never got the chance." She sniffed hard and wiped her eyes on the dish towel. A small piece of onion was caught in her helmet-like hair, but Christian didn't say anything to distract her from more confessions.

"I'm so sorry to hear about all of this. By the way, was your son at home on the day of the murders?'

"No. He went back up to school that day. Actually Tabby was up there visiting him as well. Originally Tabby was going to spend the day with Cassie, but then their plans changed. I'm so grateful. I know it sounds terrible, but just think if my daughter had been there. He might have killed her, too."

Christian nodded thoughtfully. "You know, I'm confused. I thought your son's name was Jerry, like your husband."

"Oh, yes. He was christened Jerald Joseph and we called him J.J.. My husband traveled a lot until Tabby was born, so back then it was just me and J.J."

Christian glanced at her watch and stood up. "One more thing. I understand that your husband owns a red Mustang."

"Well, yes, sort of. It's in my husband's name, but it actually belongs to our son. We bought it for him for his birthday last fall. It had been completely restored by a friend of ours."

"Really. May I ask your friend's name?" Christian's skin began to itch with anticipation. She knew the answer before the woman could speak the words.

"Jason Roads. Actually he's the youth pastor at the church where our kids attend. He's young and very innovative. He has a car detailing business, but he also restores cars from time to time."

Christian wanted to cry out as the rush of success raced through her veins. Instead she calmly replied, "I can't stay any longer, but I'd really like to talk to Tabby when she has a few minutes. I'd like to talk to her about our plans for a memorial plaque. Do you think I could use your restroom before I go?"

"Certainly. Oh, wait, the powder room is out of commission. You'll have to go upstairs. The third door on your right."

The woman turned back to her chopping as Christian headed up the stairs. She was hoping for this bit of luck. She wandered down the hall, careful to listen for footsteps. Eventually she came to the bathroom which was attached to two bedrooms, Pete and Jill style. She walked in and opened both doors to either side. One appeared to be a girl's room and the other, a boy's room. How odd that Tabby and J.J. were forced to share a bathroom, she thought as she locked the bathroom door from the hallway. To her relief, Tabby's bedroom's main door was closed. She stepped into her room and began to look around for a jewelry box. The room was a complete mess, unlike her deceased friend's room which had been fairly tidy for a teenager. Clothes were piled in corners, plates of food splayed around the carpeted floor, piles of books and empty GAP shopping bags filled another corner while the queen-sized bed was left unmade. Though the room was done in a jungle motif, due to the clutter, there was little ambience from the expensive furnishings and décor.

Finally Christian spied a small cloisonné jewelry box on the dresser next to the door. Quickly she stepped over to it and opened the box stuffed to the brim. She dumped out the box and shoved the items around on the dresser top until she found what she was looking for. Just then, she heard a door slam. She swept the remaining earrings back into the box, slipped back into the bathroom and shut the door. Flushing the toilet, she turned on the faucet and looked at herself in the mirror. *I'm becoming a damn good thief,* she congratulated herself, patting some water on her flushed face. Unfortunately her face showed the guilt too easily. She took a deep breath and forced herself to look calm. Stepping from the bathroom seconds later, she bumped into a handsome young man as she did so.

"Oh, excuse me! You must be Jerry."

The young man gave her a grin and slowly looked her up and down. "And you must be…one of Charlie's Angels?"

She laughed in spite of the circumstances. "Touché. No, actually I'm Cassie's probation officer."

"My mom told me. So what are you doing here, looking like a secret agent?"

Christian gulped. *He was too canny.* "Just trying to get some input from your sister on the plans I have to do a memorial plaque for Cassie. She was a very special girl."

"You're telling me. She was awesome." The boy began to fidget with his baseball cap uncomfortably.

"Hey, don't you drive a red Mustang? I swear that I hit your car two weeks ago. The Monday after New Year's on the day of the ice storm. Look at me and tell me you don't remember what I'm talking about."

When Jerry looked up, his face had darkened with inexplicable emotion.

"Listen. I couldn't stay at the scene, man. My insurance is sky high at the moment. I had to get out of there before the police showed up. I could see you were going to get out of the car, so I knew you'd be okay. Sorry. I was going to call you and explain, but I forgot."

"I bet. And I'm sure the damage wasn't too bad, either. What did you tell your dad?"

He looked sheepish. "I told him it was a hit and run and that I didn't get the license plate number. He felt bad for me. Actually my car is in the shop as we speak. But if you want me to pay for the damages on your car, I will. I've got some money saved up. Just don't tell my parents, ok?"

Christian held up her hand. "That's a great idea. Unfortunately for you, my car is totaled. Why don't you come by my office next week and we'll figure something out." She gave him a sloe-eyed glare that said, "don't even try to cross me."

With that, she pushed him aside and walked down the stairs. Ducking her head in the kitchen, she said good-bye to Mrs. Smithson and headed out. She'd found the earring and it looked to be a perfect match.

Ⅱ

"It's basically useless to us." Harry shook his hairless, smooth-as-a-ping-pong ball head and gave Christian a resigned gaze. "For one, you can't sneak into people's homes and collect your own evidence. And two, the matching earring could have been dropped in that bedroom months ago, or three, Tabby could own a similar pair to the one at the Maltos home. This is not conviction evidence. And correct me if I'm wrong, but earrings like these are sold all over town." He tugged at a plump earlobe where a silver crescent moon dangled from a large moonstone stud.

"Okay, so I put myself in danger for no reason. Great."

"At least you set that punk of a brother of hers straight. Dating a fifteen year old and he's how old?"

"I'm not giving up in this case, Harry. No matter what. I will not see Mr. Maltos hung out to dry."

"I think you mean, you don't want him fried. But I do have some more good news. We just finished scanning all the video footage from those two gas stations. We found a clip of Jim Maltos paying for gas at the Fred Meyers location. He was taped at exactly 2:34. I've called the prosecutor's office to let them know. So I guess he's a free man now, thanks to you."

Christian grinned joyously and threw her arms around Harry. A deep bellow of a laugh emerged from the man. "If I knew I'd get one of these, I'd have called you sooner." She blushed as she pulled away.

"Sorry," she sputtered, realizing for the first time how attractive the guy really was. Flooded with embarrassment, she grabbed her bag and headed out the door. Harry was crude, but she liked his no-nonsense approach. Furthermore, his biker-boy good looks and addiction to tattoos added an ironic twist to the by-the-book professional man.

As soon as she got to the car, she called Matt to tell him the latest news. He answered immediately, but there was a grim tone to his salutation. "Matt here. What's up?"

"It's me. What's up with you?"

"This place is driving me nuts. They just brought in a girl who should be in Carondolet Mental Health. She's ranting and raving and had to have her stomach pumped before she even got her. Apparently she beat up her mother's big screen television, but man, she's loony tunes. Crisis Response is run by a bunch of idiots."

Christian pulled into the parking lane and slowed the car to a stop. "Hey, you don't sound good. Take a deep breath, babe and think about being in my bed."

There was a long pause. "Better?"

"Yeah, but I still got eight hours to go before I'm out of here."

"So I'll stop in and cheer you up. By the way, what's the girl's name?"

"I don't know. Here, let me look it up. Shelly Nunamaker."

"It's her. The girl at the photo I took from Maltos's house. Keep her in isolation and find me a tape recorder with a microphone. Wait, there's one in my office, in my orange filing cabinet. I'll be there soon."

"Conviction depends on the evidence and due process of the law.
Edward Murrow

CHAPTER 18

♊

The fat golden candle flickered, throwing starbursts of light throughout the room. Jazz music played softly; the low, resonating moans of a saxophone echoed the steady beat of percussive rhythms. She gazed at the piece of sculpture which glowed with a warm copper sheen. Embedded shards of silver supported the elongated woman's torso. She was nearly a foot high. A magnificent siren of metal and wood, she reached down to cradle a small child in her Modigliani-like arms. The room had become more inviting with her in it. A toasted bronze patina glazed the walls. Matt had painted the room as a Valentine surprise and then added the sculpture as a final touch. His card had said that he cherished her. Christian sensed the closest thing to love that she'd felt in a long time.

An amiable hum of conversation was interrupted by occasional spikes of laughter. The cocktail party, her first since Tony had died, was going well. Kathy and Pam were engrossed in a conversation with Harry from the crime lab. Randy Rusk and Daniel sat in the corner, drinking Coronas and trading basketball trivia. Stella was flirting voraciously with Matt's attractive brother and even Rosalie had finally sat down with Matt after spending too much time preparing food in the kitchen. Christian's neighbor, Debra, and her husband, Bill, had just arrived with Sophia not far behind. Her ex-therapist had made an exception to her professional rule once Christian had confirmed to her that her therapy days were truly over. Tess Walker, a deputy prosecutor in the felonies division, and Callum O'Connor sat at the kitchen island, sharing raw oysters and office gossip. Indeed, the evening's mood was one of friendship and relaxation. As the kids on probation would say, they were totally chill. Still Christian was not completely at ease. Then her heart skipped a beat as her final and most important guest walked through the front door.

Jim Maltos looked like a familiar stranger. Time and prolonged terror had taken its toll. She hadn't seen him since January when she'd visited him in jail, shortly after his suicide attempt. He'd sent flowers and a thank-you card for her help in his exoneration. But it had been almost two months since she'd seen him in the flesh. Christian jumped up and ran to the door. She felt like a lost child anxious to see a parent. She gently hugged the man, though he seemed significantly smaller than the first time that she'd held him on that horrible night. He was, at best, a ghost of his former self. He smiled as she pulled away. The look which passed between them was not that of pity or desperation. Now they shared something in common and it had become their private bond.

"How are you, my friend?" Jim said softly, holding her eyes with his own.

"I'm good. And you?"

"Holding up, Christian. Holding up. Just wish this would be over, once and for all." His face was drawn and his eyes were blood-shot and puffy. They were the eyes of someone who cried often and hard.

Christian nodded. Since Jim's release, the case had gone cold and, with the lack of manpower in the local police departments, it would remain so. There was no direct evidence to link Jason Roads or Tabby Smithson to the crime. When he was interviewed, he indicated that the coat had belonged to Cassie's father, that he had borrowed it one time. The older man indicated that Jason was correct, but couldn't recall when he'd last lent him the Peteet. Furthermore, a young woman from the church swore that Jason was there that day.

"What can I get you to drink?" Christian asked as she took his coat and guided him into the room.

"Scotch on the rocks would be great," he replied. In the next moment, Sophia, dressed in a pale blue silk blouse and rhinestone-studded *Seven* jeans, walked up and introduced herself to Jim. A sense of relief passed through Christian as she walked away to prepare his drink. Sophia had promised Christian that when Jim arrived, she'd break the ice. Judging by the engaging smile on Jim's face, her ex-therapist had just done so with her undeniable grace.

As Christian poured the amber-colored liquor into the tumbler, she considered the murders again. Despite the case's apparent dead end, she was certain that the killer was still in their midst. And she had a hunch that the cosmic answer lie with Shelly Nunamaker. The girl had said a few things during her interview with Christian that had put the older woman's intuition on high alert. Unfortunately, shortly after they'd spoken, Shelly had experienced a complete meltdown. One of the more severe psychotic episodes, in fact, that Christian had ever witnessed. As a result, the sixteen-year-old had been immediately shipped to Eastern State Hospital for evaluation and observation. However, during the few moments that Christian had spent with Shelly, alarming words had poured from the girl's mouth like confetti. A hodge-podge of sounds and guttural groans, her responses resembled the speaking in tongues reminiscent of Jason Roads in a fundamentalist's trance. Shelly had repeated the phrase: *They be shot down to the ground, they be dead, dead with bullets in their heads* in a rap song ramble that had been whispered between her otherwise nonsensical cries. Christian had closed the unnerving interview by having Shelly sign a series of forms releasing future documents from mental health providers. At the time, it seemed a minor coup in an otherwise confusing exercise.

Though the probation officer had called the hospital several times with the hope that she might get to talk to the girl, she'd never had any success. Out of desperation, she'd sent the release form, though she was sure that any of the hospital records would be fairly vague in content.

As Christian lifted Jim's glass, she felt Matt's warm breath on her neck. "You okay, baby?"

"I'm good." She turned to face him. Normally not comfortable with public displays of affection, his sincere concern and musky scent gave her a giddy sensation. He'd become an irresistible temptation in her life and she was much better for it. Leaning forward, she kissed him.

He kissed her back, swiftly, but with a lingering sensation that spoke of love. Stepping away, she unintentionally caught Daniel's eye. A disagreeable look crept over his face, but she ignored it and made her way to Jim and Sophia who were now sitting on the couch, deep in conversation.

"Here you are!" Christian exclaimed, handing the glass over.

Jim grinned. "Cheers! It's nice to share a drink with friends. You know, I wasn't allowed to drink before. Sue wouldn't allow it. Now I have a drink, just now and then, and I'm really enjoying it. It takes the edge off sometimes, you know?"

Christian smiled agreeably, noticing that Jim, in some small way, did seem more relaxed with himself.

"You'll never guess. I signed up for scuba diving lessons this week and just found out that Jim's going to be my teacher! I'm so excited." The older woman clapped her hands like a child. Christian found it curious to watch the therapist react outside her normally low-key professional persona.

Jim blushed, turning a bright red and mumbled, "I'm a little rusty, but Bob Darnell, the scuba master, is giving me a shot at it. I used to do search and rescue, years ago."

"Now, *that's* cool," Christian replied with admiration. She knew that the type of person who was willing to dive in the Columbia River to rescue others required extraordinary commitment and unflinching courage. She had tried to do it a few years back and had panicked so badly, she'd nearly had to go to the hospital.

"Just a word of caution, Soph. When it comes to doing your final test dive, do it somewhere other than here. That river is deep, dark and very murky," Christian warned.

Sophia shook her head. "So I've been told. I'm working on Jim to meet a group of us in Mexico over Memorial Day weekend. That's where I was planning to take my completed coursework and do my final dive."

Jim blushed again. "I supposed I could go, especially now that I'm basically unemployed."

"That can be a good thing sometimes." Sophia flipped a strand of ebony hair off her shoulder. "With all that's happened, you deserve some time off."

Christian was delighted to see such an instant connection between her two friends. Excusing herself, she made her way to the kitchen to check on her Emeril-inspired crab cakes.

By midnight, the bulk of the guests had left. Only Daniel, his date and Christian and Matt remained. Daniel was borderline drunk and his date even more so.

"I think you should take my gun," Daniel roared from the couch as Christian began to clear the living room of party debris. His date was curled up in his lap asleep and didn't seem to notice his loud announcement.

"Take your gun where?" Christian paused with an empty platter in hand, and gave her partner a look of infinite patience.

"Take my gun when you go to visit Jason Roads. You got to watch out for him," he slurred.

"What makes you think I'm going to visit Jason?" Christian asked. She could hear the back door open as Matt took out another bag of garbage.

"Cuz you and I both know that kid did it. He killed those women."

Christian set down the platter on the coffee table and plopped down in the chair across from Daniel. "Do you think so? Do you really think so, Daniel?"

"You know it. I know it." At that moment, Matt yelled Christian's name.

She stood up. "Just a minute. What is it?"

Matt was standing at the back door, a look of pure disgust on his face. "Come out here, you've got to take a look at this." Christian followed him out towards the side of the garage where she kept her garbage can. The area was brightly lit where Tony had installed a large spot light on the rafter above. Matt opened the garbage can lid and she peered in. There, in a clear plastic bag, was a bloody chunk of something.

Christian shivered. "What do you think it is?"

Matt shook his head. "I pulled it out to get a closer look. It appears to be an aborted fetus. And there's a note attached."

Her knees buckled. Grabbing the garbage can for support, she tried to breathe, but the smell emanating from the can only increase her gag reflex. Matt put his arms around her waist and effortlessly lifted her. Turning her around toward the river, he said, "Now take a deep breath."

After she gained her bearings, Christian went back to the can and lifted out the plastic sack. It was marked with the Walmart logo. The infamous shopping Mecca of the poor, she thought ironically, as she gazed at the little android-like face within. Amidst the blood and tissue, the fetus peered out at her. He was three inches long and dark purple in color. Like an eggplant picked too soon, she reflected.

Hours later, after the police had taken a report and left with the horrifying little bundle, she and Matt finally finished the cleaning up. Daniel had just left with his date, sobered up by the evening's final chapter. Locking the front door, she stood alone before the large plate glass window that faced south, mulling over the evening's disturbing surprise. Who was trying to reach her and why? Could this abominable act be another girl's desperate cry for help?

She shivered. Winter was on its way out and early signs of spring had begun to appear. Delicate buds had formed on the fruit trees and the temperature was mild by mid-day. The earth's celestial companion, full and high in the sky, smiled jovially as though to welcome a change of season. Its pale light glowed softly on the sculpture that Matt had given her. The woman's face was subdued, and reflected a sense of peace that Christian felt was evasive in her own life. With a deep sigh, she ran her hand down the back of the metal piece as though she could somehow steal the contentment away from the innate and yet heavenly object.

Yet as long as Jim Maltos lived in his hell, she would live in hers. Without knowing who'd killed his family, he was unable to truly move on in his life. He was jobless as a result of all the stress and had begun to see a therapist at Christian's urging. Fortunately his company had given him a generous severance package and the life insurance policy had miraculously paid out. However, Christian knew that the more time he was without distractions, the more time he had to ruminate and grieve. She knew that from experience.

In the meantime, though Jim was not currently a suspect, she also felt no closure. Christian knew that her life had been spared and yet, despite an intense sense of gratitude, she also felt enormous guilt. She'd planned to return to the house that day and, under normal circumstances, would have without question, especially to retrieve an agency-owned cell phone. Why had she forgotten it? What or who had mysteriously interceded on her behalf? Furthermore, what was the meaning of Matt's terrifying discovery only hours ago? She knew that the remains of the baby were a message to her from someone who needed help, or conversely, as Daniel had suggested, from someone who wanted to frighten her.

And beneath the layers of questions, her instincts told her that there was a connection to the Maltos murders and the night's dramatic conclusion. Her stomach gave a slight lurch. A young woman, ripe with child, tortured into a desperate act, had come to her like a haunted creature in the night. What had it been like for this stranger to approach Christian's home, lit up and full of reveling adults with apparently no cares in the world while she still struggled with her irreversible choice? Certainly she might have rang the doorbell and asked for the young officer's help, had there not been all the cars, the music reaching out from the slight crack under the door and the faint sounds of laughter and happy conversation. Who was this young woman? Was she afraid or remorseful? The note had simply said, "He has me, too."

Christian leaned toward the statue and whispered, "Give me an answer to the riddle: what does this mean? Who is trying to tell me something?" She waited as though expecting an answer and then, feeling stupid, stood upright. As she did, she caught a man's reflection in the picture window. She turned, anticipating Matt, but the living room was dark and she could still hear the bathroom faucet running. She turned back to the window and the image remained. An icy shiver ran up her spine, but rather than to flee in fear, she forced herself to remain still. As she stared at the reflection, the man's face began to look strangely familiar. Softly she whispered, "I see you there. Why do you haunt me, Mr. Death?"

Slowly the blurred image moved closer. She knew that it was time to face this monster, or angel, which she didn't really know. The hair on her arms pricked slightly and she felt a warm wave of air circle around her. The electrical energy in the room seemed to snap with intensity. She forced herself to remain forward, knowing that if she turned around, the apparition would disappear again, maybe this time for good. As the apparition's face became clear, she stifled a shriek. Her eyes welled up and tears began to run down her cheeks in torrents. There, appearing as he had twenty-five years before, was the image of her father.

♊

"He was there," Christian insisted, burrowing deeper into Matt's arms. She wished she could climb under his skin, but not out of fear. Rather, she wanted him to understand, to feel her revelation as a visceral reality.

"Okay, so maybe all this time, this thing you have been calling, Mr. Death, has been your Dad's ghost." Matt stroked her hair in a soothing rhythm, his warm breath tickling her forehead.

"So why did he show himself now?" she wondered aloud. "He's been following me around for years. Why now?"

"Maybe you're ready now. You're older, a little wiser and more…open to him. I mean, you could have freaked, run out of the room or whatever. Instead you stayed and allowed him to reveal himself."

Christian shook her head. "And I'm safer now."

"Why's that?" Matt asked absently, gently tracing her cheekbone with his finger.

"Because." A large lump had formed in her throat. "I have someone who really loves me, for me. Before, Tony would have laughed at me. He always said I was weird and superstitious. You don't. You're okay with who I am."

"More than okay, Christian. I'm with you on this. Like I told you once, the world of spirits is something that is accepted in my culture's schema. We don't need proof for everything like white folks. We know there is another world that lives side by side with us, a world that most people ignore, or are afraid of. I think you're absolutely right, though. I am good for you." He hugged her tighter. "And besides that, I find the whole thing really cool. I think if you let him, your Dad could help you solve the Maltos murders."

"That's sort of the message I got from Maria. She didn't know about my Dad, but she knew there was some kind of energy around me and encouraged me to connect with him." Christian giggled. "I feel like a character in a M. Night Shyamalan movie."

Matt sighed. "You're an interesting woman, that's for certain. You may not be a movie star, but you are undeniably, unpredictably and, usually, unintentionally one of the most interesting women I've ever met."

"What should we do about the fetus you found tonight?"

Matt sighed. "Let the police handle it. We can't do anything about it at this point."

"What do you think that they can really do? Unless someone checks into a hospital for a botched abortion, there will probably be no trail."

Matt shook his head. "I know. Hey, I have an idea. I think you need to get your mind off things for a while," he whispered as his hand slowly slid down her torso. "How does this feel?"

♊

Harry called her several days later. "The fetus was about four months along. It appears that the mother used a derivative of a European herb once used as an abortifacient agent back before doctors did them the favor. The lab isn't willing to spend the money on trying to trace the mother, or the poison used for that matter. We just don't have the manpower. Our DNA samples for local women are very small and based on the racial features and skin tone, the baby was Caucasian and that local DNA pool is nearly non-existent. However, this might pique your interest. When I did the autopsy on that little Maltos girl, I found traces of the same poison. Is this the new thing that the kids now use to hock out babies?"

Christian shivered. The thought of one more lethal drug produced by amateurs, one which gave the power to abort, was another dark consideration in a world already dangerous for teens. "I have no clue. But what about the criminal aspect of using something like this?"

"The last time I checked, abortion was legal in Washington State. I'm not sure if there is a disposal statute, but as far as I know, Planned Parenthood basically throws their fetuses out with the trash."

"God, that's horrible. And to think that out at the All-City cemetery there's a memorial for miscarried children."

"Yeah, well, to each his own. I, myself, think that a woman should use birth control in the form of a pill. It's a lot easier and less guesswork."

"Harry! You know, sometimes we take the pill and still get pregnant."

"Oh, I'm sorry. Did I open my big mouth more than I should have?" His voice was recalcitrant.

Christian reached down and toyed with the pendant around her neck. It had been nearly seven years since she'd lost her baby.

"No. It's okay. It's just not always that easy. Anyway, I guess this is what you call a closed case, huh?"

"Yeah. Hey, thanks for the party the other night. I had a really good time. That friend of yours, Sophia, man, she's a babe. Do you think I could get her number?"

Christian chuckled. "Let me ask her first. Take care, Harry. We'll see you soon."

As she hung up, she smiled. There was one good thing that had come from that less-than-perfect night. Sophia and Jim Maltos had started dating.

♊

Maria was standing on her front steps, her face lit up with a crinkled smile. Indeed, her wide brown face was reminiscent of a homemade molasses cookie, baked until it had cracked into a myriad of sugar-coated lines. The spiritualist hobbled to the car and waited patiently as her student climbed out. She nodded with approval at the new car. "New driving, I see!" she cried in her broken English.

"Yes, my old car was in an accident. But this one is wonderful, especially for my dog." Christian grinned as Maria took her hand in her own frail one. With a determined tug, the old woman led her to the shack where spiritual concoctions brewed and minor miracles occurred.

Maria shut the door to the small enclosure. It was lit with over a dozen candles and dark curtains covered the tiny windows. The ghoulish statues of the dead appeared to be alive in the quivering light. The room smelled of chocolate and cilantro, but there were other faint scents, freshly washed clothes and a floral perfume.

She sat down in her usual chair and waited as Maria did her preliminary rituals. After a deeply moving prayer, recited in Spanish, the strange little woman crossed herself and flung holy water about the room. Then she settled on the stool opposite of Christian at a small table covered in a perfectly white linen table cloth. The delicate embroidery on the exquisite fabric was reminiscent of French handiwork, Christian thought as she squirmed slightly in her seat. Maria gazed at her with a look of unconditional acceptance, but said nothing.

As she sat there, awaiting the mentor's next cue, Christian began to relax. Then she suddenly remembered the perfume's memory. She shivered as a film of tears coated her eyes. "That was my mother's perfume," she whispered, more to herself than to the old woman.

"Yes? I believe to be, yes." Maria nodded her head with approval and smiled knowingly up at the ceiling as though colluding with an unseen God.

In the next instant, Christian felt an acute sense of departure, as though she'd been sucked into a gigantic television screen. Maria's dark little room receded from view and instead, a clear image of her mother, hanging clothes on a line in a small yard, appeared. Pale pink sheets billowed like sails, snapping occasionally in the light breeze. She felt the sensation of soft, cool grass on her skin and looked down to see a pair of grubby, little feet which were as brown as nuts. Peering up, she saw the sky above. It was a bright summer blue with puffy white clouds marking the horizon. The smell of clean laundry and peaches lingered in the dry air. Gazing down her body, Christian saw herself as a small child, who began running in and out between the sheets, laughing happily. She wanted to play a game of hide-and-go-seek! Her mother's sweet voice rose like a bell as she sang a popular song, hanging more laundry. Then her father….

Her body jerked sharply and she was back in the room. A long silence followed. Finally Maria spoke. "What you see, young one." Maria had her hands on the table. She was holding a miniature object that looked like a cheap rendition of the Pieta.

"My mother." Stuttering slightly, she continued, "My mom insisted on hanging up the laundry on sunny days. We had a clothes dryer, but she was old-fashioned in that way. I didn't remember this until now. I still hang up my clothes in my yard on sunny days. My Tony, he eventually put the line in for me. He hated the way it looked in the yard, though. He thought it made our place...made us look..."

"Poor." Maria finished for her. Christian blushed with embarrassment. She'd fought endlessly with Tony about the clothesline and had won the battle, but not without building resentment between them. Until now, she'd never understood why that damn clothesline was so important to her. It had seemed like a ridiculous obsession at the time. When Tony had first refused her request, Christian had given him the cold shoulder for nearly a month. He'd finally given in, but she'd paid the price. At social events, he had often made fun of her and told their friends that she'd been 'born in a barn' to leftist Oregon hippies and that their lifestyle was essentially white trash in his estimation.

Maria's face cracked into kindness. There was no judgment in her eyes as she murmured, "You see here. The Virgin Mary holds her dying child, our loving son of God. You, too, are dying, my friend. You must find your answers, or your heart will..." Maria closed her eyes, searching for a word. "Becomes small and..."

Christian shook her head in agreement. "You're right. I'm withering with the Maltos case. I'm dying in a way."

"Your papa. He comes to see you now?"

Christian stared at the face across the table. She was speechless. How did this woman know?

Marie nodded at her. "You see, when you open here..." The old woman put her fist to her heart, "you get help. Let him come to you. No fear of him. He has been with you all the time. You are ready."

Christian felt a sense of relief. There *were* answers, new answers. Death was not the monster she'd once believed. Death was an honorable presence which appeared in the form of her father's ghost.

"Young one, you need to follow your papa's lead. He will point you to where you must go. He says you must go back to the place where you started. Follow your first…" This time Marie pointed to her head. "You first thinking about this. It is right."

CHAPTER 19

♊

The sky was dark with rain clouds, though behind her, just outside of Ritzville, a churning dust storm roiled like a black monster. Eastern State Hospital was just south of Spokane on I-90. She knew she was at the right place as the building came into view. The bulky Pepto-Bismol-colored structure looked like every other mental health institution that had appeared in books and films over the years. The gracefully rolling lawns and spacious grounds made her wonder if crazy people needed more room to function than the average person. There was a firm commitment to security, however, noted by the iron gates and heavy electronics around the perimeter of the facility. This was one of two remaining mental hospitals in the state of Washington. The state laws pertaining to the rights of the disabled, mental or otherwise, were some of the most liberal in the country. Generally a person could not be committed against their will unless they clearly demonstrated a propensity for deliberate and imminent suicide or homicide. Due to Shelly's psychotic break and history of suicide ideation, she had been admitted, but just under the legal wire. Now that the girl had been stabilized on medications, she could leave the facility at any time. However, Christian had also made it clear that if Shelly didn't stay and finish her prescribed treatment, that the courts would be informed and her sanctions possibly more severe.

In the meantime, the attending staff continued to extend her treatment time, for financial reasons, no doubt. The fees at the hospital could run as high as ten thousand a month. Shelly's father owed a large ranch and food processing plant as well as several storage facilities. He was flush with dough. Christian guessed that the hospital's billing department had inevitably learned this and had made the decision for her long-term stay as a result. Though Shelly lived with her mother, her father was still the primary custodian, according to the divorce papers.

She parked her car in the large parking lot and hurried to the double doors, following the signs to the lobby. The drive had taken a bit longer than anticipated and visiting hours were strictly enforced. She'd made arrangements with the staff after a long conversation with Shelly's mother, a timid woman who had little emotional response to what had happened to her daughter.

The reception area smelled like ammonia and breakfast. Evidently bacon had been on the menu. A solemn-looking woman, dressed in shapeless gray tunic, spoke in a hushed voice as she introduced the visitor to the extensive list of visitation rules. She could see the teenager in an interview room, however they would be on camera as a safety precaution. They could go outside to the courtyard, but Shelly would have to have an attendant in tow. According to the woman, who seems to have her own issues with mental illness based on her flat affect and lack of eye contact, Shelly was at a level 2, which meant that there had been a recent 'incident'. Of course, she gave Christian no indication as to the incident's content. However, her voice had taken an ominous tone as she'd leaned toward Christian as though it were a big secret.

Christian was escorted into a small, sound-proof room a couple of minutes later. Shelly was already in the room. The girl was as pale as the white walls, her hair had been cropped very short and she was obviously agitated, based on her bouncing knee and clasping and unclasping of her petite hands.

"Hi, Shelly. Do you remember me?"

The girl shook her head no. Christian watched her for a moment before pressing on. Shelly was not unattractive, but had a rather mousy appearance. Her pale blonde hair stood up in spiky tuffs and her complexion was almost colorless. She had very small, straight teeth and her eyebrows had been over-plunked and then penciled on in a severe, arched line. Her eye make-up was heavy and smeared and she had a musty, unwashed odor. In a glance, the girl was a diminished version of the pop singer, Pink, perhaps after a late night out on the town.

"I'm your probation officer. I've talked to you before, but it was in detention and you were having a pretty tough time of things. How are you doing now?"

Shelly looked down at her hands. "Better, I guess. But I miss my boyfriend." She began to rock then slowly at first, but then with greater agitation. Her hands flitted to her face, scratched her nose, smoothed her hair, pulled at her eyebrows and then back to the table in rapid succession.

"Of course you do. It must get very lonely in here." Christian tried to keep her voice casual, though her inner sense of urgency hummed. Several patients hovered in the background near the window, looking either wild-eyed with the hope of scandal or drooling and confused, without any apparent awareness at all. "So who's your boyfriend?"

"Jerry Smithson. He really misses me, too. I know it."

"I'm sorry that you have to be here, honey, but you've been very sick and needed help. Do you remember what happened in detention?"

The girl gave another negative shake of the head.

"You had a violent episode and assaulted your cellmate."

Shelly's eyes lit up for a moment. "That little b-ach, Cassie. I know. She was trying to steal Jerry from me. She deserved it."

Christian felt an intense shiver run through her body, as though she'd been plunged into a tub of ice. "No, Shelly. Your cellmate's name was Lucinda." In a strange way, Lucinda did resemble Cassie Maltos.

"Have you ever hurt anyone before that?" Christian asked softly.

The girl's lips tightened into a steel line across her face. She began to pick at her cuticles.

"You know, I've been in love before, too. I know how it feels when the person you love, loves someone else."

The girl looked up, her face blazing with anger. "He didn't love her! She's a slut. Cassie can go to hell."

"Shelly, Cassie's dead."

A terrified look suddenly pierced Shelly's face. "I know."

Christian's gut clutched into a fist of anticipation. "Shelly, do you know who killed Cassie and her mother?"

The girl's eyes shone with eerie knowledge. "That is for me to know and you to never find out."

"Shelly, talk like that can result in charges against you. I know you don't want to go to prison for murder, so I'd think about what you just said to me."

"What about client privilege? They told me I don't have to say anything, that you need my consent and stuff." Her voice had started to ebb as though she was short of breath.

Christian watched the girl carefully. She had no idea what to do next. Was this all a game? The girl seemed in her right mind, but then again, sociopaths often seemed normal to the general public.

"Ok. Let's make a deal." Christian pulled out her tape recorder and a piece of paper from her briefcase. "First, I need you to sign this paper and agree to be honest. If you cooperate with me, I'll help you get out of here." Her voice was firm and her gaze constant. The report that she'd received from the hospital three days earlier had convinced her to make the two plus hour trip on a Sunday. Shelly's diagnosis was based on interview, a series of psychological assessments and a review of her prior mental health history. Her Axis I on the nationally-recognized DSM 4 was post-traumatic stress disorder with psychotic features. Bipolar Disorder was ruled out as was Borderline personality disorder. There was no indication of drug or alcohol abuse, though nicotine use was cited. Her GAF or Global Assessment of Functioning was at 35. This was low, but not unusually so for someone who'd experience a severe or acute trauma. In fact, Christian was fairly sure that her own GAF would have been scored as low, or perhaps lower after Tony died.

This diagnosis was necessary to give her pursuit validity. Had the girl been diagnosed with bi-polar, a manic episode could produce some significant inconsistencies in information. Borderline Personality disordered folks were even more unreliable. In Christian's experience, a 'borderline' would tell a lie simply for the fun of it, with no gain other than to experience pleasure from the drama that the lie might cause.

Had Shelly had either diagnosis, she wouldn't have wasted her time.

Still she cringed inside at her own measure of deceit. Her promise to Shelly had little to do with the truth. Getting the so-called deposition from the tormented teenager had required a nod of approval from the prosecutor. He'd agreed that if Shelly had any significant information to share regarding the murders, that she would inevitably be required to submit to a polygraph. Due to her highly agitated mental state, her testimony was circumspect at best. However, since Christian was still licensed as a mental health therapist in Washington, her future testimony could be considered expert. However, she was severely scolded for going to the Smithson home and was told that if she chose to do any more amateur sleuthing, Shelly would not only be pulled from her caseload, but the P.O. could be charged with interfering in the investigation.

Her hands were sweating as she watched Shelly read the consent form. It indicated that should the investigation require a polygraph that she would be willing to submit to one. Ironically, after the girl finished reading the form, she nodded and signed her name without a question.

Christian forced a smile as she clicked on the tape recorder. "Ready?"

Shelly laid her head down on the Formica table and sighed. "It is horrible, what he did. He's an evil person and he did killed Mrs. Maltos and Cassie. Ya wanna know why? 'Cuz she was with Jerry. You see, he wanted her and she wanted Jerry. That guy was crazy jealous."

Christian shook her head. "Who are you referring to, Shelly?

A disgusted sneer appeared on the girl's narrow face. "Wouldn't you like to know? I think you should try to guess. Still, if you get me out of here, I will tell you, just not until then. And you also have to convince my step-dad to let me be with Jerry again."

Christian's face grew hot. This girl was so manipulative. It was hard to believe that anything she might say would be worthy of the truth.

"Ok, so this is how it came down. We were supposed to go shopping that day. Tabby had decided that Cassie wasn't good enough for Jerry. We agreed that we would tell her something bad about Jerry, so that she would go back with Tommy. Plus Tabby was pissed that her guy was in love with Cassie. She hated Cassie for that."

"I thought that Tabby and Cassie were good friends?"

"*Were* good friends. But Tabby has this thing for him. Don't ask me why. And Cassie had slept with him a few times, so Tabby was out for blood. If you ask me, Jerry only wanted to be with her because he was trying to prove something."

"Prove something to whom?"

"To prove that he was as powerful as he is. Jerry has always hated the way all of the girls at church followed him around. He's had sex with nearly every GG. He even had sex with one of the visiting pastors' daughters. And Jerry's a normal guy, you know. For a long time, he looked up to *him.* Then, when he found out what he was really like, it freaked out Jerry."

"So if Jerry didn't like the way that the killer treated women, why didn't he reported *him* to the police?"

Careful, Christian, don't push this. Let the girl tell you her source on her own.

"Well, he...I don't know. He's not scared of him, but I think since he was...never mind. I'm not going to say any more."

Christian made her voice sound as gentle as possible. "You poor girl. You've been carrying this information around, trying to protect the man you love. No wonder you had a meltdown. That's too much for anyone. Tell me, why did you and Jerry break up?"

The girl gazed down at the table for a long while, clutching the sides of her head and rocking slightly. Her eyes were filled with tears as she looked up.

"My stupid step-dad. He wouldn't let me see him anymore because he's so much older than me. And Jerry's a typical guy. He likes sex. Cassie would go up there on weekends and stay with him."

Christian shook her head. "That's not possible. She was on probation. Her parents knew that she wasn't allowed to travel by herself out of town."

Shelly gave her a look of scorn mixed with pity. "You probation officers think you know everything. How about this? Tabby and I were up at your house not long ago. I bet you didn't even know we were there. We wanted to tell you about what happened, but then Tabby chickened out on the last minute when we saw that dog of yours…he's *really* big. And as far as Cassie goes, she went up to WSU all the time. Her parents thought she was spending the night with Tabby. They lied for her."

"Who lied?"

"Tabby's parents. They were sick of my parents threatening to turn Jerry into the police for going out with little Miss Underage here, so when he started seeing Cassie, they decided to hide it from her parents so that they wouldn't have the same problem all over again. Of course, Jerry and I had plenty of phone sex. I was the one who he really wanted to be with."

Christian wanted to scream. How could decent-appearing adults collude with their children like this? Furthermore, this girl had an uncanny ability to say it all without a trace of personal pride or sense of privacy. And unlike most teens, her bragging commentary didn't seem to be for the sake of shock value. She simply expressed herself that way.

"So how did Jason get the gun?" Christian said the name, watching for the girl's reaction.

Shelly shrugged, but the tenor of her voice was now strained with tears. "I don't really know. I know that Cassie had shown him her dad's gun a few times, so he probably knew where it was and stole it. That day, a bunch of us girls were supposed to go shopping and then Tabby cancelled on the last minute and said that Jason had called her and that they were going over to Cassie's to have a little talk with her. She seemed really angry about something. Tabby can be like that. If she's mad at you, watch out."

"So you're sure that Tabby went over there that day?"

"Didn't I just say that? I was hanging out with Jerry and he got a call from his sister sometime later that afternoon. She was screaming to come get her at Cassie's house, so we went over to pick her up."

"In Jerry's car?"

"Yeah. Anyway we didn't even get all the way to Cassie's house. When we turned onto 21st Avenue, Tabby was running down the street. She was totally freaked out."

"Where was Jason?"

"He was already gone. He actually left her there, at Cassie's. He probably wanted the cops to think that she did it. And that's why we didn't go to the cops. Cuz Jerry said that Jason would get people to lie for him, like Kelly from the church and then Tabby would get the blame for what he did."

"So when you picked up Tabby, what did she say?"

"Nothing. She wouldn't stop crying and then we just went to the river and smoked some reefer and when she finally calmed down, Jerry took her back to Pullman with him."

"Has she talked to you about it since?"

Shelly shook her head and looked away as a door slammed. "Great. It's snack time. And no, she doesn't talk about anything. Tabby's really good at pretending nothing has happened. One time she beat me up, just because she'd heard that I'd cheated on her brother. I didn't, but afterwards, she acted like she never touched me."

Christian was trembling all over now. The girl, despite her challenges, had verified what she'd believed all along. Just then, the sound of a bell rang and the girl stood up.

"That's good enough. We get brownies today and I want some." The moment offered her no words. She looked helplessly on, wishing for some stronger evidence. A mentally ill patient's word was about as good as a hollow bat. There was no power behind its thrust. As the girl turned to leave, she looked back over her shoulder at Christian. Her eyes radiated a simple answer as she said, "I have no reason to help you. I have no reason other than to protect Jerry. But I hate the guy as much as anyone could. I was his first. The poison that he gave me killed my baby, just like it did Cassie's and the others. *And* it made me sick for weeks. He doesn't know this, but I buried her. She deserves to have her memory."

Christian felt her head balloon. "Oh, Shelly. When did this happen?"

"A long time ago now. I was about twelve or maybe thirteen. He doesn't believe in using birth control. He's all about spreading his glorious seed. He has sex with every girl he can get his hands on. To tell you the truth, I was a complete sucker. He has this way about him and I fell into his trap. Then, when we get pregnant, he forces...." The girl paused to wipe a stray tear from her left cheek. "Anyway, when I get out, I will take you there. I will show you where I buried my baby."

The girl shuffled away out of the room. As she did, Christian closed her eyes and said a little prayer. "Please let this be enough." Opening her eyes moments later, Christian was surprised to find that Shelly had returned and was standing before her.

She reached down and tenderly took Christian's hand. "There are a few more of us that this happened to. Go to the church on Tuesday nights, after the girls' fellowship. He will be there with someone. But, Ms. Vargas, be careful. He's a very scary dude."

With that, Shelly Nunamaker left in search of brownies.

CHAPTER 20

♊

The Tuesday morning staff meeting started out with the usual ribbing. Daniel had forgotten to bring treats, and as the group of twenty probation officers relied on the weekly gathering's morning fare as their first meal of the day, there was no mercy for the guy.

"You're a cheap sucker, Daniel. What's with no snacks, buddy?" Doug Stamp cried. He was the drug court tracker, who weighed over two hundred and fifty pounds and was known for his foot fetish. He insisted on getting weekly pedicures, a strange fact that had been discovered by one of the female probation officers when she'd run into him at her favorite salon. The poor man had never lived it down.

"Up yours, Stamp. Go get your feet done. Pink polish would be beautiful on those fat, smelly toes." A roar of laughter filled the room as well as grumbling from those who were hungry and in no mood for jokes.

The topic of the day was logging gang entries into the juvenile tracking computer system, better known as JTS. The gangs in the Tri-City area were rampant and gang-related murders had been on the rise. Only eight months prior, a beloved coach had been stabbed to death as part of a juvenile gang initiation. The community was understandably mortified by the murder and as a result, the courts had instituted some stringent policies with regards to juvenile gang activity.

"The youth's monikers should be logged on the personal information page as well as any verified tats and, of course, known tagging activity," the gang advisor stated, as Christian's mind continued to wander a few minutes into the meeting. She was thinking about her vision at Maria's and the way that the memory seemed to cling to her like hope. Her father, whose presence was now recognized by someone other than herself, was also in the forefront of her mind. She had begun to pray to him at night, in front of the statue that Matt had given her. It was a quiet little ritual which included a single white candle and Bear. The dog seemed to thrive on her whispered words, and sat next to her, his tail slowly slapping the floor in a rhythmic counterpart to her singsong words.

Stella, who was sitting next to her at the far end of the table, nudged her softly. "Hey, where have you been?"

"What do you mean?"

"Girl, you've been checked out ever since your cocktail party. I talked to Matt yesterday and he's really worried about you. You've got to let the Maltos case go now. Jim is not a suspect anymore and from what I hear, he and your therapist have really hit it off."

Christian turned and gazed into Stella's eyes. "Thanks for your concern, Stell. I know I've been less than a good friend. It's just that it's too hard to explain."

Stella glanced over at their boss. Michael was shooting them the evil eye for talking. She shrugged and grabbed her calendar. Quickly she scribbled, "Lunch today? Thai. Please!!!"

Christian nodded and turned back to the meeting's speaker. Rick Jorgenson was a calm and sensible presence in their often high-strung or otherwise quirky probation staff. He deserved their respect and attention. She made a note to talk to him later about the gang aspect of cults. As an ex-communicated Mormon, he was the resident expert on such things.

By noon, Christian was ready to get out of the office, particularly because she'd skipped breakfast in lieu of the staff meeting's snacks, which never materialized. It had been a busy morning and she was sick of preparing court documents. She grabbed her coat and purse and headed out the door to Thai Delight.

Stella was waiting in a far corner booth at their favorite restaurant. The lunch buffet drew many court and county employees due to its expediency and ample choices. Christian was in no mood to run into work buddies, however, so she quickly scanned the room, ready to call Stella's cell for a change in venue if necessary. Because it was a Tuesday, the exotically-decorated restaurant was fairly empty. For her, it was the ambience of the place that she enjoyed above all else. There was nowhere else in the Tri-Cities that she felt so transported into another time and place. Gong-like bells played the strange Asian music that sent a wave of relaxation through her the minute that she'd walk through the door. Large marble statues of Buddha and gold-threaded tapestries filled the space which was otherwise a converted I-HOP from the 1980s. Incense burned in intricately carved bronze bowls and a large fountain, laced with ferns and floating water lilies filled the entryway. The Thai staff, silk-clad and serene, were always gracious and the food was consistently delicious.

Stella waved and stood up. "I took the liberty of ordering you some Thai iced tea. I know you love it. They just brought out the yellow curry and a fresh batch of satay chicken. Let's hit the buffet before this place fills up."

Christian took off her coat and immediately followed her friend to the buffet where they piled their plates with the spicy, aromatic food.

"Well," Stella began once they'd sat down. "I've missed you. What have you been doing and where in the hell is your head?"

Christian gazed at her friend and tried to figure out where to start. Finally she took a deep breathe and said, "Jason Roads is their killer. I have verbal testimony to prove it. However, I need more and Stella, if it takes me a lifetime, I *will* get it."

"What about Matt?"

"What about him?"

"Look, you told me three weeks ago that he was the most wonderful man you'd ever met. To be honest, I was shocked, only because you've kept Tony on a pedestal for so long. Now you have this guy who is crazy about you and has all the right stuff as they say, and you are more attentive to a murderer." Stella rolled her eyes dramatically.

"Whoa! Wait a minute. Matt understands this completely. He has no problems with my desire to solve this case."

"Oh really? Well, if you hadn't noticed, you've lost probably ten pounds, you are as skinny as a rail and frankly, not a lot of fun to be around. You keep to yourself and hell, if I was him, I'd be getting really tired of it."

Christian felt the anger rise from deep in her gut to the top of her skull. Stella had been her friend for a long time and was never one for mincing her words. However, this type of scolding was uncalled for.

"You know, I love you like a sister, and I can take your feedback most of the time, but right now, you're the one who is out of line.

Matt *is* worried about me. You don't think I know that? But he also understands that this is a process that I must complete. I have shared more with him in the last four months than I ever did with Tony and that is a good thing. You say that I've always put Tony on a pedestal and you're right. Matt has changed all that. And he loves me, really loves me for me. I can tell him anything, no matter how weird, and he always makes a connection to what I'm trying to tell him. Tony would just laugh at me. I can't believe I'm really saying this aloud, but Stell, if Matt were to ask me to marry him, I think I'd say yes, without hesitation."

Stella grinned from ear to ear. "So you love him, too. Wow, Chrissie, I never in a million years expected to hear this. You... getting married again? I would have bet my pathetic pension that you'd never marry again after Tony died. *Wow.* That's all I can say."

Christian's eyes filled with tears. "I know the Maltos murders are my obsession. But you didn't know those women and you weren't supposed to be there when they were killed. What if I'd been there, with the county car in the driveway? Would Jason had come in? And if he had, would Sue Maltos had reacted to him like she did. No, probably not. And even if she had, I'd have been there, to help calm things down. And Cassie would have been up-stairs with us rather than in her room downstairs."

Stella held up her hand. "Wait a minute. I don't have a clue what you're talking about. Why don't you start at the beginning?"

♊

By the time that Christian arrived home for work, her neck and shoulders felt like someone had taken a sledgehammer to them. Telling Stella the entire story, from the night of the murders until the present, had helped to solidify the facts in her mind, but had also been heinous journey into the land of failure. Her friend was right. She had to finish this and move on with her life. Recognizing how stuck she'd actually become was obvious to her now. Christian drove into the garage and pressed the button to close the garage door. Climbing out of her car, she thought back on the night of the party again. She and Matt had scoured the perimeter of the house, looking for any clue as to the identity of their visitor, but to no avail. She'd asked the neighbors if they'd seen anything, but Deb and her husband had been in her living room at the time and the neighbors across the street had been out of town.

Bear was nowhere to be seen as she came into the house. She thought it was odd that he had not met her at the door. She walked into the kitchen and found him on his haunches, busily chewing on something. She greeted him with a pat on the head. He looked up momentarily and then returned to chewing voraciously on a large, rawhide bone. She glanced down, mumbling, "Where did you get that?"

Christian had stopped buying Bear the expensive rawhide bones because he devoured them nearly whole. In the past, she'd had to take him to the vet twice to have the things removed from his stomach. She bent down and took the bone from the dog. He groaned impatiently, but relented. Pulling a recently purchased packet of stew meat from the refrigerator, she opened it, pouring the contents into his dog bowl. "This will have to do, buddy."

She gazed at the soggy bone in her hand. It was a fancy variety that her veterinarian sold, which was advertised as an organic product. She recognized the brand's symbol of a bull's head embossed on the bone's middle section.

Closing her eyes, she felt a vague memory tug at the outreaches of her mind. She had seen this type of bone at someone's home recently. She turned it over in her hands to see if it had been buried. In the past, whenever Bear had buried these bones, the crevasses of the rawhide's design would end up containing more dirt than a small potted plant. She noticed that the bone was completely clean, except for Bear's slobber.

She thought back again as she wandered over to the large whiteboard that was marked with all of her investigative notations. Halfway down the far left column was the name Smithson. She snapped her fingers as Bear wandered in from the kitchen, licking his lips happily.

"That's it. The Smithson's dog was chewing on one of these when I was visiting last week," she said, taking the slimy bone from the dog. Bear looked longingly at the prize, following her as she jumped up and ran into the computer room. Quickly she typed the name of the brand, *Vitamight Canine Treats* onto the google search engine bar. The name of the company came up. She pressed *cache* and opened to their home page. Two more clicks and she'd found the local distributors for their products. Her vet was the only merchandiser listed.

Bear continued to gaze at her with rapt attention, as though she was his god, mother and girlfriend all rolled into one. He gave a regretful sigh. Christian gazed down at him. "Hey, sorry. Here you go." Placing the bone on the floor in front of him, she picked up the phone. The receptionist at Dr. Grayson's office had become somewhat of a friend over the years. She was certain that if she used a little charm, she could find out whatever she needed to know.

"I just talked to her." Christian said to Matt on the phone just minutes later. "She said that the last person to buy one of those bones was Tabby Smithson. She said she remember it because Tabby wanted to put the bone on her mother's credit card and they wouldn't allow it without her mother's approval. Jill then suggested that they call Tabby's mom, and she said that Tabby became upset and paid for it in cash instead. And Matt, she bought it on day of our party."

"I think I know where you're going with this. You think that Tabby brought a bone for Bear, to keep him happy while she left her little message in the garbage can?"

"Which confirms what I thought before."

"What's that, Sherlock?"

Christian grinned. Matt had taken to calling her Sherlock which she found both amusing and endearing.

"My dear fellow," she continued in her best English accent. "Have you forgotten the strange case of the Vargas property trespassers?"

Matt laughed. "Actually, now that you mention it, I do," he replied in a cockney twang. "So you believe your mysterious trespassers were casing the joint for a future crime?"

"Evidently so, my dear Watson. Evidently so."

♊

Later than night, upon opening the garage door, she could see her breath from the immediate chill. Soon to be freezing outside, it was one of those late spring nights when the day had offered the sweet auspices of spring, but the evening had brought temperatures that could kill. The full moon looks like the character from Pete-in-the-Box commercials, she mused, gazing up as Bear climbed into the Subaru.

The car was actually a nice change from her old Volkswagen. The hatchback was very convenient for Bear. Low to the ground, but roomy enough for the dog, he was able to jump in without a hitch, despite his handicap. Matt had helped her to find the car and later, he'd custom-designed her music system. She smiled as her high-quality speakers filled the car with a new Dave Matthews tune. She'd added that feature after Jerry Smithson showed up at her office with five hundred dollars, which had covered her insurance deductible. The young man was very wary during their meeting, but Christian had made a point of hinting at her knowledge of his part in the Maltos murders. Though she'd been tempted to report him for the hit and run, it now seemed pointless. He seemed to have some remorse. Furthermore, she needed Jerry to testify against Jason Roads and a felony hit and run would not encourage that.

She considered her progress. Despite Shelly's signed statement and taped testimony, the prosecutor's office hadn't reopened the case. According to the lead prosecutor for adult matters, Shelly's mental state was questionable and, as a result, her statements could be thrown out of court by an astute defense attorney. Additionally, Shelly had tried to slit her wrists after Christian had left the hospital and was now a bigger liability than asset.

As she turned off the highway and headed closer to her destination, Christian thought about Matt. He was the best thing to come along in ages and she didn't like to deceive him, but he would have tried to prevent her from going on this clandestine excursion. In her mind, she had to find one more witness to Jason's cruel and cunning exploits. Cassie was dead, Shelly was mentally ill and the abortion victim's mother had had no further contact with her, so it was a still a weak case at best.

Christian and Matt had scoured her property in the hopes of finding another clue as to the identity of the mother of the dumped fetus. If Shelly was telling the truth, the poison that Jason forced her to take to induce the early labor could have remained in the mother's system for a while, but not necessarily transfer to the fetus. Without knowing the identity of the mother, time had become the enemy. Furthermore, Harry had explained that even when mothers took illegal drugs, the unborn baby's blood often didn't show use. "It's like secondhand smoke. It can kill you eventually, but the affected person doesn't necessarily have direct signs of tobacco use, such as stained teeth or a nicotine odor."

Christian had mulled over the situation since she'd visited Shelly Nunamaker. Finally she'd decided that it was time to act alone. Bear would have to serve as her bodyguard. She'd trained the dog to come to a certain command. Her plan was to park her car in the adjacent parking lot, close enough to the church so that if she needed his help, Bear would hear her. By leaving the Subaru's passenger window completely rolled down and placing a stick in the backdoor of the church, she could call for her dog and he would jump out of the car's window and push his way into the church via the open door. The plan seemed foolproof. Fortunately, when she was scared, Bear would be a force to be reckoned with.

The church was dark when they arrived. The dashboard clock glowed the time of day. It was seven minutes to midnight. Christian turned her headlights out as she entered the parking lot and scanned the grounds. There were two cars parked near the front doors of the church. The church van was parked to the side of the building. Whoever was left in the church would undoubtedly exit through the front to reach their cars.

As she drove closer, she could see that one of the cars belonged to Jason and the other was one that had been parked there before. The bright blue Honda Civic LXI had been there when she and Matt had gone to Sunday services. She wondered if the car belonged to the young woman who had been in Jason's office that morning.

There were no street lights where she parked the car. The darkness seemed to drop like a heavy weight as she zipped up her coat and carefully opened her car door. With a shiver, she whispered to Bear to stay put and then apologized for having to leave the door open. The dog was unlikely to be cold, she reminded herself, patting his furry head as she said goodbye.

Tiptoeing towards the backdoor of the church, she realized that she hadn't thought this through. What if the back door had already been locked for the evening? Sure enough when she tried to open it, it didn't budge. With a hiss of frustration, she paused to gather her thoughts. Was there another way to reach the back door without having to enter the sanctuary?

She glanced around at the outside of the building. When Jason had taken her into the church from that door, they had turned left and walked down a hallway before turning into the main lobby which led into the sanctuary. There had been a kitchen on the other side of the main doors, which probably had another entrance via the hallway to the right of the back door. Christian retraced her steps, focusing on the small windows along the building. When the windows stopped, she was forced to turn the corner and head back to where she'd parked the car. She continued slowly along until she noticed a piece of metal that stuck out from the outer wall. Stepping closer, she noticed it was a vent for an oven fan. The kitchen had to be on the other side of the wall, which meant that if she could enter the church from the main doors undetected, she could slip through the kitchen and down the hall to unlock the back door.

Bear put his head out the window and whined softly. "Shhh!" Christian warned. The dog immediately put his head back into the car. He knew her tone of voice well enough to know when she was perturbed. The sound of a train's whistle could be heard in the distance, but there was no traffic along the road that bordered the church.

The entrance of the church was easily visible from the road. She glanced around as she turned the corner and headed to the set of glass doors. Fortunately they only had a double bolt and otherwise could be pushed or pulled by handles. No knob to turn made her entrance easier. She pressed her face against the glass and peered in. The sanctuary was dimly lit. A hall light lit up the passage to the kitchen. She'd have to pass the open doors leading directly into the sanctuary in order to reach it. Slowly she pushed open the front door and listened for voices. It was quiet as she slipped in and hurried toward the kitchen where she propped open the door.

The area was quite large and a small island counter sat in the middle of it. Stepping toward the far side of the room where another door appeared, she heard loud voices coming down the corridor. In a panic, she dropped to her knees and crawled to the far side of the island. A large refrigerator sat along the eastern wall. The voices continued to increase in volume. Her heart was pounding and she suddenly felt slick with fear as she crouched further under the island top and pressed herself against its cabinetry.

"It's in here. Stop your ridiculous crying." There was a pause and then a girl's voice responded tearfully.

"Why can't we just get married? I wouldn't have done it with you if I didn't think you'd be there for me."

"Shut up, you stupid woman." The voices grew louder.

The kitchen door swung open and from where she crouched, Christian could see two sets of feet. Jason stomped into the room, evidently furious about something. She held her breath and slowly reached into her pocket.

The refrigerator door opened and the sound of clanking glass echoed through the large room. Finally Jason said, "Here it is. Kelly, it's easy. You just drink this stuff tonight and the problem will be gone tomorrow."

"No. I won't drink it. It's wrong to kill your baby. You said, that if anything happened, you'd stick by me." Kelly's voice was a pathetic whimper. Suddenly she issued a little squeal as Jason growled. "You will drink this stuff, if I have to hold you down and pour into your throat, do you hear me?"

Kelly's whimpers rose into sobs. "No. I don't want to be like the other GGs. I am better than that. Let me go."

The sound of a smack was followed by a scream and Kelly was on the floor. Christian instinctively crawled from her hiding spot to find Jason kicking her mercilessly. Grabbing her pepper spray, the probation officer instantly felt another item in her pocket. Pulling it out, she blew on it as hard as she could. Her dog's whistle would get him here, one way or the other.

Standing up, she pointed the spray in Jason's direction. She yelled his name and he slowly turned around, his face an instant mask of surprise. "What are you doing in here?" His voice sounded muffled and drawn as though he were being pulled underwater.

Christian was three feet from Jason as she pressed the button of the pepper spray. At first, nothing came out. He began to laugh, an evil bellow that filled the room with dire warning. His eyes glittered like lethal shards of glass and his waxy complexion gleamed mask-like. Moving towards her, Jason became a terrifying pantomime of his former self. He grabbed her outstretched hand and yanked her towards him. The act was so powerful that she was flung forward like a rag doll. A loud snapping sound from her shoulder echoed through her body as she became dizzy with pain, but a surge of fear kept her from falling. Ducking her head, she kneed him as hard as she could in the groin. Meanwhile Kelly was screaming for help.

"Call the police," Christian yelled as Jason groaned with pain. Reaching into her pocket with her other hand, Christian tried to grab her cell phone, but it was no use. Her arm simply wouldn't cooperate. "Get my dog," she cried. Just then, Jason raised his right fist and slugged the P.O. in the face. She saw white flashing light as pain seared through her head. Her eye felt like it was going to burst. She felt herself falling, but lifting the can again, she sprayed blindly. The aerosol finally kicked in. Jason screamed and began to choke, but the small amount of poison didn't have the effect that Christian had hoped for. Jason lurched wildly in her direction, tackling her to the ground.

Christian heard the sound of a door open as the room began to close in around her. Then there was a rushing sound in her ears as Jason pounded her face again. She kicked and squirmed to get free, but his hands were around her throat. She fought to breathe as he pressed his fingers deeper into her skin. Then, suddenly, he was falling towards her, his face coming within inches of her own. She could smell a wooly scent and hear an angry growl as Bear's teeth clamped down on Jason's neck. The man screamed and thrashed, trying to get the dog away from him, but Bear was invincible. The dog held on and dragged Jason by the neck until he had pulled the man off of Christian. He shook Jason like a rag doll while the man howled in pain.

"Tell him to stop," Jason begged through clenched teeth.

"He can eat you or you can tell Kelly here exactly what happened to Cassie and Sue Maltos." Christian gasped. Kelly had vanished.

Jason howled again as Bear stood on his back, completely pinning him to the floor.

"Take him, Bear." At the command, the dog's teeth sunk deeper into Jason's neck. At that point, Kelly stepped back into the room.

"I called them," she stammered.

"Tell me about the Maltos murders, or I'll tell Bear to start ripping," Christian ordered again.

"I killed them, okay! I killed Cassie and her mom!"

Kelly's eyes grew wide as Christian gave one more command. "Lie down, Bear."

The dog continued to hold onto Jason's neck, but now laid himself down so that he was essentially covering the young man's body with his own. Jason flailed and kicked as Christian jumped up and swiftly opened the utility closet. Though she could hardly see, she found an extension cord which she grabbed, motioning to Kelly to help.

Jason had curled up into a ball and was trying his hardest to kick the dog. Christian quickly moved to tie his feet, though his thrashing made it difficult. Sweat and blood dripped into her eyes as she fought his movement, but Bear hadn't loosened his grip on the man, who was now sobbing with defeat. Kelly finally reacted by grabbing one of his legs while Christian was able to sit on the other. First they tied his hands together and then, pulling his feet up, they bound them tightly together with the remaining length of cord.

Christian couldn't keep her eyes open any more. Her shoulder was screaming with pain and her head hurt so badly that she thought she might vomit. Slowly she slid to the floor. The cold linoleum felt good on her face. She fought to stay awake, but it was no use. Bear began to lick her nose, but his touch couldn't stop the feeling that she was being sucked down a hole. The last thing that she heard was the sound of sirens far away.

There is no rest for the wicked.
Anonymous

CHAPTER 21

♊

Christian was lying in the hospital bed, with a nurse poking and prodding, when she heard his voice. Two large icepacks covered her eyes, but that didn't stop the tear squeezed out of each. She felt his hand on her knee as he bent down and whispered, "I love you." His kiss on her lips was soft and careful, but she still felt a sting.

Trying to stop her tears, Christian replied, "I'm sorry. I'm sorry I didn't call you first." Her throat was raw and it hurt to talk.

The sound of rollers moving across a linoleum floor competed with the beep of a machine as Matt took her hand. "You are so lucky, Christian. He could have killed you."

"But he didn't!" she whispered.

"Thanks to Bear!"

"I know. That's why I took him along. By the way, I love you, too." Christian focused on her body for a moment. She could move her arms and legs, but her shoulder was throbbing. She groaned in pain as she tried to roll over.

"Hey, you need to stay still!" she heard as the nurse's plump face came into view.

"But it hurts," Christian whimpered, feeling as though she might be sick.

"You're due for your next shot. Here, honey, this should help," the kindly woman replied. In seconds, the sensation of peace filled her as a warm blanket of pain medication rolled down her body and she was out.

When Christian awoke, Matt was still there, sitting by her bedside. The beeping sound had gone and soft voices could be heard. "She's good. They've checked for a concussion and broken limbs. Its two black eyes and a dislocated shoulder for our intrepid warrior. She's darn lucky." She heard Matt say. Then Michael's voice.

"Man, if I knew she'd had guts like that, I would have put her in charge of SAP. She's one tough little gal." Despite her vague dislike of the man, she suddenly sensed his admiration and liked it.

"Can she hear us?" Michael continued.

"Yes, I can," she replied, her voice still scratchy and raw. "And no, I don't want the SAP program, thank you very much!" she added, trying to offer a smile.

"You're not such a pretty sight right now. Take as much time as you need, but call me tomorrow," Michael said. "I've got to get back to the office now."

"Thanks for coming by."

"No problem. The gang sends their love. See you soon, I hope."

After he left, Christian started to giggle. "I didn't think that man would ever give me kudos for anything. I had to get kicked to the curb to get a complement!" She tried to smile, but her mouth hurt. She managed a small grin.

"He's not the only one who's proud of you. You're looking, or trying to look, at your biggest fan. And you should hear what the newspaper wrote about you. Here, let me read it to you."

Juvenile probation counselor, Christian Vargas, used her guts and cunning to catch a killer. After months of unanswered questions and a lack of suspects, Christian Vargas was able to get a confession to the murders of Sue and Cassie Maltos from the girl's youth pastor, Jason Roads. But not without some help. Christian's well-trained dog, Bear, was at her side. This is the second time that the local police have had this woman and her dog to thank for their assistance in solving a crime in our community."

"Stop, that's enough. You know I can't stand the media and that paper is no exception."

Matt chuckled. "What you mean is, you can't stand being the center of attention. But that's going to be the way it is, for a while anyway."

"So what happened?"

"Jason's in jail. He's had his first appearance yesterday."

"Wait, what day is it?"

"Thursday."

"What? I've been in here since Tuesday night?"

"Honey, you've been in and out. That guy beat you up pretty bad. I can't believe you were able to tie him up, with the way you looked when you came in here. That shoulder alone should have put you out of commission."

She started to ask about her shoulder when her brother appeared at the door. "Oh my god, look at you. Better already! I wondered if you were ever going to wake up. You were quite the sleeping beauty."

She gave Scott a grimace as he bent down to give her a kiss on the cheek. "Well, it appears that your appearance *and* attitude has improved since Tuesday night."

"*Great.* Hey, Matt, give me the mirror and the brush in my purse, please!" Matt shook his head as he handed her a small mirror. She gazed at herself briefly as she brushed out her hair. "Geez, how many people have seen me like this?" Christian exclaimed, as a sudden realization flooded her.

"Let's see, almost everyone from work, most of your neighbors, and at least four of your probation kids," Daniel sauntered into the room. Despite Matt's presence, he walked over and planted a kiss on Christian's swollen lips.

"Ouch. That hurts, not to mention it's not allowed." She shot Daniel the squint-eye, but there wasn't much effort behind it. Matt offered no reaction, nor did Scott.

Daniel raised his hand in the victory sign and slugged Matt softly on the arm. "I told you I'd get away with it at least once in my lifetime," Daniel joked.

"So what's that supposed to mean?" Christian looked from one man to the other.

Daniel looked down at her. "I made a bet with your boyfriend here that I'd get at least one kiss out of you before you two tied the knot. I knew that you'd have to be incapacitated or dead in order to do it, so I took my chance when I had it."

"Very funny. What's with the tying of the knot comment anyway?"

Daniel shrugged as Matt looked awkwardly up at the ceiling. Eventually Scott raised his hand. "This is getting too deep for me. I'm going downstairs to get a latte. Anyone else want one?"

There were detailed orders, the pulling of wallets and passing of cash. As Scott turned to leave, he said, "Daniel, come with me. I can't carry four coffees without hurting myself."

After the men had left the room, Matt looked at Christian sheepishly. "So I guess you forgot. And I guess I had bad timing."

Christian gazed at him. One glance in the mirror had left her relieved to see that though it looked like a heavy-handed make-up artist had gone to work on her eyes and her lips resembled the commercials for collagen injections, she didn't look as bad as she'd expected.

"Please explain!" she insisted. Gently he took her right hand into his own. His grip was firm and reassuring and a sense of safety permeated her being.

"Maybe we should wait to talk about this when you're feeling better."

"I don't think so. What about Daniel's comment?"

Matt sighed and began to explain. "I know it's soon, but I have this thing about wanting to do the right thing. After you asked me to move in a few weeks ago, I talked to my mom. She's raised us to be traditional and she doesn't approve of us living with our partners without a marriage certificate, or at least an engagement ring. So I bought a ring and I brought it here yesterday, when you were awake. I thought you were okay when I asked you to marry me. You said yes, but, I'll understand if you want to change your mind, under the circumstances."

Christian tried to lift her left hand, but her shoulder wouldn't cooperate. Her eyes filled with tears as she whispered, "I remember now. I can feel the ring on my finger. Please, help me lift my hand so I can see it!"

Cautiously and with utmost care, Matt took her left hand and lifted it close to her face. She gazed at the glistening piece of jewelry on her finger. It was a large, radiant-cut diamond set in a narrow platinum band. It fit her finger perfectly. She couldn't speak for a long moment. Evidently she'd been more drugged up on pain meds than either of them had realized, yet the warm memory of his proclamation of love and promise to be faithful resonated like an old song. Christian nodded slowly. "I remember now."

He replied, "Do you like it?"

Christian gazed at this wonderful, kind man. "It's absolutely perfect. I don't know what to say, Matt."

Matt stared into her eyes. "It's a Canadian diamond, so you don't have to worry. No conflict diamond for you, honey." Christian could see the light sheen of perspiration on his forehead. He rarely showed his nerves in that way. "I just hope you'll still say yes." His eyes became shiny as he continued. "I love you. I respect you and God knows, I want to take care of you. You're such an amazing woman, but I'm not a guy who can live in limbo. I guess I'm an anomaly in today's world. I actually like commitment." He paused and gave a nervous chuckle. "I've never wanted to marry anyone before now. I give you me, Christian. I know I'm just a Black man from lynching country. Maybe that isn't so appealing, but I'm also smart, I work hard and I believe in being faithful. If that's not enough, I don't know what is."

Christian swallowed hard. She felt light and happy despite the stabbing pain that raced up her arm as she reached forward and pulled him to her. "Kiss me, Matt."

He put his lips tentatively on hers. She pressed back, ignoring the pain and opened her mouth as his tongue touched hers. Their kiss went on for a long time and her heart began to race for the want of him.

When he pulled away, she whispered, "I love you and I want this, too. I've been so afraid of loving someone else, but something has changed for me since you came into my life. You've always been there for me." she paused, her heart wracked with guilt and love and something indefinable. "I guess I need to think. My mind is so confused."

The handsome man standing before was everything she'd ever wanted. It just felt too soon and there were the risks of being with someone like her. Should she place another person in danger? Matt's warm brown skin slowly, almost imperceptibly, began to darken. Rejection marked his features as his eyes slowly traveled to the floor.

"So, I'm pushing you. I'm sorry. I can wait. The ring can wait." He slipped the box from her hand and quickly put it into his pocket.

"I'm not saying 'no'," Christian started and then fell silent. They gazed at one another with emotions now too strong for words. Just when she thought she might start to cry, Daniel walked back into the room.

"Here's your coffee. It looks like you two have been up to something," Daniel charged.

"We're fine." Christian's voice was sharp, but measured. Daniel looked from one to the other and seemed to take in the significance of her reply.

"Sorry if I walked in on something important, but Tabby Smithson is outside. She wants to talk to you."

Christian looked at Matt. "I think I should talk to her alone. Will you guys give us a few minutes?"

"The Sonics are playing on the tube in the waiting room. Call my cell when you want us back," Matt replied. He gently squeezed her hand and smiled. Then leaning forward, he murmured in her ear, "You're mine."

After the men shuffled out, Christian waited for a few minutes. Finally Tabby entered the room. Her face was puffy and red and her navy blue running suit looked crumpled. Her hair was pulled up in a haphazard ponytail and there was a drag to her step. "Hi. How are you doing?" Her face first registered honest shock at Christian's appearance. Then she quickly switched her gaze to casual indifference.

"I'm doing better, I guess. How are you?" Christian gestured to the chair next to the bed. "Here, sit down."

Tabby sat down and looked around the room, refusing to make eye contact. Christian waited her out. Tabby was one of the strangest girls that she'd met in a long time. Her interest was directed at the television on the opposite wall, which was on, but muted. A Jerry Springer episode was playing. A cluster of people were sitting in a row next to the talk show host. On the lower part of the screen, a running commentary stated the issue: *middle-age mother sleeps with son's girlfriend.* The trio looked strangely titillated by the opportunity to be on television. All appeared to weigh over three hundred pounds and were copiously adored with tattoos. "Do you like to watch Oprah?" Tabby asked, her gaze glued to the silent screen.

"No, not particularly. Why?"

"I don't know. I watch it most days after school. She says some good things sometimes and I really like that doctor guy on it."

"Dr. Phil?"

"Yeah, him."

Silence beat down on them like hot sun, but the girl did not leave. "What do you like about Dr. Phil?" Christian's exhaustion challenged her desire to spend another moment with Tabby.

"I like the way he talks about relationships and honesty. I have to tell you something, Ms. Vargas. It's really, really bad."

"Is it about Jason?"

"Yes…Jason and me."

"You are the one who brought me the dead baby that night." Christian said the phrase as matter-a-fact as she might discuss the weather. She realized in that instance that her father was with her, his presence there, reassuring her thoughts and actions.

Tabby's fragile features crumbled like parchment paper as anguish filled the space between them. She stared as tears rolled down her cheeks. Soon her face was dripping. Long trails of tears snaked down her neck and onto the fabric of her sweatshirt. She didn't make a sound, but her body convulsed with emotion. Christian strained to sit up straighter and with her good hand, grabbed Tabby's arm and pulled her toward her.

"Come here, Tabby," she whispered as the girl fell against her and wept. Deep sobs wracked her body as Christian softly stroked her head and continue to reassure her. "It's okay, Tabby. You can cry. It hurts to lose your baby and it hurts to lose your friend."

Finally, after a long while, the girl rose off the woman. Christian's hair and skin was wet with the girl's tears. The young one stared down at her hands for a long time and then began to speak.

"I went with him that day. He was going to tell her it was over. Jason knew that she might be pregnant. Cassie was vindictive and could make things worse for us. We didn't know that her mom was home. We didn't see her car there." Her hands trembled and her mouth twitched slightly as she explained.

"I was with him in the bedroom when he grabbed the gun away from Mrs. Maltos. She had told him she knew about his lies, his talking in tongues and that she was going to reveal him to our pastor. He shot her at least twice before Cassie came upstairs. I begged him to stop and told Cassie to run, to get away. I tried to push him down, but he smacked me in the face and I fell. Then I scrambled out of the room before he could kill me, too. I heard the gun shots and ran. He was wearing my brother's sweater and I thought that he'd try to blame my brother. I was so scared. I called my brother to come get me and after we dropped off Shelly, we kept going, all the way to Pullman. We spent the weekend there. He made me call our mom and tell her that we were already in Pullman, even though we were barely out of Kennewick, so she'd tell the cops that I'd been out of town. That's why she told you that I wasn't there that day."

Christian took the girl's hand. "I need you to tell the police about this." Tabby's eyes grew wide with fear. "But I thought he already confessed. That's what the newspaper said."

"Yes, Tabby, but they will need collaborating evidence. He's claiming that he confessed under duress; that I forced him to. He said that the bullet casing was planted by your brother. His prints were not on the gun and the neighbors reported seeing your brother's car in the neighborhood, so the investigative team could not even place him at the scene. It will be up to you to tell the whole story. You will probably do some time in Juvy, but maybe not. You were also under duress by the sounds of things."

"But the evidence is gone. He has a car detailing business. He cleaned his car up right afterwards. He told me. And he tried to give back the bloody sweater, but I washed it. It belonged to my brother." The girl dove into a new round of tears, now sobbing loudly. Then she stopped and stared at Christian. "His boots. His work boots. They are in the janitor's closet at the church. Maybe they have some blood on them. I know he was wearing them that day."

She nodded affirmatively. "Tabby, you're a smart girl. So you know that we'll need some honest testimony. You can talk to the prosecutor and I will make sure that you are protected from criminal charges."

"Actually I will," Scott said as he stepped into the room. "My partner and I will act as your attorney, Tabby. You can be assured that we will strike a deal for you. We need that guy behind bars and you can help us do that. You are a brave girl for coming here today," Scott said, his sonorous voice lending confidence to the girl. She smiled slightly.

"Ok, I have something else that might help." Tabby reached into her purse as Scott and Christian exchanged glances of disbelief. This was too good to be true.

"Here. I got these out of his office at church. They were hidden pretty well, but I knew about them, so I kept looking. I finally found the envelope taped under the bottom of his desk. I tried not to touch them too much." Tabby shoved a manila envelope in Scott's direction. He gingerly opened it, and then paused to grab a pair of rubber gloves from the nurse's station.

"No sense in contaminating the evidence." He carefully slid out the contents. "There's a good chance that we can pulled some fingerprints off these." In his hand were several photographs of young women, each wearing a pink sweater like the one that Christian had found in Cassie's closet. Many were marked with large X's and next to them was a date.

Scott turned the photographs toward Christian. "What do you think this means?"

She gazed at each girl, recognizing Cassie, Tabby, Shelly and the plump receptionist from the ugly scene at the church only days before. There were several other photos, ten in all.

Tabby pointed to a photo of one girl with long black hair and a small nose piercing. "She moved away after he did it to her. No one knows where she went."

Scott paused. "Did what?"

"Got her pregnant and made her drink the poison." Tabby pointed to another photograph. "This girl, she kept her baby. She lives in Texas now."

"How did she get away from him?"

"She was the daughter of a visiting pastor. From what Jason told me, they didn't find out she was pregnant until she got back home. He's really scared she's going to tell on him, but I don't think she will. Before she left, he scared the holy daylights out of her."

"Do you know her name?"

"That's Casey McGraw. She lives in Austin, I think."

"The dates, those are all Sundays." Christian had been studying the pattern and realized that she had to be right.

"Yeah. He said that the only way the Holy Spirit would come to him, so he could speak at the sermons, speak in tongues, I mean, was if he…uh, had sex with one of us. Then, whenever he found out we were pregnant, he was like, crazy, that day in church. Everyone believed he had the gift then."

"Everyone but Sue Maltos." Christian fell quiet.

"Yeah. Cassie told me once that her mom hated Jason. I don't think she probably hated anyone in the world, but she didn't trust him and told me once to stay away from him, that he was a fake."

"Who's this last girl?" Christian pointed to a beautiful, young woman with dark red hair and pale skin who looked like she should be on the cover of Vogue.

Another deluge of tears started as Tabby blubbered, "She was my best friend. Jill Thompson. He did a number on her. She killed herself about two years ago." Christian stared for a long time at the photograph, eventually recollecting the story of a young woman who was found naked and dead in a cherry orchard. She had killed herself with one of her father's guns. They'd found her near a homemade altar that she'd built. There had been a good-bye note saying that Jesus had requested that she come home.

"Jason was horrible to her and she really believed in his powers, but she wouldn't sleep with him, so he made her feel bad. He told her that she was denying God by not sleeping with him. He drove her crazy and harassed her constantly. Finally she gave in to him. She called me that night, after they had sex. She was totally freaked out. It was against her beliefs, you know. Jill killed herself the next day. She was so ashamed. She was really into God. To tell you the truth, she was the best of all of us Gi Gis, or as I liked to call us, the Gemini Girls."

Scott flipped through the remaining pictures. "What about these girls? There are no Xs over their names."

"He hasn't gotten to them yet. See, when you first join our cell, the Gemini Girls, you have to go through this initiation thing at one of the meetings. You can ask any of the girls. He makes you do weird stuff like drinking a drop of his blood and then you have to lie down on this altar and he puts his hands on you. He says it's a cleansing ceremony." Christian jerked involuntarily, remembering the day in the church when Jason had done a similar process to her.

Tabby stopped and looked at her. "Are you alright?" Christian nodded, impatient to hear the rest.

"Go on," Scott encouraged, sending his sister a questioning glance.

"So then you get a pink sweater that he's bought especially for you, except all of us have one. He takes you into his office after one of the meetings, after he's sent everyone else home and he, like…" Tabby paused and looked up at the ceiling, her face flushed crimson with embarrassment. "Then he pulls out his…you know….and gets his stuff all over the sweater. It's really gross. You're not supposed to wash it after that."

"Then what?" Her brother had begun to take notes.

"Then he keeps working on you. He says that God needs him to put his seed in you and that you will get more grace from it. You know what I mean by that?"

Scott shook his head. "We both do. So you had to have sex with him and then you eventually got pregnant."

Tabby nodded, her tears welling again. "Yeah, but not right away. See, we were dating all last year, but we kept it a secret, of course, because of his age. Then after a while, all we did was fight."

"Fight about what?' Christian never took her eyes from the girl's. In that moment, she felt a deep tenderness for Tabby. She'd gotten trapped by Jason, who was clearly a sexual predator who knew how to manipulate young women.

The girl gave a violent shudder, as though an unseen force was shaking the truth out of her. "I wanted to keep my virginity. I believe…did believe that you should stay a virgin until you get married. After a while, Jason gave up on me because I wouldn't sleep with him. That's when he started dating Cassie."

"And she would sleep with him?" Scott pursued her like the defense attorney that he was.

Tabby nodded vigorously. "She probably slept with him the first night. He's very sexy when he wants to be and she's such a slut... was."

"Was she really, Tabby? Think about it. How was it different for you? Maybe Cassie was just young and curious and manipulated by a cunning psychopath who she believed loved her?" Scott said pointedly. Christian looked at her brother and read his mind like she'd done frequently over the years. She knew that if Tabby was called as a witness during the impending trial, her derisive opinions about Cassie's sexual behaviors could have a negative impact on her testimony.

The girl sighed heavily and wrung her hands. A putrid desperation leaked from her, poisonous and invisible, like the odor of someone dying. "I know I shouldn't say that. She was my friend, but I was so jealous. I couldn't stand that they were together. I tried everything to get them to break up. And at the point, I'd decided that I'd do anything that Jason asked of me. He said that we might be able to be together if I'd have sex with Cassie in front of him. He was into that kind of stuff...ménage something. So one night, when he was hiding in the choir robe closet, I tried to seduce Cassie myself. He said that if she went for it just once, that he'd break up with her to be with me. But she thought I was completely crazy and got really mad at me. Then I remembered that Cassie had always had a huge crush on my older brother. Jerry knew how much I wanted to be with Jason so he agreed to help me out. They hooked up and she dumped Jason. It was my last chance to get Jason back and it worked. Right before Cassie got killed, he came back to me. But this time, I gave in. I had to. The bad thing was that I got pregnant the second time we had sex, before I could get on some decent birth control. He made me stay pregnant for a few months, until I started to show. He liked sex more then because my breasts were bigger." Tabby dropped her head in embarrassment. "I know. It's sickening. He was rough sometimes, too. He began to scare me. I wanted to get married, but he just laughed at me. He said that he would deny that he was the father and if I tried to get a DNA test, he'd leave and go back down south where I'd never find him. The pregnancy was horrible. I was sick all the time. Eventually I freaked out and took the stuff… you know, the stuff that made me have miscarriage. I didn't want to have a baby on my own."

"This is a lot of information, Tabby." Scott said gently. "I need to talk to the prosecutor immediately. But don't worry. Just leave it up to me. Stay here and keep my sister company. In fact, do something with her hair, will you? She looks like she's been in one of those Tri-City windstorms I'm always hearing about."

Wiping her eyes, Tabby giggled nervously at his description and looked at Christian for an answer.

She would have preferred to kick her brother than to oblige him. "Great! There's a brush and an elastic band in my purse, Tabby. Would you be so kind as to braid my hair for me?"

Tabby found the brush and helped Christian to sit up as Scott left the room, dialing his phone as he did so. She slowly began to brush the older woman's hair. They were silent for a long time and then Christian recalled a question that had been nagging in the back of her mind.

"Tabby, let me see your ears."

"Why?" The girl stepped back and looked at her strangely.

"Do you have pierced ears?"

The girl relaxed and leaned in so Christian could have a closer look. "Yes."

"So you were there." Christian said more to herself than to the younger woman, recalling the earring that Bear had found under Sue Maltos's dresser.

"What?"

"We found one of your earrings at the scene. I saw the matching one in your jewelry box at home."

"You what? Wow. I didn't think probation officers did that kind of thing."

EPILOGUE

April 20, 2006

♊

The five days that they had spent with Matt's relatives in and around New Orleans had been both thrilling and discouraging to Christian. There was little change in the city from the documentary photographs that she'd seen in *Time* magazine, but fortunately Matt's family lived outside of the metropolis to the northwest and had therefore escaped the heinous impact of Katrina. At first, she had been nervous to meet Matt's extended family, but by the week's end, she'd fallen in love with all of them. Now the thought of spending two weeks sailing with Matt to the British Virgin Islands offered the most delicious anticipation that she'd felt in years. He'd convinced his captain friend to allow him to deliver the sleek, mono-hull racing vessel to Tortola for some minor repairs. On the way, Matt had promised to take her to the famous rock formations on Virgin Gorda and a number of the outlying islands before they completed their journey. From his vivid descriptions, the scuba diving alone promised to be an experience of a lifetime.

Earlier that afternoon, after they'd loaded up the boat with supplies and checked the weather reports, Matt had sailed the boat out of the harbor and set course to the southeast. Christian could see that he was in his element as she took his direction, helping to hoist the mainsail and jib before settling down with a glass of wine on deck. It was a balmy 82 degrees and promised to stay that way for at least another week. Matt smiled admirably as she slipped out of her shorts and stretched out in her new Vera Wang bikini.

"You look like a million bucks," he cried. "Come over here and give me a kiss."

"That sounds dangerous," Christian replied teasingly.

"No more dangerous than what I'm going to do to you tonight in bed," Matt replied boldly. She grinned and blew him a kiss instead.

Then, releasing a contented sigh, she thought of home and then, naturally, of the Maltos trial. The proceedings were in the tenth day and things for Jason Roads couldn't be going any worse. He had opted to act as his own defense and from the daily reports that she'd received from her brother, he was digging himself into a hole worthy of hell. Shortly after Tabby's confessions, Detective Jensen secured a search warrant and seized Jason's car. Though the killer had detailed it as Tabby had explained, the investigation team's infra-red lights had picked up several blood stains that he'd missed in the clean-up. That, along with the sweaters, the earrings, his bloody work boots, several of the Gemini Girls' testimonies as well has the DNA test proving paternity of Casey McGraw's baby had solidified the prosecutor's case. And the two homicides were only the beginning. Several statutory rape charges were pending.

Making her way to the bow of the boat, she reached for her windbreaker that was secured around a cleat. Pulling out a packet of postcards from the large inside pocket, Christian glanced around for a pen. It was time to finished writing a card to Maria. The photograph of a glowing moon rising over the Caribbean Sea seemed appropriate for the amazing little seer who had helped the probation officer to believe in the power of intuition. She wouldn't hesitate to call upon *La curandera* in the future, she thought, smiling to herself. As she flipped through the cards, a folded note dropped into her hand. Curious, she opened the note. It read:

September 15, 2005
Dear Christian,

I know I was a pain today and I'm really sorry. Sometimes, it's pure torture to be so close to you and not be able to touch you, or tell you how I feel. I guess I've been in love with you all along, since you first got hired here. I know my feelings have only increased with each day. It's no wonder I can't make my marriage work. But don't blame yourself It's my problem and my aching pleasure at the same time. I just hope that someday you will feel my love for you and return it back to me.

In my place of secrets, you're my girl. Daniel.

Christian felt her face flush a bright crimson as her heart swooped down into her lower belly and hovered there. She stayed very still, holding the sensation, and wondering as to its true meaning. Suddenly it was very clear. What was it with her body, always trying to screw up her life, trying to tell things she didn't want to hear? She read the note again, slower and almost luxuriously, knowing that Matt was far enough away that he would see her guilt fighting with desire. Did her face show this shameful moment? She turned so that her back was to Matt, though he was busy with the navigational maps.

No wonder she had refused Matt's proposal of marriage. She chewed on the inside of her cheek, trying to get her pounding heart back to normal. There was no way she was in love with Daniel. She was absolutely crazy about Matt. It was flattery that had captured her and that was an embarrassing admission at best. No, she had no interest in Daniel. That was for certain. She ripped the note up into tiny pieces and glanced back at Matt. He was still staring at the chart. She cursed her poor environmental choice and tossed the pieces overboard. They sunk quickly in the surf. There, she said to herself. That is the end of that. She missed one piece, however, which fluttered back and, as if by magic, slipped back into her open purse, from which she'd taken a pen.

A soft breeze swept through her hair and the sun warmed her skin, making it easier to push all thoughts of Daniel aside. She sent a prayer out for Jim. His new relationship with Sophia was evidently going well. From her last phone call to her new friend, the therapist had said that she'd rearranged her appointment schedule in order to be at the trial with Jim. Silently she congratulated herself for hanging in there and solving what seemed to be an unsolvable crime. Somewhere in the back of her mind, a quiet voice murmured that this wouldn't be the last time that she'd assist in solving a case. But whatever the future brought, she wanted to appreciate the moment and the man who had changed her life. She gazed over at Matt, trying to catch his eye, but he was looking at the map and setting their course. Closing her eyes, she focused instead on her father for a moment. Soon his handsome face appeared in her mind's eye. He was smiling at her and she could hear him say, "Rewards are sweet for the righteous. You deserve this, my darling girl." She laughed at her overactive imagination and opened her eyes, gazing up into the sky. As she did, the innocuous cloud bank on her right separated and a perfect rainbow suddenly appeared.

"Would you look at that!" Matt exclaimed. "A rainbow without rain. Now that's a first."

Christian smiled at him and replied knowingly, "And based on my most recent experience, it won't be the last."

Except from Torena's next mystery thriller for the Zodiac series
to be published in 2014
The Capricorn Kidnapping
By Torena J. O'Rorke

Christian Vargas crouched on the damp sand, her indigo eyes scanning the muddy riverbank for clues of the missing toddler. Brackish water pooled near her feet and a stiff breeze whipped angrily, knotting her long chestnut hair. Black and blue clouds hung like theater drapes over the White Bluffs. Another downpour was just minutes away.

Bear sniffed anxiously along the water's edge. His shiny black snout pushed at the ground as he began to dig. She stood and followed her enormous, three-legged dog, her gut churning at the thought of what they might find that morning. The two-year-old female had vanished from the steps of her grandmother's front porch the night before. Six deputies had been searching since dawn before they'd called out her amateur search and rescue team. The county's trained canine was apparently at the vet.

The juvenile probation officer knew something that the cops didn't know, not yet anyway. Two other little ones from the

Tri-Cities were missing as well. Christian, who was just thirty years old, had spent over five years at the juvenile justice agency and had worked in nearly every department. Recently she'd heard from Jill Thomas, a big-mouthed staff assistant in the dependency court, that two foster kids had gone missing a couple of days prior. Par for the course, neither child had been mentioned on the news. From her strange dream the night before, the prescient young widow sensed that there was a link to every disappearance. Now she just had to convince the smug prosecutor and the team of inept sheriff deputies of that fact.

The first child, a girl just shy of her third birthday and the second child, a female infant of six months, had also disappeared from Pasco, the most rural of the three small cities. According to Jill Thomas, the first case had happened two days prior and was written off as a parental abduction. The toddler had been left with a neighbor while the foster mother went to run an errand. A tall blonde man resembling the baby's father had convinced the neighbor it was his visitation time and took the child. By the time, the mother had returned home and reported the abduction to the police, the Amber Alert had been issued, but five hours from the time of the kidnapping greatly lowered the chances of finding the child.

The second case was also attributed to a parent kidnapping, however this time it was the Mexican relative-placement foster family who had fled with the child after abuse allegations had been made, prompting a CPS investigation. Five days had passed since the last CPS visit. There was no doubt they had made it to Mexico and would therefore never been seen again. Yet the third disappearance was the most suspicious of the three. The victim's family

lived nearly twenty miles out of town on a thirty-five hundred acre
farm. A random kidnapping was an unlikely scenario. The parents
were able to account for the time and were completely inconsol-
able. Lost babies brought back terrifying memories for the young
Irish-American probation officer as well.

She glanced back at Oz Rellim. The tall, handsome Benton
County prosecutor stood a head above a group of uniformed men,
comparing notes and occasionally glancing in her direction. The
parents stood off near a grouping of cars, crying hysterically. Their
baby was the youngest of eight in the large Catholic family and
their first adopted child..

From the north, bruised clouds marched over the sky's sullen face. The late winter storm was still brewing. The river's edge
was murky, laced in milfoil, the insidious fresh water seaweed that
plagued three local waterways of the Columbia, Snake and Yakima
rivers. A pair of paper white cranes flew overhead, on their way to
several of the Hanford Reach islands that provided a protective
habitat. Snoqualmie Pass, two and half hours west in the Cascade
Mountains, had been buried in another six feet of snow. It was
early spring and the ski resorts were celebrating.

When the authorities had requested Christian Vargas's volun-
tary services on that day in early April, she'd been on her way to
a day on the ski slopes. The Broten Ranch was a combination of
orchards, potato fields, irrigation canals and residences on a block
of land bordering the Franklin county side of the Columbia River.
Her dog knew the area well after successfully finding an injured
hunter in October. Bear, a five-year-old rambunctious St. Bernard
mix, was used by local law enforcement on missing person cases
from time to time. Most of the cases were easily solved. A child

wandering away from their yard or an Alzheimers patient determined to find their way home.

Bear began to dig deeper, his highly-sensitive nose covered in
mud and debris. Christian gave a short whistle and signaled to
Rellim to join her. "I think he might have found something here."

The ambitious prosecutor famous for a ninety-seven percent
conviction rate jogged over to where the dog was working, but
Christian had beaten him to the spot. He gazed down into her
eyes. "By the way, it's nice to see you again. It's been a while."

She blushed. "You, too. I thought you were going to have my
neck the last time we met."

"True, you did a number to my department, but hey, you
solved the case." He gave her a warm smile and knelt down to
look at something in the sand. Why was he here anyway? This was
a Franklin County matter. When he stood up, she saw the thread
of fear in his otherwise boyish face. She couldn't forgive him for
what he'd done to her on the witness stand; the way he'd been the
master of the inquisition into her personal life during the trial
that convicted a four-time killer the year before. "I'm sure you're
wondering why I'm here. Tom is out of town on vacation and his
deputies are, frankly, a bunch of novices."

She shrugged, gazing out at the turbulent water. "How long
have you been doing this?" he asked, watching as her dog moved
to another part of the beach.

"Doing what? Solving crimes or spending my Sunday mornings
in the freezing cold with a bunch of irritating cops?" She tried to
sound lighthearted, but the man who was indirectly her boss made
her nervous.

He chuckled. "Well, I was hoping they were one and the same
today."

Giving up her line of defense, she finally grinned. "If there's anything down there, he'll find it." Her anxiety spiked. Was there was something sticking out of the sand?

"Are you ok?" He leaned into her, protecting her from the wind.

"Fine." She kept her eye on the burrowing dog.

"All the trouble you've gone through and knowing you, the trouble you could get into." His tone was now playful.

"I took quite a fall from grace, you know." She swallowed hard, remembering her manager's tongue-lashing and subsequent warning letter in her personnel file as a result of the notorious case.

As the dog gave a little yelp, the storm broke. The sharp crack of thunder echoed down the plateau to the muddy riverbank. A purple bone of clouds, like a drunk's face after a bar fight, crept menacingly towards them. A deluge followed a few seconds later. Christian pulled up her hood and ducked under the spindly limb of a Russian Olive tree, watching the raindrops dance on the slick face of the river. Rellim scurried over next to her. He was close to her now. His hot breath smelled like peppermint and something sweet, maybe chewing tobacco as he spoke. "Jeez, and I thought I might get a real run in today." His tanned face lifted away. "Hey looks like your hero might have found something." She called the dog over. In his mouth was a dirty piece of fabric.

"Let me." Rellim pulled out a pair of synthetic gloves and bagged the item. Then he looked closely at it through the plastic. Still the rain fell. She gave Bear a treat for his find. The intimate contact to the prosecutor was intense. She rarely found herself this close to a man. He nodded. "Look, here. There are initials on this."

The rest of the team had raced away, up the bank to where their various cars were lined up along the orchard border. They were completely alone. She gazed up at his soft pillowed lips as he scrutinized the evidence. He was ignoring her on purpose. The sensation of attraction between them was palatable.

The cloud burst stopped as suddenly as it begun. She moved away before his men could return and see them together. Bear followed her, snorting with excitement. She crouched down to her only true companion, praising him lavishly. The moist sand beneath her feet was slippery. She began to fall forward, but Oz's hand was on her shoulder, steadying her. She stood up and gazed into his solemn brown eyes. Their corners crinkled with surprise. "Caught ya!"

Christian hesitated now as Bear trotted over to an outcropping at the water's edge. From where she stood, she could tell he'd found some more evidence. She crept over the rocks to the animal. "I have a bad feeling," she yelled over her shoulder. "I think the baby was kidnapped."

Rellim was right behind her, his face registering shock. "Why would you say that?"

"Someone brought her down here. "Look here, this looks like fresh paint." She led him down towards the shoreline. On the edge of a jagged rock, there was a line of blue paint, as though the bottom of a boat had been pushed away hastily.

He seemed unconvinced, though he knelt down, studied the mark and whistled at some of the men to come down. She could see the doubt in his eyes. After several recent gang killings, a stolen child was the last thing that their community needed. She was instantly furious. Denial was the source of so many mistakes. Furthermore, no one ever took her intuitive feelings seriously. The world was full of Doubting Thomases, her partner, Daniel, often reminded her. She was gifted and cursed at the same time. Without some form of proof, she was just another self-proclaimed prophet.

"We need to issue an Amber Alert." Her voice was sharp with fear.

"It's probably too late." Rellim rubbed his chin, now covered with a day's stubble. He stared out at the river, deep in thought.

"What do you mean?"

"The call came too late. The parents said she was in her crib last night, but neither remembered to check her room before they went to bed."

"What's with these big families anyway?" She choked as though strangled by anger.

Rellim sighed heavily. "You have to wonder. It's been over eight hours since anyone in the family last laid eyes on her. The parents didn't call us until three this morning. They tried to find her on their own. That is half the problem with using the Alert. People don't report soon enough."

"You think this is a drowning." Christian wasn't asking a question.

He neatly captured her unspoken assumptions. "Kidnapping investigations take time and money." His tone was cool. "But there is more that than. Investigations like those inevitably take a toll on our emotional and physical resources. At this point in time, I'm assuming that the baby drowned. However, if you're so sure you can 'sleuth a different truth', as the pros say…" he paused for impact. "Then, knowing you the little that I do, I'd say you're probably going to go for it." Rellim laughed softly. She wanted to slug him.

♊

Christian left for work early Monday morning. The sun was just crawling over the horizon, turning the sky the glorious colors of mandarin orange and raspberry. The skyline had cleared from the storm, though the roadway was littered with tree branches and bits of trash. As she pulled out of her garage and turned off her small road that bordered the Yakima River, she glanced up at Rattlesnake Mountain to the west. A slight dusting of snow clung to its smooth hump.

The juvenile justice center was dark when she cruised up on her motorcycle, though she could see by the single light that her partner was already at his desk. She walked in a few minutes later. Daniel had a Starbucks latte waiting for her.

"Hey, thanks." She smiled warmly at her roguish office mate. A former military cop, Daniel was addicted to three things, the gym, solving crime and Christian. He still held a candle for his incorrigible partner after a previous sexual interlude that marked their history together. For the sake of professionalism, Christian pretended that the erotic moment had never happened. Often it was apparent that Daniel hadn't been able to tame his feelings quite as well.

"Hi. So how long were you looking for the kid?" He handed her the coffee, his wide- set amber eyes prodding. No sense plunging into weekend niceties. She knew he didn't want to know about her possible dating activities, though she could honestly say there were none.

"Good Morning. How was your weekend?" She pulled off her leather gloves and turned on her computer.

He looked away, taking a swig of his hot brew. "Fine. Ran a half marathon on Saturday. Played some pool last night at Joe's. Ran into Cap'n Pete."

"I should have known that Devin would tell you." She didn't care for Police Captain Pete Devin, a Pasco middle-aged good ole' boy, who had worked his way up the ranks on the laurels of his high school football antics After a sip of coffee, she shrugged off her leather Peteet and hung it on the hook behind the door.

"Well?"

"I don't know where it stands. It took them a couple of hours to investigate the area. Once Bear found the baby blanket, they started taking us seriously. When we first got to the child's home, Rellim was in no mood to follow Bear. The river's nearly two miles from their house, but once again, my dog was right. Now we need to find out if there were any fishermen or boaters out that day. The child was obviously taken away by boat."

"That's not what I heard. The authorities believe she simply wandered away and drowned. The Tri-Cities scuba search and rescue were called out this morning. I saw a couple of helicopters, too." Daniel's face registered earnest despair. He looked particularly handsome. His square-jawed face glowed with a new skier's tan. A sporty pale yellow polo shirt accented his eyes. She turned away and began shuffling files.

"Tom Haber's crew is idiots."

"Why do you say that?"

"Because it's a ridiculous theory. Even Rellim had to agree. That baby couldn't have navigated the terrain from her front porch to the river. There are several obstacles between the two, including an irrigation canal. If she'd drowned, that would be where it happened."

"I don't think so." Daniel seemed to be egging for an argument.

"Why?" She kept her voice calm.

"Because the canal is empty."

Now she felt like the idiot. They hadn't walked a straight line from the house to the river. Instead Bear had gone due north before tracking back. At one point he appeared to have lost the child's trail. She'd only known that the canal was there from a

Google Earth map.

"Ok, so the baby didn't drown in the canal, but believe me, Daniel, there is no way a child of that age could have wandered that far."

"What was that story you told me once of you running away from your aunt's house when you first got there? Weren't you about three years old at the time?"

"That's different. I had a motive. I want to find my family. And I was found on a main road."

"So what if this little girl had motive to run away? Who knows? I'm just telling you in so many words to let this go. Before you know it, you're going to be in the middle of something dangerous."

"So. We've been there before."

Daniel chuckled. "Love that word, we. The last time *you* dragged me into danger, I promised myself it was the *last* time. You are obsessed. I'm not going there."

"Whatever." Christian was tired of the verbal foreplay. She reached up and began to twist a chunk of her wavy hair. Her nerves were strung tight with the understanding that she was once again getting swept up in a terrifying web. Certain that the three babies had been kidnapped, she had no choice but to take action, no matter how clandestine that might be.

"Marie wants to see you asap."

"Is that an order?" She tossed the cord of hair over her shoulder in irritation. Why didn't she just shut up?

He chuckled. "A little touchy, aren't you? What, did Rellim get under your skin yesterday?" Daniel waited for a moment. When she refused to answer, he said softly, "Actually that is a request. My grandmother is simply worried about you."

"Sorry," Christian grumbled.

Daniel stood up and walked behind her to get into a filing cabinet. She could smell his Hugo cologne. She was hoping he might touch her, but instead he sighed heavily. A long silence was punctuated with a relieving reply. "Ok, I'm in on the investigation. Where are you going to start?"

Christian smiled victoriously. She'd won this round. "In the Blocks, at Hog Heaven probably." The Blocks was a wealthy farming area west of Pasco. Her partner had grown up near there. Due to the fact that his step-father was half Irish, his was an unusual sir name for a family of Hispanic migrant farmer workers. The O'Callahans had worked for pennies while many of the Franklin county farmers had made bank. His attitude regarding that redneck community was chilly at best.

"What? A bunch of drunks out in the Blocks who hang out in an old barn?"

"Airplane hangar."

"Say again?"

"Hog Heaven is an airplane hangar and every farmer this side of Walla Walla hangs out there. If there was anyone out on the river on Saturday, somebody who frequents Hog Heaven will be the one to know."

The enticing scent finally moved away from the filing cabinet, leaving her pheromones to flounder. "I'll go out there with you. Just tell me when."

"We'll have to wait until Friday night. That's karaoke night."

"You gonna sing?"

"No. You are." Though known for his exquisite tenor voice, it generally took a few shots of tequila before Daniel could be coaxed into a performance.

"We'll see about that. Do you want me to let Devin know about your plans to investigate this one?"

"Don't you dare, unless you want me to cancel our Wednesday night dinner," Christian shot back hastily. Daniel and she had a standing date on Wednesday nights. He had insisted after their caseloads had become unbearable and that a social break was in order. Several of the other probation officers had joined them originally, but over time the numbers had dropped. Now it was just the two of them. She avoided any overtures of intimacy by arranging her own transportation, though once a few weeks prior, he'd almost managed to kiss her good night.

Her partner stalled in the doorway, his neatly-creased khakis, along with the fitted brown leather blazer gave him a west coast preppie look. She'd admired him for a second too long and he knew it. No doubt her pale Celtic skin turned the color of a pomegranate as she looked away.

"I was thinking we could try that new Sushi restaurant this week."

She flashed him a deep-dimpled smile. "Okay, but stay away from Devin. He's a snake. *We* don't need his help quite yet."

They headed off in separate directions a few minutes later. Daniel had been placed in charge of the Special Apprehension Unit, which was a cop and probation officer warrant sweep team. Knowing O'Callahan, the juvenile detention building, which held sixty kids on a good day, would be full of gangbangers by evening. Christian had a few house calls to make, as well as a couple of court appearances, but before the day was over, she'd made contact with her friend, Harry, a crime lab tech with a penchant for the probation officer's premonitions. One phone call later and she had confirmation that the baby's blanket had indeed belonged to the missing child, Anacelia Tia Arequipay-Broten, 25 months old.

Ⅱ

Christian eventually found time to go upstairs to talk to her friend, Kathy, who had recently taken the manager's position in the dependency department, a specialized program for children in the state foster care system. Under budgeted and overworked, the small four person team relied primarily on volunteers. According to the scuttlebutt, all of the fifty-two volunteers had been called in for interviews on the first two disappearances. She wondered if her call to Rellim that morning, pointing out the foster child connection in the first two, had been the motivating factor in that decision. Kathy, an over-achieving lesbian who had been a close friend for nearly seven years, was at her desk.

"Hi. How are you holding up?' Christian sat down and offered a sympathetic smile. Her friend's normally cheery round face sagged noticeably.

"Not good. Was this your idea?" Her small, pale blue eyes searched the probation officer's darker ones.

"Look, so far there's only one connection between those two babies and that's your department." Though her subordinate, the younger woman was determined to stand her ground.

Kathy nodded, her demeanor bordering on despair. "I know, but you also know that we're as clean as a whistle when it comes to screening our folks. There's not a speeding ticket among them."

"Yes, but they have family members and you know that at least some of them talk about their cases." This was the last thing Christian wanted right now. Kathy had been her biggest ally during the notorious case the previous spring, one in which the unflappable P.O., as probation officers were informally called, had gone underground to uncover a Satanic cult against her administration's knowledge. Had Kathy not gone to bat for her edgy friend, Christian would have undoubtedly lost her job.

"And I thought you were going to stay out of police investigations." Kathy shook her head in frustration.

"I can't now that Bear has been involved. And believe me, I'm going to get to the bottom of this last one, though I think all three missing girls are connected somehow."

"Whoa, just one minute. I am not, I repeated *not* going to put my ass on the line for you again, Vargas.'

"I just think we need to look."

Kathy's hand went up to Christian's face. "Stop. Get out of my office, now. I'm not having this conversation with you, you got that?"

The manager's face turned crimson, her small eyes bugging with repressed fury. "Out." Kathy stood up, her broad, six-foot-two frame towering over her charge.

Christian had never seen her friend so angry. She rose up sheepishly, her lean, five-foot-eight frame diminutive next to the manager's hefty one.

"I…" but the words emptied from her mind like feces down an open sewer. She suddenly felt just as dirty.

Trudging back to her office, her intuition bleeping like an answering machine, Christian went over the facts in her mind, trying to connect the wires of association. Meanwhile the Pasco police department was focused on investigating recent sex offender releases from regional prisons. It was nearly five o'clock and drug court was having a graduation ceremony. She waited until the front lobby was packed before she made her move.

The vault combination was known to only three people in the Benton Franklin Juvenile Justice Center. By the next day, the social files on the missing children would be confiscated for the case, if they weren't already. The vault's tiny space held thousands of social files for the young criminals and child dependents of the provincial community known for its association with the first atomic bomb and, in more recent history, a burgeoning wine industry. She had about ten minutes to do her research. Fortunately, the receptionist had a distraction. There were sixteen people who had lined up to sign in for court. Silently, Christian ducked into the vault and slipped behind the first wall of files. She began a race against time. The rising sweat of nerve and determination made her feel clammy as she scanned the alphabetical tabs. This moment was simply a sprint in the inevitably long marathon ahead of her.

The first file under the name, Mara Santos, was a thick as a cereal box. She leafed through the dependency proceedings, now four years in duration. There was nothing unusual about the paperwork, nor the parent of the child. Serena Santos was a drug addict who'd already lost three other children to the system. To her dismay, the information that she was looking for was not in the file. The alleged father was just one of many Jimmy Banks listed on the worldwide web. There was no forwarding address or phone number for the man. The authorities believed that he had taken the toddler and fled the county three days after their social worker had reported that the three-year old little girl was sick and needed immediate medical care. The police had not worked fast enough and it was Christian's assumption that if the allegations were indeed true, the man and child were probably several states away by now.

She moved down the line to the next file. Gina Torres had been born to a sixteen year old mother, Juanita, who had a long juvenile record. A homeless felon, the baby's mother reportedly had ties with gangs, so when Gina was born, the state had immediately stepped in and turned the child over to her maternal grandparents who were both illegals, but had fostered several of their grandchildren in the past. The department had been investigating the family when the grandparents and child had gone missing.

Frustration knotted her guts as her blood pressure began to rise. Voices filled the small space as Kathy came to the vault entrance, speaking to Laura, the evening receptionist. "I'll need these files by tomorrow morning. Put them on my desk and lock my door before you leave. I've got to meet with Officer Gihan now, otherwise I'd do it myself."

She clenched her fists and prayed for a reprieve. If she were lucky, Laura, a woman in her sixties with a bad hip, would be in no hurry to get the files, though from where she hid, she could see the bulky woman moving forward with the list. Christian knew she'd face serious consequences if she was caught in the vault without permission. After a freelance defense attorney had lost several important files, the agency had instituted a new policy on vault access. Only the receptionist on duty by manager's request was allowed in the jam-packed ten-by-ten room. If Laura was to report such a breech to Kathy, she would be forced to take action. Christian's forehead beaded with sweat as the seconds moved like ancient stone. Then, as if on cue, the phone rang. Laura turned and left.

Five more minutes. That was how much time she was willing to risk. She spun around and faced the opposite wall. The file was amazingly still in its place. Anacelia Arequipay was born to a prostitute who had immediately adopted out the child to the Brotens. The hard-working Brotens were devastated by the sudden disappearance of the child. They had begged for an Amber Alert, though the policy department was buying time, expecting to find the child on a washed-up beach somewhere.

In the meantime, Christian had worked through the night on Sunday trying to come up with a connection between the three children. Though much of the information was on the computer, she was looking for the address of the third victim's uncle. Checking the bi-county I-Leads system earlier that day, she'd discovered that the man had been in prison on felony kidnapping charges back in the nineties. Then she saw something unexpected. There was another file under that unusual last name, Arequipay. Instantly she knew it belonged to Juanita, Anacelia's estranged mother.

She shoved the fourth file under her cashmere sweater and slowly moved to the front of the vault as the court buzzer rang. Laura would be done checking in the defendants. Knowing her, she would take her fifteen minute break, leaving the glass-enclosed reception area empty. Just long enough to get out of the vault.

The man known as Stic drove his truck slowly down to the beach. Stic had to go back, if only to subdue the incessant replay of events in his mind. Hidden from the main road, this spot should have been an easy launch, but instead it had become a nightmare. The fussy child had thrown a temper tantrum when he'd taken her from the car seat. It was amazing that he'd gotten her out of the house at all. Thank God the rest of the family had been out in the barn when he'd arrived to take the child. Cradling her tender, squirming body in his arms, he'd trudged down to the water and tried to hand her over to Alex from the embankment. The little girl, struggling against him, had thrown him off balance and he'd lost his footing. He'd slipped and fallen, his head crashing on the sharp edge of a boulder. In the same moment, the toddler flew from his grasp, landing between the boat and the rocks. He'd scrambled to his knees, but had gotten scared. A poor swimmer, he'd frozen in terror as the boat plunged forward against its own wake. In the next second, the child had disappeared under the water. As Alex had attempted to spin the boat around, he'd seen the foaming blood and pale bits of body tissue. He'd closed his eyes, screamed for mercy, but it was too late. In eternity's moment, he understood. She'd been sucked under and chewed up by the propeller.

Alex had nearly killed him then. Jamming the ski boat into gear, he'd ridden it up against the rocks towards his supine friend, the fiberglass bottom grinding viciously against the stone's hard surface. Jumping out of the Reinell, Alex had slapped him across the face, knocking him back again. Over and over, he'd pummeled his partner's face until it was made raw with abuse. Stic had tasted blood, but didn't fight back.

He'd deserved such punishment. For a long time, the small man with a limp hadn't move. Finally Alex had hauled him up and had thrown him into the back of the boat. Outrage and horror, at both their failure and the child's fate, had severed his reason. It was too much to believe. After picking up a floating arm, he'd rolled into a ball and sobbed as they roared away from the beach.

www.ingramcontent.com/pod-product-compliance
Lightning Source LLC
Chambersburg PA
CBHW060349260626
47160CB00006B/2246